A BLOODLINE OF SECRETS

THE UNIFICATION

An Original Sin Novel
Book 2

A

Bloodline

of

Secrets

THE UNIFICATION

Daniellle D. Drummond

Cover Art by Lexie at Selkkie Designs

Hard Cover and title page artwork by Juniper Hartmann

Interior art by Juniper Hartmann

Interior art by Anastasia Mirolubova

Interior design and formatting by Danielle D. Drummond

Map design by Winter Cutt

Editing by Charla Ayers

PAPERBACK ISBN: 9781763765122

HARDCOVER ISBN: 9798270474294

HARDCOVER D/J ISBN: 9781763765139

Playlist

When I daydream about the world I'm creating, music becomes my muse, inspiring me to breathe life into my characters. It helps me tap into deeper emotions, visualise scenes as they unfold, and find the creative energy to tackle even the most challenging chapters. If music resonates with your creative process too, or if you simply enjoy listening while you read, hop over to Spotify and explore the incredible artists who helped shape the world I've brought to life for you.

Author's Note and Content Warnings

A Bloodline of Secrets: The Unification is a book of fiction. Any description or representation of any person or place in this work is fictional, and any resemblance is purely coincidental.

This book contains heavy themes of emotional abuse and manipulation, drug use, violence, kidnapping, self sacrificial rituals and death, both on and off page. The FMC goes through a lot of trauma in this book and it is not entirely dealt with. Your mental health matters so please take note and use your discretion before choosing to delve into the world of Elyndria and please be kind to yourself while reading this. This book also contains explicit sexual content.

STAR-BORNE ACADEMY
THALASSIA
DYTHALIS
ORPHELIOS
FERI
RIVER PLYE
NEOPOLIS
ARCHANOR
SERPENT'S SEA
VALSTROME
FENRIERA
WELVERYN
QUESPELIA
OKSANA
ACREAZ
N
LOURNE

MOUNTAINS OF G'PHEN
OWENSTOWN
DEAD FOREST
WHITE FOREST
EDRUS
RIA
THE BARRONS
BLETHYN SE
WYSTRINE
DOR DESE
ELYNDRIA

For the girls who lost their way in the darkness. . .
Sometimes the darkness is our greatest strength, do not fear it, embrace it. For when the darkness loves you, you are no longer lost, but finally found.

She tip-toed quietly through the night, fearful of making a sound, and waking the wild monsters that reside inside her heart.
For once aroused, she knew not how to tame them.
—Dee Dee Paturzo

CHAPTER 1

Quentin

She was screaming his name, and it ripped Quentin Ishaan from his slumber. Was this some new nightmare? She was catatonic when he got her back to the pack's manor and laid her down to rest. Her only words were, *"I'm sorry." She* was sorry? He was a Godsdamn asshole, and he should have stayed away.

Groaning, Quentin peeled his heavy lids open. He looked over to where Paege once lay beside him. His nest was destroyed, but it was the empty blanket he had cocooned her in that stopped his heart. She was no longer in the overly large bed. He sat up and scanned the expansive bedroom to find pillows and blankets strewn across the room. The morning sun beamed through the opened windows, her rays caressing and teasing him with a sense of joy and adventure. But there would be no adventure or joy, not today. Maybe not ever again. He shrugged it off. While he loved the day, the night was where he felt alive, especially in the presence of the all-powerful moon. It was a Wolf thing. They thrived in the dark.

It hadn't been long since he brought Paege into his home. Since he laid her down and closed his eyes. Since leaving after Guy was killed.

It wasn't supposed to happen like this.

Quentin blinked. The memories of the fight and Guy dying hit him like an avalanche, the debris of his actions burying him one stone at a time. His brother was the only one he had ever truly trusted. The only one he would have given his life for. Everything he had done to this point was to keep his brother safe. Guy was a much better male than he ever was. A much better son. Brother. Wolf. Guy deserved far better than he was ever given.

He closed his heavy eyes and leaned back, trying to relieve the pressure in his tightening chest. He pushed the unfurling anger deep into his core. She screamed once more, and it yanked him from his thoughts and back to the present moment.

No, not a dream.

Quentin sat upright again, and his eyes snapped open, landing on the source of the sound. He found her lying on the floor at the end of the bed. "Paege?" he asked as he swung his legs over the edge of the bed and willed his tired and aching body to stay upright.

"Quentin? Please help me," she pleaded. Paege looked up to him with watery emerald eyes. Her delicate face was still covered in grime and blood from the battle they had just faced. Both were too tired and broken to clean up.

"Fuck, Paege. What's going on?" Quentin helplessly watched in shock as she writhed around in pain, unable to come to her aid. Paege's limbs contorted in all the wrong ways. He didn't know what to do. Quentin's brain scrambled for any understanding of what was happening.

Finally, it clicked. He had seen this before. Hels, he had experienced this before. Quentin pushed himself off the bed, then stilled and stared in disbelief.

It can't be.

She was half Human and half Fae. This was impossible. But how could he ignore what his memories were showing him? What was happening right before his very eyes? After all, she did take a life. She killed Ric. Quentin pushed down the need to help her and trusted what his instincts told him. What he knew with every inch of his being.

For a beat, he tried to reject it, but he watched in utter disbelief as she shifted.

As she Emerged.

First, Paege's face morphed, and her mouth became elongated as her muzzle formed. The rest of her body followed, twisting and contorting. Her body changed before his eyes. When her coat filled out, his heart thundered heavily in his chest with awe right before it split open in pain. Because once the painstaking Emergence had finished, there she stood as a regal, beautiful Wolf. Her coat was thick, white, and ran into grey, pointed ears. The grey tip on her tail and her striking emerald-green eyes were like none he'd ever seen before—except for one. His stomach knotted and twisted as he pieced together what he saw.

Paege was not only a Wolf; she was the perfect image of Guy. How could this be? What did it mean? "Paege, if you can hear me, nod," Quentin told her with a shaky voice as he took a nervous step toward her.

Paege bowed her beautiful head, so he continued toward her, and surprisingly, she moved to meet him. Quentin didn't want to startle her, though. He wasn't even sure she knew what just happened—what was happening to her—and he'd hate for her to run or attack him before she shifted back and he could explain. He stayed calm, letting his breath fall into a calming rhythm while he waited for her to approach him in her own time. He slowly closed the gap between them, matching every step she took with one of his own. When Paege reached him, he held out his hand and brushed his fingers against her cheek. She nuzzled into him, allowing Quentin to cup her face.

His body relaxed. "You. Are. Beautiful," Quentin sighed.

He stared into her deep emerald-green eyes for a moment, and Quentin swore he saw the flicker of a flame ignite inside them. It all made sense, he supposed. More pieces fell into place as he watched her. Was this why his father asked him to keep an eye on *her*? She wasn't human at all. She was a Wolf.

Quentin couldn't move. He tried. Gods, did he try, but it was like his bones had turned to a heavy metal that held him to the spot like a statue. He attempted to reconcile what he saw before him, but it made him sick to consider.

He was sent to watch her. To keep an eye on her. She was part of something much bigger.

Visions swam through his mind, weaving between his thoughts. Memories he had long forgotten burst to life as if he were experiencing them for the first time.

He didn't know. How could he? Yes, he had willingly done what his father asked, even contributing to the insanity of his plan, but it was clear that he was missing something. There was so much he hadn't been told.

He would have to find out.

His chest tightened, and he blinked twice. He couldn't deny that she was downright beautiful. "Paege, you're a Wolf."

Upon Quentin's words, Paege shifted back into her Fae form and collapsed on the bedroom floor. He sank and grabbed her, wrapping her in his arms. He wasn't sure she would want him to hold her after everything he had done, but he couldn't let her go. Not now. Maybe not ever.

Paege flinched, her body recoiling for a split second, but then she reciprocated his embrace and buried her head in his chest. Just as quickly as it broke, his heart selfishly started to heal. But hers probably never would. Gods, she smelled like fresh wildflowers and salty air, and it reminded him of home. Without hesitation, he relaxed into her, unsure of what else to do, what else to say, and how else to act. After everything, he never expected this. Sure, he knew there was something different about her. Knew there was something else.

Quentin felt her heart pounding against his body, and she let out a long, rattled breath. His body shuddered in response, mirroring hers.

Fuck.

Paege tilted her head toward his and looked at him through her long lashes with eyes full of confusion and discomfort. Quentin studied her face. He took in the curve of her full lips, the little freckles that butterflied across her button nose, her defined cheeks with one little dimple on the left side, and her wide green eyes, once full of life and kindness, now full of darkness and grief.

He did this.

She had been through so much these past few months, but here she was still fighting, still surviving, and Quentin's chest cracked open thinking of all the grief and pain she must have felt. All the trauma she had been dealt. He considered how strong she must be not to give up at all.

It didn't matter that when he said those three words to her before they went to battle, she didn't say them back. How could she love anyone when she had never truly loved herself? She has been used, abused, and lied to her entire life—by him, too. After what he had done, he didn't deserve those three words. Not from her or anyone. It didn't matter that he thought he was doing the right thing or that he thought he was protecting everyone. It didn't matter that he felt something for her, and that his feelings could have been true one day. All that mattered was that he lied to her. He betrayed her and put her in danger like everyone else. How would he ever get her to trust him again? Because now, more than ever, he needed her to.

Quentin pushed down the hurt and swallowed his pride. His loyalty lay with his father. With the pack. With the Wolves. Brushing the hair from her face, he returned her gaze. She didn't deserve this. Any of this.

"Quentin?" When she finally spoke his name, his chest ached from a dark place he never expected.

He did this. He broke her. And while he knew he had to, he took no pleasure from it. "Yes, Books?"

"What's happening?" she asked in a raspy voice.

What's happening? What's fucking happening? He had no idea. "What do you remember?"

"I remember." She paused, and he watched her face. Her eyes darted around the room as if scanning her memory bank, looking for answers. Then they widened. "I remember pain. I remember seeing wolves in my sleep. I remember. . .I remember." She paused again, and he didn't speak, waiting. He wanted her to remember. He needed her to come to the recognition herself; it would be less traumatic that way. "Oh, the Gods," she pulled herself back from his embrace. "Quentin, I think I'm a Wolf."

CHAPTER 2

"I don't understand," I cry as I pull myself from Quentin's arms and wrap myself in a blanket that's fallen from the bed. "How is this possible? I'm half Human, not Wolf. Human!"

"I don't know, Paege," Quentin finally speaks. He sweeps the hair out of his eyes, and a broken male stares back at me. He lost his best friend. His brother. He lost members of his pack. His friends.

And although he doesn't know it yet, he's lost me.

My heart fractures as I study his face and infinite grey-blue eyes. I trusted him, and he betrayed me. He followed me on orders from the king to keep an eye on me. He infiltrated my life and pretended to be my friend, to care. Why me? It doesn't matter. What matters is that everything I thought we had was a lie.

And what about Guy? Why would he not tell Guy any of this? He was his best friend, his brother, his fight-or-die, and Guy was just as shocked to hear Quentin's words as I was.

For some reason, I trusted Guy more than I trusted anyone. And now he's gone.

They are both gone.

And what about the fact Quentin said he loved me just before our lives imploded? How could he say such a thing, after everything that had unfolded in the day before? Was it just another lie? Was it another tactic to gain my trust and believe him?

I think back on his words. I don't believe them. I can't. There was something selfish in the way he spoke them. He wasn't asking for them to be returned, no, but he was expecting something of me. My forgiveness. His betrayal punches me in the ribs. I wish the words were true, but no matter how hard I try, I just don't believe them.

Despite how angry, confused, or hurt I am, I still want nothing more than to blind myself from the truth and hold him once more, ease him of his pain. Damn empathy. But I can't. I am falling apart. My life is crumbling around me. The debris is crushing me, suffocating me, sucking the air out of my lungs, and I'm using every ounce of energy I possess to keep myself together.

My world, as I know it, is gone.

I have taken a life.

Guy is dead.

I am a Wolf.

My bloody hands tremble uncontrollably by my sides, and with one, I grasp the charm hanging from my neck, searching for anything to make sense. My dad must have been a Wolf, but who was he? A cloud looms over every memory I have and every story I was told as I rummage through my mind, playing the plethora of conversations I had with my mum about the man I had thought was my father. But that man I had been told of, the man that I loved, doesn't exist, or doesn't exist as I know him.

"Paege?" Quentin's voice breaks my thoughts and brings me back to the present. "Paege, I need to ask you something." I look at him from my knees. He runs trembling hands through his blood-caked hair and sighs a rattled breath. "What do you know about Guy?"

This question isn't what I expected, but I answer anyway, curious about where he's going with this. "He's your friend, your brother." I push through the lump forming in my throat. "His dad was king—"

"No, not that," Quentin interrupts. "What do you know about his *Wolf*?"

"Nothing." I had only seen his wolf a handful of times, and even when we had talked about it, he never said much. None of the Wolves did.

"It was different," he murmurs under his breath as if trying to protect a secret from being exposed.

My mind drifts back to what Quentin said when Guy Emerged and to when I witnessed his shift in the woodlands. It *was* different. His Wolf was white as the winter snow and larger than the rest. His eyes, though, were the same. His emerald eyes, so different from the rest. Even in his humanoid form, he was not like the other Wolves. There was always something pure and kind inside him. He wore his Wolf with grace, not brutality. He had honour. He had heart.

Tugging the blanket tighter around me, I reply apprehensively, "Yes, it was."

"Paege?" Quentin drawls. "You saw your Wolf, right? You merged with her."

Like Zephyra's winds, flashes of my Wolf rush me. White fur, green eyes, her size, her beauty. She was familiar. She felt like home when I touched her, when she merged with me. Suddenly, images of Guy's wolf appear next to her. They are alike. Eerily so. But it can't be. My mind is deceiving me. I've had so much trauma these past few months, my brain must have finally cracked. It's broken. I'm out of my mind, coo-coo fucking crazy.

Or. . .is everything finally making sense?

I force myself to push through all the anguish just to see him, Guy, in his humanoid form. His emerald-green eyes and brown hair. His softer features and higher cheekbones, even the single dimple when he laughs. His ability to calm me in the most insane situations. He always felt familiar.

But surely not. Not this.

Something in my chest twists as I grab hold of one particular memory. A hand to his heart, with a promise he made. There is only one other person, besides me, who does that. Mum.

A tear bursts from its well as I force myself to remember his last moment, his last words. *I never understood our love, our connection, until now. I wish I got to love you longer.*

Quentin paces the room as my life, I suppose, *our* lives, continually explode with blow after blow.

"It can't be. It can't be possible," I cry out.

"Why not?"

"Because it can't be!" I screech. The reality, though, is that it very well could be possible, but every time I think about it, I feel sick. The visions when the book released my memories from the cage they had been kept in, and now this. It means my mum lied to me my entire life. She lied to Amerax, too.

"Think about it, Paege. Guy lost his mum when he was young, and you lost your dad. You both look so similar, Gods." He runs his hands through his hair. "I can't believe I never noticed it before." He stops pacing the room and turns to me. "And your Wolves are identical. Not similar. *Identical.*" He over-enunciates every syllable. "They could be the same damn Wolf," he exhales.

"I need to see my mum," I weep as I fumble to my feet. "She knows something. She has answers, and I need to know."

"I agree. We can leave today. I can get us passes through the Portals."

"No," I snap. "I need to see her alone. I have so much to tell her, and you have—" I pause, shaking my hand in the air, gesturing to the rooms beyond. "There's still the matter with the Wolves," my voice cracks, and I swallow hard, knowing that we still have three dead Scorpion Wolves, including one of their alphas, to exchange for three of ours, including Guy, my. . .

No. I can't say it yet.

"Paege, I understand, I do." His eyes dart to the floor for the briefest moment, and he swallows thickly before returning my gaze. "But I'm not letting you do this alone. No one should have to do this alone. I promise I'll stay far away while you talk, but I *am* coming with you. The pack can deal with the exchanges. It will take a few days anyway, and then by the time we get back, we can give them their cremation."

"Quentin?"

"Paege, this is non-negotiable. I am joining you, alright?" he says firmly as he stands tall and holds his ground.

"This isn't some mission from your father?" The second the words escape from my lips, I regret them. Quentin's eyes sharpen, but his shoulders round. Regret and remorse build on his defences, and I want to take it back, but I can't.

Silence.

"It's alright. Paege, I'm—"

I cut him off, shaking my head before he says what I think he's going to say. "Don't. Later."

He nods.

I don't have space to deal with Quentin's betrayal when my mother's is rising to the surface. Even if he did apologise, it doesn't change what he did. It doesn't change that he lied to me and deceived me, and that his actions may very well have led us to where we are right now. What I can't figure out is if he's sorry about me or if he's only sorry about Guy.

The battle between my heart and my head has never been more indiscernible, and I have no idea which one is going to win this round. I take a deep breath and say the first thing that comes to my mind. "Alright, we leave at noon."

CHAPTER 3

We exit the portal—me landing on my ass again—and Quentin and I silently walk the dusty roads to where I grew up. He hasn't spoken much since we left. Neither of us has. The uncomfortableness of the situation scratches at me from under my skin, irritating and nauseating. Guy's death. Taking a life. Quentin's betrayal. My mother's secrets. I'm surprised I'm even able to put one foot in front of the other right now.

The lush green paddock that surrounds our property is overgrown but still neat. A herd of horses grazes the long grass, and the fresh, brisk air, perfumed by the wildflowers in my mother's garden, quells the storm brewing inside me. A white horse at the end of the paddock slowly lifts his head, a vision of grace. His mane glistens in the sun like a waterfall of snowy silk, and he turns to face us.

I whistle loudly and call, "Whisky!" He pins his ears back and flicks his tail before trotting over to us, tall and proud. My loyal stallion. My best friend growing up. My Camarillo.

"You have a horse?"

"Yes." I breathe in the sight of him as he approaches with steady beats of his hooves across the luscious field.

A smile ghosts across his face. "I didn't know."

It wasn't just a statement; it had the hint of a question he didn't want to ask: "Why haven't you ever mentioned it to me?" And why haven't I? My relationship with Quentin has never been about sharing.

"Why would you?" I respond quietly without taking my eyes off the giant snowy beast. He is pure muscle, and each one ripples in the winter sun, glistening him with its rays.

Whisky whinnies a greeting, whipping his tail around as he pushes his head between my hands and toward my face.

"I missed you, too, boy," I say, running my hands through his long, silken mane. He whinnies again and dances his front hooves in excitement. "Quentin, this is Whisky. Whisky, this is Quentin." I jokingly introduce them, wondering if Quentin has ever ridden a horse or if he has ever spent time with them. He doesn't strike me as the horse type. Do Wolves even ride horses?

Whisky eyes Quentin with a judgmental glare and turns back to me and brays as he digs his head into my chest again. "Alright, boy, I'll come back shortly for a ride, alright?" I kiss him on his nose and run my hands down his glossy neck, his muscles flinching beneath my touch. With one final neigh, he turns and trots proudly back to the old oak tree in the paddock.

Nostalgia wraps around me like a comfortable blanket as Quentin and I stroll toward the house. "I was always the weird kid when growing up here, you know. The half-*Human* Fae," I blurt out. Alright, it appears I am now sharing. Quentin doesn't answer. He meanders silently beside me, keeping his steps in rhythm with mine, not missing a beat. "I didn't fit in anywhere, and I didn't have many friends. So, I lived my life in books, reading about history, adventures, other species, other realms, and Humans." I take a long, deliberate breath. "I used to read stories about princesses riding white horses on wild adventures, and I always admired their beauty and elegance. I even named my favourite stuffed animal, Whitey, after the horse I hoped to have someday."

A burst of fresh fruitiness envelopes me as an emotion I haven't felt in some time infiltrates my senses, and I cock my head towards Quentin. He lets a chuckle escape his lips. "Whitey?" he teases.

"I was five." My cheeks tug higher. "So, when Amerax brought Whisky home after he was rescued on a mission, I was in awe of him. We fell in love and became best friends." Hundreds of calming memories of me with Whisky flood my mind, and I giggle like a child, transported through time. "I even tried to sneak him into the house a few times."

"Sounds like you have a bond," he says flatly, and the amusement is abruptly masked by something else I can't quite place. It's murky, dark, and it wraps heavily around my heart. *Guy.*

"We do," I say in a foolish attempt to push the memories of Guy from my mind, shielding myself from Quentin's emotions as they whip around in a frenzy. Because suddenly, it's all real. The reason I have come home. The reason we are here. "Gods, I miss him. He's probably the only thing I miss about home."

"That can't be true, Books," Quentin probes with an arched brow.

"No, I suppose it's not," I sigh. It wasn't, but here I stand, my world, my home, an unfamiliar place I once thought was my pillar of strength, my centre of truth. Not anymore.

We reach the old stone house. The twin gargoyles guarding the home stare at me with a judgmental glare. Unease skitters down my spine, and my hand lingers in the air just above the handle. As if Quentin feels the truth of my hesitation, he asks, "Do you want me to come in, or should I wait out here?"

My eyes squeeze together for a moment, thinking about his question, my heart and head once more battling it out. Do I want him to come in? I don't know if I can trust him at all, especially with whatever I am going to find out and what he would do with that truth. My jaw tightens at the thought. Anxiety fuels the beating of my heart as it becomes heavier, harder, louder. What comes next will change my very existence, and I don't know if I can do it alone. I don't know if I want Quentin by my side either. Opening my eyes, a brief smile sweeps across his lips, but it quickly dissipates as I shake my head in a silent no and walk into my childhood home alone.

I don't know for sure, but I swear she knew I was coming. The air is thick with an uncomfortable silence when I first enter the kitchen. Mum doesn't flinch when I tell her Quentin is outside, but her large, caramel eyes thin with judgment as I sit at the table. Floral scents fill the room as the tea brewing on the stove starts to whistle.

This should be easy, shouldn't it? But as time stretches on and on, and the longer we sit in a bubble that's about to burst, I realise that this isn't just about me. I have to tell her about Guy. His death. Suddenly, it is all much harder to speak.

It's not until I take a sip of tea that Mum says with worried eyes, "Paegence, what is it you're not telling me?"

"Well, Mum," I rebuff, trying to keep my emotions in check, "I could ask you the same question."

The events of the past evening come spewing out of my lips in an explosion.

The Scorpions looking for Guy and me.

Guy dying.

Me killing a Wolf.

Me emerging as a Wolf.

How Guy's Wolf and mine are different from the other Wolves, but the same as each other.

Then there is the curse and her memories. I don't even think I have the energy to bring that up, because quite frankly, this is enough. I know I will eventually. Just not tonight.

With the truth stretching dangerously taut between us, her face shifts from the graceful, elegant Fae with no worries, bar a couple of troublemaking twins at the academy, to one who bears pain and guilt. Her emotions are shielded, but I don't need to feel them. Her face shows every single one, as it twists with secrets she has long buried.

She gracefully stands, flips her snowy blonde braid over her shoulder, removes a bottle of CrystalFyre from the chiller, and pours us two generous drinks. She proffers me one glass as she takes a sip of hers before sitting again. I immediately accept the drink and gulp back two large mouthfuls before blurting out the question that's been burning on my tongue for the past few hours.

"Who's my father?"

CHAPTER 4

"I think you know the answer to that question, but for you to understand, I need to take you back to the beginning."

I lean back in the chair, nursing my glass and waiting for the truth of who I am.

"Before you were born, I was an artist. Many, many years ago, I was commissioned by the royal family, Tiergan Braxtion specifically, to create some artwork, family portraits, stills, and landscapes to fill the palace with life. It was an opportunity of a lifetime. My first day at the palace, I met this dashing young male. His name was Ruh, and we became friends. He was the son of the king's advisor, and I was just a lowly artist employed by the Braxtions, but we spent many afternoons walking the grounds, talking, laughing, and getting to know each other. He was charming, funny, rebellious." Her eyes dart to the door. "Much like your friend out there."

A gasp fills the room as I realise Ruh is Ruhaul, Quentin's father, the King of Elyndria. I grab the CrystalFyre and fill another glass. My mother was friends with Quentin's father. I pour the liquid down my throat, trying to loosen the knot in my stomach.

"One afternoon, Ruh invited me to an event, not as his date, though. We were never anything more than friends. It was not yet taboo for Wolves and Fae to be close, but it was still unusual. I understood going to an event with Wolves could be dangerous, but Ruh was going to be there, and I knew him as kind and protective. So, I agreed." She leans in on her elbow, and I think she is leaning into the past, too.

"It was miserable, and I should have known before I even stepped through those doors. The Wolves were loud and unruly. Ruh was drunk and selfish, too busy trying to bed the plethora of female Wolves to even notice when a very large, very drunk Wolf tried to accost me. And my Fae powers, being passive like yours, were no good to me."

Mum struggles through a story that has clearly left its mark, but it still doesn't give me the answers I am looking for, that I need. "This is all fascinating, Mum, but it's not what I need to know."

Mum places a hand over mine as if to shush me. A smile graces her face, but it's not the warm, loving smile that I've turned to for comfort on many nights. It's one of someone trying to remember something good in an ocean of sadness.

"It was then that I met him. Vharkus."

Her eyes caramel glisten, the sadness of this story still clear as a sunny day, but the smile, the smile is different. The pain of whatever she was feeling a moment ago seems to have vanished just by saying his name.

"Of course, we had *formally* met in the palace. I had painted his portrait, but I never *met* him." She takes another sip of her drink, her throat bobbing hard as if swallowing down the emotions she has kept buried for so long before continuing. "I won't bore you with the details, but he helped me that night, and we became friends."

"Ruh became cold and distant after that night, but Vharkus and I spent almost every day together. He was smart, friendly, and misunderstood. He wasn't like the other Wolves I had met. He was kinder and gentler. We read books under the large oak trees, he taught me about Wolf things, and I taught him about Fae. We hiked waterfalls, travelled to other territories, had picnics by the sea, and watched many sunsets—and just as many sunrises. Our friendship lasted many years. Long after I had finished my work at the palace."

"Were you—" I cut myself off. What was I even going to ask? Were you lovers? Did you date? My mother, the wife of a Star-Borne, was a Fae who lived by rules and thrived in control.

"Not at first, Paegence. No. But I remember the night it changed like it was yesterday. Vharkus and I were always a little flirtatious with each other, but we knew better. I was Fae, and he was Wolf. We could never be anything more than friends. I was dating a dashing Fae by the name of Alistair, and I had been spending less time with Vharkus. We had a terrible argument one winter's eve. A bad storm was coming in, and Alistair wanted me to travel to the Neopolis from Orphelious to see him. Vharkus warned me that it was too dangerous. He wanted me to stay at the palace with him while the storm passed. It was as if Zephyra herself was trying to destroy the lands.

"I was stubborn and independent, and while I wasn't sure if I loved Alistair, my heart and intuition told me to go to Vharkus. I ignored everything and left for the Neopolis." She takes a slow sip of her drink as if cherishing the story, the memories.

"It was dangerous and stupid. The weather was wild that night. To this day, I've never seen anything like the tornadoes that raced across the kingdom in a wild frenzy that night. I hadn't made it out of Orphelious before I became trapped in a family of tornadoes with nowhere to go. Luckily for me, Vharkus was as stubborn as I was and had me followed by a unit of Israykiel Guards. When they saw me trapped and in trouble, they got me safely back to Vharkus. I knew then that I loved him." A small chuckle escapes her lips.

"Of course, Vharkus was punished for using the Guards for such frivolous work, but to me, he was a hero. It was difficult enough to hide our relationship when he was just the king's son, but when Tiergan died and Vharkus became king, it was much harder. It strained our relationship. We fought, we cried, and our time together was sparse, but we loved each other. Neither of us wanted to give the other one up. Until. . .”

“Until you fell pregnant?” I ask shakily.

“We thought it was impossible. A Fae and a Wolf? There had to be a mistake. But it wasn’t. When I gave birth to you both, it was like all my dreams had been answered.”

I drop my glass and gasp in shock. “Twins?” I ask.

“A boy and a girl.”

“Twins?” I ask again.

“Yes, Paege, you and Guy are twins,” she says calmly.

My world spins. I just thought we were brother and sister. I had not even prepared myself for the possibility of twins. But we are the same age, our birthdays are the same time of year, and Mum has given birth to a second set of twins since.

Twins.

Tears well in my eyes. Guy was not just my brother; he was my twin. He was a part of me, and now he’s gone. Gone before I ever got to truly know him. I wish I could go back and meet him again for the first time. Gods, I wish I had more time with him.

“How can you—” I begin.

She interrupts, “We thought we were doing the right thing by you, by both of you, Paege. A female Wolf cannot become alpha, nor can they rule on the throne. We didn’t know what anyone would do about you being the only known half-Wolf, so Vharkus and I thought it best that I take you far from the kingdom to keep you safe. He said he would take Guy and raise him as a Wolf. I didn’t know what Fae or Wolf characteristics you would possess or what gifts you would receive, but I did know that I needed to keep you from ever spilling blood. So, I packed up and moved us to the Neopolis, trying to keep our secret and keep you safe. That was until Vharkus was murdered, and I met Amerax.” She places her hand over mine. “And I love Amerax, I truly do. He has done nothing but try to keep you safe since the day I met him. He has kept your secret, our secret, for all these years, and I knew he would protect you to the death."

Rage, pure white-hot rage burns like a wildfire in my gut, and my Wolf stirs beneath my skin, urging me to release her, to wreak havoc. I pull my hand from her grasp. "I had a father, a brother, a twin. I am a Wolf, and you let me think I was nothing but a broken human in a Fae body. An abomination. You let me think I was a nobody, too fragile and too weak to survive this world."

"No, I did what I thought was—" Mum starts.

"I was an heir!" I scream at her, the fury of her betrayal and secrets forcing itself out.

Mum's eyes go wide, and she shakes her head. "No, no. You were not. Guy was."

"Fucking semantics!" I spit. She took everything from me. Yes, I heard her. She thought she was doing the right thing, but she broke me in the process. I have felt nothing but small and inferior my entire life. Beings judged me, pitied me. Their emotions sour every part of my being.

"Paegence!"

"Oh, don't give me that. You know what you did," I bite back.

"Amerax and I decided that we would move here to this village in Orphelious without many Fae in hopes that we could keep you safe from harm and keep you from changing into a Wolf. When you said you were going to move to the Neopolis for school, I was terrified for you. But I suppose I was more worried for myself that my truth would come out and you would finally find out what I had been hiding all these years." Her face softens, but my heart doesn't.

"And I'm sorry for that. I'm also sorry that I lied to you and kept all these secrets, but most of all, I'm sorry I never got to meet my son and the brave male that he became. I'm sorry that you only met him accidentally. That you never got to know him as your brother. That's on me. That was my choice, and I can never make it up to you. I can never make that right. But Paege, I need you to know that everything I have done, everything that Vharkus and I chose, was to keep you safe. Don't think for one second that he didn't love you because he did. But Vharkus understood that if the other Wolves knew you existed, you would be in danger, and he needed to keep you safe. Everything he did, he did for your safety. And he was killed for it."

"Guy, your son, was killed for it, too," I hurl at her. I bent and broke myself to fit this Godsdamn world. I could have had a different life, a better life, and she took that from me.

She winces, letting her guilt paint her face into a different female. Suddenly, the face of my mother is replaced by a stranger. "They would never have let you live. I had to save you."

"Save me?" I scoff. "Is that what you call it? I struggled every single day. I was alone!"

My mother, now a faceless stranger, doesn't say anything. A silver tear falls from her unrecognisable face. "Paege," she whispers in a plea to forgive her. But I can't, not now. Maybe not ever.

Standing, I say one last thing to the female who gave me life. "I don't know who you are, but you are not my mother."

CHAPTER 5

Alone, with a BarleyAle in my hand, I find myself slumped against the veranda banister, thinking about everything: *King Braxtion was my father. Guy Braxtion was my twin. King Ishaan was her friend.*

I sit upright. Does the king know who I am? If he and Vharkus were so close, if he and my mother were, does he know? Could that be why the Scorpions were looking for us? Did they know somehow that we were related? And what the fuck do they think I have?

There are too many unanswered questions. I need to know more. I need to ask her more, but today isn't the day. My emotions are steadily rising like the ocean tide at the full moon, and I'm not too sure how much more I can take. I can't entirely blame my mother for trying to protect me. For all her faults, loving and protecting me has never been one. But this, this was too much, and to be honest, I don't think I want to forgive her just yet. For the first time in my life, I want to feel every bit of anger and betrayal as it fuels my heart beat.

My Wolf growls in ire as Quentin strolls up from the paddocks with an unbuttoned shirt exposing his tattooed chest. It ripples under the afternoon sun as he sweeps his hand through his hair, loosening shards of grass that have woven their way through his strands. Unfazed and relaxed like he doesn't have a care in the world.

How can he be so calm? How can he hide all emotion? How can he be guilt-free after everything that has happened?

"That horse of yours is a crazy one. Should have named him Frisky, not Whisky." He laughs too casually for my liking as he approaches the steps I'm sitting on, and I bristle.

"Yes, he is," I reply flatly, not moving from my seat.

His eyes instantly lose their sparkle. "Is everything alright?" Quentin rests his arm on the balustrade. "Did you get the answers you were looking for?"

"I think so. Some of them anyway," I say in an attempt to dismiss him, but I'm not successful.

He stares down at me, and his brows arch pushing for more. I press my lips together. "Do you want to talk about it?"

"No—" I snap. *Not with you,* is what I want to say. My anger at him, at my mother bubbling away under my skin. Instead, I opt for, "Not yet. I'm still processing it all."

Quentin drops down next to me on the steps and shoulder bumps me. "Whenever you're ready, Books."

Forcing a smile, I hum in response. The air between us is thick and heavy. Things between us are complicated enough right now. Everything is complicated. For whatever reason, I still have a connection to Quentin, a tether drawing me to him I need to sever because I doubt I will ever be able to fully trust him again. But I am a Wolf now, I need answers and time. He is the only Wolf I know, and with everything going on, one thing remains: I don't belong anywhere.

My mother retired early without so much as a goodnight, and I ushered Quentin into my childhood room after too many ales on the balcony in silence. Quentin and I lie silently in my old bed.

Thousands of memories surround us here. Many of them are new, and many are no longer true. It's conflicting and confusing.

As I lie here awkwardly, I feel every rise and fall of my chest with every deliberate breath I take. The past couple of days weigh heavily on my shoulders, and I desperately want to revisit the possibility of King Ishaan working with the Scorpions, but I fear that Quentin will once again lash out, and things are strained enough between us as it is.

My emotions have drained me this afternoon, and I'm not ready for another onslaught. Between Guy's death, my Emergence, and the story of my mother's past, the emotional roller coaster has left me depleted. I've endured more in this past day than most would in a lifetime.

But is it fair for me to sweep my concerns under the mat? I know they say ignorance is bliss, but is it really? Because from where I'm sitting, if the death and carnage that lies before us is any indication of what's to come, I'd rather be prepared and know exactly who my enemy is and what's coming than be blindsided once more.

So, I open my eyes, inhale slowly, and hold it before I drive an even bigger wedge between us. "Quentin, you awake?" I whisper.

"I am, Books. Are you?" I let out a stifled laugh. "What's on your mind?" He rolls to his side, facing me. The new moon casts the room in darkness, and without its light, I can't see his face, but I can make out the outline of his body as my eyes adjust.

"Too much," I exhale. "But I want to ask you something."

"Alright. . ."

"Before I do, I need you to promise you won't overreact, and you'll just listen?"

"For Edom's sake, Books. That sounds ominous. If you've got something to say, just say it." I can hear the frustration in his voice already.

"Not without you promising," I add.

"Alright, *I won't react*," he says sarcastically.

"Promise?"

"Yes, Paege, I promise," he repeats. I muse for a long moment over the questions burning fiercely inside. This could change everything. "Gods, just say it already. You're making me nervous," Quentin snaps.

"Sorry," I whisper. "Are you absolutely sure your dad doesn't have anything to do with things?"

"Are you fucking kidding me with this shit, Paege?" Quentin barks, and he sits upright in the bed, and I mirror his actions. A scorching flame ignites, and the burning behind my cage sears me with every breath I take.

"No, please, Quentin, just listen to me. You promised," I plead as a need to relieve his anger wars with my need to get answers.

"I can't believe you!"

"Quentin, just listen to me, please. If I'm wrong, I'm wrong, and I will accept that, and I'll apologise for ever making you listen to my crazy theories, but I do need you to hear me out." Out of pure instinct, I rest my hand on his chest, then quickly snap it back.

"Paege, do you understand what you're asking of me?"

"I do," I whisper, heat rushing to my palms.

"Do you? Really?" he asks.

"Yes. I would hate it if someone were accusing my family of such atrocities, but I just can't ignore the facts, especially now."

"And what facts are those, Paege?" Quentin queries.

I deliberate for a moment. Quentin's anger is brewing, and it's making my stomach twist in knots. "How did the Scorpions know where we were camped? It was just us. A Crescent Wolf Pack night. . .*and me*. I didn't say anything. Guy didn't either. But you did. You and Bridget told your dad, right?"

"Of course, we did, but that doesn't mean. . ." He trails off.

"I know, I know," I interrupt.

But Quentin interrupts me right back. "And like you said, they have a Witch working for them. Maybe she. . ." Quentin pauses again, the anger finally subsiding, and I know he's truly considering things as the burning turns sticky and sweet, and worry lines appear on his forehead.

"Yes, they do," I confirm. I draw out my following words gently, "*And* your dad has been keeping a Witch captive, a Seer." I swallow hard, waiting for Quentin to reciprocate, but surprisingly, he doesn't. So, I continue. "Why does your dad have a Witch held captive? And not just any Witch, but the very Witch *I* visited the night I met you. Why did he ask you to follow me?"

I hear Quentin take a shallow breath. "Paege, please. He wouldn't." Quentin's voice cracks as he says my name, and emotions swell in my chest because I know he isn't pleading for my benefit. He's pleading for Guy's. "What is it with you and this Seer anyway? What did she tell you?"

The memory prickles at the back of my head, just out of reach. An uncomfortable truth I don't want to face. Lies, betrayal, death, and new beginnings. A two-faced male. At first, I thought it was about Sylas, but could it have been about Quentin? I hesitate a moment. "Nothing she told me was of any importance," I lie with a steady voice. "Not about this anyway. It was about Sylas."

"Hm," is his only response. But his disbelief pokes into my chest like an icy finger. *Lies.* I ignore it and swiftly continue because we need to consider all of this. I need to be prepared. I need to know the truth, no matter how horrible or harsh the reality is. "Why were they only looking for Guy and me? They were going to let the rest of the pack go. Now we know Guy and I are twins, doesn't it seem odd?"

"Odd, yes, but none of these are *facts*. Only questions and assumptions."

"Is it though? I'm sorry, Quentin. I know this isn't fair for you, but I need you to just think about it. Consider the possibility."

"Paege," he sighs. "I . . ."

My interrogation affects him. A conflict brews inside of him, debating what's true and what's not. Guilt, shame, anger, sadness, and disbelief all emanate from him in waves, and I know I've gone too far tonight. I should have left it until morning.

I sigh and say the only reasonable thing I've said this evening since we came to bed, "Forget it." With that, I hear his heart hammer like thunder during a storm. That's new. Is that some new Wolf trait? Has Quentin always been able to hear mine? My cheeks flush from embarrassment. I've never been any good at keeping my emotions hidden, but it feels like a violation, especially since he's never said as such. I clear my throat. "You don't need to answer anything tonight. It's been a long few days. I'm tired and emotional. Let's just go to sleep," I add, trying to save myself from this emotional carousel I placed myself on.

He just nods and lies back down, rolling over and facing away from me. The wedge between us grows larger with every breath he takes. I can't sleep. So, I lay here listening to Quentin's breathing get slower and deeper until I know he's fast asleep. Gods, how can he even sleep after everything? My mind is like an open book, pages and pages of information laid out before me, not knowing where to begin or what to focus on.

There is, however, still one big question looming, and I need to understand. I need to know. So, I slip out of the bed and quietly exit the room, climbing down the stairs silently, trying not to wake the house. The fire burns in the fireplace, illuminating the lounge and casting shadows that dance around the room. I warm my hands by the coals for a moment before I pad to the exit and step into the inky darkness of the night. As my feet touch the earth, my heart somersaults in my chest, anxiety pouring over me with every breath I take.

Oh, Gods, what are you doing, Paege?

I look up and search the endless skies. Thousands upon thousands of stars illuminate the moonless night. My heart tumbles again, and my stomach twists. I have no idea what I'm doing, no idea how to make this happen or if it's possible, but something deep down inside is telling me to do it.

I slip my nightdress off over my head and stand bare, exposed, and vulnerable. I take in a long, steadying breath and close my eyes, and there she is. My Wolf. I smile as she walks over to me, and my instinct tells me to reach for her, so I do. As my hand brushes over her, the magic explodes within me, filling my body with stardust, illuminating every atom and molecule of my very being, evolving into my very existence. Everything inside and around me hums, and my skin begins to tingle.

I'm suddenly weightless and calm. There is power inside me like I've never felt before, and I need to release it. I open my mouth and bellow an almighty howl, allowing my Wolf to consume me.

I'm free.

As I open my eyes, the world is different. It looks the same, but it's not. Colours of the world are brighter, bolder. It's night, but I can see everything as clear as day. Everything around the edges is a little morphed, like I'm looking through a crystal prism, light refracting, rainbows swirling around at the corners of my eyes. It's not dizzying. In fact, it feels perfectly *normal*.

The gentle breeze blows through the treetops in the paddock far off. Every leaf rustles loudly as they flow, shift, and brush against each other. The musty scent of horses carries across the paddock, bringing with it the fresh smell of cut grass, the perfume of the flowers, and fresh pine from the distant trees and mixes with the smoke billowing from the chimney. Each smell is unique and distinguishable from the next.

And while I'm a Wolf, I'm also still me. My mind is Paege. Paegence Vailenbyrg, broken hybrid, alone. How is this possible? Guy and his father, *my* father, were, as far as we all knew, Crescent Pack Wolves, yet I've shifted under the new moon?

It dawns on me that I know nothing about the Wolves. Nothing real anyway. I know what Quentin and Guy shared with me, tidbits and tall tales. Nothing real or helpful in a situation like this.

Unexpectedly, I sense something move in the house behind me, and I realise someone is coming. I don't have time to figure anything more out. I let go of my Wolf, and my body becomes heavy, and my world effortlessly changes as it shifts back to normal.

"What the fuck?" he growls.

I turn to see Quentin standing there, eyes wide, mouth agape, and I don't need to feel his emotions to know exactly what he's thinking. Because I'm thinking it, too.

What the Hels type of Wolf am I?

CHAPTER 6

Quentin looks a mess as he stands on the veranda watching me after I just shifted under the new moon. His sandy blond hair is dishevelled, and a new darkness appears under his eyes.

"How did you? What?" Is all he says.

"I don't know," I respond almost immediately as I frantically grab my nightdress and pull it over my body, suddenly very aware that I am naked and he is. . .Quentin. But there is no lust in his eyes. It's betrayal, a look I know all too well. I need to explain myself, but what would I say? I don't even know how this happened. "I just had a feeling."

"So, instead of talking to me about it, you decided to what?" Quentin shrugs and raises a brow. "Just come test a theory?" he snaps, and a flash of searing jealousy seeps from him.

"That's not fair!" I retort, anger rising from the depths of my stomach.

"So, what then?" he snaps again, sweeping the hair from his grey eyes.

"I don't know," I say again. "Honestly, I couldn't sleep and kept thinking about everything you had said." Quentin raises both his brows this time. "You know, about our Wolves being different, and I wondered." I sigh. "So, yes, I came out here and gave it a go. I didn't know what would happen. What's the big deal anyway?"

"What's the big deal? Damn it, Paege, you're seriously telling me that you don't have any idea what this means?"

I muse over his question for a moment and consider the possible ramifications of what I just learnt. Yes, my Wolf is different, but there are five different packs. I could belong to any of them. I don't get what the big deal is. "No, actually, I don't! Because you and Guy kept your *Wolf business* to yourselves. You told me nothing, so I know nothing!" I bark. "If you're so worried, feel free to share your insightful wisdom with me."

"You're only half Wolf Paege, not full! And half Fae as well, remember?" His eyes bore into me, like his statement is supposed to trigger something, but I just roll my eyes at him because he still isn't telling me anything I don't already know. "Gods, Paege, are you really that ignorant? As a member of the Crescent Wolf Pack, I could possibly protect you. I could make the pack fall in line and accept you, but. . ." He swallows hard, and I can see his Adam's apple bob. "But as another pack member, I have no sway with how they will treat this violation of our culture. Not to mention what my father would do."

My stomach tightens, and heat rises through my body. My Wolf growls. Violation? I've never been angrier in my life. "I am not a violation of your precious Wolf culture," I snarl slowly, making every word clear. "I had no idea what I was doing. I still have no idea what I'm doing. So, instead of criticising me and treating me like a Godsdamn abomination, how about you help me!" I roar, baring my teeth, and my Wolf growls in unison.

"That's what I have been trying to do since the day we met!"

"Helping? That's what you call this? Helping?" I scream. I don't know if it's all the grief and trauma catching up with me or if it's Quentin's emotions flooding over me. I sure as the Hels don't know if it's the new Wolf existing within my soul, begging to come out and be set free, but I see red, and I want to rip his fucking throat out.

Quentin must notice the ire in my eyes, because he shifts his body, and puts his hands in the air as if he surrenders. "Whoa, Paege, it's alright," he says soothingly, trying to calm me down. "Just breathe."

"It's not alright. None of this is alright!" I yell, and my world spins out of control. I don't know which way is up. "Yesterday, Guy died, *I* killed someone, and I found out I'm a Wolf. Today, I learn that Guy is my twin, not just my brother, my twin, and my father was—" My voice cracks, and I swallow hard trying to keep the lump forming in my throat from growing and the tears welling up in my eyes. "And you. . ." I scowl, teeth baring, but I pause, taking a few long, deep breaths.

"And I what?" Quentin challenges me. His emotions shift, and the thick, oily sensation of anger seeps from his veins, turning acidic as his fear stings my throat.

"And you betrayed me," I snarl with a cold fury.

I drop my head, and my shoulders slump forward. The rage slowly subsides as an old friend, grief, decides to show up, and with it, my bleeding heart sinks.

"Paege," Quentin sighs and bows his head. He hesitantly walks toward me and tries to take my hand, but I pull back. I won't allow him to touch me, to manipulate me with his emotions or mine.

"Don't," I whisper, not looking up at his beautifully cruel face.

I know he's sorry; it pours from his heart like a deluge of salty tears with every beat it takes. I know in my soul that he truly didn't mean to do me any harm, but that doesn't change the fact that he did. He betrayed and lied to me. Honestly, all I've been doing my entire life is excusing others' bad behaviours. Quite frankly, I've had enough.

Today, I discovered that my mother, the one person in this entire world I trusted and loved unconditionally, has lied to me my entire life about my father and my brother. She hid from me who I truly was. I spent my entire life feeling like I didn't belong, like I never fit in, trying to find that piece of me that was missing. And while it turns out my real father is still dead, my answer was right there in Guy.

Then I think back to my time with Sylas, the male I thought I truly loved. All the times he betrayed me, *and all the times I forgave him*. He manipulated our entire relationship. I had no control. He compelled me to forgive his transgressions and his bad behaviour. He took away my liberties, and I was violated time and time again. When I finally found the strength to leave, he kidnapped and tortured me, branding me forever. Brandings that keep me from ever being intimate with another.

So, even if I could look past Quentin's actions, even if I do believe he thought he was looking out for my best interests and trying to protect me, even if I could find it within my heart to forgive him, what would that look like? How would it work? Because I can't be with him. I can never fully give myself to him. To anyone. Not anymore. Sylas made sure of that. With this final understanding, reality slaps me in the face, tightening the knot twisting in my belly and fracturing my heart in two.

"What can I do?" Quentin asks. "How can I help you?"

I look up to Quentin's face, and his soft eyes are full of pity, as I walk slowly toward him. When I reach him, I let my fingers gently brush against his one last time. I let out a heavy breath. "You can leave me alone," I respond in a whispery, strained voice before continuing past him and walking inside the house, closing the door on him. . . On us.

CHAPTER 7

We twirl around each other, the sun beating down on us as our wooden swords smack together in unison—clank, clank, clank. I gobble down air and take a small step back, lowering my sword for a moment as I regain my strength. We've been playing this game all afternoon, and the weight of the wooden sword is becoming heavy in my little hands.

"Are you too tired to continue, Princess?" he taunts, his single dimple just like mine appearing with his grin.

I hold my sword back up, using both hands just like Amerax had taught me. "Never, Prince! I will fight you until my last breath." I lunge for him, and he jumps out of the way, bringing his sword up to meet mine again with a clank.

"When I best you, I will lock you in the dungeons to be forgotten about forever," he laughs.

"You will never be able to best me, Prince," I reply with a giggle. "I am too fast." I swing at him again, and our wooden swords smack. "I am too skilled." Another smack, "Too smart." Smack.

We still, our swords kissing. Neither one of us moves. His emerald-green eyes glisten in the sunlight, and a small bead of sweat drops to his brow.

"Honey, it's time to go."

We relax our swords to our sides as the summer song in my mother's voice carries softly across the garden like petals floating through the air. We both look up. Mum stands with the silver-haired female, one of the two who come with him every year.

"I'll see you next year?" he asks as he drops his sword to the ground and runs off to the tall, dark-haired male who always watches us play from the balcony while my mum and the other one talk.

"Guy?" I call out after him, as something in my chest pulls tight.

He stops and pivots to face me. "Yes, Paege?"

"Happy birthday."

Guy runs back to me, and when he reaches me, he wraps his arms around, pulling me in for a hug. "You, too, little sis."

He takes off running back to the black-haired male and silver-haired female, and then they are gone.

CHAPTER 8

It's been a week since I've been back in the Neopolis, and this new anger that simmers deep inside does not want to be quelled. Quentin quietly left that night. He didn't argue or resist. He packed his bag and went back to the pack manor in Quespelia.

I returned to the Neopolis a day later, and waiting for me at the doorstep of my apartment was Guy's leather jacket neatly folded, his gaudy ring sitting atop, with a formal letter letting me know that when Guy's body had been returned, I would be notified for the cremation ceremony. When I checked the spare room, all their remaining things had been removed except a few rogue items left of Guy's. It splintered my broken heart into thousands of pieces, and I cried for an entire day, grieving the loss of both Guy, my brother, and Quentin, whatever the Hels he was or could have been.

I have spent the last days erratically going through tomes and flipping through journals while at work in the archives, searching for pictures of my father or anything giving me glimpses into his life, to tell me who he was. Not just a king to this forsaken kingdom, but the male he once was. I didn't find much, but whatever I did find, I stared at it, getting lost in the pages. Lost in the glimpse of what I didn't have. Could I have saved him from whatever he did to seal his fate? If I had known, could I have saved Guy, too?

It was a worthless, hopeless search, I know, but one I couldn't bring myself to stop. I look like him. Same green eyes and same small nose. The same flat hair. She spent my entire life fucking lying about what was now plainly obvious. I was King Braxtion's, Vharkus's, child. Guy's twin sister. I suppose when you aren't looking for it, even the most obvious signs can be well-hidden behind the curtains of lies when they are woven tightly shut. Now they are drawn, and the similarities are evident.

Guy's death has changed me. It's not just the Wolf I've awoken within, and it's not just the loss of the twin I never knew I had. I had easily taken a life that night in a single act of revenge and without any remorse. Pure. Violent. Wrath. Yes, Ric had killed many innocents, and he deserved everything I inflicted on him, but that is *so* not the point. It's not me. It was not the Paege I knew. Not the Paege I thought I was. I've now seen a darkness inside of me that scares me to my very core, and I can't help but wonder if the last few months have left a mark deeper than I first thought. Or if it's something entirely different, like the Wolf that's always been there, waiting to be released?

I've not mentioned anything to my friends about my link to Guy yet. I know they will all have questions. Many of which I am not yet ready to face, and most I don't have the answers to. Maybe I'll bring it up with Mhelodie tomorrow when I see her. After all, she does know the secret of the Crescent Wolf curse and the memories of our fallen Fae. But how will she react when she finds out I'm a Wolf? A Braxtion Wolf at that. We still don't know if it's Braxtion or Ishaan blood that triggered the curse, but one of them is the key to breaking it, and knowing I am the last remaining Braxtion, I don't know what that will mean or who I can trust.

Since I've returned, I've been petrified to look for my Wolf. I know she's there. Her magic surges through my veins, craving to be let free, but Quentin put the fear of the Gods in me that night with his words about the packs. Now, every time I have the urge to close my eyes and reach for her, I hear his words playing on repeat, so I fight the impulse and try to dampen her control. Which is a lot harder than it sounds.

I've never been good at being alone, yet here I am, again, lounging in the mezzanine as the sun sets, looking out over the darkening Neopolis. Alone. Physically and emotionally exhausted, ruminating over everything—*over and over*—again.

Dread slaps into me, and I bolt upright. I haven't heard about Guy's ceremony, and it's been a week. As if it is second nature, I grab my scribe and initiate a message to Quentin, who, regardless of our situation, promised to let me know when it was being held.

Me: What's happening with Guy's ceremony? Haven't heard anything as promised - P

But before I send the message, I come to my senses and delete the words I typed.

My pulse races as I stare at the last messages we exchanged. They were just simple words, but they made me feel safe and hopeful. A lump forms in my throat. I swallow, trying to lessen the pressure building in my chest, and in a masochistic move, I close Quentin's message thread and open Guy's.

Salty tears cascade down my cheeks as I read the final exchange between us. I allow them to flow freely, breaking free from their pools like a waterfall after the rain. *Enough,* I try to tell myself, but it's never enough. I should have done more. I drop the scribe from my hands and look back out to the Neopolis, trying to calm the panic and anguish crashing over me like the undulating waves of the Blethen Sea in the middle of a maelstrom. As the city lights sparkle against a backdrop of purples and reds like stars after a midnight storm, I don't calm. Guy will never see this again. He will never hear singing birds at sunrise, children playing in the woodlands, or laughter in the streets. He will never feel the warmth of a hug or smell the new bloom of a spring's flowers. He will never get to have another sip of DesertFyre, eat gridcakes again, or hear his favourite song—which he tells everyone is a heavy metal song by one of our most famous Wolf bands ShapeShifter, but really, it's one of their covers of a classic song from long before.

With that thought, I stand and make my way to the room he made his own. I grab his heavily worn leather jacket from the bed and bring it to my face. Its softness caresses my cheeks, and I breathe in the only remaining thing I have left of him, his scent. It's sweet and syrupy, like the gridcakes he used to make me. I take his ring and place it on my thumb. The metal tingles warm against my skin, like it has every other time I've worn it the past few days. I let the heaviness of Guy's death consume me, and the darkness I've been trying to ignore overrides me. He should be here. He should be alive. I failed him. We all failed him. It pulls me beneath the swirling waves like a powerful whirlpool of emotions that I want to drown in.

But then *she's* there, my Wolf. Her powerful presence drags me back to shore, rescuing me from the emotional vortex I'm descending into. As I stare into her hypnotic emerald-green eyes, the burden in my aching body lifts. A stillness washes over me, gentle and caressingly, and I effortlessly drift off to sleep, but what waits for me on the other side is nothing peaceful.

The metallic taste of blood wraps itself around my tongue as I pull myself through the thick, muddy puddles that separate me from my twin. Wind fiercely whips across my body, and rain stings my eyes, eyes that resist the urge to blink away the discomfort and disengage from the target they have locked onto. My muscles ache, and my bones groan as I crawl forward, but I refuse to succumb to the pain.

I refuse to give up. Emerald eyes return my gaze, lifeless and still, and bile crawls up my throat. Every breath I take rattles as the gaping wound in my chest bleeds, filling my lungs with blood, not air.

As the rain finally stops, the mud thickens, making every movement heavier and unsteady, and my mindset wavers for just a moment. The heaviness in my body is winning the battle with my head, with my heart. I'm close to his body now. I just need to make it a little further. I gain another inch. Inches, that's all I'm travelling, mere inches. Just as I'm about to reach him, I hold out a trembling arm, stretching my limb out, my muscles pulling taut and joints throbbing as I try to touch him. I'm so close. As my hand finally touches his, I let out a long, rattled breath as my body collapses in relief. I made it.

But then my heart stops beating as I watch in horror as his body disintegrates into a pile of ash right before my eyes.

No!

I blink, one, two, three times as a thumping on my door startles me awake. Sweat beads across my forehead, and I search for my stifled breath. *Just a dream, Paege.* Another variation of the nightmare that plagues my sleep.

Streams of sunlight caress my skin as I take in my surroundings. I'm in Guy's bedroom, curled up in a ball on the bed, cradling his jacket around me as if I were trying to feel him one last time. The door pounds again, one, two, five bangs, and it takes me a moment to get myself moving, my breath still shaky and shallow from my nightmare.

After placing Guy's ring back in the drawer, I approach the door apprehensively. By the position of the sun, I know Mhelodie isn't due to be here for a while. Asheron wasn't planning on being in the Neopolis this weekend, unless we had confirmation about Guy's cremation. Lumeilia was visiting her parents in Orphelious this weekend. There is no one it could be.

Closing my eyes, I ask quietly, "Who is it?" but I get no answer. "Hello?" I ask again a little louder. Still no answer. I unlock the door and swing it open, and my heart kicks me hard as I see a familiar figure walking through the garden back toward the gates. Frozen by my anxiety, I watch him reach the gates. What do I do? What do I do? Do I call out and invite him in? Do I let him walk away? That damn battle plays out again, and my temples tighten. When I finally exhale, his name slips out with it. "Quentin?"

He pauses mid step, but doesn't turn around straight away. It's a breath or two before he slowly pivots, and a small smile escapes from his lips. He hurriedly strides back, his smile growing with every step. When he finally reaches me, he just wraps his arms around me and whispers, "I'm sorry."

I don't flinch or pull away, but I don't reciprocate.

Stiffening, he pulls away from me, and his eyes study my face. I watch uncomfortably as they dart between my eyes, down to my lips, and further down before I notice the slight blush to his cheek, and he returns his gaze quickly to mine. "It's good to see you," he says on a long breath. "I know you wanted me to stay away, but I needed to see you. I hope you don't mind."

Confusion sets in. He came back of his own will. I told him to stay away, to leave me alone, but here he is, needing to see me. No one has ever come back for me before. No one has ever chosen me before. With Sylas, it was a compulsion, a siren song. It was a sick need to control. But with Quentin. . . Had he thought of my last words to him? Had he considered his father's stake in all of this?

No, that voice in my head screams at me. *No,* my Wolf growls. *Don't trust him,* she says. *You have control now.*

I'm still so fucking angry at him. Furious. Everything feels like a lie, and I can't trust anything he says. Still, he's not easy to turn away from. Some small part of me isn't ready to let him go. He's one of the two connections I have left to Guy. I can't walk away from that, not yet. And I'm a Wolf. No matter how I look at it, no matter how hard

I try to suppress it, I can't ignore the truth simmering beneath my skin, howling from the depths of my soul. If I've learnt anything over this past week, I have no idea how to navigate this or what it means. I have no pack. I belong nowhere. Something inside of me inherently knows it's not supposed to be this way. I need someone. He's the only Wolf I know. I need *him*, even if I don't want to. Even if I can't trust him with my heart, maybe I can trust him with this. Why is everything so Godsdamn complicated? I know life isn't meant to be easy or straightforward. It's a maze of possibilities and insecurities, of choices and hope.

Stepping aside, I pray to Zephyra herself that I'm making the right decision and let hope in. Quentin takes a seat at my dining table. Neither of us speaks while I wait for the water to boil and the coffee to brew. Time stretches on and on and on until I pour us both a cup and hand him one. He's completely dishevelled, like he hasn't slept or bathed since I last saw him.

"What are you doing here, Quentin?" I ask as I sit opposite him, my mug scolding my hands while I cup it with anticipation.

"I know I said I would stay away, and after the way we left things, I wasn't sure you would want to see or speak to me. But I needed to see you. I need to speak to you."

"Alright," I drawl, curiosity clawing at me like a cat.

"I actually don't know how to say this."

My stomach knots like a hundred barbs of wire are twisting within. What could be so hard to say that even Quentin Ishaan can't find the words? I hold my breath with the anticipation still burning inside me. And if I had known what was to follow, I think I would have poured us a DesertFyre, not coffee.

"Guy's missing," he reveals.

"What?" I drop my coffee mug onto the table. Coffee spills over the edges just like my emotions this week. It pools on the wood in a dirty puddle, but I ignore it. "What do you mean by *missing*?"

"Missing, as in no one knows where he is."

"I know what missing means, Quentin," I snap. "I mean, how is this possible? Didn't you get him back at the exchange?" My mind scrambles to make sense of what I am hearing.

"No, we got Deekon and Monella back, but the Scorpions said Guy's body went missing the day after combat." Quentin shifts around in his chair, and he sweeps the hair from his eyes, "I've been to check out the Scorpion's Manors and the Omega Dens. He isn't there."

"Well, where the Hels is he, Quentin? A dead body doesn't just disappear by itself?" I snap because, seriously, they don't.

"Don't you think I know that Paege? If I knew where he was, do you think we would be having this conversation?" he bites back, and fair enough. I know I am being a bitch, but after everything that has happened, now Guy's body is missing.

I sigh and respond, "No, but his body can't have just disappeared; someone must know something?"

"I agree."

I'm a little shocked he's agreeing with me, but still, he gives me no solid answer. "Well, who?" He takes a sip of his coffee and stares at me, eyes and face expressionless. It's the best damn poker face I've ever seen. "Have you spoken to your *dad*?" I internally grimace as I say the words. I didn't want to bring his dad up, especially after our last conversation about him, but I don't think now is the time to be subtle about things. "He must have some sort of influence in these sorts of situations?"

Three painstakingly slow breaths pass before he finally speaks again. "He said it's pack business, not royal business." He darts his eyes away from mine, knowing full well how I am going to react to that comment.

"You can't be serious? Isn't your dad still the alpha? That makes it his business." I slam my hands down on the table, giving into the anger that keeps rearing its ugly head, and my palms sting briefly from the force.

"I know, Paege. Something's not right. Dad, he's being. . .evasive."

I nearly fall out of my chair. *I knew it,* I internally scream at him. Every part of me wants to say, "I told you so," and revel in how right I am. But the look Quentin gives and his emotions bleeding into me make me pause. It's not remorse, but it's close enough. Betrayal.

I sigh. Whether it be my Fae gift, my Wolf, or my own damned heart, my instinct is to comfort him, but what would that solve? How will that help us? Comforting him won't help us find my twin's body. Just because Quentin is too ignorant to see his own father for who he truly is doesn't mean I have to continue to placate the truth for him. He's a big boy, the son of an alpha. The fucking heir apparent.

"I know, Paege. Trust me, I know." As he says the words, my chest tightens. "You have no idea how sorry I am about the way I acted when you tried to tell me, but I think I finally believe you. Things don't add up, and right now, I think you're the only person I can trust. That's why I came."

"Good. I am glad you are finally seeing things the way I do. Maybe we can be honest now and start putting the pieces of this puzzle together. Guy was your brother, but he was mine, too. My twin. I refuse to let anyone, your dad included, get in the way of me finding him."

CHAPTER 9

Quentin spends the morning filling me in about his multiple pleas to his father, asking for his aid in locating Guy's missing body, and all the ways his father evaded him. I take the opportunity to quiz Quentin about what exactly his father had asked of him earlier this spring with his secret mission to protect me. That doesn't go down as well as I want. In fact, I don't get anything close to an explanation. Just another apology and more excuses before he storms off to the spare room, slamming the door.

My father is the king. What he asks of me is between him and me, and I don't have a choice but to obey his commands. But his intentions were moral, and my intentions were good.

While Quentin sulks in Guy's room like a pup with his ego bruised, I ready myself for Mhelodie's visit. How am I going to explain Quentin being here *again* after I had told her that we were not going to be seeing the Wolves anymore outside of Guy's cremation? I cannot believe that Guy's body is missing, and no one has any idea what has happened or even cares enough to help. I'm trapped in a revolving door when it comes to Quentin and the Wolves, and I wonder when I'll eventually exit and where I will end up.

And then there is still the looming issue of me also being a Wolf. When did my life become so bloody complicated? Right about the same time I *'met'* the wolves, I suppose.

It's noon when Mhelodie knocks on my door, and when I answer, I'm surprised to see Mhelodie standing with Sydney, her new Witch friend. "Come in," I say eagerly, trying to quell the anxiousness that threatens to squeeze the life out of me.

"Why, thank you, Princess," Sydney sings in her thick, rounded accent before gracefully waltzing through the door.

I raise my brows at Mhelodie as she follows—again carrying a pile of books—and she smiles and shrugs. Mhelodie places the books on the table, and I glance over them. On the top is an old tome written in an ancient language I've not seen before, and as an archive assistant, I am fairly versed in many tongues. While I scan the pile, I notice the red leather book halfway down.

Before Sydney and Mhelodie get a chance to sit, Guy's bedroom door swings open, revealing Quentin, and everyone freezes as if time is stuck. He throws a mischievous grin our way. "Hello, Witches," Quentin sings, and he strolls over to the table and picks up the first book. "What's all this?" he asks, and I swear I see Sydney bite her bottom lip.

"Sydney," the Witch says by way of introducing herself, and she holds up the back of her hand to Quentin. My mind flips as I watch him take it in his own and smile broadly before placing a gentle kiss on her hand.

"Quentin," he responds in a rather obnoxious tone. "It's a pleasure." He walks to my kitchen and helps himself to a coffee.

"I didn't realise we would have such company. If I had known—" Sydney looks down at her body and snaps her fingers. "That's better." She smiles, and before my eyes, her outfit changes, transforming from the modest cloth dress she was wearing into a deep blue velvet corset and long-sleeved dress, which makes her stunning auburn hair shine a deeper shade of red and her skin look even more porcelain.

Impressive!

Quentin doesn't seem to notice. I turn back to face Mhelodie, who is still staring at a shirtless Quintin in my kitchen. I follow her gaze and force myself to disregard any arising feelings. I clear my throat loudly and wait for her attention to return to me, but it's not until Quentin leaves the room and closes the bathroom door that I get both their attention.

"Um, Paege, what's going on there?" Mhelodie whispers. She throws me a cheeky grin while wiggling her brows. "I thought you said. . ."

I hold my hand up and interrupt her before she has a chance to finish that sentence. "Nothing." I shake my head. "He's here because of Guy."

"Oh." Mhelodie's voice drops. "His ceremony?"

"No, actually. He's missing," I say, trying to hold the sadness and anger at bay.

"Missing?" Sydney interrupts. "Hm, that's unfortunate."

"Oh, Paege, I'm sorry. What can we do to help?" Mhelodie adds, and she reaches out to take my hand, but as she touches me, my magic reaches for her, and the space between zaps, shocking us both.

"What was that?" I ask, confused as I pull myself from her reach.

"What's going on with you?" Mhelodie asks back. "Something's different," she says as she scans my face, and her eyes widen.

My heart races wildly, and anxiety starts creeping in. I haven't yet decided if I am going to tell Mhelodie or not. "Nothing," I blurt out before I find an answer.

"That's not entirely true now, is it, Princess?" Sydney says nonchalantly, and I can't help but feel she knows something. Oh, fuck, does she know? Can she feel it? I know Sydney is a strong, presumably old, Witch. Can she feel my Wolf's magic? Can she tell I've changed? Can Mhelodie?

"But I'm sure Paege will fill us in when she is ready," Sydney adds. "Right now, I think we should be focusing on this." She runs her hand over the dark leather-bound tome on top of the pile with the ancient gold symbols embossed on the front.

"What is that?" I ask, happy and relieved to change the subject.

Mhelodie's eyes widen once more, and I swear I see the golden hue of her eyes swirl. "So, this is *The Book of Revelations.* It talks about ancient Eagles, an all-seeing eye, if you will. Eagles who not only see the future but also see the truth."

"You can read that?" I ask, pointing to the book, impressed.

Mhelodie smiles and continues, "The Eagles are apparently not of this world, therefore immune to the magics bestowed on our lands."

"Alright." I nod, listening to every word she says.

"Sydney and I were thinking, what if the Eagles know the truth? What if they can break the spell that made us forget? Or can they find the dagger to break the curse?"

Do we finally have a lead? Can we find the answers that Guy was looking for? The organ in my chest cracks. Guy, who is dead. Guy, who wasn't even a Crescent Wolf. But Quentin is. I owe it to him to keep looking, don't I? I owe it to the Fae, the kingdom, at least. They, *we,* didn't ask for this. The memory of the Seer and her tarot cards seeps into my mind, the empress card flashing before my eyes. Is this what she meant by the empress? Is this my rebirth, my final destination, embracing the world with care and wisdom? Death was surely about Guy. I certainly feel like I died that day. The rest, well, that was about Sylas, I'm sure.

"Mhelodie, Sydney, you're both Goddesses!" I exclaim excitedly.

"I wouldn't get too excited just yet, Princess," Sydney interjects. "These Eagles, they live between the realms, and the only way to access them is to find the gate."

"What's the gate?" I ask, with intrigue and a little apprehension.

"A portal of sorts, but a gate to another world, another realm." Sydney pauses, and I notice Mhelodie's eyes lose their sparkle before Sydney finishes. "Which is apparently near impossible to find."

"Of course, it is." I slam my hands down on the table for a second time today. My palms sting from the impact.

"It could be a Watergate, a Windgate, an Earthgate, or a even a Firegate. . ." Sydney continues as if she's only muttering to herself.

"Don't worry, Paege, we'll figure it out," Mhelodie says while Sydney continues to ramble on. She brings her hand to mine, but before she touches me, she freezes and darts her eyes up to mine. "Paege, can you feel that?"

I pull my hand back and close my eyes to see my Wolf standing there, inviting me to touch her, release her. Instead of giving in to the temptation, I open my eyes, and I try to push her away, trying to dampen the magic she emits. My Wolf growls. *She* growls.

"Paege? You're different. You've changed. . .I can feel it," she adds.

Shit, shit, shit, shit.

"It's nothing. We can talk about it later. Right now, I just need to focus on this." I swallow, "and Guy," I add, hoping it's enough to drag her attention away from me.

"Of course, Princess," Sydney responds. "Anything to help you and Guy," she drawls. "Clearly, he meant much to you."

With all the commotion, I don't even notice the bathroom door open. It's not until I hear his voice that I realise he's in the room with us. "What trouble are the three of you stirring?" Quentin jokes as he strides toward us—this time fully clothed. The grey long-sleeved V-neck shirt fits him like a glove, as do his denim pants, showing off every single taut muscle concealed beneath. He rolls his shirt up to his elbow, exposing the tattoo that travels down his arm, and my pulse quickens. . .again. *Am I ever going to be able to squash these feelings?* There's no denying it; he is good to look at. Handsome in all the right ways. *But that means nothing,* I chide myself. *It's just a physical attraction.*

"We are just discussing the crescent moon curse," Mhelodie answers. I'm about to object when she winks at me. Mhelodie and Sydney explain to Quentin the details about the curse without any hesitation. At first, I think, *what the Hels are they thinking?* I distinctly remember us agreeing *not to* say anything, but it soon becomes clear that Quentin can't remember any of the details about the curse due to its magic.

"You're saying you can break the curse with a dagger and the blood of the ones who triggered the curse, but you don't know where the dagger is or whose blood that actually requires?" Quentin asks. "This doesn't sound too hard at all," he adds sarcastically, and then a concerned look washes over his face. I know that he will forget this conversation shortly, but my heart aches seeing him churn over the information and come to the realisation that it's either his blood or mine that is needed to break the curse.

"Quentin, it won't come to that," I say, hoping that he trusts my words to bring him some peace before his memory is wiped, but I guess it doesn't matter because once again, his memory is wiped. Just like every other time.

"Won't come to what?" he asks. It's been three times now. The details of the curse are gone, and his mind is at ease. By the look on Sydney's face, I can't help but wonder if the Witch is having too much fun with all of this.

"So, do we know where these Eagles are or where the gate is, at least?" I ask, steering the conversation back around to how we are going to solve this problem.

"Well, we don't know where exactly, Princess, but we believe they are in the Mountains of G'phyn."

"Who's in the Mountains of G'phyn?" Quentin enquires, as he scratches behind his ear and scrunches his face in confusion.

"The Eagles," I answer shortly and then return my attention to Sydney. "The Mountains of G'phyn are un-magic lands. How can the Eagles be there? How can the Eagles access their magic if there is no magic there to access?" I ask, pointedly, also confused by the information Sydney is sharing.

"The Eagles are in the In-Between, another plane that can only be accessed via a gate. The gate will transfer you to the In-Between, where the Eagles have access to their magic. The gate is in the Mountains of G'phyn somewhere. How the gate itself exists within the mountains, we do not know, but I assume it would be similar to the gate to the Human realm that lies beyond the mountains," Sydney answers.

"It probably has something to do with it being an entrance to a plain where magic *does* exist," Mhelodie adds.

"And the Eagles will be able to help us find another way to break the curse? Without having to use the dagger on. . ." I swallow and look at Quentin, who is studying me closely, and I can't bring myself to say it, so I don't.

"Ah, sorry, but use what dagger on who now?" Quentin asks again. I swear this is getting annoying.

"Why, the dagger to break the curse of course," Sydney replies in a cheerful tone, and she grins as she leans over the table and wipes the hair from his eyes and pats him on the head like a good little pet.

For the love of Zephyra, she's having way too much fun with this.

Mhelodie rolls her eyes and then answers my question. "Honestly, Paege, we don't know exactly what the Eagles will be able to tell you, but they see and know all. They are our best shot."

"Alright." I nod. "So, when are you going?" I ask, eager to find out when we can get some answers.

"Oh, Princess, I fear you misunderstand us. We are not to travel to the Eagles." She lets out a little laugh.

"Alright, then how are we going to get the information?" Now I'm the confused one because if they aren't going, then who is?

"We," Sydney drawls, "are not." Her chestnut eyes glisten. "You, my dear, are."

"What?" I jump out of my seat, and my chair crashes behind me. "Me?"

"The Eagles will only reveal themselves to whom the enigma relates. This is your mission, Princess. *You* must be the one who seeks them out."

Are they out of their freaking minds? Me? I can't possibly do this. I can barely look after myself here in the safe confines of the Neopolis and my apartment, and they want me to travel through the White Forest, through the Dead Forest, and then climb and explore the caves of the Mountains of G'phyn to look for a gate we don't even know would look like. All for a sacrifice that could break the curse of the kingdom.

No. Fucking. Way.

CHAPTER 10

"You've got to be fucking kidding me? Sorry, Mhelodie, but me? Me? You've met me, right?" *I can't do this. It's bad enough knowing what may come, but this. . .* I breathe deeply to calm my racing heart, just as Amerax taught me, and I nervously reach for the charm my mother gifted me, zipping it along the chain that hangs around my neck.

Oh, the Gods. Oh, the Gods.

The charm bites at my fingers, and I immediately drop it. *Damned static!*

"I'm with Books on this one," Quentin chimes in. "You can't seriously think she's capable of going. . ." A blank look washes over his face. "Where are you going?" he asks, once again muddled by the conversation being held around him.

"Shush, deary," Sydney intercepts again. "The grown-ups are talking," she says to an ever-forgetful Quentin.

"I wasn't a fan of this plan to start with either, Paege. But there isn't any other way." My stomach twists. "But I have come up with an idea to help you out." Mhelodie smiles widely. "Besides, you can take Quentin with you; it concerns him, too."

I quickly glance at Quentin, who's darting his eyes between the three of us, looking more perplexed than ever.

"What? Mister Forgetful over there?" I point to Quentin, who grimaces, looking a bit wounded by my comment and still befuddled. "What a great help he's going to be. He can't even remember this conversation." I roll my eyes.

"Why, you just need to give him another reason for going to seek out the Eagles, and the memory will stick. Besides," Sydney drawls with her thick, rounded accent, "with your newfound magic, Princess, you shouldn't need as much help as you think." She raises an eyebrow at me and stands to walk toward the kitchen.

"What magic?" Mhelodie enquires as I finally pick up my discarded chair. "I knew something was going on."

"It's nothing," I respond, trying to ignore the grenade Sydney just planted, but do so with little luck because Quentin pulls the pin.

"You know, Books being a Wolf and Guy being her twin."

"That you remember!" I snap, and Quentin can see my frustration, and he mouths, "*Sorry*" to me before he also stands and walks toward Sydney, who is motioning for him to join her.

"You're a Wolf? A Wolf?" Mhelodie exclaims loudly, her face contorting into something that resembles fear mixed with confusion. "Why didn't you ever tell me?"

"I only just found out a week ago," I reply, trying to swallow the lump appearing in my throat.

"How? What does this mean?"

"I don't know, Mhelodie. All I know is Guy was my twin brother, I am a Wolf, and my whole life as I know it is one big fucking lie," I bark, trying to hold back the tears that want to escape my eyes.

"You're a Wolf," Mhelodie sighs. "And Guy's your twin?" She runs her hands over her face, tucks a gold ringlet behind her ear, and sighs again. "Wow. I mean. Wow!"

She studies my face for a moment, and then I think the reality that I must have taken a life hits her. That my father was King Braxtion, a Crescent Wolf—*supposedly*—and she cries, "Oh, the Gods, Paege, I'm so sorry. What can I do?"

It's too late. The rage is already brewing. "You can help me figure out how to get to the Eagles so I can break this damn curse," I respond bluntly. Mhelodie's golden eyes widen with the shock of my abrupt outburst. "Sorry, that was not about you," I add because I know none of this is Mhelodie's fault. She's only doing what Guy and I asked of her in the first place. I opened this whole can of worms, and it's too late to put the lid back on.

"Well, that I can do." Mhelodie nods and smiles, relieving me of my frustrations. "I already have half a plan. The rest we can work out together." Her eyes dart across the room. "But what do we tell Quentin?" in a voice not much louder than a whisper.

I haven't even decided if I am going to take him with me, but this is much bigger than us. It's bigger than Guy. Maybe taking Quentin with me wouldn't be so bad. I could use this time to learn what I can about being a Wolf. Learn what I can about him and his father. I can't do this alone. If I'm being honest with myself, I don't want to do it alone.

Sighing, I reluctantly give in. "Leave him to me. I think I have an idea." Quentin may not remember anything that relates to why or how the curse was made and the details about breaking it, but we all can remember that there is a curse. I'm sure the secret to getting the memory to stick is not to mention the details. Plus, I am not a Crescent Wolf. My Wolf is something entirely different, something unknown. I suppose I could also tell him I am seeking the Eagles' help about my Wolf. About Guy's Wolf. That should be enough to keep Quentin's memories intact and give him enough motivation to come with me on this ridiculous mission. And if they truly are all-seeing, all-knowing, then maybe they can also help us locate Guy's body.

Maybe.

What a dangerous word. It inspires hope and assumes possibilities. Yes, "maybe" is a dangerous word indeed, but one I badly want to hold onto. "So, what's this plan of yours?" I ask.

"Alright." Mhelodie draws in a long breath. "There are no portals into Owenstown or the Mountains of G'phyn. So, the only way in is to travel through The Dead Forest. The Dead Forest is a *dead forest*. No technology works there. No scribes. You will be going in blind," Mhelodie starts.

"Oh, great, that's comforting!"

"But I have come up with an idea, and I think it's absolutely the best idea ever."

"Which is?" I query hesitantly and wait for what feels like an entire day before Mhelodie reaches into her bag and pulls out two journals and two pens and places them on the table.

"Journaling? Your solution is journaling?" I ask, probably sounding a little too cynical, because seriously, *what the Hels, Mhelodie?*

"Yes, but not just any journaling." She stares at me like she's waiting for me to figure it out, but I have no clue where she's going with this.

"Mhelodie, you're killing me here. Just tell me, please because I have no idea what you're trying to say."

"Well, we won't be able to message each other, but what if we can write?"

"You want me to send you a letter?" I scrunch my nose up at the journals. I wouldn't even know how to send a letter. I've never had to consider it.

Mhelodie snorts out a little laugh. "No, silly. I want you to journal." She smiles, and her eyes light up. "Everything you or I write in one journal will magically transfer over to the other. I can help you from here. Whatever you need, directions, help, or even just a friend to talk to. You write it in here with this pen, and I will get it in my book instantly. Then I can reply to you."

"That's an ingenious idea, Mhelodie." Jumping out of my seat, I wrap my arms around her, and the air zaps between us as our bodies collide, but I don't care. I don't flinch or pull back because this beautiful, amazingly talented Witch is my best friend, and she needs to know just how much I love her. I kiss her on the cheek. "I love you!"

"I know." Mhelodie pulls away, her face a little pink, probably because I just suffocated her. "Don't get too excited. You can't travel by portal to get there. You are going to have to go on foot, and it's going to take a long while. Weeks, possibly longer depending on the weather. But there's no other way."

"What about riding?" I ask, thinking I may have a solution for that.

"You could probably take a Centaurion to get out of the city and to the White Forest, but. . ."

"No, I mean a horse," I interrupt. "Can I ride my horse, Whisky?"

"Oh, yes of course, that's a great idea, Paege. That will save you heaps of time. Just be careful, those forests are dangerous places."

"Yes, I remember. We've been told our entire lives the dark magics that possess the lands and the dangerous creatures that once roamed there. But they *are* extinct now, right?"

"I think so," Mhelodie replies, not very convincingly. Wonderful, she only thinks so. Hopefully, whatever is in the forest, Quentin and I can survive it.

"Oh," Mhelodie gasps. "If you leave a few days before the waning crescent moon, by the time you get to the dead forest, you should have almost two weeks of Quentin, I mean *you both*," she corrects herself, "being able to shift into your Wolf, which will give you more protection and full access to your Wolf magics. *That* will come in handy."

I haven't told Mhelodie I am not a Crescent Wolf and that I can shift at any time. I haven't told anyone except for Quentin, and for now, I am leaving it at that. I need to speak to the Eagles and see what they know before I feel safe sharing any of this.

Porcelain clinks, and I look up to the kitchen where Sydney and Quentin are making more coffee. I smile as I watch Sydney make a fuss over Quentin, and he blushes in a coy manner every time she touches him. I find myself intrigued by his behaviour. It's not romantic in the least; it's something completely different.

As Sydney and Quentin finish making the coffee and return to the table, I pull myself back from my stray thoughts, focusing my attention on Mhelodie. "Well, definitely sounds like we have the start of a plan," I say.

"What plan?" Quentin asks as he sits, handing me a coffee and smiling.

"You know, just the plan where you and Paege are going to go to the Mountains of G'phyn to seek out the Eagles in the In-Between, so you can find the magic dagger to break the crescent moon curse," Mhelodie replies light-heartedly.

"Hm," Quentin answers casually, and he takes a sip of his coffee. As soon as he swallows, his glassy grey eyes go wide, and he darts his stare between the three of us. "Hang on, we're doing what?" he cries out, and Mhelodie, Sydney and I start laughing.

CHAPTER 11

I sit by the River Plye staring aimlessly into the crystalline waters, waiting for Mhelodie and thinking about the particulars of our upcoming trip to the Mountains of G'phyn.

I've taken an extended leave of absence from the museum, which Blaire was only too willing to accommodate. In fact, her exact words were, *"After everything you've been through this past year, I'm surprised it's only now you're requesting some time off."*

And only the Gods know when The Pit will reopen.

We are heading back to Orphelious, my family home. I haven't seen or spoken to my mother since that night, but going home is a crucial part of our plans. I'm still not ready to face my mother, but I have to. A ball of fury burns ferociously in my belly, fuelling my anger and betrayal, blocking any chance of forgiveness. What kind of daughter does that make me? Should I forgive her? To some small degree, I understand what she did and why she did it. I don't want to, but as every day passes, and the more I learn about the Wolves, I know deep down she was trying to protect me. Yet the carnage of my life wants to tell me she never did. It made things worse. It made me weak. I am a product of her making.

Quentin has been coming and going for the last month, alternating between spending time with his family and the pack at the den and spending time with me planning for this trip. Although we have been spending all this time together, it's still been awkward and uncomfortable. The tension between us rises and falls daily. Every time I see his Godsdamn face, my pulse quickens, and I have to use every ounce of my energy not to react. As for Quentin's emotions, they shift as frequently as the ocean's tide. So, I'm training to maintain my focus. I need to be prepared for anything out there, and after what happened with Guy, I am not taking any chances. I've already lost three friends in this messed-up shit. I can't bear to lose any more. So, I need to push all my other feelings down and bury them because mine and Quentin's lives just might depend on it.

Reflecting on the details of the plans we've forged, my pulse thumps loudly behind my ears as I consider one crucial piece of the plan that is still missing. How the Hels are we supposed to find the gate that takes us to In-Between, to the Eagles, when it's so well hidden that even Witches with the strongest of magics can't locate it? A sense of impending doom washes over me.

I am totally fucked.

I'm lost in my myriad of anxiety-building thoughts when someone lightly taps on my shoulder, and as I look up, I see a beautiful face smiling down at me, and my lips pull into a smile.

"Mhelodie!" I shriek while jumping up, and I wrap my arms around her, her warmth embracing me back.

"Hi." She sits down next to me on the bench seat and sighs. "We don't spend enough time down here," she adds. "I always forget how calming it is to watch the river."

I understand exactly what she means. There is something magical about the Plye. Its crystal-clear turquoise water sparkles in the sun, reflecting bursts of light like the stars above, and it's so deep you will never see the riverbed. It's intoxicating to look at. There are myths of an underwater city where the water Nymphs used to reside, but the water Nymphs haven't lived in our lands for thousands of years. According to lore, they abandoned our kingdom for richer waters, and they haven't returned.

"So," I drawl. "Question. What's going on with these powers of yours?" I enquire. "Because damn, they are strong!" I add.

"I know, right?" Mhelodie replies, her face lighting up like a Hels Day tree. "Yours are, too."

Ignoring her comment because I have no idea exactly how strong I am, I ask, "Did you have any clue?"

"I had no idea. I was determined to become a healer."

"I know." Mhelodie has wanted to become a healer for as long as I can remember. When I met her on my first day of Collegium, she spent hours telling me all about healers. I remember how her face lit up, and how her voice would get high-pitched and squeaky every time she would discuss it. It was the cutest thing. It still is.

"My new magic came out when I Ascended on my Sacred Birthday." Her hands clasp together tightly in her lap, her focus not drifting from the water ahead. "My magic is stronger than I ever anticipated, than anyone anticipated."

"That's great though, isn't it? Doesn't it open more opportunities for you?"

"It is, and it does." She shifts on the seat and angles herself to look at me. "But it's also scary. Did I tell you how I read the book?"

"No, actually, you didn't." Mhelodie and Sydney just turned up at my home one day with some answers, but no explanation, and I haven't dwelled on it much. I figured Mhelodie would tell me when the time was right, and I've had way more important things to be worrying about than how Mhelodie read the book, but I am glad she's finally starting to open up about it and talk to me again. The group has been distant in recent weeks.

Mhelodie draws in a long breath and whispers, "It's blood magic. Remember the art gallery with the Lumeilia's sculptures?" How can I forget? It's one of the three most terrifying nights of my life. "I used it then, as I'd been reading about it, and I was so scared. I honestly didn't know if it would work. Then, after my Ascension, I could feel it, my blood, I mean. It was like a living thing, pulsing in my veins."

Like a spooked wild horse, my heart jolts. "Blood magic?"

"Yes," she sighs, and her shoulders sag as if letting go of a heavy weight, and her gaze drops to her feet, which dangle from the seat. I can't help but wonder if that's in fear of her own magic's strength or of what it means. Blood magic is rare and dangerous if not done correctly. Blood Witches are rarer. I haven't been able to read her emotions since her Ascension.

"What does it mean?" I ask anxiously.

"It means. . ." Mhelodie pauses, and I sense her hesitation. "We still don't know what it means." *Fear.* "I don't have a clue what I'm doing. I mean, why can I lift the spells off the book but not the one off your back?" Perhaps I imagine it, but a searing heat slashes across my back where the scars mark my skin, and Mhelodie's eyes fall back to the grass in front of us. "I'm sorry, but I am still trying. I promise I will never give up." It's an apology she doesn't need to make and a promise she doesn't need to keep.

"Hm." I nod in response, unable to find the words. The scars are a daily reminder of what Sylas did to me, but I try not to think about them and what they represent. Especially now that Quentin is back in my life. There are just some things that aren't worth agonising over, and I decided a long time ago that this was one of them. Because if I do, it just reminds me of the one thing that I can never have again, and that brings me more hurt and anger than I can even begin to admit. *Nope, Paege. Lock that shit up and throw away the key.* Damn, that safe is getting kind of full.

"Gods, things are vastly different now, Paege. I don't know how to navigate it all. I'm lucky I have Sydney to help me, but. . ." She trails off, deep in thought.

"What?" Her demeanour shifts, the light in her instantly diminishing.

"It's Lu-Lu. Things between us are straining."

I'll admit, I never even considered how this could all be affecting them. It's not like things have ever been easy for them, but if Mhelodie's as strong as she's suggesting and a blood Witch, she won't be staying in the Neopolis. She will be expected to live out in Cedrus with a coven, and while Witches and Fae co-exist peacefully, I am not too sure they will be accepting of this situation. Like things aren't complicated enough.

"I'm sure things will be fine," I say, trying to sound convincing, but I can tell she doesn't believe me. How can she when I don't even believe it myself? If I've learnt anything over the past few months, it is that shit can go wrong in an instant, and nothing lasts forever. I think of my family and friends and the sacrifices I might have to make, and wonder how in the Hels did we get here? Just six months ago, we were all drinking, dancing, having fun, and living our best lives. Now, I'm a Wolf with an excommunicated king as a father and a dead twin brother. Asheron lost his FaeMate, and Mhelodie is some all-powerful Witch. I think about the book, the curse, the pulsing scars on my back, and all the blood that's been spilled, and a paralysing fear thrums between my temples. Fear of the future and what will become. Fear of losing anyone else. Fear of losing myself.

CHAPTER 12

The sun is barely starting to rise when I jump into the Centaurion, the bruised purple sky healing on the horizon into a light shade of pink, and ride to the portal halls. I sit quietly, nervously rubbing my hands up and down my denim pants and watching the city pass me by, while saying goodbye to my old life. For a moment, the roaring Wolf inside me fights to take control, as I, too, fight back the anxiety coiling around my chest like a viper. I am to meet Quentin at the portal halls, and we are stopping at the campsite before we head off to Orphelious. We're visiting Guy's tombstone. I pull my hooded cloak tightly around my body to stifle the shudder creeping across my body.

One month has gone by, and Guy's body has never been found. He has never come home. On the last crescent moon, Quentin and the Crescent Wolf Pack spent their nights at the campsite in the woodlands, where they made a headstone by the tree where my hammock hung in memory of Guy and the others. I'm grateful, and I want nothing more than to visit my brother. He was a good male. He was honourable, kind, beloved. Yet we all failed him, and my heart bleeds a river of guilt for him every day since he has been gone.

It was tough hearing that story. It felt like my heart was cleaving apart all over again. Why Quentin didn't bother to tell me that was their plan is beyond me. I would have gone. But I'm equally grateful I now have a place to visit him. Especially since I still don't belong anywhere in this Godsdamn world. Swap Human out for Wolf, and I'm still an abomination. Only now I have one more loss to add to that list.

I haven't reached for my Wolf since the night after I merged with her. She's always with me. She's in every breath, every emotion, and every movement I make. But I still don't know who I am or what Wolf pack I belong to. I am completely untethered every time I close my eyes and see her. My magic is strong, stronger than I ever imagined, and I spin out of control. It scares me to my core. Especially because I still have my Sacred Birthday coming up, and only Zephyra herself knows what's going to happen on my Unification. It's a thought I am not quite ready to entertain, so I bury it under everything else I am facing, as I travel through the streets of the Neopolis toward the last place Guy was alive. I have no idea if I'm ready for what lies before me.

My heart thrums hard when I reach the portal halls, anticipation flooding my veins. The statues and gargoyles that are stationed by the metal doors watch me upon my approach. Things may be strained and awkward between Quentin and me, but I need him. He's my only connection to Guy, and regardless of all our issues, I still want to help him. I suppose I'm a sucker like that.

I zig-zag through the crowd of the lower level of the portal halls, and my eyes dart across the various faces, looking for Quentin. A bruising grip on my shoulder has me nearly jumping out of my skin. "I'm sorry, Miss Paege, I didn't mean to scare you," the large Lupa-Centaur says as I turn to face him. The Lupa-Centaurs are unusual beings with a Centaur body and Wolf-like, humanoid faces. It's unnerving. I suppose that's why the king has them stationed around all the portal halls and houses. The Lupa-Centaur's voice is much softer than his grip on my shoulder. "The prince. . ." I raise a brow at the formality, and he clears his throat. "Quentin Ishaan asked me to give you a message. He said, I am to escort you through the royal portals, and he shall meet you at your destination."

Disappointment squeezes tightly around my chest, restricting the next breath I try to take. Why am I not surprised? I nod. We say nothing else as we climb the portal halls' spiral stairs and throw ourselves into the portal.

The trip is long and tiresome, and it's early afternoon by the time I arrive in the woodlands at Quespelia. But at least this time, I don't land on my ass. Sheamus, the Lupa-Centaur, leaves me to traverse the final distance to the campsite alone, and the fury of Quentin's abandonment rears its ugly head as I step around the large boulder into the familiar campsite. That fury is quickly replaced with grief as my eyes survey the campsite.

The log that Deekon died upon. The boulder where Monella's life slowly drained from her body. The spot where Guy painfully lost his life. Where I violently took another. And then, finally, my eyes land on the three headstones. I swallow hard, shaking my head to bury the emotions of Guy. Of all of it.

I don't see Quentin anywhere. The campfire's lit, and the same tent from my past visit here is erected in the same spot. Aside from the missing other tents, it's exactly the same. An audible sigh releases from my chest. I'm about to take another step toward the tent when Quentin appears from inside, wearing tightly woven black pants with deep pockets and a knitted wool tunic. As he exits, his eyes snag on me, and he stills as if unsure of how I will react. Then he smiles, revealing his perfectly elongated canines, and his grey eyes widen, reflecting the afternoon sun.

Shit! My heart flutters with the familiar pull to him. How the Hels am I supposed to spend the next few weeks with him? My eyes dart between Quentin and the headstones, honing in on Guy's, and all my emotions bleed together in a tangled mess. *He's here because I need him to help me with my Wolf*, I remind myself. But he's also here because of Guy. My Wolf howls.

To hell with it!

I drop my pack to the hard earth.

"You made it in good time," he says as I stride toward him and wrap my arms around his body and bury my head in his chest. He hugs me back, and for a minute, I let the warmth of his embrace settle the complicated knot of emotions in my stomach, taking from him what I need in this moment. To feel comfort. When I finally withdraw, he asks, "Are you alright, Books?"

I clear my throat. "Yes, I'm fine,"

Leaving him with my stuff, I walk over to the headstone, and I run my hand over the words etched into cold grey stone.

Guy Braxtion

24

Brother, Friend, Wolf

Gone Too Soon

But Never Forgotten

The words aren't enough, but I suppose it's all we have. I place a kiss on my fingers and transfer it to the headstone before I walk back to the fire and sit down next to Quentin, who hands me a BarleyAle.

"Thanks," I say, and I take a sip, letting the frothy, bitter liquid activate all my senses in my mouth and nose.

"I miss him, too, Books, every day," he sighs, staring into the fire. "Are you ready for this?"

I let a slight chuckle escape my lips. *Am I ready for this? I've never felt more unprepared and out of my league in my entire life.*

"Yes, me too," Quentin responds as if he were reading my every thought.

"Are we crazy?" I ask, taking a sip of my drink.

"Probably," Quentin replies without a second thought. "But I don't think we have any other option if we want to find out about your Wolf pack, about Guy, and about this damn curse."

"I know, you're right. I just feel. . ."

"It's going to be fine," Quentin interrupts. "We're not going in blind. We've got a plan, and if things get too rough, we'll just turn back around."

"You know that's not an option, Quentin," I retort shortly.

"The Hels it's not, Paege," Quentin snaps. "If there is any real trouble, we're out of there!"

My jaw clenches as my shoulder blades pull together, tensing the muscles in my back and neck. There is no possible way I cannot go through with this. There's too much at stake. If Quentin wants to bail, then he can go, but I'm seeing this through to the end. Just as I'm about to say as much, he continues, a lot more softly this time, obviously sensing my irritation. "Look, I know things are complicated between us, Books, but I'm not about to put us in any real danger," he says before casually taking a sip of his BarleyAle.

Frustration bubbles up like molten lava from deep in my stomach, but I push it down. I know he means well, and I certainly don't want to cause any more awkwardness between us. So, I breathe deeply and try to let it go. Though I can't help but wonder if this little pep talk is as much for his benefit as it is mine.

The evening passes quite pleasantly. We took a walk through the woods earlier this evening, and since then, we've sat around the fire, eating dinner, discussing the plans, and reminiscing about Guy and the other Wolves. As I watched Quentin talk about Guy, no matter what he says about this mission, there is no way in Hels he will be turning around and going home. The fury in his eyes burns, a mirror to my own.

It's late, and I'm slightly buzzed from the AmberFyre I just finished. Standing, I sip the last mouthful, welcoming the spicy heat that warms my throat as it makes its way down into my belly. "I think I'm going to bed," I say with a yawn.

"Me too," Quentin replies. "We've got a long day ahead of us tomorrow." He stands, sweeping the hair from his face. "You've got the back room. I'm taking the front."

I catch his eyes. The fire dancing in his pupils makes the hard exterior I'm trying to forge around my heart melt a little. Just a little. I'm buzzed enough to let my guards down and tell him to lie with me tonight but not buzzed enough to forget about my predicament. I need not confuse things right now. Plus, I'm still angry at him for, well, everything. So, without a word, I turn on my heel and walk towards the tent, aware that Quentin is following a few steps behind me.

Settling myself in my bedroll, I listen as Quentin lets himself into the tent. The air is heavy around me as I lie silently, my heart drumming away loudly, aware that only a thin piece of canvas separates the two of us. I search for his emotions, wondering if he, too, is struggling with being so close but so far apart, but I don't feel anything. In fact, I haven't felt any emotions from him all day.

What the fuck?

My mind scrambles as I search for a reason why. And nothing comes to the surface. Theoretically, Quentin should be able to shield himself during the crescent moon when he has access to his Wolf, but it's not the crescent moon. So, what the fuck is going on?

I slowly get up and poke my head through the canvas. "Quentin?"

"Books?"

"You still awake?"

"No, I'm fast asleep," he chuckles, not lifting his head.

"I can't feel you."

"Huh?" he mumbles.

"I can't feel you," I repeat.

"That's because you're in the other room, Books." He yawns.

"No," I drawl a little frustrated at myself for not articulating it clearly, but also at him for not understanding what I'm trying to say. "*I. Can't. Feel. You,*" I repeat over-enunciating each word.

Quentin sits up and lights his lantern, then pats the space next to him. Without hesitation, I move and sit down next to him. Holding up the back of his hand, the one with the crescent moon tattoo, he wriggles his fingers. His middle finger now wears a thick silver ring that takes up the entire space between his knuckles, and it's etched with dark markings.

"What's that?" I ask curiously. I want to reach out and touch it, but I don't.

"It's an iron band etched with runes. I had Mhelodie make it."

My brows arch high. "What does it do?"

"I've been doing some research after the night in the safe room. I wanted to understand why that room locked out your Fae gifts. I discovered that iron acts as a shield." Stunned, all I can do is blink as I inspect the ring on his hand. I can't believe he did that.

"And the runes?" I ask quietly.

"She added them. Apparently, the runes and the iron act as my own personal shield, and as long as I'm wearing it, you won't be overwhelmed by my emotions."

"You did this?" I whisper again.

"Well, yes, Books. I know how hard it is for you, and if we are going to be spending so much time together, in an already highly stressful environment, I didn't want to add to your burden." He says it casually, like it's not a big deal. But it is a big deal.

"You did this." I exhale as tears pool in the corners of my eyes. No one has ever done anything like this for me. No one. Hels, Beings rarely shield themselves from me when they can. And, while in most situations I'm perfectly capable of dealing with it, when emotions get charged, it's hard to manage.

"It's nothing, Books." He shrugs as if he truly believes the words he just said. It's something. I just don't know what yet.

"Thank you." Leaning in, I gently place a kiss on his cheek, then quickly pull away.

The hopeful look in Quentin's eyes tightens the emotions strangling my heart. He did this for him as much as he did for me. Without explanation, I stand. The weight of Quentin's stare follows me as I make my way back to my room, and it lingers as I slip back into my bedroll.

Even if a part of me wanted to forgive him, it wouldn't solve anything. Even if I did go back out there and curl into him and let him relieve me of my guilt and grief, I still don't trust him. He's not here for that. He's here for one thing and one thing only. To help me.

Ignoring the tug in my chest, threatening to push me back into his arms, I aimlessly stare at the ceiling until the faint glow of the light is extinguished.

Do not trust him, I remind myself. I'd rather drown. But that gesture, as small as it was, presses heavily on my chest, restricting my breath. It means so much more, and I don't know what to do with that.

Nothing, I decide as I roll to the side, facing away from the canvas that separates us. Nothing.

CHAPTER 13

I will myself to move, but my bones stiffen, and my muscles seize as bile stings my throat. I watch in horror as she screams. Her broken Fae body writhes on the muddied ground before me. Her emerald eyes beg for help. The gaping wound from her bare ribs oozes with blood. But it's not the bleeding or the wound that has her terrified; it's the heat from the flames that lick against her skin as they grow larger, larger around her, the fire entrapping her as if a wild beast caught in a cage.

A searing pain erupts from my hands as I clench my fists tighter, trying to contain the fury firing throughout my body. I look down as the embers fight for their freedom once more. The heat pulses from my fingertips against my palms, and I don't know how much more I can take. The sickening smell of burning skin twists my stomach as bile rises once more.

My hands glow brighter as I bite down on the urge to let go, to release the flames that want to explode from my body. The young Fae stops fighting, and as she turns to look at me, a single tear falls from her familiar emerald eyes, down her face, and she holds her hand out to me. My body pulls toward hers like a magnet, and long talons gently graze at my mind's door, willing me to let go, to release. I try to fight it, but her power is strong, stronger than mine.

"Trust me," a gentle female voice whispers inside my mind, and I tilt my head down toward my hands and watch in terror as my fingers uncurl, releasing my balled-up fists, and fire explodes from my fingertips. A fire that burns so bright and hot that it engulfs my broken and bleeding body and leaves nothing behind but a pile of smouldering cinders.

Gasping for air, I'm violently ripped from my sleep. I suck in one, two, three hastened breaths before finally recognising where I am and my mind starts to steady.

Just another nightmare, Paege. Just another one of your fucking nightmares.

Quentin's already up, and by the looks of things, he has been for some time. His bedroll is gone, and his absence cracks a small hole in my chest.

The sun's rays peek through the crack in the tent opening, and a soft breeze gently strokes my face. My mouth salivates as the scent of coffee wafts toward me. Sitting up, I find a steaming mug and some warmed oats on the floor next to me. My stomach grumbles from the hunger the smell has awakened within. I dig in without hesitation.

Full of oats, I grab my coffee and exit the tent. I scan the campsite, and as beautiful as it is here, it feels empty without the Wolf pack filling the woodlands with belly laughs and roars. Quentin is nowhere to be seen. I sit by the fire and savour the fresh morning air mixing with burning wood as it envelops me. It's invigorating, and all my senses spring to life. My Wolf loves the smell, too. She settles inside, calm and relaxed. Her complacency is unnerving, to say the least, when I am more accustomed to her fury.

I sigh as I think about what the day holds before me. We are travelling by portal to Orphelious to collect Whisky and a horse for Quentin, which puts the final part of our plan together. And I'll be seeing Mum. I haven't seen or spoken to her since I was there last. I haven't had a lot to say. It's not only because I am still angry with her, but it's also that I am still processing everything. I have questions to ask her, but I am probably more scared than anything else of what else she has been hiding from me. I don't understand how she has her memories of the past. Her stories continue to plague my dreams, and I don't know what it all means. Every time I allow myself to think about it more, waves of anxiety ripple over me, and I find myself spinning out of control.

I haven't any clue what I'm going to say to her when I see her, but that is a later problem. Quentin returns, seemingly refreshed, pulling me from my thoughts. We pack up the campsite, and he takes off on another walk, this time pulling his scribe out. Always taking off, that one.

My eyes drift towards Guy's headstone, and I find myself wandering over to it. Even though the sun rests high above, the air is still cool, and there isn't much movement around. The winter flowers are starting to bloom, and pockets of white, yellow, and violet flowers are sprouting out of the ground that's now covered in burnt orange leaves. They are delicate and pretty, and I pick a few along my walk, tying them together with the hair band that I had around my wrist.

As I sit down by Guy's headstone, I place the flowers on the ground. The silence of the morning and the stillness of the woods force me to pause, and my emotions flood me, wanting to erupt like an angry volcano. Gods, I miss him so much. We should have done more. Tears prickle my eyes, and I sigh. I begin to talk to the twin brother I lost too soon because, in the weirdest way, I feel as if he's here with me.

"Guy," I sigh. "I hope you like your headstone. I know it's not much, but it's right for it to be here. I miss you so much. I think about you every day. I failed you. Everyone failed you. I'm sorry." A single tear falls, and I wipe it away. "You deserved better. I'm heading to the Mountains of G'phyn with Quentin to try to get some answers. I know it won't bring you back, but. . ." I sigh. "It was supposed to be us. I'm lost, and I'm still not sure if I can trust Quentin"—I swallow the emotions choking me,—"or myself," I murmur under my breath.

"I'm scared, Guy. If I find the truth, I don't know if I'll be strong enough to do what's needed to break the curse. I wish you were here to help me. I'm spinning out of control, and I could never explain it before. But. . .but you always grounded me. I suppose I now know why. My twin," I whisper into the wind picking up around me. "I need you. I love you. But I will see you again. I promise." I place my hand over my heart in true Vailenbyrg-style, and I rest my head against the cool headstone, and the words of an old Fae song my mother used to sing to me begin to roll off my tongue.

> *In quiet hours of grief, where sorrow softly treads.*
> *We speak of lost tomorrows, and of Angels, it is said.*
> *With faith as my compass, through this journey we embark.*
> *The heart may bleed in silence, but your memory lights the dark.*
> *In the quiet of the night, when all the worlds asleep.*
> *We feel their warmth, we see their light, in promises they keep.*
> *They're stars that never fade, when shadows merge and blend.*
> *They're guardians in the night, their watch will never end.*

A rustling in the leaves behind me pulls me from my moment with Guy, and I turn around to see Quentin standing there. "Fuck, sorry," he says as I wipe the tears from my face. "Books. That, that was beautiful," he breathes.

"How long?" I sniff, rubbing the tears from my face with the back of my hand.

"Not long," Quentin interrupts me. "Just when you started. . ." He looks over my shoulder, and I turn back to face Guy's headstone, and I place a gentle kiss on it before standing up and walking over to where Quentin stands. "I didn't mean to interrupt. You have an angelic voice," he says, his voice quiet and raspy. Quentin's eyes burn deeply into mine, his look reflecting something between awe and admiration. Embarrassment prickles my cheeks with a warm blush.

I used to sing with my family and our friends before I moved to the Neopolis. Nothing serious, just for fun. It was a way to pass the time in a tiny village with not much else to do. Quentin is the first to hear my voice in over six years, and all I want right now is for the world to open up and swallow me whole.

"Are we ready?" I ask, trying to change the subject, shift his focus, anything to pull his attention away from me.

"Ah, yes, almost," he says. "Do you need more time?"

I shake my head and swallow hard, trying to force the lump forming in my throat away. Quentin steps forward, enveloping me in his arms. "I miss him, too, Books," he mutters softly into my ear, and his body relaxes into mine as he lets out a long throaty sigh. "I miss him, too."

CHAPTER 14

Unknown

Five days. He hadn't slept in five days, or so he thought. The relentless heat of the never-setting sun beat down on him as he walked mile after mile through the sandy desert. Not another soul was in sight. A memory pressed in on him again, and he folded over as a pain bloomed behind his temples, crippling him.

Green eyes, rimmed with silver tears.

A sword.

A Wolf.

A girl.

A scream.

What did it all mean? When the images finally stopped, the pain receded, and he stood upright again. Sucking in a breath through gritted teeth, he composed himself and continued on his journey.

He didn't know who he was. He didn't know where he was. He didn't know how he got here, but a little niggling told him he had to head north, toward the mountains that loomed overhead far in the distance. He would find his answers there. Not that he was sure it was north, but it felt right. It felt like it was north. Dark grey clouds swarmed its rocky peaks like a hawk circling its prey, and he was drawn that way. So, that's where he was headed.

His feet ached, and his muscles burned. His skin was raw and sore to the touch. Maybe there, he would find some reprieve from this heat. Maybe there, the sun might finally set. Maybe there, he would find answers.

He swallowed, his mouth dry as sandpaper, and the coppery tang of warm blood coated his tongue with a sticky wetness. He hated how his blood felt on his tongue. It felt good, giving his body the illusion of hydration. Still, he smiled, and when the cracks along his lips split, that illusion faded.

Water. He needed water. For five days or however long it had been, he had not seen one lake or river, not one body of water. The lands were barren. He didn't know how much longer he could survive out here. But isn't that how every day had gone?

He walked and walked until his body could not hold him up anymore. When his limbs were achy and stiff, when his eyes were dry and heavy, when his breath was short and shallow, he would collapse. When he finally succumbed to the pain and the exhaustion took over, he would tumble to the earth and pass out, only to wake again, fully healed and refreshed. But not safe. He was never safe. That he knew. He was not home, wherever that was. No, he was always here.

And so, the day would start again. And he would walk and walk and walk, looking for whatever it was that he was looking for. Whatever it was that was on those mountains.

Whoever it was that would save him.

CHAPTER 15

We arrive at my family home a little after lunch. The house I grew up in is modest, especially for an Israykiel Guard. Mostly, the Star-Borne families live closer to Quespelia or the Academy in spacious manors surrounded by thick forest lands. We could have had so much more, but Mum never wanted for more; she wanted land for horses and to be close to Quespelia, so Amerax obliged.

The first thing we do when we arrive is stroll over to the paddock where Whisky is patiently waiting. Whisky swishes his tail at the sight of me, but with the anxiety of seeing Mum for the first time since I told her she wasn't my mother, I find myself leaving Quentin at the paddock and walking toward my home. Glistening petals of violet, burnt yellow, fuchsia, and indigo litter the garden beds surrounding the cottage house. The strange gargoyle statues still guard the home. One thing about the Fae, they will always have their gargoyles. The Neopolis is littered with them, and most family homes have at least one pair guarding their doors.

The chimney's billowing smoke is the only sign of life inside. Otherwise, it is eerily empty.

"Hi, Mum," I call out as I push open the front door and walk into the warm living area. I dump my bags by the settee and cross the room to the sputtering fire, the glowing embers almost disintegrating into a pile of ash. I place another couple of logs into the fireplace and follow my nose to the kitchen, where I can smell freshly baked bread. I've never been good at cooking. I tend to live off takeaways or the street food vendors in the city, so coming home to a house that smells like freshly cooked meals is a treat every single time. I half expect to find Mum sitting at the dining table reading a book with a cup of tea and a coffee ready for me, but the kitchen is vacant. The kettle is warm but almost empty, so I refill it and set it on the stove while grabbing a couple of mugs to make some freshly brewed coffee.

While the kettle heats, I climb the stairs to the second floor to the bedrooms and make my way down the hall. I take my time, touching my mother's various artworks and paintings that represent the stages of our lives, trying to connect myself to something I may have missed. I wish she would hide them. No one wants to see themselves as an awkward child, especially when you look different to the rest. And now, I understand why. I pause, my eyes lazily locating a picture of myself when I was about sixteen, and now that I see myself with new eyes, I can see the Wolf features clearly. My jaw is more defined, the angles harsher. My eyes are bright but still different. My hair colour is dull and boring, unlike the Fae, and it's not naturally sleek and shiny—its unruly and hard to tame most of the time. My body is shorter and more muscular, unlike the Fae girls who are tall with legs as long as Atlas, curvy and perfectly proportioned. I used to shrug all these differences off as being Human. Now, I can see the Wolf; she was always there. I was just blinded by the lies.

My gaze snags on a set of rough carvings in the batten board alongside the painting. Tracing my finger over them, I make out what looks like an infinity symbol next to the letters B, H, & S, one I don't remember seeing as a child. Yet they look worn. Suddenly, I become aware of my breathing, every expansion and compression of my lungs becomes faster, shallower, and it draws a dull ache from my chest. Something's not right. It's too quiet, and it sets my teeth on edge. I continue to walk down the hall, and the growl of my Wolf rolls through me. I close my eyes, and I see her there. She's drawing me toward her, pulling me in with her magnificent strength and hypnotising eyes, but I take a long, deep breath and manage to resist her power, like I have consistently done since my second shift. She recedes, but not before releasing a final warning to stay alert.

When I reach my parents' room, I gently nudge the door open. I'm startled by a tall figure looking out the window down to the field below where Quentin is. "Excuse me?"

The male turns around, and my heart skips a beat.

Literally. Skips. A. Beat.

The brutally beautiful Fae is dressed in combat leathers similar to what I've seen my dad wear throughout my life, and he is armed to the teeth. An Israykiel Guard. While he doesn't look that much older than me, he could be anywhere between thirty to five hundred. He towers over me in height, his intimidating presence making me feel even more insignificant than I already do, which I didn't think was even possible. The years of combat have been kind to him. His unmarred bronzed skin shimmers under the daylight pouring through the window, illuminating him in a halo of light and casting him like an angel of death. His black wavy hair sits just above his shoulders, and it reflected shades of blues when the sunlight hits it. But it's his face that has the breath caught in my chest. Perfect. The dimple between his chin, his enchanting dark amber eyes with hues of red and gold pop against the cool undertones of his hair, and the silver arrow piercing through his right brow makes it appear to arch a little higher than the left. It's all perfect.

"You're excused," he says with a rich, powerful voice and a serious look on his face, and it's those two words that snap me out of my hypnotic state.

"Me? I'm not the one snooping around in here!" I bite. He may be an Israykiel Guard, but what the Hels is he doing in my mother's room?

"Not snooping, just. . ." He clears his throat and looks back out the window. "Waiting."

"Waiting? For whom? Amerax isn't here, he's stationed in Quespelia at the moment, and Mu—"

"Not Amerax. I know exactly where he is." He interrupts. "Synthony." His voice drops off and softens. "I'm waiting for Synthony."

"In her room?" I ask cautiously.

"No, I came up here because—" He cuts himself off once more, but this time he doesn't finish, he just takes a few steps toward me, eyes widening. "And you are?" He grins wickedly, arching his pierced brow.

"I think the better question is, who the Hels are you, and what are you doing in my mother's room?"

His eyes widen. "Your mother's room?" he asks intriguingly, his voice a little softer than before. He looks me up and down, and the look in those enchanting amber eyes makes me want to step back, his gaze exposing me. I nervously shift my weight between my feet before he throws another smirk my way again, the weight of his attention completely overpowering me.

"I'm Lazarus Cadieux, Israykiel Guard." He takes one step closer, positioning himself next to me, and he leans down. "But you already knew that." He adds and steps out the door and down the hall toward to stairs. My stomach executes a flip worthy of an acrobat.

Who in the Hels is that?

When I regain my composure, I approach the window and send Quentin a quick message.

Me: Get inside now. I need you.

Watching him in the distance from above, I see as he receives my message. It feels like it takes him an eternity to react accordingly, but it's only a quick moment before he moves. When he does, he moves like the wind, bolting toward the house as if his—*or my*—life depends on it.

Fine, maybe I could have been a little less urgent in my message. But no, there was a strange male in my Mum's room, and she seems to be missing.

My mum is missing.

Blood rushes my ears at the realisation, and I squeeze my eyes shut in response.

No, not again. I can't do this again.

My breaths come in short and sharp, and a subtle coppery tang coats my tongue. My world tilts around me, so I sit on the edge of my mother's bed, trying to regain my composure.

No, keep it together, Paege, I will myself. I don't even know if Mum is missing. *You're being irrational. She could be anywhere.*

A high-pitched whistle travels up to the bedroom and jerks me back from my temporary insanity. The kettle. Then I hear a familiar growl, and a cacophony of sounds, things breaking, furniture grunting, and I jump to my feet. Quentin has apparently made it to the kitchen and met Lazarus.

I arrive downstairs in time to find Lazarus holding Quentin up against a wall with a dagger held to his throat. The kettle is whistling aggressively and erupting over the stove but not dousing the flames.

"Yours?" Lazarus drawls, his face and eyes showing nothing but indignation.

"Mine?" I query, my brows furrow.

"Books," Quentin rasps, fury flashing in his eyes.

"Oh, shit, yes. Mine," I screech, and just like that, Lazarus lets Quentin go.

The second Lazarus releases his grip and steps away, Quentin lunges back toward Lazarus., who snaps his arm out with preternatural speed and grabs Quentin by the throat. He has a few inches on Quentin, and with his long Fae limbs, he holds him at an unreachable distance with ease. Quentin gasps as he fights to release himself from

Lazarus's grip, and his face starts going a light shade of blue. I freeze. What the Hels is going on here?

"I know exactly who you are, Wolf, but don't think I won't take you out if you don't settle the fuck down," he growls and he releases Quentin for a second time.

I rush toward Quentin. "Are you alright?

"I'm fine!" Quentin coughs and he brushes my incoming hands away from him.

Spinning, I demand, "Who the fuck are you?"

"I told you, Paege, I'm Lazarus." He smirks as if this is some sort of game.

"What are you doing here? And how do you know who I am?"

"Didn't we cover this already?" He huffs as he sheaths his dagger away. "I was looking for Synthony." And then he fucking grins at Quentin before answering me, "And you told me who you were, remember? When we were upstairs in the bedroom." He winks. He fucking winks!

"You what?" Quentin asks, grey eyes wide with fury or jealousy or I don't know. It's hard to place his emotions without feeling them, but he is pissed.

"No!" I hold my finger up. "No. I found him snooping in my mum's room," I answer and turn back to Lazarus, baring my teeth. "I want to know why."

"Is she always like this?" Lazarus asks Quentin. "All bossy and annoying?"

Quentin fucking smiles and huffs. I raise my brows letting him know my disapproval of his response, and he pulls the amused look from his face.

"Oi, star-boy," I snap at Lazarus. I'm so fucking angry right now. He has let himself into my home, my mother's room, he attacked Quentin, and now, insults me. Who the Hels does he think he is? "I want some real answers now."

"And I've given them to you. It's not my problem if you're not listening." Lazarus walks over to the whistling kettle and removes it from the stove, and the sudden silence is a welcome relief. I can hear my thoughts once more.

"Books, what's going on here?" Quentin asks, brushing the strewn hair from his face.

"I don't know," I snap back. "Where's my mum?" I bark at Lazarus.

"Paege, I don't know," Lazarus responds in a gentler manner as he casually pours three cups of coffee and sets them down on the table. "But if you sit down, and put your pet here on a leash, maybe we can figure things out."

After I manage to settle Quentin down, following yet another insult hurled by Lazarus, we apprehensively sit at the dining table, waiting for Lazarus to give us a proper explanation. Instead, he throws icy stares toward Quentin, almost egging him on for another round of poke-the-Wolf.

"Lazarus, can you please tell me what's going on?" I ask politely, hoping that my change in tone might encourage some cooperation from him, but something tells me he's uncooperative at even the best of times.

Lazarus gets up and silently walks to the kitchen window. "Are you both going somewhere?" he asks as he scans the paddocks outside.

I turn to face Quentin, and he shakes his head at me, warning me not to say anything. Instead, I try to coax a response out of him. "Lazarus, why are you here?"

"I told you already, Paege. I came here looking for your mother." His words are softer now, and it unsettles me. "Where are you going?" he asks again.

"Do you know where Synthony is?" Quentin asks with a raspy voice, probably from the grip Lazarus had on his throat.

Lazarus doesn't answer Quentin, but he turns and faces me "Does anyone else know you were coming here today?"

The sound of war drums fills my ears, and my stomach twists in knots. Quentin jumps out of his chair, stumbling ungracefully towards Lazarus once more while growling. "Are you threatening her, star-boy?" he drawls.

"*Tut, tut, tut.* I wouldn't do that," Lazarus commands as Quentin lunges at him with a kitchen knife he somehow managed to get in his hands on.

"I'm stronger and older than you, Wolf." Quentin stops in his tracks but doesn't drop the knife. He continues to hold it up defensively, but Lazarus seems unfazed. "And why does everyone keep calling me *star-boy* as if it's some sort of insult?" he scoffs.

"Enough you two!" I demand once more. "Quentin, sit down, and give me that!" I motion to the knife. "A kitchen knife, really?" I mutter and roll my eyes, and he reluctantly hands it to me as he sits back down. Surely, he knows that a kitchen knife will do absolutely nothing to an Israykiel Guard.

"And you, stop antagonising him," I bark at Lazarus like a bloody parent in a Godsdamn playground trying to keep two schoolyard bullies from killing each other.

Lazarus draws in a long breath and slowly exhales—and loudly—before softly speaking again, as if trying to appease me. "You didn't answer me. Did anyone know you were coming here today?"

"No," I answer. "It was only us. Why?"

"No one?" he asks again.

"No one," I snap again. My irritation, my Wolf, wants to come out, but I shove them both down. The last thing I need is for an Israykiel Guard to know of my truth.

"Not even Synthony?" Lazarus clarifies.

"Now who's not listening?" Quentin huffs under his breath.

I shoot him a *shut the fuck up* look before confirming, "No," I sigh. "Not even Mum," I respond as my heart slowly sinks inch by inch into the inky darkness in my gut. Oh, Gods where is she? I should have told her I was coming. Maybe Lazarus is overreacting. Although Lazarus's face remains neutral, there is something there, something deeper, that tells me this isn't a maybe situation. My throat constricts, an invisible noose tightening around it.

He nods and looks out the window again, taking another sip of his coffee. "Are you both staying here tonight?"

"That was the plan," Quentin reluctantly answers.

"Good," he says. He steps back toward us, placing the coffee mug he's been nursing on the table that Quentin and I are sitting at. "I need to make contact with. . . I will be right back," he declares, and before either Quentin or I can respond, he marches out of the room.

When Lazarus is outside, I slowly turn to face Quentin. Swallowing down my fear, I ask, "What were you thinking?"

"What was I thinking? What were you thinking, Paege? That, that. . ." The contempt is clear in his voice, and it yanks the fear right out of me.

"Yes?" I drawl.

"We can't trust him; you know that, right?"

I pause for a moment to think about his question. He might be acting rude and conceited. *Does that remind you of anyone, Paege?* But he's an Israykiel Guard, he's Star-Borne, and my family are Star-Borne—the ones that have loved me and protected me my entire life. The only ones my mum has ever trusted. And Quentin's distrust is born of nothing more than his own prejudice toward our kind. Toward Fae.

"Actually, I don't know that. He's a Star-Borne, a Guard. He knows Amerax and my mum. I think he might be one of the few we can trust."

"Him?" Quentin spits in disbelief. "Him?"

"I'm not suggesting we invite him over for dinner parties and drinks"—*or share our travel plans with him*—"but I think he could be helpful, so we need to be nice to him. Please?" I beg. "I need to at least get out of him what he wants with my mum." Relaxing my muscles, I paste a broad smile across my face. I need to get Quentin onboard with this because all the backhanded swipes and attempted fights aren't going to get us anywhere.

"Fine, I can be polite, but just for the record, I don't like him, and I don't trust him."

"That's alright. I'm not a big fan of you either, Wolf," Lazarus responds as he walks back into the kitchen.

Great.

"Now that we've established that, I'm going to stay here tonight with you both and. . ." Lazarus's eyes dart away from mine, as if deciding how much to say. "And wait for Synthony." *What is he hiding?* "And I'm getting word to Amerax."

The knot inside twists tighter and tighter with every word Lazarus says, nothing relieving me of my paranoid delusions that something is wrong and my mother is in danger. It's not like her to disappear without a word. "Lazarus," I say with a wobbly voice. "Are you concerned that my mum is missing?"

He whips his head to face me. "Missing?" Lazarus softens his voice now, too, and something in him shifts, becoming less abrasive. "No, I don't believe Synth is missing, but I'm not entirely sure *you're* safe either."

"Me?" I ask.

At the same time Quentin asks, "Why?"

"Don't ask me why, Wolf. Just trust me, alright?" Lazarus retorts.

"Lazarus, can you please tell *me* why?" I add because it seems that no matter what Quentin asks, he's never going to get an answer. I don't know if it's an alpha male thing, or a Wolf thing, but this is going to get tiring soon if they can't work it out.

"Let's just say I can sense these things. Think of it as one of my many, *many* gifts."

Quentin and I exchange quick glances, and the frustration simmers behind in his eyes. *Well, great; just what I need.* Lazarus leaves us again and stokes the fire in the lounge while Quentin and I remain seated at the table.

"I don't have a good feeling about this," Quentin mutters under his breath while rubbing his neck, and I agree. Something isn't adding up. I'm not scared of Lazarus. In fact, it's quite the opposite. Something inside me is telling me to trust him, but he's being sketchy as the Hels, and I can't quite put my finger on what he's hiding. I'm certain it has to do with my mum. He knows more than he's letting on, but one thing I know to be true is the Israykiel Guards would never, I mean never, hurt a Fae, let alone my mother. So, no matter what, I need to get Lazarus to trust me just enough for him to tell me something, regardless of how small it is.

And I have a feeling that's going to be a lot harder than I expect it to be.

CHAPTER 16

After showering, I head outside with my morning coffee and watch a shirtless Quentin, his tattooed skin glistening in the morning sun, as he loads the horses in preparation for our journey. My heart warms at the sight.

Last night, Quentin and I shared my old bed again. We never spoke. The uneasiness of the afternoon events shrouds over us with every lazy breath, but we lay there, facing each other, arms draped over each other, effortlessly and comfortably. Things are a lot less strained between us since I kissed him the night at the campsite. A bridge has been built across the canyon that's been growing between us, and while we still both stand on either side, I am connected to him again, closer to him. It's comforting knowing he isn't out of reach anymore. I'm putting distance between us in a romantic sense, but now, there's room for something else to take root, and I can cross that bridge at any time.

He has spent the morning reorganising our things for the trip, re-packing our duffels, and saddling the horses. I'm surprised he knows what he's doing. He picked Jesstar, a beautiful silver mare, for our journey. She's strong, loyal, a little bit sassy, and one of my favourite horses. If I didn't have Whisky, she would have been my second choice.

Buried in my thoughts, a deep voice from behind startles me. "What time are you heading off?"

"I don't know," I respond casually in an attempt not to show my growing discomfort at his presence.

He hums. "You never did say where you were going."

I bristle. "You're right, I didn't." I take another sip of my coffee. "And I'm not going to. Sorry."

"Well, if I had to guess, I would say the Dead Forest."

I spin around to face Lazarus. "What?"

"The Dead Forest." He smirks. "There's only one reason to take horses on a trip, especially when you've got access to portals." He nods towards Quentin, who is now brushing down Whisky's mane. "You're going somewhere only *they* can get you."

Stunned, my eyes widen at his speculation. Of course, he would figure it out. He's a Star-Borne Israykiel Guard, he knows all the land, and he's probably travelled the Dead Forest many times in the past.

"What I can't figure out is why the king's son is going to the Dead Forest with a—" I wait for the word to fall from his lips. Instead, he says, "With you." He raises his pierced eyebrow and grins at me curiously.

"With me?" I snap, heat violently bubbling up through my body. "You mean with a *halfling*?" I say through gritted teeth at the insult he didn't say, but I know he meant it with every carefully avoided word. I expected a lot of things from Lazarus, but to refer to me as a halfling, I was not expecting.

His brow drops, the smile leaving his face, leaving something like pain behind in its place. "Paege, you misunderstand me. . ." He takes a careful step forward, closing the gap between us, and with his height, I have to tilt my head back to meet his gaze. "I don't understand why *you*, Synthony's daughter, would be going with *him*?"

Shame blushes my cheeks. I suppose he wouldn't be referring to me as a halfling since he's allegedly a friend of my mum's, and there is no way my mother would allow anyone in her life if they thought like that.

"So, tell me," Lazarus continues, as if oblivious to my shame. "Why are you going to the Dead Forest with Prince Charming over there?"

Lazarus's words cause me to gasp. It's the first time since we decided to come on this quest that I've registered Quentin as the prince. In my mind, he has just been Quentin. But he *is* the prince. He is King Ruhaul Ishaan's firstborn son, which makes him Heir Apparent to the Godsdamn throne. The Crown Prince of Elyndria. And here I am, bringing him along on this mission to discover the true history of our Kingdom, who the true royal family is, and who killed them. A mission that may result in the dethroning of King Ishaan, *may result in his death, too,* which means Quentin will be stripped of his title.

And I'm just realising this now. *Shit, what mess have I gotten myself into?*

Finishing my coffee, I place the empty mug on the balustrade as I turn back to face Quentin, who is now brushing Jesstar's mane and talking to her as if they are old friends, and I rub at my chest where pain ignites. I swallow my emotions for a second time in as many minutes because I can't think about this right now.

I don't have to work too hard to pull myself out of it because Lazarus's next words are sobering. "Nothing good comes of the Dead Forest, and nothing good lies beyond. So, you're either off to do something very stupid or something very dangerous. I can't help you if you don't tell me."

"Help me?" I spin around, facing him again.

"I'm pretty sure nothing I say is going to deter you from embarking on what I'm going to assume is a death mission. So, why don't you tell me what's going on, Paege, so I can help you instead?"

"You don't know anything," I scoff. I'm sick of his games. He is the one withholding from me.

"I know enough to recognise that you two are over your heads with whatever you're planning." He isn't wrong. I have had this feeling for weeks now. My head is buried thousands of feet below the ground, and I am suffocating in fear.

"But why would you want to help us when you don't even know us?" I say apprehensively. He certainly doesn't like us. Last night was the most awkward and uncomfortable evening I think I've ever spent in my own house. Between Quentin refusing to speak or acknowledge Lazarus and Lazarus doing everything he could think of to irritate Quentin, I can't imagine why Lazarus wants to help us out of the kindness of his own heart. The three of us awkwardly ate at the dining table: Quentin throwing me icy stares, and Lazarus throwing ones of fire. Finally, when the evening was late enough, I dragged Quentin to my room and locked us in to avoid any more conflict. Which didn't serve me too well because then I spent the rest of the night sharing a bed with Quentin Ishaan.

I swear his eyes flash red as he smirks and raises that damn pierced eyebrow. "Oh, but I do, little wolf, I know exactly who you *both* are." As the words roll off his tongue, my Wolf sits up with attention, and waves of anxiety ripple over me. He knows more than something. A lot more than he was originally giving away. Mum had trusted him enough to tell him that I am a Wolf?

Does that mean he knows who my father is? Who Guy is? Gods, I have so many questions. "How?" I drop my voice, which is stupid because the two Beings here with me know my secret, and there isn't anyone else around for miles.

He leans in closer to me, his eyes locking on mine and whispers, "How do you think?"

I don't know what it is about him. He's aggravating as Hels, and he's rude and conceited, but, Gods, is he captivating. A rush of warmth graces my cheeks, and as I take in a long breath to try to calm myself, the scent of leather and sweet spices overwhelms me, and something in my belly flutters.

I lean in closer to him, breathing him in. His scent coils itself around me as I wrap myself around him. My body arches toward his, and his hard body presses firmly against mine. Heat transfers between us in pulses. My traitorous heart races in its cage, begging to be released, to be set free. I tilt my head up to his, my eyes meeting his hypnotic gaze, and his breath warm against my lips sends a shiver rushing. . .wait—

I step backwards, a foot loses its hold, and I grasp for purchase as I tumble backward. A hand clasps mine, jerking me upright. Breath wooshes out of my lungs, heavy and ragged, as he settles me back on the veranda. My cheeks blush a deeper shade of pink at the touch.

Get yourself together, Paege.

"Thank you," I mutter, refusing to look him in the eyes again. Because what in the Hels was that?

A sinful grin spreads wide across his face. "Oh, you are very welcome, Paege."

In that moment, I have no idea how, but I'm completely sure that whatever just happened to me, he is completely to blame, but the words I want to hurl at him lodge in my throat.

He takes a few steps back and leans against the wall of the house, casually crossing his arms to disarm me, but there is nothing casual about the male Star-Borne standing before me. His devilish smirk doesn't leave his face. "Look, if you aren't going to tell me what you two are doing, maybe I should just come with you?" He shrugs.

"Come with us?" I bark a humourless laugh. "Why would you think we would ever agree to that?"

"I don't think *he* would," he drawls, nodding behind me toward Quentin. "But I have a feeling that you're a lot smarter than to look a gift horse in the mouth." *Did he seriously just refer to himself as a gift horse?*

"And what gift would that be?" I sneer, no one is conceited enough to be saying what I think he's saying?

"Why, me, of course." He winks.

Alright, he is. "You?"

"I'm a Star-Borne Israykiel Guard. I have insurmountable magic. I'm strong, I'm fast, I know the Dead Forest." Goosebumps prickle across my skin in the silence while he deliberates his next words. "And I know the mountains beyond."

I cough, clearing my throat. Shit, does he know where we are going and what we are doing? No, no. There is no possible way he could know that. There are exactly five beings that know what we are doing. We haven't told another living soul, not even Asheron. There is no way he could know. I push away that thought.

He kicks off the wall and smiles. "Right, that settles things. I'll go get myself a horse then, shall I?"

As he passes me to go down to the paddocks, I grab his arm and stop him. "Why are you doing this?" I question, confused and in need of a real answer. I'm grateful for the offer to help, but why would he want to? He doesn't know me, he doesn't even like me, and he certainly doesn't like Quentin. There is no reason for him to be doing any of this.

He doesn't answer me or look at me. He just stares behind me toward the paddock, toward Quentin.

"Why are you helping me?" I ask again, tilting my head up to study his face, looking for a sign of anything that will give away his true reasoning.

He leans in, still not taking his eyes off the paddock behind me. "Because you need my help, Paege."

"I don't even know you," I challenge.

He angles his head toward mine and smirks as he whispers in my ear, "But you want to."

Shocked, I drop my hand, letting go of Lazarus's arm, and he lets a chuckle escape before he steps down the stairs. "When I'm ready, we can head off," he sings, and I turn around to follow him, to tell him no, but instead, I come face to face with a blood-red and wide-eyed Quentin.

"You have got to be fucking kidding me?"

CHAPTER 17

"No fucking way!" Quentin roars again. "There is no way I am going anywhere with Captain Leather Pants out there." He crosses his arms and stands his ground.

"Seriously? Captain Leather Pants? What's with you two?" I roll my eyes and wait for a response, but Quentin just uncrosses his arms and digs his hands deep into his jean pockets and shrugs.

I sigh and walk over to him. "Look, I'm not entirely happy about all this either, but he has a good point."

"Which is?" he drawls.

"We have no idea what lies beyond the White Forest, and we may not be prepared for it at all." I try to swallow the laugh trying to escape my lips as I continue, "But *Captain Leather Pants* does." I pause briefly, working hard to keep a straight face and trying to stifle the laughter bubbling up. "I think he can help us. We can use him."

Quentin shrugs again, his grey eyes of steel refusing to meet mine, looking anywhere but me. I take another step toward him and tilt my head, trying to catch his gaze. When he finally surrenders, a smile stretches across my face, and a sense of relief washes over me when he smiles in return, even if it doesn't reach his eyes.

"Thank you," I whisper as I wrap my arms around his body and bury my head into his chest. "I promise we'll cut him loose if he turns out to be a liability or unhelpful."

"Promise?" Quentin pushes, and I swear I can hear a glimmer of hope in his voice.

I pull back, stepping away from the Wolf who is starting to slowly regain my trust, and place my hand on my heart, true Vailenbyrg-style. "Promise."

That smile falters for the briefest of moments, something akin to grief rippling across his features before fading. Guy. This stupid gesture that is sacred between Mum and me suddenly becomes much more. It was clearly something between Mum and Vharkus. Mum and Dad. A crippling weight bears down on me, crushing me beneath the very grief I just witnessed splash across Quentin's face.

I sigh.

As if he can see the pain in my eyes in corporeal form, Quentin reaches for my hand, but I step away. Although a bridge has been built, his touch, the touch of the male that started all of this, cannot bring me comfort, not in this moment. Understanding sweeps across his features, and he nods.

Needing things and the subject to change, I say, "So, are we ready to head off soon? I think we should try to make it to the river's edge before nightfall."

"As long as *Lazarus* doesn't hold us up too much longer, we'll make it in time," he sneers, emphasising Lazarus's name just to prove a point, but I ignore it because I need him to get past whatever it is that's causing this disdain toward him.

"I'm going to try to get a message to Mum and Dad again before we leave," I say, pivoting to go inside. I'm still worried, and I just need to know she's alright.

Quentin silently nods, brushing sandy blond hair off his face as I walk past him, then he gently takes my hand. "Are we alright, Books?"

My heart and body stop dead in their tracks. A breath doesn't even leave my body, and tightness between my blades pulls. Quentin and I haven't broached the subject about us in a while, and although the bridge has been built, connecting us once more, I'm unsure just how alright we are. There are still so many unknowns and unspoken obstacles. So, I do what I do best these days, and that's swallow hard and push down all my emotions and concerns.

I tilt my head. "Of course." I offer a soft yet insincere smile and squeeze his hand. "Why?"

He shrugs me off and loosens his grip on my hand. "No reason." The thrumming behind my ears lessens, but the knot in my stomach and the tightness between my blades doesn't shift. Ignoring it, I gently reclaim my hand and smile once again before going to send these damn messages.

We are closing in on the river's edge along the eastern flank of Orphelious after a solid day of riding, only stopping for a hydration break at a couple of pools along the way. It's late afternoon, and the bleary winter's sun will set shortly. We need to find a spot to set up camp for the night.

We follow Lazarus, who somehow ended up being our guide, and his brilliant chestnut mare, Lilith, *the irony isn't lost on me there.* Making our way toward the river, a shadowed figure appears, leaning against one of the old weeping willows by the river's shore. Blood rushes to my ears as panic ripples over me. My first instinct is to warn the group, to squeeze my knees and thighs around Whisky's muscled torso, instructing him to run and gallop back up the hill as fast as I possibly can. But Lazarus, who I'm sure can see the figure too, doesn't react and continues travelling toward them. As we continue, my gaze lingers on the shadowy figure. The unease begins to lift, and I feel something familiar about them. The stance, the way they kick off from against the tree and begin taking long, casual strides toward us. They are a few hundred strides away, but as they get closer, my heart starts skipping.

Asheron.

I barely let Whisky reach him before I dismount and run toward him, arms splayed out in a full *'I'm going to wrap myself around you and never let go'* manner.

"Whoa, settle down, firecracker," Asheron laughs as I envelop myself around him.

"What are you doing here?" I squeal as I burrow into him even more.

"I got a heads up that you may have been headed this way."

I withdraw and steal a glance over my shoulder towards Lazarus, who is pretending to ignore the two of us. "Really?" I drawl.

"Really," Asheron confirms casually. "He's one of the good ones, Paege."

"We'll see," I respond light-heartedly, but Asheron seems to take offence at my remark.

He puts his hands on my shoulders, holding me firm in my place, and his brows furrow. "You trust me?"

"Of course," I exclaim. I trust Asheron more than I trust anyone in the world these days. He's one of the few Beings in my life who has never hidden a single thing from me or ever lied to me. I trust him with my life.

"Then trust him, too," he quips as his mouth turns one of the goofiest smiles I've seen him from him a long time. He casually puts his arm around my shoulder, leading me toward Quentin. "So, what's with all the weaponry? You look prepared to fight a war."

"Well—" I start to explain, but think better of it. I want to tell Asheron everything, but I haven't seen him in so long, and there are too many explanations that I don't even know where to start. Instead we walk in silence, Asheron graciously not pushing me for an answer. We reach Quentin, who has been watching us intensely, and before I even get a chance to say something, Asheron slides his arm from my shoulders.

"Q." Asheron nods.

"Asheron." Quentin nods back.

What's it with these two also? At least they're not trying to kill each other. Sighing, I take my canteen from my saddle pack and take a sip, while Asheron greets Lazarus with a warm brotherly hug.

Quentin snickers under his breath as he continues to eye the two Star-Borne Fae. I roll my eyes at him as I start to unpack to set up camp.

"Leave it," Lazarus calls out from across the clearing. "There's a small village a little way up the river with food and an inn. We'll be staying there tonight."

"Did you know about this?" I enquire with Quentin.

He huffs. "Do you honestly think he would have told me anything?"

"No," I confess.

"But I won't say no to a proper meal and a bed if it's on offer." He takes a sip from his canteen, and leans in and kisses my cheek as if it's second nature. I blink, my heart a frozen object in my chest, unable to decide what to do with what just happened. Quentin doesn't give it a second thought. He turns to Jesstar, giving her a brush down her long mane with splayed fingers. She stomps her front hoof down and brays, demanding more.

Ignoring what just happened as best I can, I focus on re-securing the load I just loosened, and mutter to myself, "Alright, keeping the horses packed."

It's a short ride to a small village that sits north along the riverside. In fact, one could hardly call it a village. There is a small inn with possibly ten rooms, and an old, well-maintained rock tavern attached with rooms on the second and third floors above. The rest of the village consists of a small food mart and five rickety shacks along the river's edge. If I had to guess, this place exists purely for wayward travellers. I can't even imagine they get too many of them around here. But like Quentin, I will not say no to a proper meal and a bed—if you could even call it that—as it may be our last for some time.

While Asheron and Lazarus go inside to enquire about rooms and a meal for the night, Quentin and I unload the horses and secure them to the hitching posts. Two troughs bracket the posts, one with apples and carrot scraps mixed with hay, and the other holds grains. A third one is full of water. A few woollen blankets rest over a saddle beam behind the troughs—at least we know the horses will be well fed and rested before we head off tomorrow.

The village is deserted. There is an eerie emptiness to it that makes the hair on the back of my neck stand on end. I haven't seen one Fae or other Being since we arrived. It's unnerving; even the tavern itself appears empty. However, the vacant room sign says full, which I find hard to believe. A short moment later, Asheron and Lazarus stand at the large wooden door of the tavern, motioning for us to enter.

Crossing the threshold, my body tingles as if the blood in my veins is fizzing with an old, unfamiliar energy. It hums against my skin, inviting me to enter. Pressure presses against my body, thick and warm, as though I'm stepping through the very fabric of time itself. It all happens too quickly, but it's there, and the moment my foot reconnects with the ground, my jaw drops as I now stand at the entrance of what I can only describe as a grand palace.

I expected to walk into an old, run-down bar with a fireplace, some wobbly, liquor-soaked wooden tables and chairs, occupied by a few drunken locals and travellers. But the establishment is nothing like I have ever seen before. It's spectacular. I turn to look at Quentin, and his face mirrors what I feel. His eyes widen with wonderment, and I watch as his dropped jaw gradually curves down into an enormous frown. Huh? I know he's used to palaces and the like, but he seriously can't be scoffing at this place. I wish he weren't wearing that ring. I've had no read over his emotions for days now.

Shaking off the confusion about Quentin's facial expression, I refocus my attention. We've walked into a grand foyer that is three times the size it should be based on how it looked from the outside. Marbled flooring leads to the reception desk, which is flanked by two large gargoyles. Two curved wooden staircases fall from the floors above, covered with floral woven carpet in rich colours of maroons, pinks, purples, and greens, and are draped with matching flowering vines. Trumpet vines and wisteria hang from the mahogany banisters while crystal chandeliers filled with candles swing from the rose ceilings, warmly lighting the space before us. Tapestries and artwork fill the stone walls between the framed floor-to-ceiling stained-glass windows by the entrance.

I've never seen anything so grand in my life. "But how?" I ask no one in particular.

"It's warded," Asheron answers under his breath as he walks over to me. "Shall we?" he asks, proffering me his arm and arching an eyebrow that lets a slight grin form on the same side of his face.

"Oh, we shall," I sing in delight, threading my arm through his. I turn to face Quentin, who is still frowning at what we are seeing, and I offer him my hand. He brushes the fringe off his face and takes my hand without questioning, allowing Asheron to escort us through the reception. We head toward the back of the *tavern* into an enormous hall, which would only be fit for a royal ball.

My skin prickles with electricity as I study the room in awe. I want to stay and spend a long, uninterrupted moment in this space, imagining the marvellous parties that must be held here, the dancing, the drinking, the music, the ball gowns and suits. But, to my disappointment, we don't stop. Lazarus is up ahead, opening another set of large mahogany doors. As he does, a rush of cool, fresh air washes over me, and the sweet sound of music and laughter gently envelops me as we walk out onto a sprawling balcony filled with dozens of Fae, overlooking a ravine. A ravine that, I am certain, did not exist when we arrived.

CHAPTER 18

"Have you ever seen anything like it?" I whisper to Quentin as we make our way through the crowded balcony to find an empty table.

"Yes, Paege, I've seen many run-down, decrepit inns in my time. Just because I am a royal doesn't mean I haven't experienced the other side of life at least once. It's actually similar to some areas in Anchanor, the port city."

"Decrepit? It's no—" I start, but Asheron tugs me back as Lazarus ushers Quentin through the crowd, and they take a seat at a round wooden table.

"What is this place, Asheron? And why does Quentin think it's subpar?"

Asheron grins and tilts his head toward mine and whispers, "Welcome to Ferinini, Paege."

"Ferinini?"

"Yes. It's home to the Star-Borne. This was once the Court of the Star-Borne. It's kept concealed by magics, heavily guarded to protect us from unwanted attention, and only those whom we grant access can see it for what it really is."

"And who is that?" I ask, my mind still in a hazy fog of awe as I watch a tiny firefly flutter toward me, its light growing brighter as it nears.

"It shall only reveal itself to those with Fae blood."

I snap my attention back to Asheron. "But I never gave you my blood. You don't have it. . ." I start frantically. Did Lazarus somehow steal my blood? Did Asheron?

"No, Paege, we haven't taken your blood without you knowing." I sigh in relief. "The magic knows you are Fae. It knows your truth. So, it reveals its truth to you."

"How is that?" I mutter. Asheron doesn't respond as I return my gaze to the magical space around me. Across the river, on the other side of the ravine, large brick and stone villas covered in jasmine vines and wisteria are built into the cliff faces. Their large glass windows with balconies protrude over the water, and cobblestone paths weave between the homes from the shoreline up to the cliff's edge above. They look like jigsaw pieces, all leading to colourful doorways and connecting all the estates. Fireflies fill the sky, gently lighting all the dark spaces that aren't lit by the warm street lanterns and fairy lights that hang from the large trees around the water's edge. The air is perfumed by the jasmine vines that weave and climb around every column, balustrade, and rock face.

It's beautiful. It's breathtaking. *And it's hidden.* "It's magical," I sigh.

"It's not a bad place to call home," he chimes.

"Wait. This is where you live?"

"Of course. Where did you think I lived?"

"At the Academy," I respond, pinching my brows in confusion. "And then you have your place in the Neopolis."

Asheron casually nods, considering my statement. "Huh, and where exactly do you think the Academy is? I'm surprised Amerax or Synthony never told you about it."

I shake my head, too blown away by all of this to find the words to answer. "So, why is all this hidden again?"

"As I already said, it's to keep us safe from unwanted attention."

"To keep us safe from the likes of him," an unwanted voice speaks sharply, and I roll my eyes.

"You mean the Wolves?" I pivot facing Lazarus, his handsome face looking every bit the warrior he is. Beautifully brutal.

"I mean *him*," he growls. "It's guarded, using ancient magic to protect us from him and his kind. Magic long forgotten to the realm, except to the true guardians of this kingdom." The Star-Borne, he doesn't say, but that is what he means.

"So, he can't see this?"

"No, and you can't tell him either," Asheron says bluntly.

"I don't want to lie to him." Even though it's all I feel like I've been doing for weeks.

"Well, you have to. This place is sacred. It must be protected, and Wolves have a history of taking things that don't belong to them," Lazarus fumes.

A low grumble emits from my belly, my Wolf clearly not happy with Lazarus's statement, but he has a point to some degree. The Wolves history is sketchy, and knowing what I now know, I'm not sure we should trust them with this. "I, um. . ." I worry my bottom lip, the weight of the situation pushing me further into the darkness that is slowly consuming my soul. A lie. Another lie. I've never lied until this damn curse came into my life. Not until I started down this path of figuring out how to break it. That little ball of fury in my belly starts to grow brighter, and my Wolf stirs. Not until Quentin came into my life.

"You either lie or you leave, and you can go camp on the water's edge. It's no skin off my nose. But whatever you decide, decide it quickly," Lazarus says sharply.

"We stay," I say, pushing past both the males and heading over towards Quentin, who is sitting rather uncomfortably in what appears to be a comfortable chair. While this situation is completely infuriating, I can't help but be a little amused by the precarious situation we are in with Quentin. Does that make me a horrible Being? I internally reprimand myself as I answer both yes and no to that question.

"There was nowhere else we could have stayed?" Quentin asks no one in particular as we sit at the table. Lazarus grabs our bags and hands them to a young Fae who follows us to the table. The Fae obliges, carrying our bags past us and entering a room further up the balcony on the left.

"No, Wolf. It's either this or the river," Lazarus snaps as he seats himself down on the other side of Quentin next to me.

I hear a growl emit from Quentin's chest, and my teeth grind. I suspect Asheron and Lazarus took a huge chance revealing this to me, and the last thing I want to do is make a scene, especially one that involves Wolves. I put a hand on his knee and squeeze it gently, silently requesting him to calm down and let it go. I, too, would be pissed if I thought we were staying in a rickety inn. I wonder what he sees exactly.

As we sit here in silence, the four of us awkwardly avoiding each other's gaze, I find myself wondering about Lazarus and how much he knows. I wonder if he's like my mother, who has memories of events she shouldn't, and I'm curious how much Asheron knows, too. I have the sudden urge to speak with Asheron. I need to tell him everything about Guy and King Braxtion, my Wolf, the curse, and our journey. I need to find out what he knows because he must know something. Lazarus wouldn't have invited him here if he didn't. By the way Lazarus and Asheron are looking around right now, scanning the faces of the Fae who are socialising around us, something tells me now isn't the time. Now is the time to try and relax and enjoy our evening with *friends*. Yes, later.

"It's not that bad. It's one of the safest places along the river. It's kind of a notorious hub for Fae travellers," Asheron continues.

"This place?" Quentin queries, not bothering to hide his distaste for this place that is clearly painted across his face. Rude.

"Yes, this place," Lazarus scowls as if offended by Quentin's remarks. Which is ridiculous because he knows what Quentin is seeing.

"We don't let many other kinds in here, Quentin. This place is sacred to our kind, but we're trusting you," Asheron adds calmly, as if trying to keep the peace for my sake. Or maybe it's for their sake, as a few Star-borne turn to face us. Shit, shit, shit. I slink down into the chair, its velvety cushions protecting me from their judgment.

Quentin raises one brow slowly. "Why? This place is—"

"Because Paege trusts you, and I trust Paege. She's one of us." Asheron pauses for a moment, watching Quentin, and the air thickens around me, an intensity flowing between the two males.

"So, don't go letting her down," Lazarus grumbles under his breath. It's such a sweet yet vicious sound, and the hairs stand on the back of my neck.

I sit myself upright. My Wolf is suspiciously quiet as I drag my eyes across the three males seated around me, and worry unfurls inside my chest. Am I exposing Ferinini, the Star-Borne's home to danger? Regardless of Quentin's actions lately, I don't trust him any more than I did a few weeks ago, and the fact remains that his father cannot be trusted. If it came down to it, I still don't know if Quentin would choose all of this, us, *me*, over his father. At the end of the day, blood is thicker than water.

While various assortments of foods and drinks get delivered to our table, none of which were ordered, Lazarus tells me he heard from Amerax. Mum is fine and at the Academy, dealing with a mess the twins have gotten themselves into. Asheron confirms his message with a nod. Apparently, Asheron was the messenger. This news has the knot that's been twisting in my stomach for two days relaxing, and the slight nausea that has been brewing dissipating, leaving behind an emptiness that can only be filled with the food that is sitting in front of me. When I think about it, I haven't eaten that much these past few days; my anxiety and nerves haven't allowed it.

VineBrew and Fyres flow, and my palate is overwhelmed by all the diverse flavours of the Kingdom: sweet, savoury, spicy, and sour. There are various meats on sticks, fried cheesy balls, baked potatoes, breads with zingy dips, pickled vegetables, fresh fruits, and pastries. I try a little bit of everything.

Quentin had stew and Ale. He actually had stew. The Fae brought a bowl of steaming hot stew for him and a pitcher of frothy BarleyAle, and he consumed it like a starving male. According to Lazarus, we all ate stew, too. I really should feel bad.

After dinner, Lazarus joins a group of Star-Borne dressed in similar combat leathers on the other side of the balcony. Some are Israykiel Guard, and some are not yet activated. As I look around, I notice there are a lot more Star-Borne here than I first realised, also in civilian wear. They can be easy to miss at first glance when their black razor feather wings are tucked away and their Star-Borne marks covered. They look a lot like normal Fae, a tiny bit taller, but not much else.

I glance at Asheron, and he nods to Quentin next to me. I turn to find a tired Wolf, nursing a half-drunk glass of warm BarleyAle in his hands, sunk deep into the chair with his eyes half closed. His face looks softer than it has in recent weeks. With his jaw slack and his sandy hair swept across his forehead, he appears less angry. He looks like the Quentin I thought I knew. My nose stings. He isn't that male, though, is he?

"Quentin, are you done with that?" I ask, as I try to gently peel his fingers from the glass.

He hums and lifts his lids. "Sorry, I was just listening to the chatter and not thinking about too much to be honest. I can't believe I closed my eyes and nearly fell asleep in this place. Paege, how could you let me fall asleep?"

"Excuse me? I didn't let you do anything. You're a grown ass Wolf, Quentin Ishaan, and I am not your mother nor your—" I cut myself off, not wanting ,or knowing how to finish that statement.

He sighs, and I watch as his lips curve up into that mischievous grin I have not seen in a long time, and I can tell all the BarleyAle he's consumed has taken a toll on his Wolf brain. "There she is," he croons, "I've missed that fire."

My cheeks heat, and a molten fire ignites deep in my core. Gods, I've missed that Quentin, too, but the start of a familiar burn sears across my back, and I know I need to tame that fire down.

"Is my room close by?" Quentin asks casually as he stands, brushing the hair from his weary eyes.

"It is." Asheron digs his hand into his pants pockets, searching for something. "Take the third door down and climb the stairs two floors. That's your accommodation for the night." He hands me a large silver key on an ivory ring.

My mouth drops open in shock, and I shift nervously in my seat. He must sense my discomfort because he quickly adds, "I'm sorry. I just assumed you two. . ." My eyes dart to Quentin, and he just smirks and shrugs. "Quentin, you can have my room, and I'll bunk with the firecracker." Asheron winks and throws a cheeky laugh my way, and my face turns even redder.

I snap the key out of Asheron's hand and shake my head at him. "*Ha-Ha,*" I add mockingly.

I stand to leave with Quentin when Asheron says, "Actually, Paege will be up in a moment. I need to speak to her. *Alone.*"

The anxiety that I have managed to stave off for the past few hours comes rushing back, coiling around my chest. Quentin takes the key from my hand and nods. If Asheron's words irritated him or got to him in any way, he doesn't show it. The nonchalant expression on his face gives nothing away. He doesn't say anything either. He just taps the table with his fingers and walks off. No goodnight, no goodbye, nothing.

I slowly sit back down. "Aren't you going to say *goodnight, Quentin*?" I somewhat jokingly call out after him as he leaves the table. *Because rude!*

"Goodnight, Quentin," he sings mockingly, and he saunters away, exaggeratedly swinging his hips in a move I know all too well, and I can't help but laugh.

"What was that about?" Asheron queries as he slides into Quentin's vacant seat and relaxes.

"Nothing," I sigh as I watch Quentin count the doors as he makes his way down the balcony and disappears behind a large yellow door he pulls open. "Won't he get lost? Or aren't you scared he'll end up somewhere he shouldn't be?" I ask.

"No, he'll end up exactly where he needs to be," Asheron dismisses, as if it's no big deal at all that he just sent off one Being they don't want to know their secrets.

"I have something I need to tell you, and I'm not too sure if you're going to like it," I blurt out as Quentin disappears out of sight.

"If it's to do with a certain Wolf, I'm afraid the pup's already out of the bag," he chuckles.

"No," I respond, but then clarify, "Well, yes, but not *that* Wolf. Besides, I don't even know what's going on there."

"Ah huh," is all Asheron supplies in return.

"*Nothing* is happening there, or there isn't anymore," I reassure Asheron. Or maybe I am just trying to reassure myself. Because Gods knows what's happening there. But that isn't what I need to say. I muse for a moment longer, considering how he might react to the news I've been keeping from him these past few weeks. It's not like I didn't want to tell him. I just didn't know *how* to tell him. How to tell any of them. "No, it's not about him. It's about me."

"It's alright, Paege." Asheron takes my hand and squeezes it. He leans in and lowers his voice, not much louder than a whisper, "I have something I need to tell you, too."

"You do?" I ask cautiously, my insides twisting into a knot.

He arches his brows and whispers, "I know."

I don't take another breath. I freeze, the blood in my veins turning to ice. "What do you mean, you know?" I manage to mutter out. Because I'm unsure exactly what Asheron is referring to, but if it's what I think, how much does he know? And how?

"I know everything, Paege."

I swear the second the words leave Asheron's lips, my heart stops beating, dead in my chest. He knows everything? Is anyone else keeping any fucking secrets from me?

"You have no idea how sorry I am, but it changes nothing."

"It changes everything, Asheron!" I snap, anger, my old friend starting to make an appearance, and my Wolf wants to make a damn scene, urging me to reach for her and let her consume me. "You had better start talking now. I want to know exactly what you know, how you know, and for how long. And do not leave anything out! Because I swear to the Gods, Asheron, you do not want to get on the wrong side of me! Not anymore!" I growl, and it's not my own voice. It's hers.

Asheron's eyes soften with sorrow, and he opens himself up to me in that moment, showering me in love, guilt, and sorrow, a plea for a cease-fire. While I appreciate the gesture, I've never once doubted Asheron's love for me. It's all the lies and secrecy, and the damn hits just keep on coming.

"It started the night of the attack at the Gallery, when Remi died. I was so lost, Paege. I had fought the damn bond for years. I didn't want Remi to have to deal with this life. I thought she deserved more than that. The night I walked away, I made her a promise. And after. . ." He shakes his head, platinum hair falling over his face, as if trying to shake the memories loose from his mind. "I eventually wanted to see her. I was ready to speak to her. So, I invited her to Lumeilia's event. It was the worst decision of my life. When I left with her body, I took her home and then came here to see Laz. I can't tell you why he told me. This fucking Apex Code stops me from revealing so much to you. But he knew who you were and referred to you as a Wolf. I challenged him, but you know Laz."

"I don't actually," I mumble under my breath.

"I don't know how he knows, but after I returned home, when I came to see you, it was right there. I could see it. It was like a veil had been lifted from my vision, and I could see clearly."

"Why?" I croak out as my eyes begin to moisten with tears. I trusted him more than I trusted anyone else. Even Mhelodie and Lumeilia. We've had a bond since the day I met him. He's looked out for me more than anyone, and he's never steered me wrong. I could go to him with any trouble, no matter how big or small. "Why didn't you tell me?" I croak.

"I wanted to tell you. Gods, I wanted to, but every time I opened my damn mouth to speak, I was blocked. It was a constant war between my head and my body. Instead, I drank, and—Well, you know the rest." He hangs his head in shame. Emotions, thick and murky like mud and oil—both mine and his—barrel over me, and my vision swims. "After that, I stayed away because I couldn't face you. Not because you're a Wolf, but because I hated that I knew this and couldn't tell you. I hated that I had to keep it from you. I'm sorry, Paege. I swear I didn't know about Guy, though. Not until after you did."

Every part of me splinters like fissures forming in drying mud, and I want to scream into the void. And my Wolf, she howls, her magic humming beneath my skin, urging to be released. But there's no denying the remorse permeating from him. He didn't have a choice. I can see it in the way his violet eyes dampen with grief for Remi, with guilt for knowing this big secret about me and with hope that I can forgive him.

"I know my father sent you to keep an eye on me in the Neopolis," I tell him. "You didn't know then?"

His eyes blow wide, surprised by my statement. "No, Paege. I swear. Our friendship is real. I promise you that."

I know it is. I've known it from the beginning. I've already had my suspicions about my father, and Asheron has always made sure he's revealed his feelings and intentions for me were pure by gifting me glimpses of his emotions. I will never deny that.

"Will you ever be able to forgive me?" He reaches across the table and takes my trembling hand in his. The cracking of his voice and the shimmer of his tears have my heart kick-starting in my chest. This is killing him.

Can I forgive him, though? It's not like he's been hiding this truth from me for years; it's been months at best. It won't be easy, but my forgiveness would be as much for him as it would be for me. Holding onto all this anger isn't easy, and I don't like the way it burns away at my insides, darkening my soul with every strike. If I can find a way to keep Quentin in my life after everything he did, how can I not find a way to forgive Asheron?

"Yes," I finally answer.

On a sigh of relief, he says, "Thank you." I realise he's been holding his breath this whole time.

I offer him the warmest smile I can muster before saying, "I need to get some rest. I'll see you tomorrow."

Asheron doesn't argue. He just nods and watches me stand. As I walk away, he calls my name. I turn to face him, and his porcelain skin glistens from the sweat beading across his skin under the faint balcony lights. "You know I love you, right?"

"I do. And I love you, too, Asheron." Then I leave to try and put all the broken pieces of my life back together, the only way I know how. By breaking this damned curse.

As I open the large double doors to mine and Quentin's room, Asheron's words play endlessly in my head. The bedroom, like everywhere else here, is spacious. The lights from Ferinini sparkle through the floor-to-ceiling stained-glass windows, and the light from the fire burning hot in the fireplace provides me with enough light to find my way to the four-post king-sized bed, where Quentin lies silently, and it's calling my name. But I push the heaviness in my body and mind aside and force myself to freshen up in the bathroom before lying down next to Quentin.

The bathroom is marbled with a large clawfoot bath and shower, and a smaller stained-glass window in the shape of a star on the riverside wall above the bath provides just enough light for me to shower and change. Oh, I would give anything for a bath, but I don't have the time for that this evening. Tiredness is overcoming me, so I take a mental note to come back and visit this place another time.

Once dry, I quietly climb into the large bed and close my eyes, willing myself into a deep slumber, but Quentin unexpectedly rolls over and faces me. "Everything alright?" he whispers sleepily.

"Sorry, I thought you were asleep. I didn't mean to wake you." I yawn.

"I was awake. How did things go with Asheron?" he pries gently.

"It was *interesting*," Quentin doesn't respond. He holds my gaze, his grey eyes urging me to trust him and share my burdens.

I sigh before taking in another long breath, and I tell him everything in one long, jumbled mess.

"He what?" Quentin gasps, his eyes hardening at the news I just shared.

"Yup. He found out during the days he went missing after Remi died."

"And he never thought to tell you?"

"No," I reply, not wanting to betray the Guards about their Apex Code. "And guess who it was that told him. Our lovely new friend, Lazarus."

"Have I told you today how much I dislike him?" Quentin scoffs, and I can't help but chuckle at his admission. It's not as if this is new information. The two of them are starting to make an art form out of insulting each other, but hearing him acknowledge it in a light-hearted way eases me somewhat about our journey. Maybe I won't have to worry about them killing each other before the Dead Forest or Mountains of G'phyn have a chance to try.

"He's promised no one else knows, and that he would keep it that way. So, that's something"

"I suppose," Quentin adds, and he squeezes my hand in support of my revelations.

"Oh, and he also swears he didn't know Guy was my twin until recently. I have a sneaking suspicion that may have been Mhelodie's handiwork, but he never gave her up."

Quentin huffs. "There's a lot to unpack there, Books. How are you feeling, really?"

"To be honest, I am just exhausted by it all and talked out. I told him that it was all fine and I loved him. And here I am."

"So, all's forgiven, just like that?" Quentin says with harsh judgment in his tone.

"No. Not *just like that*," I snap with a sudden urge to pull myself back from Quentin as I resent his assumption that I'm flippantly ignoring Asheron's indiscretions. I'm not. I've thoroughly thought this through. "I've forgiven a lot worse from those who mean a lot less to me," I say with a not-so-subtle hint. "I'm sure holding onto all this anger is no good for me. I just want to let it go."

I hold Quentin's gaze. The soft lights from the stained-glass window dance along his angled lines and clenched jaw like glistening gemstones. I watch as his face slowly relaxes again. "Fair enough," he whispers as he closes his eyes and squeezes my hand once more in an effort of support, but I know he isn't supportive of this. He's jealous that I can easily forgive Asheron but not him. "Fair enough," he repeats, and I hope to the Gods he drops it because I am too exhausted to deal with him, too, and we have a long trip ahead of us. I can't keep carrying the weight of everyone else's troubles along with my own.

To my relief, he doesn't say another word. When I hear his breathing slow and his hand loosen its grip on mine, I know he's finally asleep. I finally allow myself to close my eyes, praying I follow in his footsteps and gently drift off to a peaceful slumber.

CHAPTER 19

I wake more refreshed than I have in a long time. No nightmares. It takes me a moment to gather my thoughts, and when I try to move, I realise I'm pinned down by a large, but equally comforting Wolf. Though the bed is large enough to fit four of us in here, somehow Quentin and I ended up with legs and arms entwined on one side of the bed. One of his legs is draped over mine, his arm wrapped around my body, and my head is buried against his chest. Probably because he thinks we are in a derelict inn in the middle of nowhere.

I try to gently slide myself out from his embrace, but he just pulls me in closer and murmurs something undiscernible. It reminds me of an innocent child dreaming, and I can't help but melt into him. It's in moments like these that the troubles between us disappear, and I wish that we could stay like this forever. We are slowly rebuilding things, and as I lie here studying his face, running my eyes over his perfect lips that once took me to places of pure ecstasy, whispering my name with such desperation, I close the space between us further. A slight burning sensation starts to rise in my back, and I'm pulled from this hypnotic state. My scars remind me of the male he truly is, and I can't allow myself to get lost in the dream that it could ever be anything more than just this.

I try to uncurl myself from Quentin's embrace again, and this time when he speaks, I hear him clear as day. "Don't," he pleads in a rough voice that has me curling my toes.

"I have to," I whisper back.

"No," he pleads again, holding on a little tighter. When I wriggle myself free, he harrumphs and lets go, rolling over to the centre of the bed.

I sit up for a moment and take in my surroundings. In the darkness last night, I didn't see much of the room, but now, with the early morning light shining through the colourful, flowered windows, I can see just how beautiful and large this room is, and it's just as elegant as the rest of this inn.

There is a velvet maroon and gold hemmed chase at the foot of the mahogany and ivory four-post bed. A distressed, round wooden dining table sits between four velvet wingback chairs in colours of emerald-green, dark grey, maroon, and sapphire blue. A chestnut bureau sits next to the fireplace opposite the bed. The stone wall is decorated with landscape artworks between the floor-to-ceiling stained-glass windows, and a large, royal carpet in similar colours to the dining chairs covers the stone floor at the foot of the bed. Along the far, right wall sits an armoire and an elegant vanity table with drawers and two piles of clothes that appear to be unbadged combat leathers. There are at least two sets per person with boots, and it occurs to me that Asheron, *or Lazarus,* has provided us with clothing that is more suited to our journey than the denim and jackets we have clothed ourselves in.

I take another quick shower, not because I need one, but because it may be the last chance I get in a while. I braid my wet hair and dress in the combat leathers left out for me: fleece-lined white tunic, leather laced corset, weatherproof leather patch jacket, armoured tactical pants, and knee-high military boots. As far as clothes go, they are considerably comfortable and warm. Once dressed, I head out to the dining balcony below, leaving Quentin to continue resting. It's early, and we have plenty of time to make it to the White Forest, so there is no need to rush.

The cool morning air stings my face and awakens all my senses. Ferinini looks spectacular in the daylight. The sun glistens off the crystal-clear water of the river, and the various colours of the villas bring the mossy ravine to life. I spot a few small streams and waterfalls cascading down the ravine face, separating groups of villas, but they all remain connected with bridge crossings. The air is filled with the scent of the fragrant jasmine vines mixed with the smoke bellowing out from chimneys set behind the cliff's edge and *coffee.*

I follow my nose, and as I approach the table we occupied last night, I find Asheron and Lazarus already there with a pot of coffee and the largest stack of gridcakes with fresh fruit I've ever seen.

"Morning," I sing in my most cheery voice because even though I'm heading off on a possible death mission today, I am incredibly confident. Something about knowing Mum is safe, a good night's sleep, and a belly full of food has my anxiety fading.

"Someone's chipper," Asheron chimes back. "Are we all good, Paege?" he asks coyly.

"Of course." I smile and lean down, placing a gentle kiss on his cheek before taking a seat beside him and opposite Lazarus, who is studying me with one brow furrowed and the pierced one raised. His eyes narrow as if he's questioning my mood. I force the smile into a full-blown toothy grin because I won't allow him to ruin my good mood, no matter the reason.

"Point taken," Lazarus responds before grabbing a plate and placing some fresh berries, melon, and banana with a couple of gridcakes on it and handing the plate to me.

Hm, I wasn't expecting that.

Offering a more sincere smile this time, in gratitude, I accept the plate of food he prepared for me.

"Sleep well?" Lazarus enquires. "Good to see the clothes fit."

"I did. Really well. And yes, thank you." I run my hands over the leather, marvelling at the softness beneath my skin before turning toward Asheron. "These are comfortable and with the built-in sheaths, I don't need to wear any halters," I say before dropping a couple of blueberries in my mouth. The berry bursts, filling my mouth with a sweetness like no other. The fruit, the food, the smells, everything here is more intense. Even the colours. "These berries are incredible. What's with that?" I grab a few more, popping them in between my lips.

"Good. Eat up because this might be the last meal like this for some time. I'm afraid our accommodation at the foot of the mountains may not be so *accommodating* anymore," Lazarus says as I take a mouthful of gridcake.

I snap my head up because I had no idea he had organised accommodations, but also, why would they no longer be accommodating? "What's going on?" I ask, darting my eyes between them both and placing my utensils back on the table because suddenly, I'm not so hungry.

"We got word overnight that the king's locking down Owenstown."

My stomach knots at the words. "What? Why?"

Asheron adds, "We don't know, but Lazarus's legion has also been called back to Quespelia. And the Lupa-Centaurs that guard the mountains have been told to lock down. No one enters or leaves," his voice sounding a little shaky.

The roar of blood in my ears drowns out the sound of the rapids below, and my tongue presses against the roof of my mouth. "Well, what the fuck does that mean for us?"

"It means that things got a little more complicated but not impossible," Lazarus responds a little arrogantly.

Swallowing down the lump that's now starting to form in my throat as walls start to close in around me from all angles, I ask Lazarus, "So, you're heading back then?" I hold my breath in anticipation for his response because as annoying as he is, his assistance might actually be the difference between surviving this whole ordeal and dying before we even make it to the mountains.

Lazarus smirks. "I do what I want, when I want, and I answer to no one."

Regardless of his arrogance, I'm relieved by his answer, but it doesn't prevent the massive tidal wave of anxiety that is now trying to drown me. I swallow hard again and breathe deeply, keeping myself from spilling over the edge into despair.

"Do you think there is an outside force coming? The Humans? Something else?" *Or is this about me?* I think to myself. Because it's a Godsdamned big coincidence that the king is locking down the lands to which we are travelling, and if I've learnt anything by now, there is no such thing as a coincidence.

"Honestly, Paege, we don't know, and we probably won't know for a few days, maybe weeks at least," Asheron responds, his voice still shaky as hell, which is not instilling any confidence in me.

"What do we do?" I ask just as shakily because Godsdamn, my good mood and confidence just got squashed by a king-sized monster.

"We do nothing; we change nothing. We leave today as planned. Asheron will get word to us if we need," Lazarus commands.

"How? We won't have access to any. . ." I stop myself before I finish the sentence because from the looks on their faces, they know about the journal. "My journal?" I groan, "You know about my journal!"

"See, I knew you were more than just that charming mouth of yours and good looks. The little Wolf is also smart." Lazarus goads in amusement.

"Don't think for one second you're going to have access to it. Whatever Asheron needs to send, it goes through me and Mhelodie. You understand me?" I bark, irritation taking up a permanent residence in my belly.

"No one's taking your journal, Paege," Asheron chuckles, and he rests his hand on mine. "But I'm not a guard yet. I can't communicate with Lazarus via *other means, so. . .*" he drawls, "what Lazarus is asking is, *can we please communicate using your journal?*" He smiles and bats his long lashes at me in an attempt to quell my sudden burst of anger. Which works, of course, because Godsdamn it, I can't truly stay angry at my best friend for too long.

The next moments at the table are the longest of my life. The three of us eat under a blanket of uncertainty while I quietly ruminate over the information that was just shared, trying to make sense of what it all means and how it will affect our plans *and our safety* moving forward.

When Quentin appears at the table, not dressed in the clothes left out for him, *typical,* he smiles but doesn't greet any of us. He silently fills a plate of gridcakes and fruit and sits down casually. His blond hair flops over his face as he starts to eat, completely unaware of what the conversation held moments before his arrival. My stomach churns as I consider whether I need to repeat everything I just learnt, and if so, who knows how he will react. There's a good chance he will abandon our plans, *abandon me,* and head back to Quespelia. I'd like to think that he wouldn't after everything we've been through, but if history tells me anything, when his *dad* calls, he goes running.

And I'm certain his dad will be calling.

CHAPTER 20

"Get in there," I huff while I shove my jacket into my already overflowing pack, and Quentin snickers at my frustration.

"I told you to travel light," Quentin jibes as he rips the jacket from my grasp and shoves it into his own pack.

I open my mouth to respond with some snarky comment, but the words fall dead on my tongue as *one, two, three* light taps on the bedroom door interrupt me. "Paege?"

Asheron stands in the slightly open doorway. Worry wears on his handsome face. His violet eyes appear soft, but it's his forced smile that gives it away. He motions for me to join him out on the balcony. I throw a glance over my shoulder to Quentin, a silent question stretching between us.

"Go, I can finish packing, but don't take too long. I need to get out of this flea-infested inn as soon as possible." He scrunches up his nose at the idea of dragging this stay out any longer. I bite down a laugh as it tries to bubble up inside.

Asheron meanders over to the balcony's edge, tucking his silver locks behind his ears and rests his arms on the balustrade. I follow. "What's going on?" I urge, leaning over the railing next to him and looking down to the ravine below. This place is mesmerising. How do the Star-Borne ever get anything done while here? Every moment

I'm here, I find myself getting lost in the beauty of this place. The hidden sanctuary to the Fae, nestled amongst the forest edge and the beauty of the land. With every breath of fresh air, with every crash of the rushing waters below, or the gentle touch of the sun's rays on my face, my mind runs away, determined to stay lost and never return to the harsh reality that lies beyond the walls.

"I wanted to make sure you're alright, that *we're* alright. . ." He reaches into his jacket and retrieves two gilded daggers. Daggers that resemble the swords Amerax had made for me. Just as beautiful, just as deadly. The hilts are perfect for my smaller hands, and the pommel is ivory and gold, jewelled with emerald stones. "And give you these."

"Asheron, what—" I gasp as he fluidly flips them in his hand before offering me the hilts. I hesitate for a quick moment before accepting. "They are beautiful. Where did you get them?"

"They were Synthony's."

I jolt at the sound of my mother's name, looking up to him, and I'm met with cautious violet eyes. My chest tightens. "*Were* Mum's?" I hold his gaze, and his throat bobs. "What aren't you telling me, Asheron?" I ask apprehensively. It's as if he has something he wants to say, but he's holding back from me.

"Nothing." Asheron shakes his head, breaking our connection, and I immediately know he *is* hiding something. I've known him for seven years, and I know that's one of his tells when he's hiding something from someone. Until recently, I never thought that included me.

"Asheron?" My stomach twists, and I hear the familiar yet unsettling growl of my Wolf, warning me to tread carefully. A warning I heed as something is off. All conversations about my Mum have been skirted around and veiled in suspicion the last few days. Who am I kidding? All conversations about me and my past have been so these past few weeks. Ever since I found out the truth of who and what I am. Or part thereof.

"I swear, it's nothing," Asheron confirms.

"Then what do you mean *were* my mum's?"

"Before you," Asheron swallows his next words.

"Asheron," I urge.

"Before you and Guy," he corrects, and I now understand his hesitation. It's not about Mum; it's about Guy. "She had many Star-Borne friends, Paege. In fact, she is a bit of a legend around here. And those"—he nods at the blades I hold—"*were* hers."

My attention drops to the featherlight blades gripped in my hands. Turning my hands over, I study each one closely. Each dagger's hilt is engraved with a pair of letters, one on each side. One with G and V. The other with G and H.

"Hers?" I sigh, my eyes not leaving the beautiful weapons I hold in my hands.

"Paege, are you alright?" Asheron asks again.

No. No, I am not. Nothing has felt right in weeks, in months, in years. An ache blooms in my chest, as if my heart is cracking into pieces like a porcelain cup long forgotten. "Truthfully, I don't know, Asheron," I say. "My world keeps changing, shifting. Everything feels wrong and different. I don't know who to trust. Everyone has secrets, and they are *all about me.*" My vision spots. I breathe deeply, trying to calm the storm I've been weathering for weeks, but instead of calming me, every breath I take intensifies the tension in my body. "Tell me, how would you feel?"

Asheron loosens a breath, and he runs his hands through his silvery hair, tucking it behind his ears. He faces the river. "You're right," he sighs again. "Gods, I know you're right. I would hate it." He straightens himself up and swivels to face me. "But I promise you *can* trust me, Paege, and you can trust Laz, too. I know he can be difficult, but he's been a Guard since he was sixteen. He hadn't even finished his Star-Borne training. You grow up quickly. You learn to be a soldier," he mutters. "When you're activated and thrown straight into battles after losing a parent to living the very life you're destined for, the only way to survive is to compartmentalise your emotions."

My heart splinters more at his words, and a veil that's been tainting my view on the Star-Borne lifts. I've never thought about it like *that* before. What it truly means to be a Guard. The Star-Borne families are destined to endlessly repeat history. One dies, their child or children take their place, thrown into the same life, fighting the same battle that took their parents' lives. A curse that keeps recurring with every generation.

Seems this entire Kingdom really is cursed.

No wonder Asheron denied himself the truth, refusing to admit who he truly was. His great gift of activation only comes when his father is dead. It's a cruel, ironic reality. I nod in understanding and sheath the blades in the compartments sewn into the thigh of my pants.

"I need you to trust him," he continues, "because I need you to come home. I need you alive. We all do." His beautiful violet eyes soften at the edges, tears cresting at the seams. He forces himself to smile. "I can't imagine a world without Paege Vailenbyrg in it." He wraps an arm around my shoulder and tugs me into him. A subtle vanilla scent caresses my nose, smooth like velvet. His love is warm and comforting, but it cracks something deep inside of me. Asheron has lost so much these past few months. He lost his FaeMate, Remi, and it devastated him. No wonder he's concerned. He is scared for my safe return, a worry I share, but I refuse to let it overcome me. I will not succumb to my fear.

And I will not let him lose anyone else.

I pull away from his embrace and place my hand on my chest, holding it to my heart. "I'll come home. I promise," I answer softly, then I fold back into Asheron's embrace. He rests his chin on my head, and a sigh brushes through my plaited hair as he slowly rebuilds his shields—piece by piece—until there's nothing left except the two of us with nothing more to hide.

We leave Ferinini not long after mid-morning. Before we departed, Asheron demanded that Quentin promise to protect me. His exact words were, "Look after her, and if anything happens to her, don't bother returning." A clear warning if I've ever heard one. Quentin didn't argue. He silently accepted the challenge. In fact, Quentin's been oddly quiet all morning.

It takes us all morning and most of the afternoon to reach the edge of the River Plye, the border of Orphelious and White Forest. My body quietly aches as we cross the river, Lazarus refusing to accommodate any requests for respite during our day's journey. I've been too emotionally exhausted to act as a mediator between the males, so I haven't dared attempt to start any conversations with either of them. Instead, I've been focusing on drowning out the conversations my mind's been having with itself, trying to make sense of everything I've learnt in the past day.

Just another day of revelations.

I am curious how Lazarus knows my mother, and I'm even more curious to learn about her alliance with the Star-Bornes and why she's infamous. It also makes me question her relationship with Amerax. Gods, with every discovery comes more questions, exposing more secrets and more lies. *I'm not too sure how much more I can take.*

Quentin hasn't mentioned his father, nor have I. Every time I consider having the conversation about the king's plans, anxiety presses down on my chest, constricting my breath. His father's intentions hover like a looming dark cloud, building a storm and ready to inflict chaos.

"We'll travel inland for another couple of hours before setting up camp," Lazarus calls from up ahead as Quentin and Jesstar cross the River Plye behind me.

"Can't we rest here tonight?" I moan, protesting on behalf of my legs and ass, which are silently screaming at me for some sort of relief. Lazarus doesn't respond, but he continues moving forward up ahead, Lilith slowing her stride but not missing a beat.

As we make our way into the White Forest, I can't help but notice the variety of trees. Each one's trunk is deathly white like ghosts, providing an eerie landscape for as long as the eyes can see. Some with bare branches cast an equally unnerving canopy above.

There are no paths. No laid-out routes for us to travel. We follow Lazarus through the dense forest as a tight group, manoeuvring our way around the old ghostly trees. The horses take any opening they can to move forward. The forest floor is covered in mossy rocks, old stumps, green ferns, and thickets, providing some challenging obstacles as the forest grows thicker the further we travel from the River Plye.

It's not long before we stumble upon a clearing that's suitable for a campsite, and without discussing it, I pull Whisky to a stop. I'm not used to riding non-stop in this manner, and my body feels it. My legs ache, and my arms are heavy from the last two days of riding. My stomach grumbles from hunger as I dismount ungracefully. As my feet hit the ground with a heavy thunk, my joints groan, and I welcome the numbing pain that shoots up through my legs, awakening me as the blood rushes to my extremities.

Lazarus turns Lilith around and snarls, "What do you think you're doing, Paege? We still have plenty of sunlight for riding before we can rest."

"This is just as good as any place," I snap. "I'm hungry, tired, and sore," I moan, and before I get a chance to confer with Quentin, I hear a thud and *bray* from behind me, and I know he has dismounted Jesstar in a quiet sign of his agreement.

"This clearing is fine. It's dry, flat, and well protected," Quentin calls up to Lazarus.

Lazarus growls in protest, literally growls, but he motions Lilith to trot back toward us in a reluctant surrender.

"Who died and made him king?" Quentin rebuffs hoarsely in my ear as he takes Whisky's reins from my grip and walks the two horses over to the sycamores along the border of the clearing.

"I don't know, Wolf. Isn't that something you'd be particularly familiar with yourself?" Lazarus quips back, his eyes flashing red as he dismounts from Lilith, where Quentin is now unloading the horses.

Blood pounds between my ears, and I draw in a long breath in preparation for the verbal bloodshed that is to follow, but surprisingly, Quentin doesn't bite. Instead, he opts for blatantly ignoring him.

If these two knuckleheads don't stop throwing their dicks around, we won't need to wait for the Dead Forest or the Mountains of G'phen to try and kill us. I'll be doing it for them.

CHAPTER 21

Our camp is basic: a couple of small tents with bedrolls barely large enough for two, a few lanterns placed around the clearing, and a small fire pit. Basic, but it's all we need, and all we could afford to carry without overloading the horses and sacrificing other essential supplies like food, clothes, and weaponry.

After a quick freshen up in a small stream near the camp, I sit cross-legged next to the fire, *and next to Quentin,* to get warm. I notice Lazarus standing over by the edge of the clearing, leaning against a tree and giving Quentin a wide berth. I roll my eyes at him.

"Here," Quentin proffers, as he hands me a cup of tea. "Drink this. It will keep you warm."

"Thanks," I say through chattering teeth, and I accept the enamel mug, welcoming the heat defrosting the tips of my quickly numbing fingers.

The sun's warmth struggles to reach us through the tree's canopy. It's already setting, and blue specs above the shadowy forest quickly start turning darker shades of purples and greys, the air becoming frigid. I'm suddenly incredibly grateful for the warm leathers, and at the rate the chill is filling the air, even the tiny tents are a gift. I sip the hot tea and stare aimlessly up at the darkening sky. A few clusters of stars peak through the mosaic patterns of the leaves above. Then something bright catches my attention. My eyes widen as they settle on the crescent moon.

The first night of the waning crescent phase.

The weight of Quentin's eyes presses into me, persistent and impossible to ignore. I shift my body around and bring mine to meet his. I find that mischievous wolfish grin that I love and hate beaming at me. His light steel eyes sparkle as the firelight dances in his irises.

He leans in closely, his sandy blond hair flopping over his brow. "I wondered when you would figure it out," he whispers gently into my ear, each word a caressing invitation to join him and shift under the moon.

I continue to hold his gaze, his eyes softening with each passing moment in a silent plea. I haven't reached for my Wolf since that night at my family home. I knew this was coming. I knew, eventually, the moon would hang in the sky, the perfect crescent bright and proud, and Quentin would want to shift, and he'd want me to join him. I just didn't realise it would happen so soon.

I'm not ready. She's there every day, yearning to be released, reaching for me with those warm tendrils of light. She reacts to my emotions, and it takes every bit of energy to keep her at bay, locking them and her down at every chance I get. After what happened with Quentin, something scares me about it. Her power is strong, and I'm not sure that I'm strong enough to control her. I worry she will consume me, change me.

As if peering into my chaotic mind, Quentin gently probes, "I know you're apprehensive, but you're still a Wolf, Books, and you need to figure that out at some point. Why not now?"

Why not now? Unlike the rest of the Wolves who've known their whole lives who they are, what they are, who have known no other way, who have spent their entire lives surrounded by each other, I have had a little over a month to learn and accept my truth. I still don't know what Wolf I am.

"You said it wasn't safe for me to shift after last time," I supply truthfully.

"Books," Quentin sighs. He runs his hands through his sandy hair, his wolfish smile fading. "Is that why you're avoiding this? Because of something foolish I said in a moment of anger and fear?"

"It's not only that. My Emergence was terrifying, uncontrollable, and violent, but there was so much else happening at the time, I didn't have a moment to think about it. The second time I shifted, it was my choice, and it was the freest I have ever felt in my life; I felt whole. I felt found. Of course, there was hesitancy then, too. There always is with any unknown, but, to answer your question, yes, I'm even more apprehensive now because of your meltdown. You told me I was a violation."

His expression softens around the edges, and although I can't feel his emotions, the guilt over his words is clear in his eyes. "I never intended for you to fear your Wolf. I just want you to be careful of when you shift and with whom, at least until we figure it all out." He shuffles closer to me, wrapping his muscled arm around my body, tugging me into him. "Come here," he says. I lean my head on his shoulder, and his scent, as fresh as the forest, caresses my heart.

Looking up to him through my lashes, our eyes collide. The pressure of his request demands an answer, and the longer I stare into his gaze, the harder it is to avoid. My lips part on a word, but a jolt of energy slams into me, the air thickening between us. I gasp, but the breath doesn't reach my lungs. Quentin's eyes widen, his mouth dropping open.

What the fuck is going on?

The air continues to thicken as if the oxygen is being sucked out of our surroundings. I attempt to draw in another sticky breath, but my throat constricts my airway. A cough lodges in my throat, and my chest burns as it compresses, tightening with each passing second. Quentin releases me and brings his hands to his chest, playing his ribcage like a drum, and he gasps for air.

The mug falls from my hands as they reach to my throat, grasping, searching, scratching, as I heave for every stifled breath. I close my eyes and frantically search for my Wolf, trying to ignore the fire raging in my lungs. She isn't there. My eyes snap open, and they collide with Quentin's. A quiet resolve passes over his features. His hands fall slack at his sides.

Is this the end?

No. This can't be happening, this can't be it. I didn't survive everything these past few months to die like this, suffocating in the forest. What was the point? What was the point of any of it?

As I continue to fight for breath, my vision swims. Tension squeezes behind my eyes, and panic slams into me as my body becomes heavy and tired. I can't hold on any longer. I blink, and a single tear rolls down my cheek as I accept our inevitable fates.

How can this be the end?

I'm about to succumb to death's visit, my body no longer fighting or struggling to survive, when my lungs aggressively fill with air. Quentin's coughing and gasping tells me he, too, has found relief. The world around me tilts as I descend to the ground with a heavy thud, my body convulsing as it fills with the sweet elixir of life.

"Books, are you alright?" he heaves as he continues to gasp for air.

I swallow down air like a dehydrated animal finding water. "I think so," I wheeze, sitting myself up slowly, my lungs still burning from suffocation. Both Quentin and I scan the site. Lazarus stands unfazed against the old sycamore tree by the clearing's edge, one leg bent against the tree, his arms crossed with an amused look on his face.

"You both alright over there?" he snickers as he pushes himself off the tree and strides over toward us. "Looks like you could use some help?"

"What did you do?" Quentin jumps up and rushes him, still unsteady on his feet.

"Quentin!" I scream, but it's too late, Lazarus already has Quentin against a tree, arm bent behind his back, dagger drawn and aimed at his neck.

"You need to be more careful out here," Lazarus growls. "These forests are dangerous, and it's not a playground."

"Let him go!" I demand as I jump to my feet, but I don't make a move as the world continues to lean around me.

"Paege, first lesson, don't trust anything," Lazarus orders. "And you," he snarls at Quentin. "Stop putting ridiculous and dangerous ideas in her head." Lazarus pushes up against Quentin, and he grumbles in protest. "Understood?" Quentin nods his head in agreement. "Good," Lazarus releases Quentin and strides over to me in five long steps. "There will be no shifting tonight," he demands.

Fury balls in my stomach, and heat rises through my body. "You did this?" I snarl, holding my ground, trying to control my labouring breath. Lazarus's lips twitch, but he doesn't respond. "What the fuck is wrong with you?" I roar. "You could have killed us. You nearly did!"

"You weren't going to die," he chuckles, completely unfazed by anything. The audacity of that male. What was he thinking? And how did he do that? I know the Star-Borne are strong, but that was, well, I don't even know what that was. Suddenly, everything becomes clear about our little encounter back at the house.

I rush to Quentin, pushing through the swaying blur of my surroundings. His eyes thin, darkening with rage. He shakes out his trembling body as if relieving himself of the anger and trying to control the urge to shift and unleash all kinds of wrath.

"Are you alright?" I reach out, but he pulls away. My brows pinch. Surely, he can't be angry at me.

"Tell me again why the fuck he's with us?" he demands, but before I get to answer, Lazarus does so for me.

"I'm here, Wolf," he drawls, "because I am the only one who can get her to the Eagles safely, to make sure Paege survives." The air thickens around us as he watches Quentin with amusement. "I could ask the same question of you." He raises his pierced brow and smirks a devilish grin, his eyes flashing red with fire, though the campfire is out.

I manoeuvre myself between the two males. The animosity between them intensifies with every venomous word spat, and I just hope that my body is enough to deter either one of them from lunging for the other. I do not want to end up as the filling in a Lazarus and Quentin sandwich.

Or maybe I do...

Stop it, Paege!

Emptiness rolls through my stomach as I lie in my bedroll with the journal in my hand. I wasn't in the mood for small talk or to spend any time with Lazarus after he tried to teach Quentin and me *an important lesson that* almost killed us. A lesson I still don't entirely understand the point of. I excused myself without eating and retreated to the tent.

Eager for some normal connection, I write Mhelodie a quick message in the journal, testing it out and making sure it works. Just holding the journal brings a sense of peace and connection to her. It's nice to know I can write to her whenever I need. It isn't so lonely or scary out here in the forest, knowing she's right there at the end of a letter.

Mhelodie,

How are you? I saw Asheron yesterday. He met us at a small village in Orphelious and camped with us for the night. It was nice to see him. Haven't seen him in a long while. He looks good. A lot better

than he has been in recent weeks. Happy. I hope you and Lumeilia are doing alright. Write me back when you can so I know this is working.
- P

She responds almost immediately.

Paege,
There you are! I was expecting to hear from you last night, but I saw Asheron today, and he said he had seen you. I heard you have another yummy male to keep you company, too. Lu-Lu and I want to hear all about him when you can. It's the crescent moon tonight. Have you shifted yet? I hope you're staying safe and Quentin is behaving himself.
Speak to you soon.
- M

The crescent moon?
The crescent moon.
The crescent moon. . . *Fuck.*
I put the journal away and lay in the silence. I can't stop thinking about what Quentin said earlier. Maybe it wouldn't be bad to finally shift and experience my full powers. After all, she's a part of me. I can't deny that, and lately, the more I keep her at bay, the stronger she becomes. She shifts with my thoughts, and I close my eyes for a moment. There she is, waiting. *Shit.* She slowly moves toward me, her emerald eyes sparkling with want, an eagerness I feel in my bones, and I swear I see her smile. It's as if she knows I'm ready to finally embrace her. On instinct, my body pulls toward her, and I slowly reach out. Every inch closer, my heart races faster.

I hear the zip of the tent rip, and I snap my eyes open, abandoning my foolish attempt to visit my Wolf, and I'm met with Quentin's curious face. His blue-grey eyes are wide, and that wolfish smile that I love and hate so much wears broadly on his face.

"Books?" he drawls. "What are you up to?"

"Nothing," I sheepishly respond, sitting up and freeing myself from my bedroll.

"Why do I feel as if that's not entirely true?" Quentin chortles. "Here, I brought you some food," he proffers as he passes me a mug and enters the tent.

The smell of vegetable soup fills the tent, and my stomach grumbles as my hunger awakens. He's also brought me some bread, dried meat, fruits, and a nut bar. It's not a lot, but it quells the hunger, and I am satisfied enough after I've gobbled it all down.

"Are you going to tell me what I walked in on earlier, or do I have to guess?" My face blushes, which is strange because I wasn't doing anything outlandish, but it is still rather intimate to me, the whole Wolf-shifting practice. "If I were to have a guess," he continues as he wipes the hair from his face. "I'd say you were thinking of shifting?" My eyes dart to his, widening with the embarrassment that grows thickly across my skin. "Which of course, I am totally on board with, no matter what *Tall, Dark, and Annoying* says," Quentin mocks and cocks his head, his eyes glistening with amusement. "But maybe we could find a better place than our small canvas tent, which is our only shelter for the rest of this journey, and you might want to change to save your clothes." He lets out a quiet chuckle.

Heat races across my skin. I hadn't even thought about that. I was going to shift, right here in our tent, in my bedroll, in my clothes, like the amateur I truly am.

Damn it, Paege, get your shit together.

CHAPTER 22

Frigid air rushes my face, piercing my skin like thousands of tiny needles. We've waited until the moon was high before deeming it safe. We laid silently, listening as Lazarus sat around the fire, having what I can only assume were Star-Borne telepathic conversations with other guards. We only dared to move after he retired to his tent.

The anxiety of shifting stares me dead in the eyes. It's one thing to shift momentarily, but it's another to run freely in my Wolf form, embracing her wholly, and another to be standing completely naked in front of Quentin Ishaan. Suddenly, the air isn't cold, but still, I wrap my arms around my body in an awkward attempt to keep some dignity.

My first shift was a strange experience that I don't exactly know how to put into words. I could hear myself speak inside my head as if I were speaking aloud. While my physical form had changed, my consciousness hadn't, and I pray to the Gods it remains the same.

A sigh of warmth brushes against my neck. "Are you ready?" Quentin breathes into my ear, and the butterflies that live in my stomach awaken. So does my Wolf.

"No," I respond meekly. How can I ever be prepared for what's about to happen? Two months ago, I thought I was half Human. But now, here I stand, naked in the White Forest as a Wolf. Something I never imagined.

Unexpectedly, Quentin's hand brushes across my arm, leaving a trail of heat and freeing the knot in my chest. He whispers, "Trust me."

I can't tell if it's the intimacy from Quentin's closeness, the nakedness, or the impending shift, but my pulse races beneath his touch as he gently takes my hand and squeezes it. Using every inch of willpower I have not to look down or cover myself again, I pivot to face him and force an uncomfortable smile, anticipating what might be one of the most significant moments of my life.

"Trust me," he repeats more earnestly. "On the count of three?"

I nod, and then we count. "One, two, three."

Squeezing my lids shut, the darkness consumes me, and there she stands. Perfect, majestic, and regal. She's mine, and I'm hers. She wastes no time as she makes her way to me, our magnetic draw stronger than ever. Calmness shrouds me. I reach for her, and as my bare skin touches her soft coat, electricity sizzles through my body, awakening all my senses. With a final jolt of power, magic explodes within me, every atom of my body filling with stardust, evolving into my very existence. I blink, one, two, times, and I see Quentin, a handsome and powerful grey Wolf, standing before me, with my new Wolf vision.

"Books?" I hear his voice say my name so clearly, and it startles me. Unlike in my Fae form, my body doesn't flinch, my heart doesn't thunder, my stomach doesn't flip. I have better control over my reactions. I am no longer a slave to my emotions, no longer caged by my thoughts, and that realisation frees me from my confines.

"Yes?" I answer cautiously because I'm still not sure I actually heard him speak to me or how he did.

"Are you alright?" he asks gently, and his Wolf, no, *he* steps toward me.

"Are you. . ." I tilt my head, unable to find the right words, because we can't be speaking. "Are we?"

"Yes, Books, we are communicating." He chuckles as he starts to slowly but gracefully pace around me, his eyes never leaving mine.

"How?" I shift my body, following his movements, and we coil around each other as if we are dancing, and the earth shifts beneath my paws. *I have paws*

"It's part of the magic." I swear I see his marbled blue eyes smile.

"Are you reading my mind?" I stumble on my words, unsure if I want to know the answer.

Quentin laughs as he continues to stalk around me, slow and deliberate. "Not exactly." He stops and turns to face me. "It is your thoughts, but it's all about your intention. I can't hear anything you don't intend for me to hear. It can be quite difficult to master, especially when you're not with the pack, but I think, with your Fae gifts, that is not going to be a problem for you."

Mind reading. I sigh. *Great, another way to invade someone's privacy.* But Quentin doesn't respond. He doesn't seem to hear me at all.

"What do you say I show you what it's like to be free?" And with that, he shifts his weight to his hind legs and, as effortlessly as taking a step, he pounces forward, leaping over the top of me with such force *and grace* toward the forest behind me, landing without a sound.

I pivot around to face him as he purrs, "Come on," and bounds off to the forest.

I take one small moment to savour the experience before I find my centre of gravity, allowing my weight to shift to my hind legs and in one fluid motion, I effortlessly pounce off from the ground, and I'm soaring through the air. As my front legs plant firmly on the ground a few lengths from where I stood, a small jolt scatters through my body, but it's nothing like when I run or jump in my Fae body. No, this is weightless, as if I'm defying gravity. And the speed. Oh, my Gods, the speed at which I can move is nothing I had ever imagined. As I run, my vision adjusts to the rapid acceleration of my movement. I never lose focus of my surroundings for one second, and my reflexes are heightened, too. I jump logs and boulders and dodge trees, twisting and turning as I manoeuvre my way through the dark, thick forest.

Quentin is already deeper into the forest, but I know it won't take me long to catch up with him. His scent is strong. It's woody and earthy, and I can track him easily.

"Catch me if you can." His playful words tug my mind.

"Oh, I will," I laugh in response and push off from the ground with a little extra force and quicken my speed as I glide through the White Forest with ease towards his scent.

I catch up with him within minutes, and my first instinct is to pounce. I push off and leap through the air toward him. He doesn't move as my body makes impact with him, and I tackle him to the fern-covered land. Our bodies bend and writhe together as we tussle over the muddied floor, and I pin him to the ground underneath me. Our eyes lock for a heartbeat, his electric blue eyes glistening in the moonlight, and he lets out a playful growl. I lick the side of his face and pounce off, running deeper into the forest.

"Oh, it's going to be like that?" he jokes down our mental connection as I hear and *feel* him chase after me.

"Like what?" I tease back as I continue to weave and leap my way around the moonlit woods.

I'm blindsided when Quentin tackles me from the side, and I yelp when we crash to the ground, our bodies wrestling to win this next round, rustling and rolling around, neither one of us conceding. As we continue to bend and curve around each other, laughing and teasing, I can't help but think how my body, my heart, and my mind are free. I am weightless, as if I'm floating through the atmosphere, moving between time and space. I feel *beautiful*. I've never had so much fun.

Quentin finally wins this round, pinning me to the ground. Our eyes collide again, and my body relaxes as his settles into mine, and all I want to do in this moment is get lost in the deep abyss of his eyes. Then I see those same gold tendrils of light I saw when I first Emerged slowly extend from Quentin's body. Each one is wrapped around him, cocooning him, as they reach out for me.

What is that? Though I keep the thought to myself.

Whatever it is, it makes me want to shift back into my Fae form, so I can hold Quentin, so I can kiss him, can be with him. I nuzzle my head up into his chest and let out a quiet rumble.

"Books," Quentin growls in response, his chest vibrating as he carries the sound of my name, and it makes me want to melt into him completely. The way the golden tendrils move elegantly like fine drafts of smoke wafting through the air seems as if they are going to start wrapping around me, as if they are going to bind us. Some part of me wants them to—is eager for the warmth that it brings. Then two large, black shadows fiercely jolt out from behind me, engulfing me and protecting me from the beautiful golden tendrils that are reaching out from Quentin's body.

And my body jerks.

What the fuck?

Quentin immediately retracts from me. "We should be getting back to camp," he says nonchalantly.

"What was that?" I ask as I jump to my feet now that Quentin no longer has me pinned.

"What was what, Books?" Quentin replies casually as if he has no idea what I just saw. Maybe he didn't. Maybe I was seeing things. Maybe whatever I saw has something to do with *my* Wolf pack. Because we still don't know what I am.

Oh, Gods, is my Wolf pack evil? Defective? Is that why they're extinct? I take a long breath, stilling my thoughts because I know I am spiralling in my mind, even if my Wolf's physical emotions are still in check. "Never mind. I must have imagined something," I respond, shaking off the uneasiness. "Let's get back to camp."

And just like that, our escapades in the forest are over, and we head back to camp and away from the freedom my Wolf brings.

CHAPTER 23

"Are you sure this is it?" I ask, confused as we stride into a clearing that eerily resembles the area where we set up camp but is void of any life.

"Yes," Quentin replies as he shifts back into his humanoid form, his brows crinkling with confusion.

I follow his lead, letting go of my Wolf, and I shift effortlessly back into my Fae form. "Well, where is everything?" I pivot around. "Where's Lazarus?"

"He isn't here, and neither are the horses."

"He took the horses?" I spin again to see a bare sycamore that once roped our steeds.

"Looks like it." Quentin runs his hands through his hair, still scanning the empty site.

"Why?" Anxiety ripples through me like tiny waves of hot, scalding water.

"Why does he do anything?" He pauses for a moment before he adds, "Probably to piss me off." Quentin huffs, kicking the dirt.

I continue to pivot, searching for any clues. As much as I know, he and Quentin don't get along, but surely, he wouldn't be so petty as to steal our horses and take our camps. There must be an explanation. "Maybe there was trouble, and he had to leave, and, and. . .we weren't here, so maybe he's out looking for us," I say to no one in particular, trying to ease my own anxiety.

"Or maybe he's just being a dick," Quentin seethes.

"Quentin, what are we going to do?" I ask, panic hitting me like a punch in the chest, restricting my breathing and sending me to my knees.

Quentin hurriedly strides to me and kneels before me, gently placing a hooked finger under my chin and lifting my head to face him. "Books, there's no need to worry. We're Wolves, remember? We can shift and travel fast." My eyes meet his, and it instantly calms me, and I nod in silent understanding. "We can track his Star-Borne ass with ease," he sneers as he rises to his feet and sniffs the air. "His scent is all around here."

"How do you—" I start to ask how the scent tracking works but stop myself because it's not important right now. Quentin can track him. I just need to follow his lead.

"It's easy." He shrugs, understanding my unfinished sentence. "Once you've scented someone, you can track them whenever. I scented the bastard the second he pulled a dagger on me in the house. You don't need to be in your Wolf form to scent someone, but it certainly helps with tracking."

"I suppose when you've been brought up as a Wolf, all of this becomes second nature," I mumble with irritation. Sniffing the air, I smell nothing but the musky forest. Gods, am I ever going to learn about my Wolf magic?

"You'll get the hang of it soon enough," Quentin winks at me. "I've got no doubt you'll soon be teaching me a thing or two about Wolves."

"I doubt that," I scoff. It's nice to have the vote of confidence, but there is a lot I have to learn. I'm years behind the others. "Will you teach me?" I ask, wanting to learn as much as I can as soon as possible.

"Sure." Quentin shrugs, and the chill in my veins starts to warm, and the waves of panic begin to wane. "But right now, I need to focus on Lazarus."

"Then track him." Quentin nods in response.

We shift, and I follow his lead as we travel through the forest. I watch with intrigue as he tracks Lazarus, jumping logs and weaving between trees with his nose to the ground, and I can't help but be excited to learn this new trick. In an attempt to help, I sniff the ground and the air whenever we stop, but I smell nothing but the decaying foliage of the forest and the overwhelming scent of Quentin, earthy and fresh, like pine.

It takes us the rest of the night. The sun is barely starting to rise when we finally find the new camp, and everything is set up.

The moment we arrive, Quentin and I shift and get clothed. Without hesitation, he marches over to Lazarus's tent. "Get out!" he roars, baring his canines, and I stumble back at the intensity of his voice. I've heard Quentin angry before, but this is different. This is primal.

A moment later, the tent zips open, and Lazarus crawls out and stands casually. Quentin was right. His scent now envelops me, even in my human form, now that I know how to sense it. His chest and abs are bare, chiselled perfectly, and covered in the outline of a large five-pointed star tattoo. Each point is marked with words within the star, all except the top. My gaze lingers on the ink. I've seen that star before.

"You made it," he chortles, his dark amber eyes glistening with amusement.

Quentin snarls at him, and I want to snarl, too. I am not sure what game Lazarus is playing, but he's treading on thin ice with not only Quentin but me, too. After he tried to choke us and now this, I'm beginning to think bringing him along is going to be more hassle than it's worth, and maybe we should go our separate ways.

"Careful, Wolf," Lazarus sneers. "You don't want to start a fight with me."

"And why is that exactly?" Quentin shifts his weight, furling his fingers into his palms, his knuckles whitening.

"Because you wouldn't stand a chance," he swipes harshly, as if the thought of fighting Quentin would be like fighting a small child.

"You know, I hear a lot of this. . ." Quentin brings his hand up to his face, snapping his fingers and thumb together over and over again. "Yet all I see is a few glamour tricks and a lot of childish games," Quentin retorts with casual sarcasm. "Nah." He drops his hand and turns on his heel and walks away. "You're not worth it."

I sigh in relief, even though I know this isn't over.

"Come on, Books. Let's get some rest."

"Don't get too comfortable. We'll be heading off as soon as that sun is fully up," Lazarus snickers, arching his brows in amusement and smirking.

Quentin stops dead in his tracks and cocks his head to the side, not actually looking at Lazarus but aiming his voice at him, and growls. "We'll go when we are rested and ready and not a moment before."

And I swear my heart swells to three times its size and takes off in my chest, soaring for the sky like a bird in flight as Quentin holds out his hand for mine. I gleefully take it, throwing Lazarus a 'ha-ha' smirk, and he escorts me to the tent.

After a short and restless nap, I crawl out of the tent to find the sun snuffing out the stars and barely painting the sky with brilliant strokes of pinks and blues. Still weary, I make my way to the dampening fire, its embers barely giving off any heat. The air is a little frostier, or maybe that's just the hostility between Quentin and Lazarus.

The camp is packed, with the exception of my tent. Lazarus is stalking one half of the clearing. He looks to be patrolling the border but is more likely keeping a wide berth from Quentin, who is on the other side of the clearing, casually leaning back against a paper bark tree with a keen eye on Lazarus as he paces back and forth, back and forth. *Back and forth.*

I roll my eyes at them both and ready myself for the day. Once prepared, Quentin silently packs the tent, and we head off again in a deafening silence that sets my teeth on edge. It's been close quarters with two insufferable males for days now. Well, that's not fair. Quentin has been amazing lately, but Lazarus certainly brings out his arrogant side. The last two days have been especially awkward and uncomfortable. Lazarus and Quentin never talk directly to each other, and somehow, I've become the official liaison between the two. At least no more fights have broken out, and Lazarus hasn't lashed out again, using his magic or leaving us stranded. I suppose, there's that.

Quentin and I haven't shifted again, but my Wolf is restless. She's been calling to me, urging me to free her from her cage. Instead, I've kept myself busy, training and sparring with Quentin and ignoring her silent demands. I want her out just as badly. I crave the freedom she brings me, but we have to remain focused.

"We're going to stop a little further up for the night," Lazarus calls out from up ahead.

Perplexed, I shoot my gaze to the pale blue sky. The sun still sits high above. Strange. We don't normally pull up until late afternoon. I turn my head toward Quentin, and he arches his brows and shrugs. Clearly, he's thinking the same. "Don't we want to travel as far as we can with the light?" I muse loudly enough for Lazarus to hear me, yet he ignores me. "Lazarus, will you answer me?" I plead, ushering Whisky to gain some speed so I reach his side.

"We'll talk when we rest, Paege," Lazarus dismisses me. Heat blushes my cheeks as a wild fury builds within. Something inside snaps. I've had enough.

"No, we will talk now," I demand and gain enough speed for me to veer Whisky in front of Lilith, making him pull up. "I'm sick of this. You say you want to help, but all you've done since inviting yourself along is order us around, play stupid tricks, and piss me off." I don't even bother mentioning how pissed off Quentin is because I don't think he cares about Quentin, and that might just make him gloat. I've had enough of his ego for the past few days. "I am not in your precious Guard, so stop treating me like some newbie recruit. Be straight with me!"

"That's right, Paege," he hisses at me, "you're not a Guard, and you are certainly not a recruit. A recruit has basic training. You have none," he bites, and my stomach knots. "You are not prepared for what's out there. You play your silly little games, training with swords and daggers, shifting into wolves, drawing attention to us, but none of that is going to help you in there." He nods past me into the forest behind me.

I throw a glance over Lazarus's shoulder and search for Quentin, wondering if Lazarus's words strike him like they are striking me, each one spat with such force and precision aimed at knocking me down and scaring me into submission. Quentin appears unfazed. I swallow hard, letting a long sigh escape and shift my gaze back to Lazarus. "Well, then, tell me. *Help* me, Lazarus. Stop being an ass and help me prepare!"

"You can't even do basic shielding, Paege. Most Fae your age should be able to command that at least." Lazarus's words hit harder than I expected them to. He's right, I can't shield. No one has bothered to take the time to teach me. We always thought I was half Human and not even sure I would get Fae gifts. Why bother training for something you may never have?

It wasn't until the year I started at the Collegium that my Fae gift even started presenting itself. Most Fae start getting access to some magic in their early teens. For females, it's when they have their first cycle. Being a half Fae, that didn't happen for me. I was magicless until nineteen. I barely had time to learn anything before I left, which is why my parents didn't want me to leave in the first place—or so I thought. Here I am, twenty-four and unable to command something as basic as shielding. I'm pathetic, and the look on Lazarus's face agrees.

I pull on Whisky's reins, my nails biting into my palms and my knuckles white as snow, and I turn us around. Without a word, I squeeze my thighs around Whisky's middle, instructing my loyal friend to take off into the thick forest ahead. As Whisky picks up momentum, the frigid air prickles my face, cooling down the heat in my cheeks from the anger. I don't even notice the tears streaming down my face until one tickles my jaw before it drops from my chin.

I know how far behind in training I am. I've felt insecure and inferior my entire life. When my peers started getting gifts, and I had nothing. When my school friends got to play around with their gifts in classes, and I had nothing. And at the Collegium, shielding was not something we focused on because it's common knowledge that shielding happens naturally when you have your Sacred Birthday. I don't need Lazarus reminding me how useless I am.

"Paege!" My name carries on the wind from behind me, a tone of desperation lacing it, but it's too late. I'm not stopping, not for anyone. I need space from Lazarus. I need space from both of them and respite from their constant bickering.

I just need to be alone.

So, I ride, and I don't look back.

CHAPTER 24

Whisky and I move faster than the wind in a winter storm. Embarrassment drives the desperate attempt to free myself from them, spurring me on with every humiliating thought about my shortcomings.

You can't even do basic shielding.

Faster, faster.

You play your silly little games.

Faster, further.

With every squeeze of my knees, Whisky gains more speed, and we make our way deeper into the forest, jumping and dodging trees and stumps as we go.

Space. A little bit of space is all I need.

Shadows start to infiltrate the scattered light, the shade of the forest slowly merging with the dark. Realisation slams into me. I've been riding at full speed the entire afternoon, and dusk is upon me. Shit. I wanted to be alone, but did I want to be *this* alone? Knowing that Quentin can track me, they will catch up eventually, my heart, for once, doesn't betray my mind and lets me have this moment of peace. Some time alone without me to referee may do them some good, too.

I pull Whisky to a gradual stop, scanning the area and mentally mapping my surroundings. I should start looking for a clearing to camp for the night. The trees here appear differently in the drowning light. Different shapes, different sizes. Scattered amongst the sycamore and paperbark trees, a new variety, unlike anything I have ever seen before, stands tall. Some have leaves, but many are without. All of them have impressively thick trunks. Their bark is rough and flaking, and their trunks hollowed, knotted, and twisted in varying shades of browns and greys with burls larger than a Wolf's head. Creepy.

There must be a place nearby for me to set up camp. I check my supplies, and I have my bedroll, duffel, some food, and water. Enough to survive the night or until they arrive. Determined to find a decent ground for camp, I urge Whisky to continue. He brays at me and rears back a couple of steps.

"What's up, boy?" I ask and give him a nice, big brush down his silken yet gritty neck, his muscles flexing at my touch. Whisky stomps and neighs again and rears back some more. "Come on, Whisky, just a little further, and we can stop for the night, I promise." I brush his neck again, and he pulls his head to the side and hesitantly takes a couple of steps forward.

As Whisky takes another apprehensive step forward, a twig snaps, and the sound shatters through the forest, revealing how eerily quiet it is. Too quiet. There is no sign of life around, as if the forest is holding its breath, pressing in on me. It sends a chill slithering across my bones.

"Paege?" I hear Quentin whisper into my ear from behind me. My heart jumps out of my cage. Breathing heavily, I whip my head around, expecting to meet that wolfish grin and cheeky eyes. I don't see him. Or Lazarus. Neither of them is here.

I shake off the nerves skittering across my skin, and I urge Whisky to move again. "Alright, boy, let's go." He takes another couple of uneasy steps forward and stalls again. His muscles twitch beneath my thighs, and his tail whipping is the only sound I now hear. He rears back and his front hooves crawl high above him, as if crawling for purchase, and his neigh echoes across the land. I hold on for dear life as he aggressively drops to the ground and bolts.

Whisky gallops so fast it makes my stomach flip. He's completely spooked, and no attempt to calm him or gain control is working. I pull back on the reins and squeeze my legs and feet into his muscular abdomen as hard as I possibly can. Bouncing, I can't get my ass back in the saddle securely, so I push through my knees and lock my feet in the stirrups.

My vision blurs as tears stream from my face, and I frantically try to gain control. I pull the reins back into my body, my knuckles whitening as my nails dig into my palms around the leather reins, drawing blood to the surface of my skin. Whisky doesn't relent. He keeps running further and deeper into the forest that's turning into a scene from my nightmares.

My stomach lurches as Whisky pulls up to an aggressive stop. His front legs fly into the air in front of me while he brays fiercely, the sound sending a chill through my veins before he finally stills. I hesitantly unfurl my fingers, loosening my grip on the leather lifeline I hold, and I let out a sigh of relief, relaxing at the realisation we are finally going to rest. Finally, this nightmare is ending.

Whisky bolts again, but it's too late. My body, my mind, my hands had prepared for the rest I wrongfully anticipated coming, and he throws me from my saddle in one fell swoop. Acid stings the back of my throat, and my stomach jolts into my chest as I am flung through the air as Whisky runs into the darkened woods out of reach and out of sight.

I hit the icy, muddy ground in a violent thunk, my bones cracking and groaning upon the impact. I blink frantically as my vision swims, and darkness circles me like a vulture circling its prey.

Rest, a voice coos to me, lulling me into slumber.

No, I need to get up, but my body refuses to move. Get up, get up, get up.

Rest, it says again.

And for some unknown reason, I silently agree. Yes, I need rest. I draw in a long, rattled breath and close my eyes, succumbing to the darkness inviting me to take refuge in that sweet place of relief.

"Paege, wake up."

The sound of my name being called rips me from my slumber. I snap my eyes open and groan in pain as I attempt to roll over. Where am I? My eyes slowly adjust to my surroundings, and images of Whisky running off into the woods pepper my mind. I slowly sit myself up, pushing the throbbing pain away and look around. It's completely dark. I must have been out for a little while.

"Paege, come with me." I hear that voice again—the one that woke me.

With my eyes now adjusted to the darkness, I scan my surroundings, but I don't see anyone. The crescent moon hangs high in the velvety sky, providing limited light through the ghostly treetops.

"Paege," it whispers again.

What the fuck?

I slowly stand, cradling my injured arm. Adjusting my weight, a dull ache blooms in my hip, but I pivot around, still scanning my surroundings. "Who—who's there?" I stutter.

No response.

Rubbing my head, the dull ache behind my ears throbs, and the world spins out from under me. I must have hit my head hard. I take a few unsteady steps forward, avoiding bearing weight on my injured leg, and I hear it again.

"Paege, trust no one." I snap my head around. I know I heard that.

"Hello?"

"He's going to kill you."

I pivot around again, losing my balance, my bearings, and *my mind*. "Who is?" I call out into the nothingness that surrounds me. *It's a dream. It must be a dream,* I tell myself as the panic increases, my pulse thrumming behind my eyes to a heavy throb. "Hello," I call out again.

In an attempt to ground myself, I shift my weight between my legs, but the voices keep coming. They keep speaking. The voices keep. . .keep. . .keep. . .

"It's all lies."

"He's still alive."

A vice tightens around my chest as I keep spinning around and around and around, searching, scanning, looking for an explanation. The words are everywhere but nowhere at the same time. They burn my ears, they scatter across my skin, they burrow into my mind.

"He killed your mum."

"Who did?" I cry out. I'm going insane.

"You must die so Daiz can lead you to the light. You are our saviour."

"Find Sinordra."

"Stop it, please!" I beg as tears escape my eyes and roll down my cheeks, the cold air turning them into ice as they reach my chin.

"Did you think you could escape us?"

"Kill the prince to set us free."

"You must choose right."

"Stop," I scream. I slump forward and trip over a stone, propelling myself down to the tilting ground again, my palms stinging as they take the full brunt of my fall.

"I should have killed you while I had the chance."

"Abomination."

"He is our king."

"Help me, Paege."

"Stop, please!" I scream again, but the voices keep coming.

"He's your FaeMate. Did you know? He will never forgive you."

"Please make it stop!" I can't take any more. All my worst fears, my inner grief and shame, echo on repeat into my ear. Secrets and lies, truths and dares, wishes and nightmares, and no way to tell where it starts or where it ends.

"You could have saved her, Paege. But you let that Wolf into your pants. Did it feel good to be pleasured while she died?"

"Please. . ." I beg, I beg so hard my voice cracks, my heart cracks, and my soul cracks.

"Burn, burn, burn."

"Trust no one."

"Ardronis will set us free. Will you save us all?"

"Paege help us! Help us!"

"Stop. Please, stop," I sob to myself as I pull my hands up to my ears, trying to block the words out. But no matter how many times I beg, no matter how much I plead, the voices keep coming, sometimes one by one, sometimes many over the top of each other. I'm lost, disoriented, dizzy.

"She died protecting your secret. They will all die because of you."

"Surazal is the answer you seek."

"I'm so sorry," I cry.

"Can you kill the one you love to save the ones you love? You have the weapon. Your blood is the blood that breaks the curse. Guy is the key. You must kill him before he kills you. Do not trust anyone. Let the fire burn. You must die."

"Help!" I call out, but my voice catches as the lump in my throat grows and my breath becomes laboured, the cold air burning my lungs with every sharp breath.

"You killed him. He will never forgive you. He is rotting in Hels because of you."

"No, go away. I'm sorry! I didn't mean to kill you!" I scream into the darkness. I'm utterly and completely lost, lost inside my mind, trapped in this nightmare. Trapped in my Hels.

"Quentin is going to kill you. He will kill us all."

"Stop it, please stop it." I plead.

"Paege, it's alright." A warm hand rests on my shoulder.

"Make it stop, make it stop!" I beg whoever is there to stop this madness and set me free.

"You must die to save the ones you love."

"There is nothing for you left."

"No!" The scream rips from my chest, erupting all around me.

"Paege," that soothing voice, that's different from the rest, calls again.

I'm cocooned, enveloped in a warm, silken darkness, and it cradles me like a newborn baby. I move, floating through time, soaring high into the infinite night sky, weightless and free.

Is this death? Am I finally being consumed by the darkness?

Is this how it ends?

Chapter 25

"Paege, are you with me?" That beautiful lulling voice speaks to me again.

"Mmm?" I moan.

Warmth caresses me with a safety I haven't felt in months. I don't want to wake up, but the gentle voice is still calling my name, coaxing me from my dark cocoon. I draw in a long breath, and a calming scent of leather and some sort of sweet spices fills my senses. My heart flutters quietly for a moment before settling back into place. Calm. I gently pry open my eyes, expecting to see Quentin's grey eyes, but all I see is infinite darkness. It *is* the end.

I reach out into the inkiness. My fingers meet a soft and silken blanket. One that moves, flinches with my touch. Huh?

"There she is," the familiar voice chortles as the darkness slowly dwindles as if a veil is being lifted from my eyes. Magnificent feathers appear. Magnificent, onyx feathers with iridescent hues peel away from me, slowly and steadily, as if I were a precious gift being carefully unwrapped. At the first sign of light, the cool air rushes me and prickles my skin as the expansive wings release me from their embrace.

Blinking, my eyes adjust to my surroundings. The forest is gloomy and foreboding, the dense woodlands allowing minimal light as the sun trickles through the canopy above. The trees are twisted and gnarled like the fingers of an old crone. The air is cool and thick with mist, and the damp ground beneath me smells dank. The only sounds I can hear are the rustling of leaves and the occasional hoot of an owl; even the horses are silent.

The horses.

Whisky.

I roll myself over, my lips parting on a word, but the word—whatever it was—falls dead on my tongue. The sight of Lazarus's ridiculously perfect face, crooked smile, and his pierced brow arched in amusement has a snarl erupting from my mouth instead.

"How are you doing in there?" he asks in a soft voice that I've never heard before, and it retracts my canines. He almost sounds sincere, truly concerned for my wellbeing. But I know better than that.

I take in the situation. He holds me close to him, his large arms wrap around my torso, pulling me into his surprisingly warm body. I hiss. At him. At the position we are in.

"Are you hurt?" he queries in that same velvety voice, and his forehead crinkles.

I consider his words carefully. I know I fell from Whisky quite violently. I self-scan my body, wiggling my fingers and toes and shuffling my limbs. A dull ache still throbs in my leg and shoulder, and in my head. Determined to put some space between us, I push back from him, trying to wriggle from his embrace. My heavy head bobs, and my resolve slips as the world tilts.

Lazarus resists my push, keeping his arms firm around me. "Are you hurt, Paege?" he asks again, clipping his words. His dark amber eyes narrow in frustration as they remain fixed on my face. Something in the way he stares at me has me shifting again, a desperate need to move away from the uncomfortable space constricting us. Still, he doesn't relent.

I sigh and give in to his incessant questioning. "My head and shoulder. Possibly my hip," I mutter as my eyes roll from the heaviness.

"You've been out for a while. Just rest for a bit before trying to move. We aren't in any rush." The warmth of his breath brushes against my cheek with every word he says. Too close. He's too damn close. I try to push back from Lazarus again. He rolls his eyes and clicks his tongue in disapproval. "Do you always have to be so defiant?" he huffs in irritation, shaking his head. "That's what got you into this mess in the first place."

That sentence is all I need to snap back into clear consciousness as pure rage floods my body. "Excuse you?" I smash my flattened palms into his chest, shoving my body away from his. He lets go, and I roll back, tumbling out of his embrace and smacking into the ground with a thud. A cry falls from my lips, the pain in my body roars with the impact.

Staring up at him in disbelief, he grins wickedly. "Well, if you had just listened to me, that wouldn't have hurt so much." Lazarus stands, tucking his wings away and wiping some dirt off his leather pants. "But you'll be fine. Healed soon enough, I'm sure."

"Where's Quentin?" I ask, trying to let it show how much any of this has affected me because damn me if it hasn't. Him. Everything about him is so Godsdamn irritating. He's rude and a complete and utter ass, but I need him. I sit myself up, taking in my surroundings. We are in a small, empty clearing.

"The *Wolf* is tracking Whisky. No doubt he'll come back like the obedient pup he is when he finds him."

My heart stutters. "He, he didn't want to come find me?" I mumble quietly.

"One of us had to get you out of there." He nods, pointing his nose behind me. "One had to get the horse. It made the most sense that I flew you out."

"*You* found me? Wait, you flew me out?" The weightlessness comes tumbling back.

"I will always find you, little wolf." Tension coils in my core at his words, along with the last solid memory of me being alone in the forest. Those words, my darkest fears and secrets, whispered in my ears. All my shame and deepest regrets out there, being used against me. And all the other things that don't make sense.

"What was that place, Lazarus?"

"It was the Whispering Woods," he answers shortly.

"The Whispering Woods?"

"Yes, The Whispering Woods. It's believed the souls of our once forgotten ancestors roam the forest, confused and alone. If their soul stumbles into the dead forest, they are absorbed by the essence of the dying trees. The trees use the souls as a life force for an otherwise dying existence. They whisper to you, manipulate you, and get into your head. There is no way to tell what's true and what's not. They use your fears against you, and the longer you are there, the crazier you feel. Nasty place, especially if you're unable to shield yourself. Which you would have known if you had just listened to me instead of running away like a spoiled little brat because you didn't get your way."

Firey rage boils up from deep within, and my Wolf growls. "I'm not a spoiled brat!" I roar. I drag myself up to a rickety stance, my legs wobbling as if I'd been at sea. Spots obstruct my vision, but I use all my strength to overcome the pull back to the earth and stand tall. With a lengthened spine, I take two unsteady steps toward Lazarus.

"Really? So, tell me, Paege, what had you running away by yourself then?"

I step back. "You, you. . ." I stammer. The throbbing pain in my leg intensifies as I continue to hold myself up.

"I what? I told you that you were unprepared, and you were not taking things seriously. I told you that you were unable to command basic magic," he snarls. "What did I do that was so wrong, Paege, besides speak the truth?"

He isn't wrong. This is exactly what he told me. Exactly what he said, and it's completely true. I don't like being told what to do or what my shortcomings are. My immediate reaction is to defy common sense and react in the worst possible way by leaving, running away, or acting irrationally. That's exactly what I did the night of the Pit, and the night Guy died. If I had just listened, maybe. . .maybe.

Once again, every instinct inside my body screams at me to run away. To bolt. But I swallow hard, stiffening my body, trying to control my urges.

Defiant. That's what he had called me earlier.

Defiant and out of control.

"I'm sorry." My chest collapses, and my eyes sting with tears.

"Stop apologising," he huffs. "It's not your fault you haven't had the proper training. It's not your fault that those entrusted to care for you let you down. It's not your fault that no one knew if or when or how your magic would manifest, but it needs to change. *You* need to start making changes. You need to take control. You can't run off at the first sign of conflict." He sighs, "How can you be expected to—" pausing, his eyes soften as they study my face. "Things need to change, Paege."

"Change? How?" I ask, not trying to challenge him, but I'm genuinely interested in knowing if he has a plan and if so, what that is.

"First, *we* train." Lazarus starts pacing back and forth in front of me, rubbing his large, bronzed hands together. "You need to learn patience, acceptance, and control, and you need to master shielding. You are strong, Paege, and your magic is even stronger, but you have little control over your emotions, let alone the emotions of others. There is nothing wrong with having these emotions. Use them to fuel you, to drive you, but you can't let them rule you. You need to learn to command them." He takes a few steps toward me, and my muscles tense. "It won't be easy. *I* won't be easy on you, but when you succeed, it will be rewarding."

"Strong?" I scoff, concealed by a humourless laugh at the thought that Lazarus thinks my gifts are strong. Maybe he doesn't know as much as he says he does. Annoying, yes, unpredictable, yes. But strong? No.

"Yes, strong," he says, his voice carrying a tint of awe in it, which can't be right. "You have the potential to be even stronger. I've only known a few empaths, but they all have immense power. Just like your mother."

"Mum doesn't have any active magic." I sneer. "Like mine, they are all passive."

I watch Lazarus curiously as he furrows his brows, narrowing his eyes. "Be that as it may"—he shakes his head and sighs—"you need to master your emotions and control your powers."

"Control," I mumble under my breath. Tilting my head up to look at the quickly brightening sky, I consider his proposal for a moment. I suffer pain and discomfort daily because I can't shield myself from others. How nice would it be to be able to control it rather than be at the mercy of others? How nice would it be to have peace? I drop my head back down, amber eyes meeting mine. "What's in it for you?"

"Besides you not being a liability or a royal pain in my ass?" He chuckles and crosses his arms. I raise my brows at him in displeasure. "Let's just say I've got a vested interest."

"What would that be?"

"That is none of your concern."

I scoff and fold my arms, mirroring his posture. He keeps saying he wants me to trust him, but he refuses to give me any valid reason to. "Why did you come along?"

"That is also none of your concern."

Fury balls in my stomach. He is so insufferable. "Not interested," I snap, turning on my heels to walk away.

"Why are you going to the Mountains of G'phyn?" Lazarus growls.

I stop halfway through a step, my bones freezing as if winter's ice has settled in them. I slowly place my foot down on the ground and pivot around, dropping my arms to my waist. "I think we both know that you know exactly what I'm doing. So, let's not pretend that you don't," I say, trying not to stammer my words, willing every bit of confidence to my voice that I can muster.

He harrumphs. "Then why won't you trust me?"

"Because you are still not telling me anything." I cross my arms again and stomp my foot. Lies, it's all lies. Him, Quentin, Mum, Asheron. Is there no one in my life who can tell the truth? Lazarus doesn't tell me anything, and he expects me to blindly give my trust out. The last time I did that, someone I loved died.

Lazarus sighs in clear frustration, but the features in his warrior face slacken. As he steps into my space, I drop my arms by my side. Our chests are only a heartbeat away from each other. I tilt my head back to see him through my lashes. He is so damn tall.

"Paege," he says, his voice soft like velvet, "I know your family. I work for your father"—his throat bobs—"and for Synthony. How do you think they would feel if something were to happen to you? I couldn't—" Lazarus cuts himself off, considering his words, and then he takes a step back, lengthening his spine, standing proud and tall. "I am an Israykiel Guard, a Star-Borne. It is my obligation to help you, to protect you." His lips part with a smirk. "Me training you is just a bonus."

"So, I'm an obligation?" I retort, taking an uneasy step back. I was also Quentin's obligation to his father, and look how that turned out.

He shrugs. "See it how you will." He loosens a breath and runs his hand through his onyx hair. "But make no mistake, you need to learn how to shield and become a master of your gifts. If you won't train with me, I will find another way." He shrugs.

My heart hurts as I think about my parents. Yes, they lied to me, and I'm angry at them, but I would never want them to suffer like that. And the twins, my friends, they would be devastated if something were to happen to me. I consider Lazarus's proposal. What's the harm? At least he told me a partial truth of why he's here, why he wants to train me. Which is more than most Beings lately, even if I did have to pry it from his cold, hard hands.

Master my emotions. Shield myself from others. Isn't this what I've always wanted? Isn't this what I need? Train with Lazarus. I suppose it could be worse. "Fine," I moan.

"Good girl," he chortles and winks.

I roll my eyes at him, but something akin to pride blooms in my chest at his praise. Yes, I am doing this. I am going to master my gifts.

"Now, I've said it before, but it bears repeating: You need to be careful, Paege. *You* cannot trust anyone, not even Quentin."

"Quentin?" My brows arch, and that lump appears in my throat, "Why?"

"You have no idea, do you?"

Chapter 26

"No idea about what?" I hear his voice before I hear their heavy footfalls. I pivot to see Whisky and Quentin padding across the clearing toward us. Quentin's eyes are a dark storm as he takes me in, studying me from toes to head. The weight of his stare unsettles me, and my heart thrums in rhythm to his steps as he approaches.

"I believe this one belongs to you." He proffers the reins to me. "I found him not too far from where he found you, but it took me a while to get him to trust me; otherwise, I would have returned much sooner." His eyes dart erratically between Lazarus and me as if searching for an answer to a question he didn't ask. "Is everything alright, Books?"

I nod, silently responding to him as I rest my face against Whisky's cheek, my heart instantly calming at his return. I run my hand down his smooth neck and across his body, as I search for any injuries. None.

"So, what do you have no idea about?" Quentin repeats, scowling at Lazarus as he circles us, circles Lazarus.

"Lazarus was just explaining—" I start.

"I was just telling our dear Paege here that she has no idea how dangerous things are going to get, and she needs to learn how to shield and control herself," Lazarus cuts me off, wrapping his arm around my shoulder like some old friend.

"Uh-huh." Quentin nods as I drop my shoulder from underneath Lazarus's arm and shuffle one step away. I may have agreed to train with him, but we are not friends.

"Lazarus has offered to train me," I supply, my words sounding a lot more enthusiastic than I intend them to.

"Has he now?" Quentin drawls, circling us with his hands buried deep in his pockets. His eyes are locked onto Lazarus, never leaving their mark. "Is that all he has offered?"

"What does that mean?" I shift uneasily, taking the weight from my injured leg. The pain still lingers, but I notice my injuries are healing faster than usual. Wolf healing, I realise.

"It means he has done nothing helpful so far. He let you ride off into the Whispering Woods without warning."

"He didn't let me do anything," I snap. "I rode off. My choice." I palm my chest in two quick, successive hits. "And Laz is right. I have no control over my gifts. I let my emotions rule me, and I can't shield myself. I'm completely vulnerable and unprotected."

Quentin stops pacing for a moment, his eyes narrowing at Lazarus. "Laz?" he muses with some sort of amusement in his tone. "Alright." He nods, then shifts his eyes to meet mine. "If that's what you want, then we train."

I clear my throat. "*We?*" My brows leap, and I dart my eyes between the two males.

"You train with him to learn how to shield, to learn self-control, and you train with me to master your Wolf and harness her strength, speed, and senses while in your Fae form."

"Absolutely not!" Lazarus barks, taking one step forward toward Quentin, positioning himself between me and the Wolf.

Here we go again. The alpha male bullshit that these two keep throwing at each other is growing thin. I watch in silence, anxiously zipping my charm along my golden necklace as the two males begin arguing, and the damned thing zaps me with static.

"She is half Wolf, too."

"I said no, Wolf!" Lazarus growls, and I take a step back as it pulls me from my thoughts.

"So, you want her to be able to harness her Fae gifts, but not her Wolf? Protect herself from a mental attack, but not a physical one?" Quentin scowls.

"I want her to be able to protect herself in every possible way and from every threat, but I will train her, not you"

"I am a Wolf!" Quentin roars, revealing his canines. "I am the only one here capable of training her."

"You don't need to remind me of what you are, boy," Lazarus snarls in response.

"Enough!" I shout, throwing my voice across the clearing, and it echoes through the Dead Forest, sending a murder of crows into the skies. I watch as Lazarus and Quentin still like statues, before both slowly turn to face me. Quentin sweeps his hair off his brow. I clear my throat as heat flushes my neck, and my blades pinch together in anger.

Lifting my chin, I snap, "*She* is standing right here. All this ends now!" I take a few long breaths in the silence spanning between us, trying to calm the rage boiling inside. "Quentin, Lazarus is just trying to help me, so I will train with him, and it will be a priority!" Lazarus's mouth pulls up at the edges, revealing a victory grin. "What are you smiling at?" I scoff derisively. "I will also train with Quentin when the time and the moon allows. Quentin is here whether you like it or not, but if you don't like it, then *you* can leave." I pause while I watch the smile leave his face. "Except I hope you don't," I add more softly before turning to walk away.

Lazarus grabs my arm, pulling me in close, his head tipping down toward me. "You are making a big mistake, Paege," he grumbles under his breath into my ear.

I cock my head to face him, my eyes meeting his, and I swear I see flames igniting in his pupils. "Is that a threat?" I say through gritted teeth.

"No, it's a warning," he breathes, and my heart thunders in my chest, fear rippling over me. My Wolf sits to attention and growls. He drops my arm and steps toward the horses. "I'll go set up camp. You need to rest after your ordeal in the Whispering Woods last night. We can resume our journey tomorrow."

After a long moment passes, I finally let out a long breath.

Sure, Paege, you've got everything under control.

CHAPTER 27

"**G**et up," Lazarus barks at me, his nostrils flaring and his jaw ticking in frustration over the past days of fruitless training. It's been four days since my ordeal at the Whispering Woods, and every afternoon, after we set up camp, like clockwork, Lazarus begins the assault on my mind. He walks straight in, twisting my memories, manipulating my thoughts, and overwhelming me with emotions, no matter how hard I try to push him out or shield him. And every night, after Quentin and I take to the woods, shifting, scenting, and hunting, I cry myself to sleep, the pain and exhaustion weighing heavily on me.

"Focus, Paege," he demands as I scramble to my feet, breathless and exhausted. My lungs burn with every ragged breath I take.

"Again!" I roar at him as I shift my weight, trying to steady myself on my unbalanced legs, determined not to show my weakness or fatigue.

"Maybe that's enough for today," Quentin says, not questions, as Lazarus stalks around me.

"No!" I bark to no one in particular. "Again," I pant breathlessly.

"Paege," Quentin pleads from the clearing. "I think you should rest."

Frustration spurs me. I don't understand why I can't shield. Quentin has been showing me how to access my Wolf strength and speed while in my Fae form, and I have been able to do it with ease. I no longer need to close my eyes to see her; she's always right here with me. I see her, feel her. She is me. With the slightest thought, I can access her magic. Why is shielding so Godsdamn hard?

I dig deep again, pushing my frustrations aside. I see the large iron doors. Grounding myself, I distribute my weight evenly between my feet, and with all my mental might, I slam that door shut, locking it closed with the key I conjured in my mind.

"Again," I demand ignoring the plea from Quentin. Anyone attacking me isn't going to give up because I'm tired and won't stop because I beg them to. If my ordeals with Sylas and the Scorpions taught me anything, it's that.

The fire roars in the hearth, warming the house. An aromatic breeze tickles my nose. Camomile, lavender, and a hint of liquorice. The tea my mother loves to brew right before bed. "Mum?" I call out as I casually stroll through the house and climb the stairs to the second floor to the bedrooms. I trace the hallway with my fingers as I make my way to the bedrooms. From the furthest room at the end of the hall, an orange glow flickers, skittering across the floor in a silent invitation to enter. I call out for Mum again as I continue to walk toward the room. The flames dance, hypnotic and enthralling, and they draw me toward them.

My steps become slower, heavier as I continue down the hallway towards my mother's room. A warm breeze brushes against my skin, and a sliver of ice crawls up my spine in response. My stomach twists. Something is off, not right. As I reach the threshold of my mother's room and place a hand on the slightly ajar door, I nervously call out for my mother again, "Mum?" But the only sign of life is the playful flames. My heart hammers in my chest, an unsteady beat of a war drum, as I slowly extend my arm, pushing the weight of the door into the room. It gives easily.

Dread consumes me, shackling me to the ground as I take in the sight before me. She looks so peaceful as she lies there. Her blonde hair is braided loosely, resting over her shoulder. Her caramel eyes are wide, seemingly staring through the ceiling into the endless night sky, and her hands rest across her chest. But it's the crimson pool staining the bed covers, the absence of breath raising her chest, the rotting flesh of the gaping wound on her neck, and the blackened veins that now trace her body that have me falling to my knees.

I scream and scream and scream.

The warmth of a hand gently squeezes my shoulder, and it violently rips me from my nightmare. Only it's not a nightmare. I'm huddled in the clearing of the Dead Forest. I lift my head from my shaking hands, and through tear-soaked lashes, I see Lazarus kneeling before me, eyes soft with remorse and regret. "Paege?"

"What was that?" I ask through a sob. "Why would you show me that?"

"I may have taken that too far," he says with a soft tone to his usually rough voice.

"What was it?" I snarl.

"I was trying to evoke some sort of extreme emotional response because nothing else works. You can't shield, no matter what I do."

"So, you show me visions of my mother dead in her bed?" I cry. With strength I pull from my Wolf, I slam my feet into Lazarus's chest, kicking him away from me. He doesn't resist. He stumbles backward, but he catches himself and stands, wiping dirt off his hands.

"We needed to find another way. I hoped that if I got you angry or upset enough, you would force me out, but it's not working. Nothing is working." He shakes his head and stalks away. His bitter frustration washes over me with every step he takes.

"Are you going to put your shield up?" I call out after him. "Because I can still feel your emotions."

He pauses, right before he reaches his tent. "Are you?" is all he responds with, not even looking back toward me, before unzipping his tent and seeking solace within.

"Are you alright?" Quentin asks softly as he approaches me somewhat apprehensively. His steps are slow and deliberate as if approaching a wild beast.

"I'm fine," I snap, taking a couple of quick steps away from him. I don't know if it's my own frustration or the remnants of Lazarus's emotions that leave me disturbed and angered by my lack of shielding ability, but I don't want to be coddled right now. In fact, I just want to be alone. "I'm going to go for a walk."

"Fine," is all Quentin replies with, his pale grey eyes studying me with every step back I take.

I walk from camp, searching for a stream to freshen up in. Lazarus always manages to choose a clearing with running water nearby. The deeper I travel into the Dead Forest, a sense of unease floods my veins. The trees in the Dead Forest are as ancient as Elyndria, and the ghosts of its past press down on me, drowning me in their burden. Fatigue rolls through me. The emotional onslaught from my training with Lazarus is taking its toll on my body, and my nerves are on high alert. I scan my surroundings. It seems as if the trees are closing in around me, suffocating me and robbing the frosty air from my lungs. It's now thick with mist, and the faint sound of water gently flowing carries from up ahead. Leaves rustle from my footfalls, which are the only sound around as I tread carefully.

A twig snaps, and an owl hoots. Rustling from ahead sends a chill slithering up my spine. For days now, I have felt like something is stalking us, following us, watching us from the shadows, waiting to pounce. But Quentin and I have shifted and hunted nightly, using the opportunity to train and hone my Wolf magic. We have never scented or come face to face with any sort of creature we would have to combat. We've rarely seen a rabbit or rat. Still, I unsheathe one of my mother's daggers and prepare myself for whatever may be lurking. I inhale a quiet breath, anticipating what may come. Strangely, nothing emerges. Pausing for a long breath, I wait, but all I hear is the soft babbling water up ahead, and I sigh in relief. *It was probably just my mind.* I am exhausted.

Without sheathing my blade, I cautiously resume searching for the stream, still listening, still alert, my thundering heart now the only sound I can hear. Fog thickens around my heels. The trees draw nearer, forming a skeletal canopy overhead. The late afternoon light fades, and I can barely see my hand in front of my face.

I step into a small clearing, but there is still no stream in sight. I've walked quite far, but the water sounds no closer but no further either. In the centre of the clearing stands a tree unlike any I have ever seen. Its trunk is black as the dead of the night. Its branches twist and turn like serpents suffocating their prey, and its mossy roots glimmer from the remaining rays as they sprawl widely across the ground.

That's when I see a pair of glowing green orbs, peering at me from beyond the clearing I now find myself standing in, and my Wolf sits to attention. Dagger at the ready, I use every bit of remaining energy I hold to remain calm.

"Who dares to interrupt my slumber?" a slimy voice hisses.

Ice fills my veins, freezing my feet to the ground. I should run, turn back to camp, forget the stream, but like I'm compelled, I find myself speaking "I am a. . .a traveller," I stutter, replying into the nothing.

"And what, young traveller, do you seek?" My attention is locked onto the glowing eyes as its voice fills the clearing.

I shouldn't answer. I don't know what this thing is or what it wants. Unease coils around my chest, slimy as its voice. *Trust no one,* my Wolf seems to say as she growls, but as if my brain is short-circuiting, I open my mouth and say, "I seek knowledge from the Eagles. I seek to find the gate."

Damn it, Paege. No fucking control.

"Then you have come to the right place," the voice hisses. "The gate lies beneath the surface, veiled within the icy depths of the mountains. But be warned, you are not the first to seek the gate, and you shall not be the last. For in there lies danger and magic unknown to your kind, and only the bravest and most cunning can survive. If you follow the flow of time and choose the right path, you will find what you are looking for."

"Who are you?" I ask, my voice shaking with every word and my stomach twisting with unease.

The voice falls silent. I sheath my dagger and take an apprehensive step forward past the old serpent-like tree, toward the glowing eyes. "Why are you helping me?" I ask again.

"I am not helping *you*. I do not know you. I do not care if you live or die. But I am helping this world, and I want to go home." The glow of the green eyes dampens at its last words.

It's not lost on me what the creature says. Of course, when the wards went up to keep the Humans out, it wasn't the first time they had done this. How many times had they done this before? How many other creatures are stuck here is unknown. What other realms have been cut off from ours?

"Where is home?" It's too late. Green eyes continue to fade, retreating to where they came from.

"Remember, choose the right path," the hiss whispers into the wind like a distant echo.

When the glowing orbs disappear into the inky shadows, darker than the night, a gentle spray of mist brushes against my cheek. To the left, a burst of water rolls down a large mossy boulder, filling a dried-up riverbed. A glorious stream of water appears as if it's been flowing the entire time. It gently gushes over glistening rocks, the ripples reflecting fragmented light. I lean down and let the cool water sieve through my fingers as I ponder what in the Hels just happened.

CHAPTER 28

I return to camp with my hair wet and unbound, and both Lazarus and Quentin are nowhere to be seen. Our campsite itself is in a small clearing, surrounded by the tall, unnerving trees of the Dead Forest that loom over us. The roaring fire is the only source of light we have, and its flickering flames cast eerie shadows on the trees. The tents are set up along one side of the perimeter of the clearing, looking small and vulnerable in the darkness.

Unsure if I should tell the others what just happened, I decide to keep that little encounter to myself for now since I am not certain what it was. I grab the journal from my satchel strapped to Whisky and open it. I haven't spoken to Mhelodie in a couple of days, but I need to update her on my lack of shielding progress and find out what's been going on with her and the others. I huddle closer to the fire, using the flames to light my pages, and I see that Mhelodie has already written me a message.

Paege,
Just checking in to see how you're travelling. It's been a few days since we last heard from you. You must be deep in the Dead Forest by now. Is it as scary as they all say?

Asheron has been bugging me to write you. He says he has some news, so when you get this, let me know when a good time is for you two to write each other.

How are Quentin and Lazarus? Are they still at each other's throats? How is your training coming along?

Things here are quiet. Lu-Lu and I are doing much better. I think she's finally coming to grips with my magic and change of calling. It's been hard for her, but it's not like I have a choice in any of this. Even if I did, I don't think I would change anything. Oh, Paege, I wish you were here so I could talk to you about it. I know you would understand. You know what it's like to find out you have magic beyond what you ever thought possible.

Please write to me when you can. I'm always here if you need anything.

Mhelodie

I stare at the words on the paper for a moment, rereading Mhelodie's letter. I miss my friends, and I worry for Lumeilia and Mhelodie. I wish I could be there for them right now. I close my eyes and allow my mind to take me back to when life was easier. Memories of when it was just four of us, partying, laughing, and having fun pepper my mind. It feels like a lifetime ago. We were young and free and unburdened. Now, everything is different. I am different, and I can't imagine any of us finding a way back there.

I respond.

Mhelodie,

It's good to hear from you. You have no idea. The alpha male bullshit is tiresome. I would do anything for a quiet night with you and Lumeilia. Just like the old days. When I get back, let's make that a priority! I miss you both so much.

Training is hard. I have mastered absolutely nothing and am starting to think I am somehow broken. Maybe because I am half Wolf and half Fae it's harder for me? My magic is diluted. Not pure? I don't know what to do. Do you have any suggestions? Do you think you could look into it for me? Feel free to speak to Blaire. I'm sure she would be willing to help, too.

Tell Asheron I miss him too, and he can write to me whenever he wants.

Oh, and one final thing. Have you ever heard of a creature that lives in the Dead Forest, one that hisses like a snake, has green glowing eyes, and can make things appear and disappear? I think it's following me, but it doesn't appear intent on hurting me.

I'm going to get some rest now. It's been a tough and exhausting few days, but I will write to you again tomorrow. I promise.
-P

Once I finish, I stare at the words and watch as they disappear from the page of my journal. As I wait for a few minutes to see if Mhelodie receives my message and responds, the feeling of being watched presses against me. I snap my eyes toward the gnarly trees, but I don't see anything. *No glowing green eyes.* Yet, I can't shake that something is still out there, waiting for us, watching.

Staring back at the pages, words suddenly appear, as if she's writing them in real time.

Paege,
I think I have an idea. I need to talk to Sydney, and I will get back to you soon, I promise. In the meantime, keep practising. Don't give up.
And I miss you too.
-M
Oh, and I will look into that creature for you.

I write a quick reply to say thanks and goodnight, and then I place the journal on the ground next to me and huddle in closer to the fire. Its warmth slowly dries my wet hair and heats my skin, but

I don't settle. Every rustle of the leaves and snap of a twig makes my heart stutter and my body shudder. I keep telling myself that I am exhausted and fatigued, and it's just my imagination playing tricks on me.

As I gaze into the hypnotic flames dancing in the darkness, my thoughts wander, and my eyes become heavier. I don't even notice when he sits down beside me.

"How are you feeling?" His words startle me. Flames dance in his pupils, his amber eyes burning red. His features appear harsher in the firelight. The angles of his face are sharper. As shadows cast across his face, I can see the warrior in him. Strength and control radiate from him with every breath, with every movement. The years of training and combat have barely marked his skin, but his eyes tell a different story.

I don't answer his question. I return my gaze to the fire.

"Been writing to the Witch?" he asks curtly.

"The Witch has a name," I respond, clipping my words. "Mhelodie. Not that it's any of your business, but yes, I have."

"Did *Mhelodie* have anything interesting to say?"

"What do you want, Laz?" I snap. Still not looking at him.

I hear him pull in a long breath and hold it for a moment. "I just want to see how you are after earlier. I will not apologise for it, but I do realise I may have taken things too far." Of course, he will not apologise for it. I doubt the male has ever apologised for anything in his miserable life. He's Hels bent on making sure everyone around him is just as miserable as he is. Realising he hasn't continued, I glance up at him. I assume he's waiting for me to respond, so I subtly nod, and then he continues, "I've been thinking, I think we need to take another approach to this."

"Am I broken?" I ask, running my necklace up and back along the chain as a heavy weight presses against my chest, restricting my breath. I let go of my charm as the damn thing zaps me again from the static energy filling the air around me.

"What?" Lazarus's voice cracks, and he clears his throat before continuing, "Why would you ask that?"

I shuffle around to face him and pull my knees in close. Next to Lazarus, I am usually small, but now with my knees drawn in, I feel like a mouse next to a beast. Small is how I feel inside, so I suppose it's appropriate.

"Because I can't shield." I exhale, my voice a little shaky, and tears well in my eyes. I bury my face into my knees.

"I don't think you're broken, Paege, but I do think things are different for you, so we just need to change our approach and figure out what's going to work."

"And how do we do that?" I mumble, tilting my head toward him and resting my cheek on my knee. His silver arrow piercing glows gold from the flames.

"I don't know exactly, but I may have a few ideas. I suggest that for now, you keep trying to build your shield, keep practising. Don't give up."

"You sound like Mhelodie," I snicker as I relax the grip on my knees a little. Relax into the conversation. When he isn't antagonising me *or Quentin*, he's not that bad, and maybe when all this is over, we might be able to tolerate each other. We might even become friends.

"She must be a brilliant Witch then," he sniggers, his pierced brow arching with amusement.

"Oh, she is," is all I respond with before pivoting back to face the fire, the warmth flushing my skin.

Lazarus shuffles over and snakes his arm around my shoulder, pulling me into him. "We will figure it out. I promise."

I lean into him and rest my head on his shoulder. The aromatic flavours of sweet cloves and leather stir my quiet heart, and it flutters to life as he gently runs his hand through my damp, unbound hair and knots his fingers through the ends of the drying strands. His other hand traces the length of the chain that hangs around my neck, and I am aware of every stroke of his fingers against my bare skin as they travel down between my breasts to where my charm rests. My knees drop, and my chest rises and falls with every deliberate breath I take.

Lifting my head from his shoulder, I tilt my face to meet his. His eyes are wide with a feral desire. "I don't think I've ever seen anything quite as exquisite before," Laz murmurs into my ear as his fingers clasp the charm, sending a shudder down the length of my spine. "Truly beautiful," he exhales, his breath brushing against my skin like warm silk. His lips slightly part, and I see a glimmer of his white canines as he arcs one side of his lips. Something inside me growls, making me want to bring my lips to his to taste him.

He places the charm between my heaving breasts, his eyes never leaving mine, and he traces the chain with a featherlight stroke back up my body, up the length of my neck to that sensitive spot right beneath my ear, then across my jaw until his hand cups my chin and he tilts my head back, revealing the length of my neck.

"Laz?" I gasp as his eyes trace over my exposed neck, and he licks his lips like a wild animal eager to taste his dinner. I have no idea what I'm doing, but something inside me soothingly tells me that this feels right. It is right. My eyes flutter closed, and the warmth of his lips brushes softly under my jaw as his tongue flickers against the sensitive skin there. A low groan slips between my lips, and I arch into him, my breasts aching at his touch and exposing more of my neck for him to devour.

Laz clicks his tongue. "Tsk, tsk, tsk. Greedy little wolf," he growls into my ear, and I swear I can hear the smirk in his voice growing wider on his lips.

Letting my eyes drift open, I find him hungrily watching me, eyes dark with an intensity that sends a heat pooling in my core. Under the firelight, he looks like a fallen angel, brutally perfect and regal. Gods, he *is* perfect. I reach for him, one hand cupping his face as the other twists through his long black hair. I eagerly pull him in, my lips finding his and our tongues not wasting any time as they feverishly discover each other.

The depth of my stomach tenses with every brush of his tongue against mine. His hands explore my body as if trying to commit it to memory with his touch. One traces lazy, uneven lines up and down my inner thigh, gradually going higher and higher with every stroke. The other finds its way to my breast. He cups my swollen peak, his finger and thumb squeezing my nipple through my cotton shirt as his tongue greedily ravages my mouth.

Needing a breath, I pull myself back from the kiss. My chest rises and falls to a heavy rhythm, and I study Laz's face. His amber eyes are dark and wild, and they reflect the flames dancing in his pupils. His bow-shaped lips part as he tries to control his laboured breathing, and his damn piercing slowly arches in amusement. The hand tracing my inner thigh almost finds my apex; his other hand still holds my breast.

Oh, the Gods. Why did I stop kissing him? I want to, I need to kiss him again. Before I let myself get pulled back into the deep, murky waters of whatever line we just crossed. I drop my gaze to his chest and perfect abs where his shirt hangs wide open, exposing his star tattoo across his insanely chiselled body that I want to touch. *Touch him, touch him,* that little voice whispers to me inside my head. I have no idea when or how this happened, but. . .wait—My back, my scars, they're not burning.

As if he heard my thoughts, Laz smiles widely, and he lets out a sinful laugh. I blink one, two times, and then I'm sitting alone by the fire with my knees curled up to my chest, just as I had been before this all started.

Panting heavily, I try to gather my thoughts. What in the Hels just happened? I jerk my head behind me to see Laz sauntering away toward his tent. He stops before entering and pivots around to face me, that same wide smile still worn across his arrogant face. "Night, little wolf. Always a pleasure." He dips his head, and he turns back and crawls into his tent.

Leaving me by the fire, breathless and aroused, and utterly confused as the Hels.

Chapter 29

The quiet sets my teeth on edge. The only sound in this Gods forsaken place is the rustling of leaves and the cracking of twigs underfoot as we slowly make our way through the dark forest to the foothills of the Mountains of G'phyn.

If Laz's calculations are correct, we should be arriving by late afternoon. I haven't spoken to him since last night by the fire. I'm not angry at him. I think I understand why he did what he did. He told me to keep practising my shields. He even warned me he was going to try something different. I just wasn't expecting *that*. I sure as Hels wasn't expecting to react the way I did. I'm a little uneasy, maybe even a little shy, but not angry. I haven't been able to look Quentin in the eyes either. Not that I did anything wrong. Quentin and I are not together, but the lines of our *relationship* are certainly blurred. Laz planted the images in my mind, but it's the fact that my body didn't object to them, and my marks didn't burn, that has me embarrassed and ashamed and a little confused, too. So, we have travelled by day in absolute, uncomfortable silence.

Even though we are expected to exit this Hels-hole later this afternoon, somehow the disturbing trees are denser now, and sunlight barely penetrates through the canopy. The forest floor is in a relentless state of darkness. Large stones and root systems splinter across the ground in a vein-like manner, their surfaces alive with thick layers of slippery moss, making it a challenging trek. Due to the level of difficulty, we've spent more time walking our horses than riding them. As I glance around, my vision blurs. Daemonic faces morph from the tree trunks, sending chills racing up and down my spine. I flinch, pulling back as we pass by another terrifying tree, its branches reaching out to grab at me as I pass by. Whisky bucks back, and I tug on his reins to keep him by my side. Needless to say, my anxiety has not lessened in the slightest. If anything, the knot in my stomach twists tighter and tighter as the afternoon progresses. The thick air, lined with a stench of damp earth and something decaying, stings at my lungs. It's impossible to breathe through my nerves.

Quentin is the first one to break the silence when we finally rest at a stream for the horses to rehydrate. Food supplies are growing thin, and I hope when we find our way out of this Hels-hole, there will be a place for us all to rest and feed properly before heading into the mountains. After what Laz had said in Ferinini, my expectations are realistic.

"So, are you going to tell me what's going on?" Quentin whispers harshly to me as Jetstar and Whisky spend some time drinking from the glistening stream. The streams are the only things in this horrid place that have any sort of life or light, and sunlight filters through the treetops, sending crystals across the water.

"What do you mean?" I ask casually, trying to ignore the weight pressing against my chest.

"Don't play dumb with me." He grunts as he crosses his arms across his chest. My heart stops beating for a moment. Not entirely sure what he's referring to, my mind keeps yelling at me, *he knows. He knows. He knows.* But what exactly does he know?

A lump starts to form in my throat, cutting off my voice. I swallow, "Quentin, I don't know what you're talking about."

He sweeps his mop of hair off his face. "You didn't sleep in the tent last night."

Oh that. "And?" I couldn't bare face Quentin after that encounter with Laz, and I sure as Hels wasn't going to sleep with Laz, so I shifted and slept by the fire, which was a lot more comfortable than I expected. "I just needed some space and time to myself." Not all lies, but not entirely true either.

"Space?" Quentin's grey eyes narrow slightly, and he takes a step back from me, giving me exactly what I just said I needed. Space. I nod. "Space?" he repeats as if tasting the word on his tongue.

"Yes, it's been a long few weeks," I add because I can't be sure, but I sense Quentin is a little hurt.

"I understand." He does? "Where did you sleep then?" He mumbles, darting his eyes toward Laz, who is sitting high up on a boulder brushing Lilith's mane with his fingers, and then his eyes fall back to me.

No, he doesn't know. "I shifted and slept by the fire," I scowl. My Wolf, I've realised, runs hotter than my Fae form. "I've been stuck with you both snickering and fighting for weeks with no time to myself." *And I've got a lot going on right now,* I don't add. Quentin doesn't know the depths of my worries. He thinks we are off on some adventure to get answers about my pack and find out about the Crescent Pack curse, but the reality is more than that. A whole kingdom is cursed, and either his family or mine was at the core of the curse. The weight of all this keeps me feeling as if I'm drowning in the Blethan Sea, alone, and the only person I can speak to about it isn't here.

As if he can hear the inner diatribe playing out in my mind, Quentin's face softens. "Are you alright?" He takes a step toward me.

I take a step back. "I'm fine," I reply, clipping my words. "I just need some time alone."

I'm unsure why Quentin's questioning is triggering me and giving me the sudden need to push him away. Maybe guilt. Maybe something else entirely. Quentin and I have been skirting around our relationship for weeks. We aren't together, and we can't be, but sometimes, most of the time, we act as if we are. But I don't trust him. I want to, but with his father still pulling his strings, I can't. I certainly don't trust his father, and the closer we get to the mountains, the closer we get to the truth, the more distance I want to put between us.

"No need to snap. I was just making sure you're alright. If you need space that badly, you can have the tent or the room to yourself tonight, depending on our accommodations."

"Quentin—" I start.

He holds a hand up to stop me. "It's fine, Paege, I understand," Quentin steps back, pulling Jesstar's reins and guiding the horse away from the river. He fiddles with the buckles, checking everything is secure.

"Thank you," I sigh, as he walks off.

"Wolves, it's time to go if we want to make it to the foothills before sundown. I won't know if we have accommodation until we get there," Laz calls out, interrupting my thoughts. He has already mounted Lilith, ready to go. I can tell from the look on his face, the glisten in his dark amber eyes, that he heard every single word we just said.

I roll my eyes at him, over-animating my movements, making sure he sees exactly how unimpressed I am by his behaviour. Quentin mounts Jesstar while I guide Whisky a few steps away from the stream. He neighs loudly, his voice echoing through the forest, and I swear I hear a rustling in the thickets across the stream from me, but like always, there is nothing there that I can see.

I mount Whisky and urge him to start moving because the sooner I'm out of this Hels-hole, the sooner I can get answers and end all this.

"Are you sure we are headed in the right direction?" I probe Laz for the hundredth time since we embarked on this journey. I've been asking him multiple times daily because somewhere along the line, he became our guide, and neither Quentin nor I ever questioned it. Now, it has become a bit of a joke inside my own head, as I know how much it annoys him. While we haven't got lost yet, we still haven't made it to the other side, and we should have by now—according to Laz' earlier calculations.

"Have I steered you wrong yet?" Laz dryly asks from ahead as he tugs on Lilith's reins at her hesitation to follow him.

"No, but. . ." My words fall dead on my tongue, my mouth dropping open. I see a glimmer of light pushing through the endless darkness. I lift a shaking hand out, pointing to my right.

"Is that—" Quentin pauses before finishing, obviously noticing my head nodding in response to him. "Should we cut through?" he adds curiously.

"No, we follow the line of trees," Laz replies bluntly, mounting Lilith for the final leg of this section of the exhausting journey.

Following his lead, Quinten and I mount our horses. We climb out of the tapering riverbed and move along its edge as it and the line of trees shift direction and guide us directly toward the light. With every step we take, the forest floor becomes less rocky. Moss melts away, and the trees rapidly disperse.

As we finally emerge from the forest into the light, I take in a long breath of crisp air, lungs expanding effortlessly, easing the nausea that I've felt in my stomach for days now. The sun's warmth finally prickles my skin, and I relish it. It's been over a week since I've felt the full force of the sun's rays on my skin, and I didn't even realise the extent of the cold until my numb skin tingles as it defrosts. When I see the snow-capped mountains before me, the weight that's been dragging me into a pit of despair lifts from my shoulders, and the release makes me finally smile.

I made it.

We made it.

We're standing in an open field of grass. Some patches are long and dry, and some are luscious and green. The dry riverbed continues to travel up toward the mountain, creating a clear path to a mammoth stone wall and an abandoned-looking castle beyond.

As I look up at the mountains rising behind it, their snow-capped peaks gleaming in the sunlight, a thrill of excitement ripples over me. I breathe in a lung full of air, taking a moment to appreciate how far we have come. "I can't believe we are here," I say to no one in particular.

"That was just the beginning," Laz responds wryly. "We still need to make it over the bridge, and through the keep, and then find a place in there for a couple of nights before we trek into the mountain and the cave systems below to find the gate."

I assumed he knew exactly what we were doing. I roll my eyes at him. "I know," I sigh. When he puts it like that, all the hope I was carrying suddenly disappears, and I'm left with a familiar anxiety as it ripples over me. Thanks to Laz, the moment of excitement is as fleeting as ever. Without looking at either one of them, I lean forward and run my hands down Whisky's soft mane. "Ready, boy?"

He shakes his head as if answering me. His muscles flex beneath my touch, and he brays quietly, swishing his tail around in response. My Wolf growls as if also acknowledging the new reality setting in. I take one more long, deep breath, willing myself to calm as I squeeze my knees around Whisky's torso, and we step forward to set out towards the wall and Mountains of G'phyn beyond.

Quentin and Laz trail closely behind me.

CHAPTER 30

Unknown

A screech overhead snaps his eyes open. That was new. The days all bled into one. He didn't know how long it had been. Weeks, months, possibly years. Nothing had changed. He still held no memories of the past. He didn't know who or where he was. He *still* had no hope. Yet, he walked on and on, the insanity scratching at the walls of his mind like a flea on a mange-riddled dog. He just needed to make it to those foreboding mountains. Of this, he was sure.

The terrain was unforgiving. Every day, his skin would rip apart as he forced his way over dunes and through sandstorms. But he never gave up. He *would* never give up. Not until he was safe. Not until. . .

He sat up.

The only change in this desolate environment since he first woke here was the sun. It now sits low along the horizon, dancing across the sandy edges of the land. Still, darkness never arrived. No. He lived in a place between day and night. Light and dark. Life and death. It was a constant state of dusk. Or was it dawn? He didn't know. All he knew was that he hadn't seen true darkness since—

Green eyes, rimmed with silver tears.

A sword.

A Wolf.

A girl.

A scream.

No, not a scream, a screech.

His head tilted up to the orange and purple painted sky. Muted silver stars dotted one side of the horizon. The sun assaulted him as it rolled across the other. Its new position cast long shadows around him as he stood, his eyes slowly focusing as they scanned the sandy desert.

As always, after he woke, he was healed again. Refreshed and revived. There was nothing as far as his eyes could see. As always, there was nothing. His mind played cruel tricks on him these days. The sounds of rushing rivers roared past him. Bodies of still glistening water and lush forests appeared before his eyes. He sighed. He was truly going insane. Maybe he already was.

He was about to set off again towards the mountains that never got closer when his eyes snagged on a little black dot far on the horizon to his right. He blinked. That, too, was new. He squeezed his eyes closed and shook his head, clearing the mirage from his mind. When he opened his eyes, they settled back on that little black dot again. No, now there were two. Two little black dots.

A screech cracked through the sky, and something in his gut grumbled as if a beast was rising within. He swallowed thickly. Right, he didn't imagine that. . .What the fuck was it?

His heart thumped hard, pumping blood to his muscles, flooding him with adrenaline. He tensed, unsure of what to do. He looked around the sky. There was nothing in his line of sight. The beating sound of distant wings thumped heavily across the land. Thumped heavily in his chest. *His heart*. Still, there was nothing that would be responsible for *that* sound. He knew he did not imagine it, and those two little dots on the horizon were still there. No, not two. Three. There were now three little dots.

And that's when he knew what he must do.

He needed to run.

CHAPTER 31

The journey through the fields is short-lived, as are my optimism and nerve. Standing at the edge of a large ravine that travels down to a merciless river, my heart pounds as violently as the white-water rapids thrash against the enormous boulders below. The ice-tipped wind licks at my face, and I stare wide-eyed and mouth agape at the old and unstable-looking stone bridge with no barriers that crosses it. *The only way to get to Owenstown, the village at the foot of the mountains,* Laz had said.

A greyish-brown stone castle stands proudly on the other side at the foothills of the Mountains of G'phyn behind a long stone wall that glimmers silver and gold in the quickly diminishing sunlight. Five thin, square towers with turrets reach twice the height of the tallest building of the castle and are all connected by the firm wall. Crude windows are scattered thinly around the castle, and Harpy statues man the casements in perfect symmetry along the wall and sentry towers once used for archers and artillery. The old, crumbling bridge stretching out before me leads directly to a sharp incline of stone steps that provide entry through the wall and inside the castle.

"When you get out onto the bridge, don't look down, and don't stop. Hold your horse tightly, and walk straight down the centre. The wind out there is going to be strong, so walk quickly. Don't stop when you get to the other side, no matter what you feel. Climb the stairs into the keep and wait," Laz yells out over the howling wind. I nod in response, unable to find any words that don't include *fuck that* or *no way in Hels*. There is no way I am going out there first. "Wolf, you go first, then Paege, and I will follow behind," Laz yells again as if he read my mind. But nothing he says is going to ease my nerves.

"See you on the other side, Books," Quentin chimes with a smirk and steps out onto the bridge with Jesstar without hesitation or worry. He's so perfectly balanced that if it wasn't for his sandy blond hair flicking around him, you would think he was on a casual stroll. When Quentin is at least ten lengths out, I take a deep breath and cautiously step forward, my foot hovering over the edge of the precipice between where the ground ends and the bridge begins. For a moment, I feel as if I am standing on the edge of the world with nothing but the wind and my fear to keep me company.

"Don't hesitate, Paege, you'll be fine. Just keep looking up and keep walking. Don't stop for anything," Laz repeats.

I nod and close my eyes. She's here. My Wolf. Her emerald eyes sparkle as she studies me. She pads toward me and leans her warm body against mine, and her courage and strength pour into me, giving me what I need to continue. I open my eyes and exhale as I let my foot touch the ground, taking my first step to the other side, guiding Whisky behind me. As I begin to walk across the bridge, I look at the thin line of disintegrating stone that separates me from the deep ravine below, and my heart thrashes against my cage. The river is a distant murmur, just a whisper that echoes up from the depths of the canyon.

The howling wind piercing my ears becomes more violent as I make my way further across the crumbling bridge, whipping at my face, stinging my eyes, and tugging at my hair. My braid dances behind me and fiercely rips the loose strands back from my face. Every breath is a struggle as the icy air burns my throat and lungs with every pant. Whisky pulls back, and my stomach lurches as I lose my balance and take a few unsteady steps to the edge of the stone beneath me. I freeze, as fear slips between my ribs, the ravine yawning below me.

I don't look back.

I don't look down.

I pull Whisky's rein in closer to me and take a slow, measured step toward to centre of the bridge and another step forward, and then another, and another, each one more difficult than the last as the wind pushes against my body as if to impede me from making it any further across. I push through, each step just as determined as the first, to make it across without losing my lunch or anything else.

Keep moving. One step at a time. Don't stop. Laz's words play on repeat in my mind. I shift my focus from the bridge, from the darkness below, to the keep and wall ahead of me. I don't even focus on Quentin and Jesstar upfront, who look like they are casually walking across a field. Show off. I focus on the keep, taking in every detail. The sentry towers and turrets within the wall are impressive structures made of a dark stone that blends with the nearby mountains—obviously built to withstand the harshest of conditions. They stand tall enough to provide a clear view of the surrounding area. The towers are linked by the great wall, forming what would have once been a formidable barrier against any would-be invaders.

Keep moving. Don't stop.

The towers are unmanned except for the stone Harpies that hold a keen eye on me as I struggle to cross the bridge. I can't help but wonder if they were once manned by skilled warriors who kept a watchful eye on the surrounding area day and night. Was the wall originally built to keep us out? Or keep whatever lies within the mountains out? It's hard to be sure, but something tells me it was originally built to keep us out.

Keep moving. Don't stop.

Breathlessly, I finally reach the other side of the bridge, and as I step onto not-so-solid ground, something rips at my insides, and bile rushes up from my stomach, stinging my throat. Tears fill my eyes as my blood turns to acid, and my body convulses in response to the agonising burn. I feel as if my soul, my very essence, is being torn from my body, and I use every ounce of energy to not collapse in pain or exhaustion. I swallow hard, trying to ignore the sudden emptiness that fills my vessel. A fissure forms in my chest.

Keep moving. Don't stop.

My gaze follows the path leading to the keep's entrance. The sight of the steep and narrow rocky stairs carved into the side of the ravine like a series of jagged teeth twists my stomach in knots.

Keep moving. Don't stop.

I draw in ragged breaths and cling one shaking hand to the rough stone barrier, and the other grips Whisky's rein tightly. My nails bite my palm, but we climb higher and higher. A sudden awareness of weakness that I haven't felt in weeks sets in, and my muscles groan and joints bark at me with every exhausting and gruelling step I take as I climb to keep above.

Keep moving. Don't stop.

The wall looms above. Its turrets and towers, now gigantic, rise into the clouds, casting long gloomy shadows across the stairs and ravine, bringing the darkness sooner than expected. At last, I reach the top of the stairs and step onto the keep's crumbling battlements. Through the wall, I finally allow myself to collapse, my body crying in pain and my lungs burning, gasping for breath.

Empty. I am empty and alone, and I let the tears escape my eyes as I recognise, for the second time in as many months, a part of me has been stripped away. The curse of the unmagic lands. At least this time, she will come back. My Wolf will come back. He will not.

Within the old walls of the abandoned keep, and with the absence of the howling wind, the sound of my heart thrashing behind my ears becomes deafening. Laz finally steps into the keep, his wings flaring widely as if he's stretching them. They don't retreat. With the pain gradually subsiding, I force myself to stand. Whisky nudges me with his nose in support. As I rise to my feet, my pulse still racing, I look out over the landscape from where we just came, and my breath catches as I take in the rugged beauty of the ravine and the river below.

Breathtaking, literally.

I pivot back to face Quentin and Laz, who are both standing further in the courtyard of the abandoned keep, staring wide-eyed at me from either concern or relief that I made it—*probably relief*. I wonder if they, too, felt what I felt when their magic had been ripped from their body.

After a few short minutes of silence, Laz is the first to speak. "We need to keep moving if we want to make it into town to get somewhere to sleep," he commands after he finishes taking a drink from his water canister. The sound of our footsteps echoes off the walls as we set off through the courtyard to the large doors at the far end under a large tower and turret. Doors, I assume, that grant us access to Owenstown.

The courtyard is overgrown with weeds and vines, and some of the stones beneath my feet are loose and mostly slick with moss. In the centre of the courtyard, there is a dried-up, cracked fountain, and I can't help but see the beauty that was once this place. Such a shame it was abandoned and left to rot. I notice more Harpy statues stationed around the keep. They, too, are watching me, their grey eyes following my every move.

Just as we reach the other side of the courtyard, the oversized wooden doors burst open, the rusty hinges creaking with anger. Five Lupa-Centaurs storm in armed with swords and shields as if they are going to war, and fear slithers over my bones. Laz and Quentin step toward the regal warriors, neither flinching or baulking at the sheer size or weight the warriors exhibit.

"Sarge, Prince, we were not expecting you," says the bay and white coloured male standing in the middle of the five as he steps forward toward Laz and Quentin. "If you had given word, we would have met you across the bridge and brought you and your steed in the other way."

Other way? There was another way that didn't involve almost falling to our deaths. I must remember to kill Laz, or Quentin, or both.

These Lupa-Centaurs are certainly not what I ever expected. I have only heard stories about them, the Guardians. In my mind, they are brutal, vicious and feral, but standing before me, these male beasts are strong, regal, and beautiful. Their horse-like bodies stand tall and proud, and they are more muscular than the horses we ride or the Lupa-Centaurs back in the Neopolis. Their Wolf faces are still majestic; however, the ones standing before me are crowned with ram-like horns. They are a sight to behold.

"Apologies, Perrin, we would have sent word, but we *are* here on official business," Quentin responds curtly. *Perrin? He knows these males.* "We need lodgings for two nights, if you would accommodate. Two rooms?"

"Three," I interrupt.

"Sorry. Yes, three," Quentin corrects, his eyes not meeting mine.

"Your Royal Highness, we would, but we are on strict lockdown orders," Perrin responds, his feathered white hoof pawing at the ground in front. I watch curiously as Laz lengthens his spine and a muscle in his jaw ticks, but he doesn't speak.

Quentin says, "Why do you think we are here? My father sent us, sent me. Our mission is confidential." The way he lies to them is effortless, like the story has been building in his mind for weeks. The sudden realisation stabs me in the back, brutal and painful. This is him. A master of lying.

He lied to you for months, Paege. He is still lying to you. It's all lies.

"And she is?" The chestnut Lupa-Centaur next to Perrin speaks and nods toward me. His eyes are dark and intense with distrust, and his dark tail whips around him. My breathing stalls as the intensity of the stares burns through me.

"*She* is none of your concern," Laz unexpectedly retorts with an air of authority, baring teeth at the male who just spoke.

"She's assisting us, and that is all you need to know, Samuel," Quentin adds more respectfully, addressing him by name. He does know them. Why didn't he mention any of this?

"Will you give us a moment?" Quentin speaks to Laz directly, who doesn't respond verbally; he simply manoeuvres Lilith around as if he expected the request.

"Come on." Laz motions to me to follow, and I oblige, unsure of what exactly is happening.

When we reach the fountain, I whisper to Laz, "Why aren't you over there helping him?" I stare at Quentin and the beast, conversing by the doors that lead to food, shelter, and warmth.

"Because they do not follow the command of the Guard. I have no sway over them. Don't be fooled by the charm of the Lupa-Centaurs, Paege. They blindly follow the king's orders. We do not tell them who you are under any circumstances. Do you understand?" His words crawl over me, my eyes never leaving the beasts, and my stomach twists tighter in my gut as I remember Guy's story about the Lupa-Centaurs. "Did you hear me?" Laz whisper-yells at me, clipping his words, and his gaze burns into me.

I nod, still not shifting my attention from the five Lupa-Centaurs standing between me and freedom. Something wriggles its way into my brain, a faint memory from when I was young. Amerax was heading off to do a job for the king, and my mum begged him not to go. Amerax's clear reply was, *"We are Guards of the king, Synthony. What he asks of us, we must do."* Hypocrites all of them.

Laz grabs my arm with force, his fingers squeezing tightly, and yanks me toward him, demanding a response. I wince, but he doesn't let go. "Do. You. Understand?" he snarls at me.

"Yes," I yelp, not fighting his grip because I know there is no chance I would win that, even if I did have access to my Wolf strength. I didn't realise how much I would miss her. I feel empty.

"Good." He drops my arm, and he turns back to face the beasts.

"And you?" I ask, my voice quiet and ragged.

"What about me?"

"Do you blindly follow the king?"

He doesn't answer.

I sit myself on the edge of the dilapidated fountain, rubbing my arm where Laz's grip left a throbbing ache, and stare idly into the rubble that fills the basin. Laz keeps his focus on Quentin and the beasts. Pebbles, wire, chip ceramics, and other discarded junk lay among hundreds of silver coins that blanket the basin floor. Wishes. Those coins were once wishes. Now it's just junk.

Owenstown, a place where wishes come to die. They should put that on a plaque.

I lean over and I scoop up some of the coins from the rubble. After sifting through the broken bits of ceramic and metal scraps, I pick out a brassy, old skeleton key with a little red stone encased in the filigree design of the bow. It's no doubt to one of the chambers in here. I idly finger the key, fidgeting anxiously while we wait for Quentin and the beasts to finish their conversation. After a short while, Quentin nods to his acquaintances and turns back to us, motioning for us to come.

"Looks like he came in handy after all," Laz quips, arching his pierced brow and flashing his canines at me before leaning over my shoulder and whispering in my ear, "And I told you, little wolf. I don't answer to anyone." His breath tickles my skin before he stands, playfully taking the key from my fingers, pocketing it, and he strides off toward the door.

The local Owenstown Inn is no more than ramshackle, but it provides what's needed. Beds, food, hot water, and a laundry. Three of the Lupa-Centaurs, Hawkins, Callum, and Samuel, take our steeds to the stables to get them fed, groomed, and rested. The three of us travel with Marlow and Perrin to the inn.

Stepping into the room, I set my duffel on the ground at the foot of the bed and take a sniff of myself. *Ew.* I'm going to need more than just one shower to wash away the stench from the last couple of weeks of travel. The room is small, but somehow, they have managed to fit a double-sized bed, an armoire, and a writing desk in it with room to move. The beige walls are bare save for a window above the writing desk, a small, empty shelf, and a wall scribe by the door. The pot belly in the right corner opposite the bed is already alight. The bathroom is even smaller, but it's complete with a half sunken bath, separate shower, and a flushing toilet. *Thank the Gods.* Funny how the basics become a luxury when you've been stripped of them for any given amount of time.

I jump when the door slams in the other room. Curious, I walk back to the main room and find both Laz and Quentin standing in the small room, staring at each other. Quentin snarls. "What are you both doing in here? This is my room," I say, interrupting their stand-off.

"Not anymore," Laz chides, with an air of humour in his voice. He dumps his pack on the floor by the door.

"No, apparently, it's ours. There was only one room left." Quentin drops his pack where he stands in the middle of the small room. Seriously? This isn't the Wolf den.

I cough. "Excuse me? One room, as in. . ."

"That's right, little wolf, the three of us are sharing." Laz huffs a laugh. How is he finding all this amusing?

"No, uh-uh. No way. You need to go back out there and fix whatever happened for you to lose your rooms."

"What makes you think I did anything?" Laz raises a brow and places a hand on his heart, feigning hurt.

"Because you are the one with the connections here." As the words fall from my mouth, I realise how that's not entirely true. Quentin has connections here, too, and it was his connection that got us into Owenstown to begin with. Not Laz's.

I dart my eyes to Quentin, who is staying extremely quiet, and the look on his face gives everything away. He has come to the same realisation. This was not because of Laz; it was because of him. "Fix it," I snarl, baring my teeth.

"I don't think anyone can fix this," Laz replies. "Let's just deal with it for now. We all need to rest and figure out our next move. I will take the first watch. You two can freshen up and try to get some sleep."

"What do you mean, first watch?" I question. I've heard things about Owenstown. It's where the Heretics were banished to—Witches with no active magic—so they had to syphon magic from the earth. They have no magic here, none of us do. Save for the Lupa-Centaurs, it would appear no one would be a threat to us.

"It's not safe here, Paege. You will not be safe here. I promised to protect you, so I will stay on guard while you both get some sleep."

I open my mouth to protest. "I don't need much sleep anyway," Laz adds, dismissing me.

"Why do you get first watch?" Quentin snaps, his teeth grinding together. As if the thought of Laz taking guard was one-upping him in some way. I stay quiet, watching the craziness unfold before my tired eyes. I don't care who takes first watch. I would rather they both stay out there. All I wish is for them to figure this shit out so I can have a bath. That tub might not be the biggest or nicest, but I bet it's got scalding hot water.

"Because I am a Guard. It's my job to protect her." Laz stands tall, his wings flare with pride.

"Well, she is—" A breath catches in my throat, my attention immediately back to the argument ensuing. Yes, Quentin, I am your what? But he doesn't finish that thought. "I am the Heir Apparent and the future alpha of our pack. It's also my job to protect her."

"Because of your father, right?" Laz fires back.

Quentin's grey eyes shift to blue and widen, and his nostrils flare. Then it hits me. He's jealous, and I know Laz hit his intended mark. "Enough!" I bark across the room. "That is enough."

"Alright, Wolf, if you want first shift, it's all yours," Laz concedes, and he walks to the bed, plonking himself down and begins toeing off his boots as if he had just won the battle of the century. Quentin smirks and puffs his chest out, but his face still looks wounded from Laz's remark. I internally smirk at Quentin for not seeing this for what it really is. Laz just baited him, and he bit it—hook, line, and sinker.

Quentin sweeps his fringe from his face, his eyes cold as steel, and faces me. "Paege—" he starts, but I just wave him off and close the door to the bathroom. Laz's comment didn't just hit his mark; it ricocheted, and its fragments tore into me. I run steaming hot water into the bath, pour some liquid soap into the tub, and leave it to fill, as I return to the main room.

First things first: laundry. Ignoring Laz, I walk to the armoire, the weight of his stare pressing in on me. I open the doors. A bathrobe and a wool blanket are the only two items it contains. I grab both and set them on the bed. "Why do you do that?" I ask Laz.

"Do what?"

"Bait him like that." I throw my arms into the air in a dramatic gesture. While it was kind of amusing watching Quentin fall for that, it doesn't help our situation at all. My two insufferable males are at each other's throats all the time.

"Because it's too easy," he chides.

"Am I truly in danger here?"

"Haven't you been paying attention? You are in danger wherever you go, little wolf. But no more here than anywhere else."

My brows shoot for the stars. "Then why say that?"

"Because I figured you could do with a night of rest, and I didn't want to deal with that intolerable—"

I cut him off. "Seriously, Laz, why do you have to make it so hard?"

"Hard?" Laz sits up. Throwing his weight into his enormous frame, he stands, wings flared wide, and he prowls over to me. I tilt my head back to see his features shift into the warrior I know he is. "If you think that is me being hard, then you have a lot more to learn than I thought. He is a spoiled little princeling who knows nothing of the real world. I do not trust him." He leans forward, his cheek meeting mine. "Neither should you," he breathes into my ear. My breath hitches in my throat as warmth flushes my face. He's so damn close again, and that sweet aromatic taste of spices and leather gently caresses me, and I find myself surrendering. I close my eyes, savouring the sensation. He shoves the towel robe into my chest. "Go clean up, Paege. You stink."

What the fuck is wrong with me?

I unsheathe my daggers and swords, placing them on the floor, and sit on the edge of the bath. I untie my boots, removing my swollen and sore feet from them, followed by my socks. I wiggle my toes. The action, although minor, sends a shooting pain up the arch of my foot. I wait for the pain to settle before peeling the combat leathers away from my aching body, and the blood rushes to the surface of my skin.

Once completely naked, I wrap myself in the robe and throw all my soiled clothes into my duffel to dump them in the main room, telling Laz to call for food and laundry, but he doesn't answer. The room is empty. I open the bedroom door to set my bag outside for laundry collection, and the ice-coated air scratches at my bare skin. Quentin catches my eye, standing two doors up from me, holding his scribe. Noticing me, he slowly strolls over. "How are you feeling, Books?"

"Tired. Sore. Cold." *Empty.* I pause for a moment before adding, "And smelly," I admit with a bit of a chuckle, wrapping my arms around myself, tugging the robe in tighter. He laughs and nods in agreement, so I push him in the shoulder jokingly and roll my eyes. "You're not one to judge."

I study Quentin's face, his body. He's leaner than when we left. His pants hang a little looser, and his tunic is not so tight. The skin under his eyes looks darker now, his face sallower, even under the growth covering his jaw. His shaggy fringe is annoyingly longer now, and he spends way too much energy trying to keep it out of his eyes. I wonder if he would let me cut it for him. But amongst all that, his grey eyes are glistening with that hint of blue they sometimes shine, and he manages a smile, even if it's maybe half forced.

"I will have you know, this—"he waves his hands up and down his torso and then smells himself, wrinkling his nose in what I assume is disgust—"is the smell of pure, raw, alpha masculinity, and the females love it," he says in an attempt to lighten a dark situation, but there is nothing light about any of this. He drops his smile. "You need anything?" he asks when I don't laugh in response.

"I'm fine. I just need a bath, some dinner, and a good night's sleep in what I am assuming is the world's most mediocre bed."

"With the world's most mediocre company," Quentin jabs under his breath. "I've already instructed him to sleep on the floor. So, you'll be safe."

"You've done what now?" I say as my teeth start chattering from the frigid air creeping into my bones.

"I laid out the expectations of us sharing a room with him."

Seriously? What the fuck is wrong with him? His words would have had my Wolf sitting up, paying attention. I've only had her for a handful of months, but it's as if she has always been here with me, and her absence is like a gaping hole in my soul. "I can handle myself and *any expectations* just fine," I snap. Quentin takes a step back. "And he isn't that bad. If you would only—" I cut myself off as a muscle feathers in his jaw. This is pointless. "Never mind," I say, stepping back into the door frame, towards the warmth.

"I'll see you in the morning then." He shoves his hands deep into his pockets and turns on his heel.

"See you in the morning," I mutter to myself, turning to go back into the room.

The soapy water envelopes my body like silk sheets when I submerge myself in the tub. I showered twice beforehand. Once to roughly scrub my body and shampoo my hair. The second was just to let the warm water wash over my skin, gently soaping and massaging my body where it ached the most: my thighs, my ass, my biceps, and torso. When I was certain my body was dirt, sweat, and grime free, only then did I step into the bath.

I sink myself low, the water line reaching my clavicle, and I lay my head back against the warm ceramic edge. It's not a luxury bathtub by any means, but my muscles groan in relief as I relax into the warmth. I close my eyes and let the tension melt away from my body. The smell of clean soap stings the back of my throat, but it's a welcome change to the body, horse, and dead forest odours I've been subjected to. As I lie here, the aches in my body lessening with every leisurely breath, I let my mind wander off. Thoughts of the past few weeks, months, and even years pepper my mind as the eerie quiet of the village offers no distraction.

We twirl around each other, the sun beating down on us as our wooden swords smack together in unison—clank, clank, clank. I gobble down air and take a small step back, lowering my sword for a moment as I regain my strength. We've been playing this game all afternoon, and the weight of the wooden sword is becoming heavy in my little hands.

"Are you too tired to continue, Princess?" he taunts, his single dimple just like mine appearing with his grin.

I hold my sword back up, using both hands just like Amerax had taught me. "Never, Prince! I will fight you until my last breath." I lunge for him, and he jumps out of the way, bringing his sword up to meet mine again with a clank.

"When I best you, I will lock you in the dungeons to be forgotten about forever," he laughs.

"You will never be able to best me, Prince," I reply with a giggle. "I am too fast." I swing at him again, and our wooden swords smack. "I am too skilled." Another smack. "Too smart." Smack.

We still, our swords kissing. Neither one of us moves. His emerald-green eyes glisten in the sunlight, and a small bead of sweat drops to his brow.

"Honey, it's time to go."

We relax our swords to our sides, as the summer song in my mother's voice carries softly across the garden like petals floating through the air. We both look up, and I see Mum standing with the silver-haired female, one of the two who comes with him every year.

"I'll see you next year?" he asks as he drops his sword to the ground and runs off to the tall dark-haired male, who always watches us play from the balcony, while my mum and the other one talk.

"Guy?" I call out after him, as something in my chest pulls tightly.

He stops and pivots to face me "Yes, Paege?"

"Happy birthday."

Guy runs back to me, and when he reaches me, he wraps his arms around, pulling me in for a hug. "You, too, little sis." He spins, running back to the black-haired male with the glowing red eyes and silver-haired female, and then they are gone.

I gasp for air as I snap my eyes open to the sound of three loud knocks on the bathroom door. Water splashes around me as I flay my legs around to stop myself from going under the water and get my bearings.

Him.

"Paege, are you still in there?" Laz calls again from outside, and I sit upright at the sound of his voice.

Breathless, I run my hands over my face, the callouses that have formed are now soft, and my hands are wrinkled from the extended time submerged in the bath water that is now cool.

"Paege?" Laz calls again

"Yes, sorry. Coming!" I stand, water dripping from my body, and I step out of the bath. I wrap a towel loosely around me and head to the door to take the robe off the hook. As I reach for the robe, the door swings open, and I jump back. Laz stands in the opening. "Laz!" I squeal and turn back around, facing my back to him, my wet hair flipping around me like a whip. My towel drops low down my back.

He chuckles. "Sorry, but you said come in. . ." His voice trails off.

"No, I said, *coming*."

"Oh," is all he replies. I roll my eyes at his obvious disregard for my privacy because he doesn't make any attempt to leave.

I turn back to face him, waiting for him to retreat out of the room to give me privacy to cover myself, but his gaze is fixed on me. Deadly, violent rings of fire rim his irises. His wings flare. "What happened?" he asks dryly.

"What do you mean?" I reply as I turn back to face the bath, away from those damn amber eyes judging me, studying me.

A hand wraps around my arm in a bruising grip, and I'm spinning to face him. Ire flashes in his eyes as they roam over my body, lingering on every piece of exposed flesh. My skin pebbles at every point of inspection. He releases me and marches out of the room.

I tug the robe off the back of the door, wrap it around me, and chase him out of the room. "What the Hels was that?"

He turns slowly to face me, every movement like that of a predator, calm and deliberate. "Your back. What happened?" His words send a chill crawling down my spine as he stalks over to me. His eyes narrow, but his gaze never leaves my body as he makes his way closer to me.

"Oh, it's nothing." I shift under the weight of his stare, tugging the robe tighter around my body. Lies. Big fat lies.

"It doesn't look like nothing. What. Happened?" he asks again, clipping his words, and a muscle in his jaw flickers. I look away. "*You* need to start trusting me, Paege. This won't work if you don't talk to me."

"What won't work?"

"This, you and me, and our little arrangement."

"What little arrangement? The one where you piss Quentin off, or the one where you hide things from me?"

He sighs. "I am on your side, little wolf, but I can't help you if you don't talk to me. Trust is everything between us, and you need to trust that I *will* tell you what I can when I can."

I sit on the end of the bed and draw in a long, slow breath and hold it for a beat, contemplating whether to tell Laz, and if so, how much of it. When I exhale, the words just tumble out of my mouth, and for some reason that is beyond me, I end up telling him everything. Sylas happened. He was my ex-lover, an unbound siren. Cunning and dangerous. A liar. He compelled me to trust him. To love him. He stalked me. Kidnapped me. He tortured me. Branded me.

And he's now dead.

Laz doesn't speak. For the first time since I've met him, he's speechless. He stares at the wall, and I stare at him. His wickedly handsome face is now expressionless, motionless. Even his bronzed skin is as pale as the snow that caresses the mountains outside, and his now molten red eyes are glazed with anger. Finally, he moves. He shakes his head intensely, forcing his eyes closed, and his jaw ticks as if he's trying to erase the images of my story. Of me bound and branded.

"Quentin?" Laz turns to face me, opening his eyes and arching his pierced brow inquisitively. If I said yes, would that change anything? Maybe. But it wasn't Quentin. I can't lie about that. I can't take something good that Guy did and use it to gain points for Quentin. Guy deserves better than that.

"No. Guy." A lump forms in my throat as I say his name, and I swallow, trying to push it away, but it doesn't budge.

"Your brother? I'm sorry I never got a chance to meet the Guy you knew. I only knew him as a young boy, but I heard good things about him. He would have made a good king one day, if he had been given the chance."

His words knock the breath out of me. Words I have never heard anyone ever say. Words I have never even considered. Guy would have been the next king if his father—no, our father. . .I don't let myself finish that thought. I haven't allowed myself to think of Guy much over the past couple of weeks. Every time I have, a dark cloud has washed over me, my heart cracking a little bit more, so I have kept the memory of Guy locked behind that big iron door.

"You would have served him willingly, even though he's a Wolf?" I ask, not looking up from my clenched, still wrinkly hands.

"I would choose Braxtion blood over Ishaan blood any day," he says in almost a whisper.

"Did you know him? My father, I mean." Before we left, I never got the chance to ask my mother too much about my father. I was too stunned and angry the day I found out the truth to ask anything, and I needed time and space to process everything. I wanted to ask about him before we set off, but she wasn't at home to indulge my curiosity. And my dream in the bath just now. I don't know what to make of that. Was it a dream, though? Or a memory? Had I met Guy when I was young? And then there was. . .Laz. There are so many questions, but there is no one else around to answer them.

"I did. He was a good male and king. He tried to make things. . ." Laz pauses, sighing as he shifts. He pivots his body around to face me, and his knees gently graze mine. My body sparks at the connection. "He loved your mother very much, Paege, and everything he did, he did for you. For both of you."

"But he left us. He left me," I murmur, my voice catching as I swallow back the tears.

"He did, but not because he wanted to." Laz moves his hand over my knees, and for a moment, I think he's going to take my hands, but he halts, and it wavers in midair for a heartbeat before he places it on the bed in the tiny space between us.

Neither one of us speaks for a moment, and then he stands, pushing up from the bed with his hands. "Paege, you are going to hear a lot of crazy things about your father, but please know that whatever you do hear, both your parents loved you very much, and everything they did was to protect you and Guy. Always."

"Like what?"

"I'm sorry, little wolf, that's not my story to tell."

There's a light tap on the door. Laz's lips tighten, and he walks across the room and slightly opens the door. Murmurs come from outside, and then a distinct and curt, *"Thank you,"* and when he pivots back to enter the room, he's holding a tray of food I didn't order. He places the tray on the writing desk next and closes the door.

He smiles warmly. It's the first true smile I have seen Laz give me that isn't full of mischievousness or malice. "I *choose* Braxtion blood over Ishaan blood, Paege. That includes you." He strolls to the bathroom door and, without looking back at me, he grumbles under his breath, "If Guy hadn't killed him, trust that I would have."

CHAPTER 33

I arrive at the tavern where Laz requested me to join him and Quentin for dinner at sundown. The streets are bustling with activity. The air is filled with the bouquets of vibrant perfumed flowers that adorn the buildings, and hanging lanterns illuminate the darkened streets.

As I stroll into Thorp's Tavern, the aromas of freshly cooked stews and exotic spices caress my nostrils, my mouth salivating in response, and my stomach rumbles, echoing through the empty pit inside. Food, I need more food.

Quentin and Laz are already sitting at a tall bar with a pitcher of golden liquid atop it, and both are drinking from a glass poured earlier. Neither one is talking or even looking at the other.

Well, this is going to be fun.

Quentin never returned last night, and I haven't seen him all day. Laz didn't sleep on the floor. I woke to find him next to me, asleep on the bed, cocooned in his wings. It felt oddly normal and safe with him there. I spent the first half of my day lying in bed, trying to send messages to my friends—with no magic here it was of course a useless endeavour—and waiting for my laundry to be returned. Laz had errands, so he left early. Once my clean, dry clothes had been delivered, I spent the second half of the day walking around the village, exploring the vendors that offer a wide range of products from handcrafted jewellery to finely made clothes and eating exotic fruits and local produce.

Owenstown sits right at the base of the Mountains of G'phyn, and the mountains line one entire edge of the village like a boundary. Mountains aside, Owenstown isn't that dissimilar to any other small village back in Orphelious. The cobblestone streets for pedestrian access only are lined with granite and stone buildings and townhouses, some of which are two or three stories high. Colourful street stalls house a variety of goods, and other structures populate the village on this side of the wall. All homes and businesses belong to the Lupa-Centaurs and the banished Heretics.

The townsfolk have been kind enough to indulge my curiosity about their culture and merchandise, but it hasn't been an entirely warm welcome. Most are a little wary of an outsider. Some, though, are completely indifferent. But none are aggressive or cunning like I had imagined. In fact, this place is nothing like what I assumed. The tales told when I was young made it sound like the Heretics were aggressive villains who inflicted nothing but bloodshed and chaos everywhere they went, stripping Beings and land of its magic. But this town is more civilised and safer than the Neopolis itself.

I sit down and smile curtly at the two males. Quentin and Laz both go for the pitcher of liquid at the same time and pull their hands back in sync. I roll my eyes at them both, grab the pitcher, pour myself a glass, and gesture *thanks* to the males before taking a sip. Warm AppleAle. The spicy and sweet warm liquid heats my body after the chilly walk to the tavern, and I drink back my first glass in a few large gulps.

After we eat a warm bowl of stew and bread, mostly in silence, I finally ask Laz why the summons. "I wanted to have a drink with my travel companions. What's wrong with that?" he chimes sarcastically as he refills our glasses, leaving Quentin to refill his own.

Children.

Before any of us has a chance to continue this riveting conversation, the tavern doors burst open, and the five Lupa-Centaurs that greeted us in the Keep's courtyard march directly to us. The patrons and staff pause for a moment, silence rippling through the great room as the beasts make their way through the busy tavern, until they all stand around our table. Like they realise the beasts are not there for anyone else except the three strangers that have occupied their village, the townsfolk return to their conversations, games and whatever else. I swear I hear the room sigh in relief.

"I hear you're settling in well?" Perrin speaks as he motions to the pretty young girl working behind the bar to bring him and his companions a round of drinks.

"We are, thank you," Quentin responds curtly, staring at the beast. "We will be gone the day after tomorrow but will return not too long after that for another night before we return to Quespelia," he adds.

"I am not here to talk about your travels," Perrin snarls. "You and I have a score to settle, and I am here to settle it."

My stomach lurches, his words crawling through my body like a spider. I knew this was too good to be true. I stare into my glass, waiting for what may come next, and will my tears to remain hidden. Fear is creeping in, and my pulse starts to race.

"That we do, old friend," Quentin responds, swilling the remaining liquid in his glass back and standing as he slams it on the table. "Twelve-twenty?" he asks.

"What did I tell you?" Perrin growls.

"If it's not dead hearts, it's not Arrowlets. You're getting grumpy in your old age, Perrin." Quentin snorts.

My eyes widen, and I snap my head up to watch as Perrin, Callum, Hawkins, and Quentin pad through the crowd, chatting and laughing, to the far corner of the tavern where they open a small set of wooden doors on the wall, revealing a board to throw their ridiculously miniature feathered arrows.

"Arrowlets?" I mouth to Laz, trying to contain my surprise and amusement as Marlow and Samuel come in closer, surrounding Laz and me.

"Did you get what I asked for?" Laz asks in a hushed tone to no one in particular, all signs of amusement quickly abandoning his face.

I cock my head toward him, my brows pinching in confusion as I respond, "Get what?"

But it's Marlow, a black, grey and white Lupa-Centaur who places a small object wrapped in a brown cloth on the table and slides it to Laz while Samuel keeps an eye on his companions with Quentin. "The other one is still missing."

Laz nods as he swipes the package and pockets it. "Leave that to me," he softly replies. "Do we have safe passage?" he asks.

Samuel speaks softly without taking his eyes off the group playing darts, "Yes, Sarge. Callum has ensured it. The cave entrances at the southern edge of town near the inn will provide you with the easiest access to where you need to go. It shall be unguarded between the moon's peak and sunrise, not this night, but the next. You will be able to slip in unnoticed."

Laz arches his pierced brow and tilts his head to Samuel, who huffs light-heartedly. "Why do you think we put you in that run-down piece of shit inn and not one of the nicer lodgings on this side of town? It wasn't for its five-star rating, that's for sure."

"I gathered as much, but there wasn't anything nicer you could have offered?" Laz snorts, taking a sip of his AppleAle.

"We aren't a tourist destination. You said you wanted to keep a low profile. Anything nicer would have drawn too much attention," Marlow adds. "Speaking of which, Miss?" I snap my head to Marlow, who is now addressing me directly. "We have no issues with you walking around town, but please keep to yourself, and try to stay inconspicuous. It's not safe for you here. You cannot forget that no matter how friendly they seem." He nods his head into the crowd.

"The Heretics were banished here by your kind, your ancestors. They may have made this into their home and filled it full of life and colours, but it's still their prison, and we are their guards. Do not underestimate them."

I open my mouth, close it again, and nod in response as my stomach twists in knots, and the tension between my blades tightens. Foolish. I was foolish for going out alone, asking questions around town earlier.

Laz doesn't react to Marlow's appeal. He simply asks, "And the horses?"

"The horses will be well looked after by a young Cent called Gerreid. They'll be ready for you on your return."

"Thank you, Marlow," Laz responds, dismissing them as he finishes his spiced AppleAle and refills both our glasses.

"If you need anything else, Sarge, you know where to find me. Otherwise, we will leave you to an enjoyable evening. Good luck."

After the Lupa-Centaurs leave, I stare at Laz for a moment, waiting for him to explain himself. "What?" is all he offers up.

"What was all that about?" I whisper-yell at him.

"The prince isn't the only one with connections here, but we can't trust them all. What I said yesterday remains true. I will not be sharing any more than this. They are putting themselves at great risk just by talking to us, let alone helping us. I know who we can trust; you do not."

"Do we tell. . ."

"No!" Laz snaps. "What have I been saying, Paege? We trust no one. Not even the Wolf Prince himself." He tucks a rogue strand of hair behind his ears.

"Fine," is all I can muster the courage to say, but Laz isn't done yet.

"Speaking of, I was considering your situation, and you know, there is no magic here. So, those scars on your back, the brandings, would probably hold no power here." He takes a sip of his AppleAle and looks over toward Quentin, his eyes narrowing. "Just something to consider. You can do with that information what you like."

CHAPTER 34

Sleep was minimal. I sit on the bench outside my room, staring hypnotically into the starry night sky while the wind bites at my face. Laz's words from the other night keep peppering my mind. Words powerful enough they could change things, yet I've not dared to repeat them out loud. Or act on them. But every time I consider them, the cage around my heart squeezes, and blood rushes to my head, sending my body into a state of suspension. Isn't this what I wanted? To be released from the stronghold of this jail I have been kept a prisoner in. For Quentin and me to finally be able to be together.

Yes.

No.

Quentin and I have been dancing around our relationship for months now. Neither of us has addressed the obstacles in our way or the vast distance between us that ebbs and flows like the ocean tides. Every time we manage to take a step forward, my heart begins to repair itself at the possibility that we will find our way back to each other. But as I sit here in the unmagic lands with the Mountains of G'phyn looming overhead from behind and the memories of the past soon becoming unlocked, I am left to face the harsh truth that our complications are way beyond that of my brandings.

The cage squeezes tighter.

My lungs expand uncomfortably, searing from the frozen air, and I try to slow the unsteady, wild beats in my chest. Heavy footsteps pull me back into the present moment, and I look up to see him casually strolling toward me with a huge grin on his face, holding two mugs.

"Morning," Quentin chimes as he hands me one of the two steaming cups of coffee he holds.

"I could kiss you," I blurt out as I take in the bitter aromas and warm my chilly, bare hands on the mug. The temperature would have to be close to freezing at this time of the morning. And that would be well before dawn.

Quentin smirks. "Really?" he drawls, and a rush of heat blushes my cheeks. He muses for a moment before digging his hands into his back pocket and pulling out a pair of leather gloves. "What are you willing to do for these then?" He wiggles them in front of me, his brows leaping high, and he sticks his tongue out at me.

I try to grab them from him, but he pulls them out of reach. "Wicked," I snicker, roll my eyes at him, and sit down, taking a sip of the scalding coffee. It burns my tongue, and I cough out the liquid onto the ice-glazed veranda floor.

"Careful, it's hot," Quentin chuckles.

"Thanks," I say sarcastically, my tongue stinging, and then I hold my hand out, motioning him to hand me the gloves.

"So, what do you think a pair of fleece-lined leather gloves is worth these days?" Quentin muses to himself as he studies the gloves in his hands, mocking the slip of the tongue I made earlier, refusing to hand them over. "Two kisses?"

"Really?" I tilt my head and school my features, still holding my hand out.

"Three kisses?" His eyes blow wide, and his wolfish grin grows larger.

"Quentin, seriously?" I plead in a light-hearted manner.

"Five kisses?" He draws out each word with hilarity. "No? Okay then." He shrugs and drops his hand, pivoting on his heel as if to walk away.

I put the coffee on the bench seat and jump up, lunging for him, but he shifts his body, angling his side against the front of my body so he doesn't spill his coffee, and holds the gloves out behind him, inches out of my reach.

But still I try. His laugh rumbles through him as I try to carefully manoeuvre myself around him to avoid slipping on the sleet-covered ground, but he blocks me again, the gloves moving further out of reach. I huff and fake concede, pretending I'm giving up by stepping backwards and dropping my tired lead-filled arms to my sides.

He falls for it.

Quentin, wearing a winning grin, drops his guard and his arm, and I instantly give it another attempt. This time, I shift my weight to jump around him, but instead, I slip, my foot careening along the icy floor, and the world tilts.

Shit!

Without spilling a drop of his coffee, Quentin wraps his arm around my waist and catches me before I fall, and my heart cartwheels in my chest like a Godsdamn gymnast. "Careful there, Books." Quentin helps me back up. Our eyes lock, and my cheeks blush, flushing with so much heat that I'm surprised I'm not steaming.

"I don't mean to interrupt anything, but we need to get moving," Laz's voice slaps me out of the hypnotic state I was just in, lost in Quentin's light blue eyes.

I clear my throat and step away. Quentin takes a step back toward me. He tilts his head down, his cheek almost touching mine, and he hands me the gloves, his hand brushing against mine as he does. "I've missed this, missed you," he says softly in my ear, and then he lengthens his spine. "I'll grab the bedrolls, you finish your coffee, and we can go," he says loud enough for Laz to hear.

"We need to. . ." Laz starts, but Quentin cuts him off.

"We have time," he snarls. And for the first time, I watch as Laz slowly nods, quietly accepting defeat against Quentin. Something in my gut twists.

Laz never yields.

The ice-whipped air bites at my face as we wordlessly trek down a dark, narrow alley between a couple of timeworn buildings that have clearly been abandoned. They are overgrown with vines and weeds, and any once existing windows are long gone, now just open holes. The alley, not too far from the inn, travels east toward the mountains. Our path is lit only by the sole lantern we agreed to light, and we march toward a large iron gate. It's unguarded, just like Samuel had said. Laz heaves open the heavy doors, revealing a stone passageway that leads directly into a cave at the base of the mountain. "Well, that was easier than expected," I murmur under my breath as I step out of the alley into the passageway. I expected to rock climb, traverse a mountain's edge, or do anything other than open the gates and walk right in.

Laz shoots me a silent glance that warns me to be quiet before he drags the large metal doors closed after Quentin has passed, and we travel in silence until we step into a spacious cavern the size of my apartment. The air is heavy with the smell of damp earth, and the only sounds are the music of our own footsteps echoing off the walls as we walk toward the centre of the cave. Quentin lights two more lanterns, and my heart expands, pressing firmly against its cage as I watch the space before us burst into life with rainbows of colours. The walls are damp, moss-covered, and lined with glowing crystals, casting soft, colourful light throughout the cavern. Mineral spear-like deposits hang low from the roof, throwing demonic shadows across the stone walls. On the other side of the cavern, there are two tunnels. One leading left. One leading right.

"Which way?" Quentin asks no one specifically.

"We go right," I confidently blurt. I can't explain it, but there's something there. A memory, an instruction that I can't quite remember, but I keep hearing it, and I know without a doubt it's right.

"Books, we can't just go guessing these things. What if it's left, and we spend days travelling in the wrong direction?"

Choose the right path.

"It's not left. It's right," I say matter-of-factly.

"And you know this how?" Laz also challenges me.

"I just know. I need you both to trust me."

"Right?" Quentin ponders.

"Are you serious? You are going to make this choice on a hunch?"

I'm angered at the way that Laz demands that I *trust* him, but he refuses to trust me. "It's not a hunch!" I cry, the green eyes now a clear vision in my mind's eye as it hisses once more *to choose the right path.* "Why is it so hard for you to trust me?" I ask, hands on my hips, tapping my foot against the hard stone floor, each hit echoing in harmony throughout the cavern.

Tap, tap, tap.

"It's not that I don't trust you. I just don't see you providing any reasonable explanation for it."

I scoff, "As opposed to all the other reasonable explanations for the choices any of us have made over the past few weeks?" I snap.

"What in the Hels is that supposed to mean?" Laz bites back.

"Nothing," I huff. Laz doesn't respond. He stares at me, holding my gaze and waiting for me to provide a reason. I roll my eyes and sigh. "Fine." Then I tell them about my encounter with the green-eyed creature who told me to *choose the right path,* hoping to the Gods they won't laugh at me.

"Naga. Interesting. . ." Laz muses when I finish my story.

"Huh?" Quentin queries, looking back toward the two paths.

"I thought they were long gone. . ." Laz says to no one in particular. Quentin and I don't speak. We both stare at Laz, hoping he will clarify his personal contemplations. "They haven't been seen in centuries," he finally says. "Naga-Guardians are not from this kingdom. We don't know where they came from exactly, but right around the time—They disappeared years ago. It seems, Paege, that you encountered one. Strange for it to be in the forest. They usually dwell around water."

"And what are they exactly?" Quentin asks the words I desperately want an answer to, but I can't help but stay stuck on the fact that Laz is withholding something else. Right around the time of what?

"They are serpent beasts, guardians or gatekeepers of magical secrets and treasures. Nasty creatures, too. I'm surprised it left you alive, unless it needed something from you?" Laz muses, and I shake my head in response. "Hm. They cannot lie, but they are not usually so forthcoming with information. Which is why I am inclined to say we go *left*."

"Left?" I ask, my brows leaping. "But you just said they don't lie?"

"They can't," he supplies flatly.

"Well, it told me to choose the right path," I challenge him with a scowl born from my irritation.

"I don't believe it did. Naga are guardians, protectors. It told you the truth. To pick the *correct* path, but the right path is not the correct path. Slippery, cunning creatures they are."

I open my mouth to speak and close it again, instead opting to nod in agreement or understanding or whatever. Nothing, or no one, it seems is going to give me a clear answer, no matter my protests.

"Right, now that we have determined which tunnel to take, I need to know, are there any other encounters with strange magical

creatures that we need to know about, or are you done keeping secrets?" Laz asks, as he raises his pierced brow at me disapprovingly.

"No, nothing," I respond, defeated, as I step around Laz and past Quentin toward the left tunnel, my backpack and bedroll suddenly heavy on my back.

When Quentin and Laz meet me at the entrance, I chirp in a mock enthusiastic tone, "Well, what are you both waiting for? Left tunnel it is. Let's go." I step forward without any hesitation, and the world falls away from beneath me.

Chapter 35

"Paege, watch out!" I hear his voice before I realise what's happening, but it's too late. My stomach lurches out of my body as the ground beneath me opens, and I'm falling down, down into a pit of endless darkness.

I throw my arms up to try to grab for anything at all, but there is nothing but a swirling vortex of darkness, and I hear a familiar blood-curdling scream echoing through the emptiness as I continue to fall. It's mine. The weight of my pack pulls me further into the nothingness, and my legs and arms thrash about. The air whips at me from every angle, and my mind races with fear as the world spins and whirls around me.

Just when I think all is lost, and I am about to close my eyes to succumb to the inevitable fate, a shadow appears in my blurry vision. Wings. Large, glorious, beautiful wings.

Laz.

Laz is coming for me at incredible speed.

He is coming for me.

He draws closer, reaching out for me, and I drive an arm out for him, grasping for purchase and willing the length of my arm to extend to meet his. A second later, fingers entwine with mine, then wrap around my hand, and he tugs, hauling me in close to him. I

cling to his body, holding on for my life. Once he has me secure within his grip, he quickly shifts direction and springs upward. My stomach jumps up through my throat, trying to escape along with my bellowing screams, and my heart smashes at my chest with a determined aggression.

I close my eyes and bury my head into his chest, muffling my shrieks and cries as he flies back up to the cavern above, bringing me back to life as he soars higher toward the faint light above us. My body jolts, bones and muscles groaning as we hit something hard. The world continues to roll around me, but I'm immediately enveloped in a weighted silken warmth, a feeling I know. I don't have to open my eyes to know that we're back on solid ground, and he's wrapped his feathered wings around me. I lean into him, accepting his embrace for what it is. Safety. As I gasp for air, warm tears cascade down my frosted face, but Laz's cocoon pulls me in closer, bringing me comfort and shelter.

"Paege, Paege?" I hear muffled cries, but I'm still not ready to move.

"Back off," Laz snarls.

"Let her go, Laz."

"Touch me again, Wolf, and I will throw you down that hole myself. Now back off!"

I wiggle against Laz's soft wings. They shudder, and he loosens his grip. "Are you alright in there, Paege?" he asks gently.

"I— I think so," I mutter, self-scanning my body, searching for any signs of injury or pain.

Laz releases a wing, and I open my lids. Slowly lifting my head, amber eyes, soft with worry, meet mine. His pupils dance with colours of yellows, greens, and blues from the crystal light show that the cavern is still putting on display.

"That was a bit unexpected," he chuckles playfully, and something in my chest shifts because, damn, it's the sweetest sound I've ever heard. "But at least we have determined that this is the *right* path," he adds sarcastically.

"How do you mean? This place just tried to kill me."

Laz winces. It's small and brief, and to someone not paying attention, it wouldn't be seen, but I notice it. "It isn't meant to be easy, little wolf. If there's a trap, then something doesn't want us to pass."

He's right. Of course, he's right. I roll my eyes at him, but before I get to answer, Quentin is standing over me, over us. "Books, are you alright? Can you stand?" He holds out a hand for me to take.

My brows pinch and I nod. "I'm fine." Laz releases me from my cocoon, but I don't reach for Quentin's hand. I attempt to stand, my legs wobble beneath me, and the world leans again. Before I plummet back down, Quentin grabs me and yanks me into his chest. His arms wrap tightly around me, and betrayed by my body, I rest into him. His familiar forest scent and warmth send a flurry of conflicting emotions sliding behind my ribs. What is going on here?

"You scared the living Hels out of me, Books."

I pull out of Quentin's embrace and pivot back to see Laz standing a few feet back, eyeing me. Eyeing us. "How did you? I thought we had no magic here?" I ask, confused, taking a small but significant step toward him.

"I didn't—" His throat bobs, and he steps back from me. "I figured, they are a part of me, like an arm, or a leg, so I took a chance."

"You—" My voice cracks. Laz jumped into that pit after me without knowing how much of his ability to fly is magic, and how much is pure strength and force. Without knowing if his wings could take flight.

I take another step toward him. A step away from Quentin.

He jumped.

And another step. This time, he doesn't move away.

He jumped.

I lurch forward and wrap my arms around his large frame. "You jumped." I sob gently into his chest, my eyes filling with tears.

"I jumped," he exhales, his chest collapsing as he wraps his arms around me in return. The weight of his hold settles something stirring inside. Not my Wolf. No, she hasn't been with me since we set foot into this damned place. It's something else. Something that's been stirring and unsettling me since I met him at my parents' home, and I'm not quite sure what to do with that.

Neither of us speaks for a moment while we continue to hold each other, tears rolling down my frosted cheeks until I hear Quentin clear his throat, and Laz peels me off him. "You should. . ." He nods towards Quentin, a quiet resolve etching across his features as he walks away from me and toward the big hole in the ground.

I follow him, and Quentin follows me. "So, what are we supposed to do now?" I ask the males as we stare across the open space before us.

"We keep going," Quentin responds, carefully shimmying across the narrow ledge between the tunnel wall and the gaping hole.

Well fuck, I suppose we keep going.

Laz flies me over the pit. We meet Quentin on the other side and keep moving. Cautiously. As we silently walk deeper into the mountain, the darkness swallows us whole, consuming our optimistic attitudes step by step. The tunnels become narrower and more treacherous with steep drops and jagged rocks, and small bodies of water flow through the cave systems. The channels are dark and damp with twisting passages that climb daringly high toward the peak of the mountains. Over the hours, we discover more chambers and many more traps.

We cross another pit, one of thick, bubbly inky liquid, with a few stalagmite stepping stones as the only crossing option—stepping stones that even Quentin refuses to try and jump across. So, much to Laz's disdain, he has to carry Quentin across. Which just might be the highlight of this entire trip. Watching Quentin and Laz try to figure out the logistics of how it would work has me folding over in stitches. Quentin refuses to let Laz hold him, and Laz refuses to embrace Quentin. In the end, Laz picks Quentin up like a rag doll under one arm and pretty much hurls him across the pit before he even makes it to the other side.

My humour is short-lived when we reach another spacious cavern. Much like the one at the entrance, it's a cavern without a ceiling and is filled with stars. Its beauty is undeniable, and I find myself aimlessly wandering around, looking up, mesmerised by it all. It's like nothing I have ever seen. So many stars. A heaviness overcomes me, and as I open my mouth, a yawn escapes. Tired. I'm so tired. We must have been travelling for an entire day and not even realised it. The perpetual darkness of the caves and tunnels has been robbing us of the ability to track time. We decide to pull up camp for the rest of the night until the sun rises. We unroll our bedrolls in lines, keeping ourselves huddled together to keep warm. Lying between Laz and Quentin, and without so much as a goodnight, I drift off to sleep.

Whoosh. Hiss. Whoosh. Hiss.

I wake to a rancid, rotten smell. Blinking once, twice, three times, my eyes slowly adjust to the ominous darkness around me. The night sky above is still filled with stars. I must not have slept too long. Yawning, my stomach churns, from an acidic layer lining my mouth, the sulphuric odour still filling the cavern. "Lazarus?" I whisper, rolling over to face him. "Are you awake?"

"I am now," he says around a yawn.

"Sorry." I chuckle. "What's that smell?"

"Don't know," he grumbles.

"How long do you think we slept for?"

"Don't know," he repeats.

I sit up and look at the starry night high above me. Time is as distant as the stars above since we entered the mountain's cave systems, and it felt like we were going around in circles. All I know is we have been travelling upwards, slowly. Laz follows my lead, sitting up next to me and joining me in silence. He looks up to the dark skies above. An unspoken comfort grows between us.

He jumped.

As we gaze into the stars, I catch a glimmer of a light becoming brighter, and I take a deep breath as a shooting star lights up the night sky. My awe quickly fades, and my eyes widen as I realise it's careening toward us, getting brighter and brighter, as it plummets toward us.

Then another one falls.

And another one.

"What the fuck!" I yell as a star smashes onto the frosty cavern floor. The ground shakes upon impact, and I watch in disbelief as it sizzles and steams and disperses across the rock before setting, forming a new layer of rock over the old.

Not a star. Lava.

"Shit, watch out!" I bellow as I scramble, pulling my feet out of the bedroll. Molten lava starts to randomly fall around the cave, another one slamming into the floor right behind us.

"Quentin, wake up. We have to move!" I call out as the whooshing sound becomes deafening all around me. I jump out of my bedroll without hesitation and frantically get our belongings together before the next one plunges. Quentin moves like the wind, helping Laz and me roll the bedrolls, and we dart toward the closest edge of the cavern, unsure where the next lava tear is going to drop. Waking and rapidly moving has me wondering if Quentin was truly even asleep at all. Was he lying there eavesdropping on me? On us.

"Shit, shit, shit," Quentin mumbles under his breath as I watch multiple lava streams begin to cascade from the sky, obstructing our path to the tunnel. My skin heats as warm light fills the cavern. The ground around us quakes, sizzles, and spits, and the lava pools in crevasses and cracks, marbling the floor with blistering reds, fiery oranges, and golden yellows.

How the Hels are we going to get out of this?

"What do we do now?" Quentin shouts desperately, his eyes darting rapidly around the cavern.

The cavern is alive with the sound of the lava echoing off the walls and creating a deafening symphony of sound. I mentally map the cavern and lava patterns, my breathing becoming more unsteady with every breath taken, more defeated with every second that passes. The lava appears to be searching for a way out, pulsing and reaching out with its fiery tendrils, trying to escape the confines of the cavern and is rapidly spreading toward us. My eyes follow a line to the right of me along the wall of the cavern and widen as I notice the lava is travelling toward the right, slower than the rest of the cavern.

I draw in a long breath, trying not to let the sulphuric air choke me. "This way," I declare, certain it's the way out of here. Each obstacle we have encountered so far has been extremely difficult, but not impossible to pass. I have to believe this one is the same, and the more I stare at it, the clearer it becomes. I move. Carefully. With my back in a straight line and the pack I'm carrying now pushed hard against the rocky wall, I slowly take a cautious step to my right. My breathing is rapid and unsteady while my eyes follow the path of the lava as it travels around the cave, slowly creeping closer to the edges.

Neither Laz nor Quentin questions or answers me. They silently follow my lead and begin moving toward me after I have cleared a couple of lengths. As I continue to shimmy myself along the edge of the cavern, I take note of what's happening. The lava doesn't ever make it to the edge as I move around it, and I never get near the cave entrance or exit. In fact, the entrance we walked through and the exit I thought I was heading toward have disappeared altogether. Now, the lava appears to be pooling below us. My eyes adjust to the ground below. The world tilts, and my stomach lurches. The cave edge spirals upward. I am shimmying around a ledge. The lava is now a molten lake below us.

Oh fuck!

"Um. . . Laz?" I ask, trying to steady my voice, my body, my mind.

"Keep going, Paege. Don't stop."

"But. . ."

"Just keep going, Books," Quentin agrees.

Just keep moving. How many times am I going to have to say that to myself on this trip?

Every step I take is calculated and cautious as I push all my weight to my heels, being careful not to misstep or lean too far forward. Sweat beads across my brow, the heat intensifying as every minute passes by. The lava appears to awaken, hissing, sizzling, and illuminating the walls of the cave around us while we shimmy across. All three of us cough violently, and it unsettles my balance as the sulphur burns our throats and stings our noses. Tears pool in my eyes as the lava continues to cascade past us like molten waterfalls down into the lake beneath, now possibly twenty lengths below. The danger is no further away or lessened in the least. Weightlessness overcomes me, and tears leak from my eyes as I fall backward into a black hole. I'm falling. Again.

Fuck.

I close my eyes and open my mouth, but before I get a chance for any sounds to escape my lips, my back and hips bark in pain, as I smash against the stone. My eyes snap open.

Not a black hole. Another cavern.

Relief ripples over me. The air is still acrid but lighter and easier to breathe as I gasp for breath. I roll myself over onto all fours, my hands screaming as the sharp, cold ground beneath me rips into my skin, and I crawl across the slippery ground away from the opening into *Hels*.

CHAPTER 36

Laz is the first to fall into the cavern after me. His black wings glisten with an iridescent red and golden sheen as the molten lava lake below reflects his feathers. Its effect is a stark contradiction between strikingly beautiful and deathly brutal. Just like his angular face. His amber eyes, now also burning red like the Hels beneath, open wide as he realises where we are.

Safe.

"Well, that was interesting." He smirks. "Let's never do that again." He stands and wipes his hands down his leathers. He takes a few steps toward me, throwing his pack to the ground next to mine, and he stills, looking me over from head to toe, taking me in at every curve and angle. "Are you hurt, Paege?" he asks, his voice thick and hoarse.

I swallow hard as his eyes burn into me. I'm suddenly aware of my breath and the small space between us. I don't know. "Yes"—I shake my head—"no," my voice cracks, and I instinctively reach my hand out toward him, my pulse quickening as I do. Before my hand touches his, before I can say anything else, Quentin comes falling through the wall into the cave, landing exactly where Laz landed moments ago. Where I landed moments before that. I drop my hand, taking a step back from Laz.

"What now?" Quentin asks as we take in the chamber before us.

The damp stone walls of the cavern are rough and jagged with sharp edges, and they gleam with hues of oranges and golds, throwing an eerie but mesmerising effect. On the other side of the cavern, I eye a series of caves that are unlike anything we've seen before. "I suppose we go check these out," I respond hesitantly.

"I don't think we have another choice unless we want to go back out there," Laz says, trying to reassure me that it's the only valid option we have.

I stare at the caves across the room for a moment before glancing back to where we came from. The blood rushing in my ears quells, but sweat still beads upon my brow as I weigh up our options. I'm exhausted. My body aches all over, and I don't know how much fight I have left in me. Going back out there isn't an option, but what's on the other side of these caves could be worse.

Neither Quentin nor Laz speak while my body pivots between our options: new caves or lava. With a split decision, I step toward the caves on the other side of the cavern. The males fall in step beside me. As we make our way across the cave, I notice the cavern walls surrounding the entrance are adorned with intricate carvings and paintings. They depict war-like scenes from ancient myths and legends and drawings of strange and wondrous creatures—tiny fairies to massive dragons and beasts unknown. "What's all this?" I exhale as I run my hands over the stone wall, taking in all the bizarre markings and the story they tell.

Quentin moves to the furthest cave on the left, Laz to my right, and my breath stalls at the sight of two green serpentine eyes right in the middle. The eyes are attached to a humanoid face with a forked tongue, but the head rests on the body of a snake, holding a shield and a sword. A creature I can only assume is a Naga-Guardian.

Where Quentin stands among all the drawings on the wall in front of him, I can make out a series of markings. They are straight and curved lines, triangles, and circles, all underneath five Wolf faces that form a circle. They surround one unusual creature, Wolf-like but with feathered wings. Fire erupts from the ground beneath. The phases of the moon are fading across the top. Further along the wall, other drawings and paintings I can make out include a crown engulfed in flames; twin swords; the sun and different star constellations; a cauldron; a ring and a dagger; and a key and an hourglass.

Yet it's the one cave furthest to my right, the dark one where Laz stands, that has my attention. It draws me in, calling to me. It's something I can't explain, but as I walk over to Laz, who is staring at a drawing of a half circle with an angled line and one eye in the centre, a chill slowly slithers over my body, and I as I realise what he's looking at.

The symbol of the Eye of the Eagles.

Laz turns his head to face me and smiles widely, revealing his white canines. "Paege," is all he says.

I smile back in a silent acknowledgement, and I step past him into the darkness. As my foot touches the ground within the cave, I gasp. The air is dense with magic, and the power of it courses through my veins as my skin surges with static energy. "It's definitely this way," I whisper into the darkness, and as I take another step into the cave, sconce lanterns light up with a burst of fire.

"Paege, be careful," Laz adds from behind, his voice echoing throughout the cave.

I turn to see that he has unsheathed one of his blades. He looks prepared to fight, causing dread to consume me. I nod as he walks past me, taking the lead, and I let out a long breath, waiting for Quentin to catch up before I turn back to continue making our way deeper into the cave. The sconce lanterns flicker one every few meters, bursting to life with flames as I pass them. Though magic is all around me, I quickly realise my Wolf is still gone.

"I thought these mountains were the unmagic lands?" Quentin whispers.

"They are. . . Can you feel that, too?" I reply, my skin prickling as the magic envelops me.

"The gate must leak magic out. I can feel it all around me," Laz adds from ahead, stepping softly as he moves, blades still drawn in his hands

"So, we agree: the gate must be close," I say.

Laz stills, slowly turning his head to his left, and he drops his blades to his side. "Yes, Paege, I think the gate is close." The smile that graces his face is beautiful and bathed in a light that doesn't appear to be coming from any of the lanterns. "Very close."

After a couple more steps, I realise why.

Laz is standing before a narrow tunnel, no larger than the width of our bodies, no longer than a few lengths. And on the other side, an electric blue light pulses.

As we step out of the other side of the tunnel, my pulse steadies as a crystal blue lake appears before us. The tranquil water is so clear, I can see all the way to the bottom, and the reflection of the shimmering gate and colourful stalactites on the water creates a stunning blue hue. It's as if the water is made of thousands of diamonds and the light is refracting off them in a million different directions. Down the middle of the lake, a well-built wooden path leads toward the pulsating, white and blue glowing orb underneath the surface of the water.

The gate

A Watergate.

Silence fills the space around us as the hypnotic pull of the Watergate draws me toward it, as if it has tethered itself to me with invisible chains.

"Paege?" I hear the distant call of my name, but it's so detached, I'm unsure where it's coming from. "Paege?" I hear my name again, and I'm dragged from my trance as a tightness around my arm pulls me back. "Paege?" I snap my head to the left, and I see Quentin standing beside me, his hand around my arm, tightly gripping me, his brows knitted.

"What happened?" I ask, blinking my vision back into clarity.

"I don't know. You were—" Quentin says.

"In a trance," Laz interrupts. "You were walking toward the Watergate."

"And?" I ask, confused, my eyes darting between the two males. "Isn't that the point, to go through the Watergate?"

"Books, maybe we should talk about what our plan is exactly?" Quentin adds.

I knew there was a chance Quentin would want to retreat, but I didn't think it would happen when we finally made it to the gate. I expected it when we were in the Dead Forest or even in Owenstown. Not here. The whole point of going through everything we have is to make it to this exact spot, to this moment. There is no way in the Hels I am turning back now. "The plan is and always was to go through the gate."

"No. The plan was to get here. We never discussed what would happen if or when we made it to the gate. We didn't even know what the gate would look like," Quentin retorts rather sharply.

"Well, to clarify, in case anyone isn't clear, the plan is and always has been to go through the gate. So, I am going to cross that bridge and jump into the water through that Watergate. There. Discussed," I snap, probably a bit too harshly, but I didn't endure all those ordeals the past few weeks just to talk about what would happen when we got here.

"Paege. . ."

"You heard what she said," Laz cuts him off. "She is going through the Watergate, and I'm going with her." Darkness fills

Quentin's steel eyes as they dart between Laz and me. He opens his mouth to speak, but Laz cuts him off again. "There is only one thing left to discuss, Wolf, and that is whether or not you are coming with us?"

Quentin shakes his head disapprovingly but doesn't argue further. Instead, he walks toward me, his icy eyes softening, and he takes my hands. "You should know by now, Books, that where you go, I go. I just wanted to make sure." My heart flutters at his touch, but something in the way he said those words has me pulling back from his grip. I don't know why. It feels forced. Another obligation perhaps?

"I know." I smile broadly, painting warmth on my cheeks to hide what I suspect.

"Right, we are all going through the Watergate, then. Shall we?" Laz motions toward the path.

Toward the Watergate.

Toward the unknown.

CHAPTER 37

My body is being pulled apart at the seams. Limbs stretching thin, my ears ring as the walls around me swirl and twist in dizzying fluid motions. My head throbs as if it's being squeezed between a vice, while vibrant rainbows of colours whirl across the tumultuous vortex as my stomach churns in a nauseated manner, and bile stings my throat. I feel like I may die.

The feeling is short-lived as I'm violently spat out of the whirlpool, and I smash into a hardened ground, landing on my ass with a thud. My tailbone roars, and my muscles groan as I try to regain my breath, the world around me continuing to tilt long after I am back on solid ground. Seconds later, Laz dives out of the shimmering gate, now a Windgate, rolling gracefully and standing perfectly on his feet. He smirks, his pierced brow arched as his eyes land where I still sit, awkwardly.

Asshole!

Quentin follows not long afterwards, landing skilfully on all fours as if he's about to shift into his Wolf. He stands, sweeping his hair out of his eyes and walks over to me, holding out a hand to help me up. "Thank you," I mumble, but like usual these days, I don't accept his offer. I push myself up off the soft grassy ground. My eyes widen with wonderment when I mentally map where we landed.

I tilt my head up into the sunny sky to see streaks of vibrant blues and greens, royal reds, and golds are splashed across the atmosphere. Three moons hang from the sky, one large, full moon rests directly above us, and two partial moons shine further away, one waning and one waxing. At the base of the flat lands far across the horizon, a blue, fiery sun burns brightly like icy fire and begins to rise as if it were just awoken by our presence. The land is luscious and green, and the air is perfectly tempered, perfumed with sweet floral scents. It smells like spring. It smells like home.

A high-pitched, drawn-out cry echoes throughout the land, and my chest tightens. Across the fields, I notice two exceptionally large Eagles soaring through the sky. Their wings are spread wide as they glide effortlessly on the wind. Their feathers are white and rich brown in colour with flecks of gold, shimmering in the sunlight. Their beaks are long and curved, *perfect for tearing flesh from their prey,* and their mighty talons are sharp, *capable of piercing flesh and bone with ease.*

Creatures of power and freedom. A symbol of majesty and strength.

Transfixed, I watch as they continue to gracefully fly through the sky, one of them lets out another piercing cry that echoes across the valley before us, a sound that sends a shiver crawling through my body. A sound that, no doubt, strikes fear into the hearts of all who hear it, including mine, and my bones stiffen. They are a sight to behold. As they scan the landscape, maybe searching for prey, their sharp eyes lock onto us, and my heart jerks as I watch them both effortlessly change course and start soaring down toward us.

Quentin's hand rests on my right shoulder, and he squeezes gently. "When you said Eagles, I was expecting less. . ."

"Eagles?" I ask breathlessly. I can't keep my eyes off them.

"Yes. So, how do we. . ."

"Honestly, I have no idea," I sigh, my heart still thundering away in my chest as the Eagles glide closer, growing larger than I could have imagined. "Laz?"

"This is a first for me," Laz supplies, his usual snarky tone replaced by one of uncertainty. "My only advice is to stay still. No sudden moves. Not until we know exactly what's going on." A silent agreement nods out of me. Quentin does the same.

The Eagles perform a delicate landing, not two lengths in front of us, in a graceful yet brutal manner. They must be at least ten feet tall. They could take us out in a single bite or slash of their talons. Blood wooshes in my ears, and my stomach twists with anticipation. The Eagles stand tall and proud like statues. They shake out their wings, their feathers glistening in the icy-blue sunlight, before tilting their heads. Their eyes dart between the three of us before the one on the left locks its gaze onto mine.

Its eyes are piercing and intense with a fierce intelligence that seems to look right through me. They are a deep, murky brown, almost black, and they glint in the sunlight like polished stones set deeply into its head, *probably giving it a wide field of vision to spot prey from great distances*. A shudder travels through my body. Its stare is like a magic power beam, unwavering and intense.

"You are such a lost, little winged thing."

I hear the words form in my mind, and my eyes widen. With my heart still thrashing around in a desperate attempt to escape, I turn to face Quentin, looking for some sort of comfort, but he doesn't react. I pivot to face Laz, and his brows furrow as he pins the beasts with his eyes. "Did you hear that?"

I nod, too scared to react any other way.

Quentin asks, "Hear what?"

"Have you got a secret to share?" Their words climb through me, chilling and cold, making my hair stand on end. Again, Quentin doesn't react, but as a muscle feathers in Laz's jaw, and he blinks, one, two times. I'm certain he hears what I am hearing.

"Quentin?" I ask.

"Yes?" he drawls in a way that makes me feel like I'm going insane.

"Can you not hear that?"

"I don't hear anything," Quentin's brows knot as he looks between Laz and me.

"Laz?" I ask again, trying to be certain, I am not going insane, and the voices are, in fact, real.

"When seeking answers, don't be shy. Just ask the questions that come to mind."

"Well, you heard them," Laz says, shrugging his shoulders as if these majestic birds didn't just speak into our minds.

Quentin turns to face me, his face a blank canvas. His bluer-than-blue eyes from the cool shades reflected from the three moons and sun, lock hard with mine for a moment, and his throat bobs. I've never seen him look so unsure or confused. But this is crazy. I don't understand how they are communicating with me, or how Laz and I can hear them, but it's clear Quentin can't.

I swallow hard and close my eyes, zipping my charm along my necklace, the static charge biting hard. Alright. Here goes nothing. "Who, who are you?" I stutter, aware of the sweat trickling down my temples.

"We are one but also two, just like you," a distinct female voice replies.

"Well, not exactly like you. But we, too, have one missing. . ." a male voice corrects.

"So, maybe more like you than we think," the female speaks again.

Their voices are distinct, but I have no idea which one is speaking.

"Arnrun," the female voice answers.

"And Niaxon," the male voice adds. Still no way to distinguish which one is which.

A warmth brushes against my hand, and I steal a glance to see Laz's hand brush against mine in a silent acknowledgement that he heard the reply, just like I did.

"How are we hearing you?" It's magic, that I'm sure of.

"The mind is such a powerful tool. We have powers, just like you," Arnrun speaks.

"Paege, you and I have telepathic abilities," Laz whispers to me. "That must be why."

I snap my head toward Laz. Telepathic? Is that what my powers are going to manifest into when I Unify? And how does Laz know this? Of course, he knows this. Laz knows so much more than he has ever let on.

"We can discuss this another time. Right now, we are here to talk to them," Laz adds as one of the Eagles impatiently stamps a foot. The other one blinks erratically as if they are urging me to continue.

"Where are we?" I look around at the mystical, captivating land surrounding us. The three burning suns, the crystal-clear sky, and the grass that looks unburdened.

"Dasturn is this realm's name," Arnrun says.

"We are very glad you came," Niaxon adds.

CHAPTER 38

I conclude that the Eagles are definitely communicating, but every word Arnrun and Niaxon speak is in riddles and rhymes, making it difficult to decipher what they are saying. As frustrating as it is, I have a plan. Mhelodie's journal.

After discussing my plan with the males, and the Eagles eyeing us with an uneasy impatience, Quentin reluctantly agrees to scribe the riddles, Laz repeating everything we hear from the Eagles verbatim. Leaving me to focus on asking the questions that have been burning in my mind for the past few months.

Though intimidating, I feel completely safe in their company. Their marbled eyes blink erratically for a moment, their impatience clear as I deliberate on the order of all my questions. Releasing a steady breath, I start with the most important issue at hand. Or *selfishly*, the most important to me. "What am I?"

"You are born from the ashes of the past, your love unsurpassed. You will be known for your beauty and might, for your grace and ability to take flight. You shall rise high, with wings so wide, and you shall soar across the sky," they both sing.

"You must learn how to use your wings and fly," Niaxon adds. The Eagles speak with such grace and poise, mostly in complete uni-

son, as if they are one. Their words flow like ancient poetry penned by the Gods themselves.

Well, that was ominous and unhelpful. Out of the corner of my eye, I see Quentin scrawling in the journal. Laz quietly and slowly repeats the words as the Eagles speak, ensuring he transcribes exactly what he has heard.

Satisfied that the plan is going to work, I try again, asking a more pointed question, naively hoping for a different response. A helpful response. "What Wolf pack am I from?

"You are a creature once thought to be gone. But your pack is still there; you are not alone. A pack born of fire, a pack born of ash. You all shall rise from the flames with one brilliant flash. A symbol of rebirth, of life anew. Often found in tales, ones that are not true. You have been rediscovered after years of being lost. And now you are back; it is at a great cost."

My heartbeat quickens. "What great cost? Is that why the Scorpions tried to kill me and my twin—because we are an abomination?" Laz darts a look my way. His eyes blow wide, his lips form a straight line, and he cocks his head.

"You are a creature, yes, hunted and feared. But you are not a monster, make no mistake, dear. You are rare and powerful and stronger than all. And if you survive, the crown shall fall."

Like a serpent, their words slither through my mind, coiling around me until my temples throb. "If I shall survive? What does that mean?"

"You wear the blood of the cursed. Use it to set them all free," Arnrun adds.

"I wear the blood of the cursed? Is that why the king sent the Scorpions to kill me?"

The words fall out of my mouth before I can control myself. *Fuck!* It's too late. I steal a glance toward Quentin. He drops his hand from the journal on his lap, and I watch in fear as his eyes narrow and a muscle in his jaw ticks. I can no longer feel his emotions, but

I know without a doubt he's simmering with a dark rage as his eyes slowly turn black. *Fuck. Fuck. Fuck.*

"A ruler with venom and eyes of gold once killed a king, brave and bold. He sought his power, and he wanted his throne. But the king was clever, and he was not alone. The king had an heir, who was also a twin, and their other half is hidden, safely within."

Laz picks the journal up from Quentin's lap, pulls the pen from his loosened grip, and begins to scrawl what he heard. Quentin doesn't fight or respond in any way. Like a predator, he keeps his gaze hyper-focused on me. A chill spider-walks down my spine in response. I should have known better. I should have been more tactful. I should have. . .

No, a voice in my head demands loud and clear. *Focus, Paege! We came here for the truth, no matter how harsh or unsettling it may be.*

Quentin's blackening eyes remain firmly affixed on me. I shake my head, trying to dislodge the haze that has settled upon my mind.

"What happened to the original royal Fae family?" Laz doesn't miss a beat. He asks the next question and continues to scribe as the Eagles answer, completely unfazed by my earlier line of questioning. But this question pulls Quentin from whatever trance he was in, and he, too, shakes his head, as if to clear whatever destructive thoughts control his mind and confirm what he just heard. Will Quentin remember any of this when we leave this realm? Or will the curse snap back into place and wipe his memories clean of all these unsettling questions? Or will being here with the Eagles reset his memories like the book did for me? Wait—

"There was once a ruler, a king and a queen, their bloodline so blue, their reign was supreme. But now the kingdom is gone, their last dependent unknown, but all is not lost, for they wear the stone."

"A last dependent. . ." I swallow "You mean the bloodline isn't gone?"

"The blood of a royal, once lost and alone. Their name and face are undetermined but also known. They were survived, yes, by one last royal heir. The kingdom mourned, for their fate seemed unfair. But then they were found, yet their worth is untold. A legacy revived, a future now bold."

"Swords and Stones may break my bones, but fire and ash survive me." Arnrun sings so beautifully, her voice resting heavily on my heart.

"And what stone?" Laz interjects.

"A magical stone with powers untold. Made from blood and made from bone. As fire erupts, it grants you life. But only of those who can take flight."

"What do you get when you mix wings with fire?" Arnrun chimes again.

"Is that what triggered the curse?" I add while Laz scribes what the Eagles just sang.

"In shadows veiled, a silent clash, where magic wove and a curse was cast. A war unseen, with no trace or mark, except for a new king, who arose from the dark," Arnrun replies.

"With blood it's bound, with blood it breaks," Niaxon answers curtly.

Another ominous answer. I sigh and notice the Eagle on the right cock their head toward their left, as if motioning for me to look in that direction. I follow their gaze. Quentin is no longer standing near us. He has walked off and is aggressively pacing some distance away. Emotions swell in my chest. I want to go to him and apologise for my insensitive questions. I want to check in on him and make sure he's alright. But why? Quentin has done nothing but lie to me and hide the truth. Why should I grant him anything more?

Still, I could have warned him what was coming. I could have prepared him for what I was going to ask. What answers I seek. But some selfish part of me didn't want to deal with his denial. Didn't want to fight with him. And I suppose I was scared he might have talked or *fought* me out of it.

The other Eagle puffs their wings out, pulling my attention back to them and to Laz, who is watching me closely. The Eagle is right: we don't have time to deal with Quentin's brooding. We need to get the answers we came for. "How do we break the curse?" I continue.

"There is a blade that can break the curse. Its power is strong, its magic diverse. It will clean your soul and set everyone free. From the curse that binds and won't let you be."

"Where is the blade?" Laz asks.

"Pretty little things come in all shapes and sizes," says Niaxon. If it weren't for their distinguishing voices, I would have no idea who was speaking. I still have no idea who is who. Both Eagles stand tall and proud like identical statues, not even a muscle flinching as they speak.

"How can we find it, the blade?" I ask.

"It's hidden away but lives in plain sight. Its magic is potent; its power is bright. It's somewhere you see, but you never notice. It's not hidden from view; you just need to focus. It can grant you this wish and make your dream come true. But only if you find it and know what to do."

"Know what to do? What do I need to do?" I huff in frustration.

"There is a bloodline, a lineage of old. Their power is great—their full magics untold. They are the key to the curse, the one that can break. But to find them, you must know which path to take. They are not of light. They do not renew. The ones that can save—the ones that are true—they are the answer you seek, the ones that will free. But to free them, you must choose the right family."

I throw my arms up in the air. "Can't you just tell me which bloodline breaks the curse?"

The Eagles cock their head sharply to the side and blink, but neither of them responds, clearly pleased that their previous answer was sufficient. It was not. My heart thrums in my ears, frustration building. What does any of this mean? Is it my bloodline or Quentin's that breaks the curse? None of this is helping. I steal a glance at Quentin, and my heart sinks. I need to know if there is another way. "Is there another way to break the curse?"

"A bloodline shall live; a bloodline shall fall. A bloodline of secrets shall take it all. The curse needs blood to break it free, and only blood will satisfy thee," Arnrun sings.

Laz curses next to me, but he doesn't lift his eyes from the journal. I wouldn't know what to say even if he did.

"The cards of the past are the key to the future. Whatever path you choose will bring about your answer," Niaxon adds.

Well, that's helpful. I sigh. Does that mean it doesn't matter whose bloodline it is? Their riddles and rhymes make no sense at first listen, but we have time. When we get back to Owenstown, where there is no magic, we have time to read the journals and try to figure it out before it sends the messages to Mhelodie.

Laz nods when he finishes scribing this last riddle, suggesting we are done. But there is one more thing. One last question lingering that needs to be asked. I look back over to Quentin, who is now watching Laz and me and the Eagles, completely motionless, and a lump forms in my throat as tears well in my eyes, and I allow the memories of one other to rush to my mind.

I don't allow myself to think of him often because when I do, I find it hard to control my emotions. I want to scream and fight. I want to let my Wolf take over, and I'm afraid of what I may do at that moment. So, I keep him, my memories, my what-ifs and whys, locked behind that big safe door.

Warmth envelopes my right hand, and I glance down. Laz stands by my side, my hand in his, a silent gesture of solidarity, as if he understands exactly what I am thinking. His black hair shines with deep blue tones, and his warrior face looks less hardened in this realm. Is it the cool hues washing over everything? Softening even the harshest of angles and lines. He smiles—not smirks like he usually does. He smiles. Friendly. Kindly. My heart stills for a quick moment. My chest heaves as I take in a long, unsteady breath, and Laz nods, squeezing my hand in comfort. "What happened to Guy?" I finally ask.

"It's a puzzle, yes, a mystery to solve. Your answer lies veiled in a problem to solve. You are the key to salvation, the one who can free. So, to find him, you must look inside thee. But do not fear, child, for he is safe. Lying in secret, for you, he waits."

"Little winged one, your love shall guide you to your answer," Niaxon adds. And the Eagle on the left blinks twice and nods as if finally confirming it was him who spoke.

"Do not fear our truth, child. And do not fear death. For those who bleed shall repay their debt," Arnrun finishes, the Eagle on the right blinks, and I know it was her who answered this time.

Without any other opportunity to say anything else, both Eagles release a piercing cry and graciously spring from the ground in harmony, spreading their wings strong and wide as they take to the skies. I loosen my bated breath, and Laz's grip on my hand tightens as my legs become jelly and the world tilts around me. "I got you," he says as I begin to fall. As he turns to face me, my body lurches backward, and I'm violently yanked from his grip.

"Paege," someone screams.

The last thing I remember is the look of pure shock on Laz's face.

Chapter 39

“Paege.” I hear distant shouts, and my body moans as I blink my eyes, slowly becoming aware of my surroundings. Up-side-down snow-capped mountains loom overhead, the multiple peaks glistening from the bright but cool sun, and the frosted air whips at my face.

Mountains of G'phyn.

Owenstown.

What in the Hels?

My back cries out in pain as I try to peel my angled body off my pack and swords beneath me. Vague memories of Laz and my body being ripped from his grip assault my mind. Somehow, I have travelled through another gate back to Elyndria, my home realm, completely unconsciously.

Sliding my arms out of my pack, I gently roll over, scanning my surroundings. I seem to be alone, but I am not. I am surrounded by hundreds of granite and sandstone arches. Some are grander than others, but they are all grey in fashion. I peel myself off a headstone that reads *Hera Frans Paulster*.

Owenstown Cemetery, near the northern part of town, is the opposite end to where we entered the mountains. How did I get here? Did Laz not get pulled through the gate? Did he not jump through after me? And where is Quentin? "Lazarus," I whisper-shout, trying to keep my voice from travelling too far or drawing any unwanted attention to myself. Or wake the dead from their peaceful slumber. I wait for a moment. No answer. "Laz?" I call again as I stand unsteadily, my body still groaning in protest as I move.

"I don't know where he is," a rough voice startles me from behind. I pivot to see Quentin limping toward me. His face is sullen, and the light has dampened in his usually bright eyes.

"Are you alright?" I ask, fighting the urge to run to him.

"No. I am far from alright," Quentin growls as he slowly prowls toward me.

"What's wrong?" I study him, my eyes roving over every inch of his body. A body I have traced in my mind so many times now that I know every angle. I reach out to him, and he roughly swipes me away, and my eyes widen.

"What's wrong? You have got to be shitting me right now," he bites, and my stomach twists in knots.

"I'm sorry." My voice drops as does my head as shame ripples over me. I don't need Quentin to tell me what his problem is. His demeanour and words say it all. It's about the same person every single time. His father, the king. It's the same fight that drives a wedge between us every single time.

"You. Are. Sorry? That's rich," he scoffs, barking a scathing laugh. I look up, and Quentin's eyes darken. "This fucking obsession you have with my father trying to kill you, and it's getting tiresome, Paege," he scowls, and he takes two steps forward toward me, closing the gap between us.

I take two unsteady steps back, my heart pounding hard against my chest. "It's not an obsession. I just want the truth."

"The truth?" He huffs. "You are incapable of hearing the truth. How many times have I told you that he is not responsible? Yet you still refuse to listen."

"No, *I* listen, Quentin," I roar back at him, anger flushing my face. "*I* pay attention. *I* ask the hard questions, no matter how uncomfortable or difficult they are. You walk around in denial, incapable of even considering that your *perfect* father may be involved."

"Alright then, I am listening now." He takes another step toward me "How about you explain to me exactly what the fuck is going on, Paege?" His throat bobs, and his voice takes on a hair raising tone. "Because it was clear to me today that this trip of yours was more than just about learning how to break the crescent moon curse *for me*." Fear ripples over me as I study Quentin's face. His eyes are completely devoid of any emotion except for the fury that dances in his pupils.

I have kept so much from him, but the curse wouldn't have allowed him to remember, even if I had told him. I take a step back again.

Fuck.

"Tell me," he demands, his words as emotionless as his eyes.

"I just wanted to learn the—"

"The truth, uh-huh, so you've said." He nods his head in a sardonic way.

"You—you heard the Eagles," I stammer.

"No," he cuts me off. "I heard what you asked them. I heard what *Laz* told me. And it all sounded absurd." His eyes narrow. "But in case *you* don't remember, I couldn't hear them."

Even though the Eagles did speak in riddles, some of what they said was completely clear. I am a *"thought to be extinct"* Wolf pack. A Wolf pack that is so unique, we are feared. Misunderstood. There was an original Fae royal family that was slaughtered, yet they have a remaining heir. And the curse on the kingdom can be broken, but only by the cursed blade. We just need to figure the rest out. We need to solve the bloody riddles.

"What Laz told you was the truth," I say with a shaky breath.

"Laz?" His brows leap for his hairline. "And you?"

"I told you what I could. But the curse would not allow you to remember. And—And I didn't know whose bloodline was responsible." I swallow. "Yours or mine. . ." I say, my voice full of guilt and shame.

"Are you sure that's what it is?" he growls.

"What's that supposed to mean?" I can barely get the words out.

Quentin takes another step toward me. "You. Hate. Him," he says, clipping his words. "You *all* hate him because he's a Wolf." He steps again. "Well, guess what, Paege. You're a Wolf, too."

Realisation crashes into me from the way he says it. Shortly. Sharply. Cruelly.

I am a Wolf. My father was a Wolf. He was the King of Elyndria until he betrayed our kingdom. Until he was executed, possibly betrayed by Quentin's Family. Yes, he may have had something to do with the fall of the Fae Royal bloodline, but I have to believe that if my mother, a Fae, fell in love with him, he wasn't the big bad Wolf everyone had always made him out to be.

"I know, but. . ." My voice cracks, and I take another step back. My back presses into something hard and cold. A grand tombstone.

"But what? You've let *his* kind poison your mind your entire life, and you can't see the truth."

His words slap me like a phantom hand. Fae. "I am also *his* kind in case you have forgotten. So was Guy."

"And what about your father?" Quentin takes one more step toward me, completely closing the space between us. I turn my head away from him, and his laboured breath sighs against my cheek as he leans in close to me, resting his hands on either side of the headstone and barricading me against the stone. He's trapping me like prey, and he snarls into my ear, "Do you hate him like you do mine?"

I snap my eyes up and lock onto him, a fire igniting inside, burning with a ferocity that could melt steel. I respond to his antagonising comment as it crawls over my bones like a venous spider "My. Dead. Father? That your father executed? Fuck you!" I spit.

The harshness in my words, of my tone, snaps something free in Quentin, as if slapping him into the realisation of how cruel his words were. His eyes widen, and he pushes back off the headstone, putting space between us. "Paege, I didn't mean..." His voice breaks.

"Get away from me!" I ram my hands into his hardened chest, pushing him with such force that he stumbles a few steps backward as I remember the Eagles' rhyme.

"A ruler with venom and eyes of gold once killed a king, brave and bold. The king had an heir, who was also a twin, and their other half hidden, safely within..."

It had to be about my father. Did Quentin's father kill mine because he was jealous? Was this all so that Quentin's dad, his family could take the throne? In all the stories I've heard about King Braxtion, none ever explain exactly what he did to get excommunicated. To be executed. He betrayed our kingdom. How? The question burns so brightly, so fiercely inside me. *Trust no one.*

"I'm sorry," he grumbles, taking a few steps toward me and closing the space once more.

"No. Get away from me!" I shout at him again, pushing him away from me *again*. The heat rising from the depths of my soul darkens my heart, and my stomach sinks.

Laz appears from behind the headstone, and my chest collapses in either relief or despair, probably both. He scowls, baring his teeth. "You heard her, Wolf. Step away!"

"Back off, star-boy. This has nothing to do with you," Quentin roars back.

"That's where you're wrong. It has everything to do with me." Laz steps between us.

"How do you imagine?"

I don't know when it happened, but sometime over the past few weeks, something has shifted between Laz and me. I no longer view him as the possible enemy, the hindrance to my quest. In fact, somewhere along the way, he became a crucial member of *my* pack. I rely on him. I need him here. I want him here. He has proved himself many times, and he has saved my life more than once.

But Quentin. I no longer know what part he plays in all of this. Our relationship has become so strained. It goes beyond the brandings on my back or his father trying to kill me. It has been for longer than I care to admit. Everything between us has become so muddy and unclear, I can no longer see any way out of this. Maybe it's time to truly set him free.

"I want you gone, Quentin," I say, my words tearing me asunder.

"Paege..." he begs and reaches his hand out, defying both mine and Laz's requests.

Laz clicks his tongue "Tsk, tsk, tsk. . .I wouldn't if I were you, Wolf. Unless you want me to drop you back in that mountain cave, you'd best be on your way."

"You're loving this, aren't you?" Quentin snarls through clenched teeth.

"Well, it's not the worst idea Paege has had, I will give you that."

"Leave." I exhale. My body and soul are tired, and my heart is heavy from everything.

Remi.

Sylas.

Guy.

My father.

Quentin.

The cracks in my heart are about to shatter like glass.

"Don't do this, please, Paege," he pleads one final time.

"You know, for someone who says they listen, you're doing a damn good job of proving yourself wrong," Laz retorts, snickering as Quentin takes a few steps away, dropping his head and hands in defeat.

Quentin stills, looking at the ground for the longest time, his breathing laboured as I watch his chest rise and fall with each one.

But then he slides his hands into his inside pocket of his leather jacket and pulls the journal out and shrugs.

He found it.

Did he read what the Eagles said about the bloodlines?

My mouth falls open on a word, but it falls dead on my tongue as I watch his face contort, wickedly. Lifting his gaze back to mine with arched brows and his long fringe hanging into his now black eyes, he bares his teeth with a wolfish smirk, and he throws the journal nonchalantly to the ground in front of us. "You better not come for me or my family."

"Quentin?" I choke on his name, and the breath is ripped from my grasp as if his words reached inside me and squeezed. My chest clenches violently.

"Yes, Books?"

"I will find another way. I promise." Raising my trembling hand, I place it over my heavily beating heart, true Vailenbyrg style.

"Good luck with that." His words are cold and as sharp as a blade, striking me deeply and brutally, leaving a mark I know he intends to leave. He turns on his heel and runs off into the cemetery, darting between headstones so quickly I lose sight of him. And for the second time today, the world tilts and the unrelenting darkness burrows itself into my heart as I collapse to the ground beneath me. Falling further down than ever before, down into a harrowing pit of despair.

CHAPTER 40

Two days. We have been out of the mountains and back from Dasturn for two days, and I haven't heard anything from Quentin. I am not sure what I was expecting. Maybe a note left at the inn. I don't know, but it was not absolute silence.

The warmth of the water wraps itself around me as I sink further under. I haven't left my room at the old rickety inn, and I have refused to speak to Laz about any of it. For no other reason than I have nothing to say to anyone right now. I know he has been using my scribe to try write to Mhelodie, which has been unsuccesssful due to the lack of magic. Yet he's been trying everything and anything to work out the damn riddles, which I am ever so grateful for. The journal didn't work while in Dasturn, and while here, where there is no magic, she still hasn't received the riddles in hers.

I, however, am completely useless at the moment.

One, two, three. . .six . .ten. . .twenty. . .thirty. . .sixty. . .

I grab the edge of the bathtub, the cool ceramic biting at my fingers as I pull myself out of the water, gasping for breath. Still here, feeling nothing.

Tap, tap, tap.

I ignore it. I close my eyes and draw in a long breath as I lie back down and let my naked body slide back into the warm, silky water as it caresses me like sheets made of satin, and darkness envelopes me.

One, two, three. . .six. . .ten. . .twenty. . .

Pain sears through my arm, and harsh light hammers through my eyelids as I am yanked out of the water. I gasp for air once more.

Laz stands next to the tub with his arms folded across his chest and his leather jacket unzipped, exposing a tight, white knitted shirt that highlights every curve and bump of his chiselled chest, now splattered with water.

Damn, he does look especially good tonight.

He arches his pierced brow, and his jaw ticks. "This is what you have been doing with yourself these past two days?" He sounds so judgmental.

"I've also been drinking and sleeping," I retort, my words dripping in sarcasm. While Laz and I have shared a room, he has spent most of his time patrolling Owenstown and taking guard while I've been holed up in this room, refusing to acknowledge the world beyond, including him. Every morning, I've woken to find him curled up beside me in the bed, keeping his distance, but still so damn close. I still don't know what to make of that.

"You need to pull yourself together, Paege. We don't have time for your childish antics."

I scoff, "Childish? You sound just like him." I relax my body and begin to slide back under, but Laz grabs me again, yanking me up with brute force.

"I am nothing like him, but I won't let you fall into this pit of despair you are digging for yourself, and I am not going to coddle you." His eyes travel down the length of the bath, where my naked body lies under a thinning layer of bubbles, and his lip quivers. "Get up!" he demands.

I roll my eyes at him and lean back, closing my lids as I sink back against the lip of the bathtub. Maybe if I ignore him, he will go away and leave me to enjoy my *peaceful* bath.

Apparently not.

"What do you want, little wolf?" His voice awakens something inside me.

"I want to feel something, anything, other than this. Other than fear, doubt, and. . .everything else," I confess.

"If it's a distraction that you need. . ." The purr of his voice caresses something fracturing inside me, and his hand grips my bare legs, lurching me with surprise as Laz plunges his hand between my thighs into the bathtub. I know I shouldn't want this, but I can't deny that right now, I do. His fingers snake up my thigh, and a breath hitches in my throat, then a low groan rumbles in my chest as his fingers ever so lightly brush against my core. I lean back and close my eyes, savouring the touch. It may have been a surprise, but I would be lying to myself if I were to say it was unwanted. Desire unfurls in my core. Maybe this is exactly what I need to feel again. Yes, a distraction. A low laugh reverberates around me as his fingers brush over my entrance, then stops, lingering there for a moment.

"Like this?" His fingers stroke between my thighs, fluttering against my slick entrance.

The toying of his intrusion makes me beg. "More," I demand.

A dark chuckle rumbles in his chest.

What am I doing? I know this is not real, but I want to feel something that isn't the hurt and betrayal of my past. A small moment of reprieve. A small moment of ecstasy, and he could give that to me.

"Or this?" His fingers glide up my entrance, wet heat pooling in my core, and then he presses down on that little bundle of sensitive nerves, and a moan slips out of my mouth. My thighs tremble and my core tightens as pleasure builds between my legs.

"Yes," I moan, the apex of my thighs clenching, waiting for his ministrations.

"No." He pulls the plug from its socket, and I'm cleaved back to reality. I think I might hate him.

"That's not fair," I cry out as I sit upright, glaring at the back of his head as he storms out of the bathroom.

"Not everything in life is fair, Paege."

"You know, you could have just joined me. . ." I purr teasingly. He stills, pausing for the longest moment before he pivots to face me. My body slowly becomes exposed as the water gradually drains. I should probably care that he can see me completely bare, but I don't.

"I have no intention of taking you when you are being self-destructive."

"Only when you're in my mind, uninvited?" I mumble under my breath, but just loud enough so he can hear.

He doesn't react, his eyes transfixed on mine, but I swear I see a flicker of regret in them. "We need to talk," he finally says, and he turns and walks out of the room.

I slide down the back of the tub, as the water gurgles down the drain, wishing I could disappear with it.

Oh, Gods Paege, what's wrong with you?

Wrapped in my soft towel robe, I sit on the bed. Laz leans against the wall near the fire and crosses his arms. A glass of amber liquid that mirrors the colour of his eyes dangles from his fingers. "Are you alright?"

I huff a laugh, "I am not alright, no."

"Because of?" he asks, and something in the way he asks infuriates me.

I cross my arms. "I know you don't like Quentin, but he has been here for me through all of this. . ." I swallow. "And he. . .he just left. No note. Nothing."

"If I remember correctly, you asked him to. Demanded him to leave."

"Yes, but. . ."

"But what?" He swirls his glass and takes a sip of his drink, then he pushes off from the wall and takes a few steps toward me. "How exactly did you expect this to end?" It's more of a statement than a question. He continues, "No judgment, but you kept your motives concealed. You didn't warn him about your line of questioning. And if I were to take a guess, I'd say you always thought the Ishaans were responsible for all of this."

I stand, shaking my head, rejecting his accusation. Yes, of course, I have a worrying suspicion that the Ishaans are responsible. That it's going to be Quentin's bloodline that breaks the curse. But maybe not. It is going to go one of two ways—Ishaan *or* Braxtion blood—and it still could be the Braxtion bloodline that ends all of this. That means the curse breaks with my death, and Quentin didn't seem to even care about that part. My heart dives into the pit I've been digging for myself for days.

"Don't get me wrong, I'm not a fan of the prince, but surely you expected this."

I take a few steps toward Laz, meeting him halfway across the room, and I take his glass and knock back a large gulp. AmberFyre. I relish the burn as it travels down my throat past the hollow cage where my heart used to live and settles in my empty, knotted belly. "I just thought he would consider me in all of this." I sigh and lift my gaze to his, handing him back the glass.

Laz scoffs a derisive sound. "He's a Wolf. His lifeline of concern extends to him and him alone."

Here we go again. The battle of the species. Wolves versus Fae. It always comes back to this. I'm sick of this divide. The Fae are just as bad as the Wolves, and I include myself in all of this. Before I met Guy and Quentin, before I knew the Wolves and the Crescent Wolf Pack, before I knew who I was, I distrusted and hated the Wolves as much as any other Fae. And only the Gods know where the Witches stand.

But I am half of both.

I am Wolf.

I am Fae.

"I am his kind."

"No, Paege, you are different." His eyes soften, and I swear I see him grin before he takes a sip of his drink.

Now it's my turn to scoff. I place my hand on the glass of the AmberFyre to take it from him again, but he hesitates, our hands momentarily uniting, and my stomach flutters. He cocks his head slightly, and his grin stiffens. "Very different," he repeats under his breath, and he releases the glass from his grip. He clears his throat and takes a step back. "We need to leave," he adds curtly. "Tonight or tomorrow, but we do need to leave. It's not going to be safe here for much longer. Not with Quentin. . ."

I take a large sip of the AmberFyre, draining the glass of its fiery liquid, and blood rushes to my ears, drowning out the sound of Laz's words. Not safe. The story of my life.

I nod, heeding his warning, and I hand the empty glass back to him. "Tomorrow," I mutter, and I sulk over to the unmade bed and lie down with a thump, not caring that my robe is folded open, exposing my legs. Not caring that I am still undressed or that my hair is wet. I close my eyes.

Moments later, a heavy weight cocoons my body, and the sweet scent of leather and cloves caresses my nostrils as the bed groans underneath me.

"Tomorrow," he whispers from across the bed.

Tomorrow.

CHAPTER 41

The sun, so warm and comfortable, is barely starting to peep above the mountain's peaks when I wake. Stirring slowly and peeling my heavy lids from my dry eyes, it takes me a moment to realise that I had fallen asleep still undressed under my now *undone* robe, and Laz had fallen asleep beside me. The smell of leather and sweet cloves gently wafts around me as I take it all in. He looks so peaceful lying there, his usually hardened features now soft and his wings enveloping him, obviously keeping him warm. He didn't sleep under the blankets—blankets I vaguely remember him covering me with after I plonked myself down on the bed the night before.

Even though he kept to himself like usual, our hands somehow found each other during the night, fingers interlacing. Maybe in an act of comfort. Maybe in an act of solace. I'm not sure how I feel about that. I slowly untwine my hands from Laz's, my heart and mind strangely calm. Trying not to disturb the peaceful warrior, I slither like a serpent from the bed. Once free, I quietly tiptoe like an awkward ballerina to the bathroom to freshen up and dress, preparing for our exit from Owenstown. Back to Orphelious. Back home. But is that even home? Is anywhere?

When I finally emerge from the bathroom, I find Laz awake but still lying on the bed, knee bent with an elbow resting on top. "Good morning, Paege. Feeling better?" he chimes chirpily.

"Somewhat," I moan. "I will be better after coffee," I murmur as I scan the floor of the room searching for my boots, avoiding any contact with his hypnotic eyes as the memory of his intrusion and of my brazen invitation to join me in the tub smacks me in the face.

Why the fuck do you do this to yourself, Paege?

"Paege?" I hear the bed groan as he drawls my name with enough trace of concern that it gives me pause, and I look up to him. He now sits upright, legs still stretched out long atop the blankets but crossed casually, and he cocks his head. "I need to make sure you are alright. We have a long journey ahead of us, and I want to know that you aren't going to do anything rash or risky to put us in jeopardy."

"I'm fine," I snap, clipping my words, blood rushing to my head as anger spikes in my belly. "Good to know your concern for me is about your safety and not my wellbeing."

"Paege, it is about *our* wellbeing. Your safety is my primary concern, but it also directly affects my safety, too." My cheeks flush. "So, I ask once more, are you alright?"

It's a fair assumption, and he's correct, I should feel more concern for our safety than I am giving him. Most days, it's hard for me to move past one immediate emotion to the next. I carry around so much fear and uncertainty, sometimes it's hard to see what I need. What others need, especially when their emotions aren't telling me. Is it his years of training, of honing his craft that makes him so attune to the smallest of detail, even beyond the moment? Or does knowing the exact definition of who you are, and what your destiny holds, do that to you? I hold his gaze, unblinking, searching for an answer. Maybe both. My empty chest aches, and with that ache comes a stark truth. What I need right now, is safety. I need security and stability. In myself, in my friends, in my family. In my world.

Still, I roll my eyes at him. More so to cover my own sheep-ishness than anything else. "Yes, Laz, I am fine. I want to make sure we are both safe, too. I do need coffee, though," I scoff as I eye my boots and socks warming near the pot belly.

"Already taken care of," he says casually as I make my journey across the room. "It should be here any moment with breakfast, and I've restocked our supplies so you will have enough coffee to get you through the rest of winter," Laz chuckles.

My heart hitches, and I trip over my feet, stumbling a few steps before I pivot to face him. Unable to take a breath, I just stare. There he goes again, thinking ahead. Thinking of me. . .

The rest of winter. . .Winter. Shit, I didn't even realise. "What date is it?"

"It's two days past Winter's Solstice," Laz replies casually.

In all the plotting and travelling. Through all the ordeals and trials, through all the heartache and heartbreak, I completely forgot what is arguably the most important day of my life.

Winter's Middle.

My twenty-fifth birthday.

My Unification.

Three weeks from now.

My heart wrenches. I should be doing this with Guy. We should be doing this together. Two halves, unifying as one. "We need to get back," I cry out in desperation. I frantically pace from side to side, unable to decide what to do, but I need to start gathering my belongings.

"That's what I've been saying."

I still. "No, you don't understand. My Unification is Winter's Middle."

Laz's brows furrow, like he's calculating time and dates. He stands abruptly, moving with sheer determination and intention as he strides across the room to where I stand motionless like a statue as warm, salty tears begin to pool in the corners of my eyes. "We will make it, Paege." He takes my hands and squeezes them. "I promise."

"Thank you" feels like too few words to say, but I can't find any others to express my gratitude.

So, I nod.

Winter's first snow fell overnight, and Owenstown is even more beautiful when it's dressed in white. It doesn't make for a great start for our journey home, though. After gathering our belongings, we find well-fed, rested, and cleaned Whisky and Lilith tied to a tree at the front of the inn, fully prepared for our return trip. Quentin took Jesstar, which irritates me more than I care to admit. Surely there are other horses around town that he could have taken. He knows the Lupa-Centaurs well enough; they do work for his father, the king. I'm certain Perrin would have been able to assist, providing him with another horse. Sure, it's irrational, but he took my family's horse but couldn't leave a note. Maybe Laz was right about Quentin after all.

Laz's *friends,* Marlow and Samuel, gave us a pass to leave Owenstown via the gated drawbridge at the bottom of the ravine, a much safer and less anxiety-building crossing, thank the Gods. I don't think I have it in me to cross that bridge ever again. Especially in this weather. As we make our way through the lower level of the keep, passing what I am assuming are storage chambers, cellars, and undercrofts for produce and other supplies of goods that are not so easily obtained in Owenstown, a sigh of relief travels across my shoulders. Home. We are going home.

"Marlow, thank you for all your help," Laz curtly says to the Lupa-Centaur who escorted us to the drawbridge.

"Stay safe out there, you two. There is a storm coming through, and..." He cuts himself off and muses for a moment, his eyes darting behind us, ears twitching. I notice Whisky's ears twitching, too, as Marlow continues, "Just be safe and alert."

Laz dips his head slowly, an honourable thank you before digging his heels into Lilith and urging her to move forward.

"Thank you." I smile at Marlow, showing my gratitude for their hospitality, but before I can urge Whisky to follow Laz, he grabs my arm.

"Miss, I just want to say, if you ever need anything, you can always find Samuel and me here. There may not be many of us left, but there are a few who don't blindly follow the king."

"Thank you," I repeat, unsure why his declaration of support, or should I say, dissent, was necessary.

"No, thank you." He dips his head and turns, padding off through the keep's passageways back into Owenstown.

Urging Whisky toward the drawbridge, the water below thrashes against the rocks. It's deafening, and the ice-tipped wind bites at my face, stinging my eyes as I push Whisky to cross. As we pass the threshold of Owenstown, Whisky ploughing through the deep snow, I am sucker punched and winded by an invisible attack. My stomach growls, and something deep inside me thrashes and rips my insides to pieces as my body surges from what feels like thousands of electrical zaps.

What the fuck.

I pull on Whisky's reins and rapidly dismount, trying to hold back the waves of nausea. My chest tightens. My scars on my back burn like a raging fire. My stomach growls in fits of fury. I fold myself in half as the pain intensifies, and I close my eyes, forcing the tears I didn't even know were pooling to escape their tiny puddles in my eyes.

There she is, my Wolf, clawing and howling and thrashing like a caged beast trying to free herself. I reach out to her, and she stills.

Acknowledging me, I swear I see her smile a wolfish grin, and her emerald eyes sparkle. She graciously walks toward me, and I allow her to melt into me, and I finally feel as if I am home. As if I am whole once more. As if all the pieces that were stripped away from me when I entered Owenstown are all put back together again and returned to where they belong. I sigh. I am whole.

It's alright, girl. We are fine.

A hand grabs my shoulder, and I open my eyes and find Laz standing beside me, his hand gripping me in an act of support. Worry travels across his brow as he tilts his head down to me. *Are you alright?* he seems to ask.

"I am," I breathe. "I really am," I confirm as I mentally scan my body and my Wolf, both of us feeling freer than we have in a long time.

"It can be tough the first time, losing your magic and gaining it back, I mean. I forget. It was a long time ago for me. Apologies for not considering it," Laz says as he squeezes my shoulder before helping me up to my feet. "Do you need a moment?"

"No, I am good."

We mount our steeds once more, and I follow Laz across the remaining wooden sleepers of the drawbridge and finally land on solid ground. The once green field is now a blank canvas of snow with no clear path back toward to Dead Forest. Back home.

"How long ago was the first time you went to the unmagic land?" I prod. In the weeks we have spent together, Laz has barely shared anything about himself.

"A while," he answers.

"How old are you?" If I had to guess, I would say he's at least my mother's age, two hundred years give or take.

"Older than you, little wolf."

"Well, yes, I get that." I roll my eyes at him for probably the twentieth time in as many days, but he's riding slightly in front and can't see me. "But how much older?"

"Why the sudden need to know about my age, Paege?"

"Why the secrecy?" I retort. He doesn't like to give much away. I don't like it.

"It's not a secret. I just don't know how my age is relevant at this moment."

"It's not relevant. I'm just curious. I don't know much about you."

"You know enough. . ." he drawls.

"I know nothing," I snap.

He pulls Lilith to a sudden stop, and Whisky and I need to swerve to avoid them as he pulls her around to face me. "Paege, we are about to enter the Dead Forest. Is this necessary right now?"

I don't know why, but his attempts to avoid my questions bug me. It makes me dig my heels in, wanting to push for answers.

"Yes, it kind of is," I say, my frustration lining every word.

"Alright," he sighs. "What do you want to know?"

A victorious smile creeps across my face. "How old are you?"

"Too old for you to be asking that question and not as old as your father." He smirks, revealing a pearly white canine, and he winks.

"But as old as my mother?" He doesn't answer. "How do you know Asheron?"

"Hm." He nods, and I swear I see his amber eyes flash red as his smile quickly fades. "I met Asheron through Remildiaz, actually. She was a good friend of mine. She loved him very much."

That sentence, I was not expecting. The final images of Remi's life, her death, flash before my eyes, and a hollowness fills me. How did I not consider that he was friends with Remi, Asheron's FaeMate? Of course, he was. Because if he were friends with Asheron, we would have at least heard about Laz at some point. A lump in my throat starts to form, and I'm about to apologise when Laz continues.

"I honestly don't know how he handles losing his FaeMate like that. I know they had their problems. Asheron's reasoning for why he wanted to reject the bond is completely justifiable. As a Star-Borne, our life expectancy is greatly reduced." His throat bobs. "But I had hopes they would work it out. He is young. He would have come around eventually, I am sure."

The way he says it makes me wonder if Laz had ever had a FaeMate. He bears no mating marking, from what I've seen, but I suppose it could appear anywhere. Did he lose her? Maybe she was a Star-Borne, a Guard, too. He is certainly old enough to have had a mating bond snapped into place. He has travelled and lived enough to meet her. Or did he, too, reject his mating bond like Asheron tried to? Maybe she's still around, waiting for him to change his mind. Or maybe she rejected him because of his calling. *Or because of his arrogance.* Maybe they are together, and he hasn't said anything, and she's just walking around wearing a mark, the twin to his, waiting for him to return to her.

No. Once you accept your bond, everything changes. The bond between mates becomes so intense, you basically become one, or so I've been told. He certainly doesn't act like he has a FaeMate. My cheeks heat as I think back to the bathtub. I shake off the thought, letting the frigid air chill my quickly heating body.

"I'm sorry, Laz. I didn't know," I finally get to say, bringing the conversation back around to Remi.

He shakes me off. "It's fine, Paege. How would you know?" It was more of a statement than a question. So, I don't respond.

"Come on," he says, changing the subject and urging Lilith to turn around again, back toward the foreboding Dead Forest. "We need to get moving if we want to make it to the clearing before it gets dark. Unless you have any other vitally important questions to ask?" He raises his pierced brow cheekily and smiles, trying to conceal the pain that I can see clearly because that smile never reaches his eyes.

"No," I say, shame blushing my face with heat. "No more ques-tions."

"Paege, I am an open book. I will tell you anything you want to know when we can sit as friends and enjoy each other's company, rather than trying to travel through dangerous lands in the middle of a snowstorm."

"Is that what we are? Friends?" I ask curiously, my heartstrings tugging at his words.

His raised brow arches higher, and he smiles. This time, when it reaches his eyes, they glisten, and I see those damn flames spark and dance in his pupils. "Of course, we are friends, Paege. Well, we're friends when you're not being a royal pain in my ass." He chuckles. "Yes, we are friends, if that's what you would like."

Friends. Something in my chest settles. "Yes, I think I would like that," I reply, and my lips tug upwards and my eyes crease at the edges.

"Good, now come on. Let's not waste any more time." He digs his heels into Lilith and rolls his body, and they gallop off toward the Dead Forest.

Friends, yes, I would like that very much.

I follow Laz's lead, and Whisky and I gallop off behind them.

Finally, on our way home.

CHAPTER 42

Lilith and Whisky slowly and carefully make their way over the sleet-covered ground as we follow the riverbed wall through the forest. We approach the clearing with the serpent-like tree, where I met the Naga, and my stomach twists in anticipation, waiting for the slippery creature to reappear. But as we pass by, it never does, and the invisible weight that has been pressing on my shoulders since we left Owenstown lifts. I sigh, relief flooding my veins.

When we reach the campsite clearing, I dismount Whisky. The hard earth stings my heels, and my bones groan from the familiar aches and pains of riding a horse for an entire day as I land firmly with an ungraceful thunk. The distinct earthy and fresh forest scent fills my nostrils, and it steals the calm in my bones, replacing it with tremors that could shake the earth terra protects. Quentin has been here. Of course, he has. Is this what it's going to be like for the next couple of weeks? Every trail we walk, every camp we stop at, will remind me of him, of us.

I walk around the site, his strong scent caressing me like a forbidden drug, overwhelming in some places, less so in others. It tracks out of the clearing towards the west. A distinct path back home, like a trail of breadcrumbs guiding me to Quespelia, to him. Or straight to the big bad Wolf himself, the king.

What am I going to do about the king? Is he still looking for me? Is Quentin going to tell him about all of this and where I am? I don't know where we left things. I told him that I didn't know whose bloodline breaks the curse. I told him I would find another way, but the vision of his emotionless eyes as he spoke his departing warning, *"You better not come for me or my family,"* haunts my memories.

Shit. A shudder creeps across my body. I can't think about this right now. We need to get back to Orphelious for my birthday. For my Unification. Then I can worry about what's to come.

I leave Laz to set up camp while I freshen up at the stream I visited before. Barely able to see my hand in front of my face from the dense fog, I step through the wooded area, gently manoeuvring my way across the veiny, slippery roots and rocks toward the serpent-like tree.

After a few minutes, I step into the small clearing, the fog evaporating around me, and I can't help but notice there is a distinct absence of. . .well, everything. It's as if the world has pressed pause. The usual symphony of nature is noticeably absent, replaced by an uncanny silence that amplifies with every step I take. The trees stand like silent ghosts, their branches devoid of life. It's as if time itself has frozen, the eerie stillness hanging in the air, unsettling yet intriguing.

Opening myself up, I let my senses extend from me like little tendrils stretching from my heart, but I can't sense anyone or *anything* watching us as I did last time I was here. The veiled stream is now in plain sight, and the serpent tree is exactly as I remember it. Its black trunk is as dark as the inky sky, branches twisting and turning like hundreds of snakes, and a chill slithers across my skin. I pivot, scanning the woods beyond the clearing. Still, I see nothing, feel nothing.

Shaking the unease off, I spend a few minutes freshening up by the stream, the freezing water awakening my skin as I let the liquid flow through my fingers.

"I see you have returned," a slithery voice hisses from behind me, and my bones stiffen. I slowly turn around to see the familiar forest-green orbs glowing from beyond the tree.

The Naga Guardian.

I stand, cautiously drawing my dagger, and I take a step forward, willing myself to remain calm as I remember what Laz told me about the Naga.

Beasts, not from this realm.

"Wh-what do you want?" My voice catches as I try to speak through my ragged breathing, the winter air burning my lungs with every breath taken.

"Is that any way to greet an old friend?" It cackles, but I don't answer. "I wish to know if you found what you were looking for?"

"Yes, and no. No thanks to you." I roll my eyes and instantly regret it.

"How do you mean?"

"You lied to me." I take another uneasy step toward the beast, my dagger at the ready, fingernails biting at my palm as my grip tightens around the hilt.

"I did no such thing. I cannot lie. You beings in this realm hear only what you want to hear." Then it *tsks* me as if it's telling me off, and I can't help but scoff.

"What's that supposed to mean?"

"It's unimportant. What is important is that you found the answers we all seek," it hisses, drawing out every word.

"I don't have the answers. They, like you, told me nothing but riddles and workarounds."

"Of course, you do. Look inside your heart, Paege. You've always known."

What in the Hels? How does it know my name? Watchful eyes pressed against me as we travelled through the forest, reveals itself. It was following us.

I lower my dagger, and my grip loosens. "You, you were watching me?"

Throughout our entire journey in the Dead Forest, I sensed it. I knew I wasn't alone. That we were not alone. A constant feeling of being watched gripped me the whole time. An invisible presence lingered in the shadows, unseen eyes tracing every step I took. "Yes," it hisses. "I've been watching you for a while." It was the Naga Guardian all along.

"The Whispering Woods, was that you, too?" Laz told me it was *believed* to be old souls whispering through the trees, speaking your truth, but what if he was wrong? Maybe—

"No, that wasn't me. That was the other folk."

"The other folk?"

"Hm, some are good, and some, like all Beings, are evil. I felt you when you first entered the Whispering Woods, but I was too late. You were already indisposed, but I knew exactly who you were. Why do you think I let you pass and gave you my help?"

"Your help? That's what you call it?" It hums as if perplexed by my ungrateful manner. "You gave me mixed messages, just like the Eagles. Just like everyone else. Why can't any of you just be clear?" I question, my words dripping with frustration.

"I must say, I was worried when I didn't see you with your companion the other day," the Naga muses as if it didn't hear what I just said.

Quentin. It saw Quentin.

"So, wh—?"

The Naga cuts me off again. "I do not know. You sought. You found. Now, you must act."

I take another step toward it. Thumping hard, my heart sends fiery blood through my veins. It roars in my ears, drowning out the Naga as it continues to prattle on. The Naga beast, just like all the other creatures in this forsaken place, is only interested in itself, speaking in riddles and telling half-truths. None of them *actually* helping.

Now, you must act.

Why me? Why don't they do something? They all seem to know what's going on, but no Being has ever tried to free anyone. Fire rages in the depths of my stomach as I pad closer to the beast while its slimy reptilian figure takes form. Its moss-green, scaly body moves fluently but disjointedly, as if it's moving between time and space.

It doesn't back away. I partially shift, willing myself to calm so the Naga doesn't sense my anxiety or my anger. But it's too busy talking about itself, being too self-righteous to even notice how close I'm stalking the beast.

Now, you must act.

Seems they all know the truth. So, why haven't they acted? Why haven't they attempted to get the answers themselves? Something inside of me snaps, and my Wolf roars, pushing through my resolve and taking over my body. Her rage is a living thing, born of nothing but wrath and fury, and the sweet taste of revenge.

Its illuminated serpentine eyes finally meet mine, but I don't give the beast a chance to react. My fingernails bite into my palm, and I swing my dagger high above my head, moving swiftly like an assassin in the dead of night as I slice through the air. The Naga's eyes blink only once before my blade meets the beast's neck. Inky blood oozes from the cleanly cut stump. Its head rolls from its body, landing with a sickening thunk as it hits the muddy ground. It's forked tongue flicks, and its green orbs blink erratically as its inky reptilian slits grow larger. A single tear rolls down its face. The Naga's body twitches, and I wait patiently for it to fall before taking another step toward it, cocking my head as I watch the life slowly drain from the beast's eyes.

My focus regains, and my eyes lock with the Naga's lifeless orbs. My palms sting. I drag my eyes down to my side. Limbs shaking, my white knuckles grip around the hilt of my dagger as if I'm holding on for dear life. Black blood freckles my skin.

I smile. There, I acted.

With shaking hands, I clean myself at the stream once more, splashing water on my face and scrubbing my hands of the inky goo the beast bled from its body. Tears consume me, and I hiccup a sob as I scrub the remnants of its life away as if it never existed.

I sit on a mossy rock, composing myself and making sure my Wolf is settled before I hike back to the campsite, musing over what the Naga had divulged and not what I had done. What does this make of me to kill so carelessly? Or is it careless at all? These creatures don't belong here, and they are all too quick to want to see me killed to save them all. Irritation consumes me as I consider all the riddles these creatures speak in. Why does everything have to be Godsdamn puzzle?

When I finally get back, my frustration peaks as I see a single tent pitched right next to the fire. Of course, Laz and I have to share. Quentin took the other tent, but to be fair, it's too cold for either one of us to be sleeping exposed in the elements. There probably would have been a time when I would have objected and forced Laz to sleep by the fire. Or more likely, I would shift into my Wolf and sleep by the fire. Given the circumstances and the change in our relationship, *friends,* I don't object, and I can't be bothered with an argument. So, I crawl into the tiny tent and lie down, facing him.

He draws in a long breath. "You. . .Is everything alright?" he asks.

I sigh. "Yes, Laz, everything's fine. I just. . ." I pause, considering whether I should tell Laz that I saw the Naga again, what it told me, and what I did. I'm not too sure I can explain that, let alone deal with his judgment. I sure as Hels don't understand what that means about me.

You are a creature feared. . .

"Paege?" he drawls curiously, his eyes still closed, and my stomach coils.

I opt not to mention it now. Instead, I bring up another thought I had after my magic returned. "I was just thinking, should we continue our lessons? You know, now that we can access our magic again."

His eyes leisurely open. "Hm, I was thinking about that. We can if you would like to. Otherwise, when we get back to Ferinini, we can start lessons there."

"You still want to train me when we return?" I ask, confused.

"I told you I would train you. I am nothing if not a male of my word."

"Thank you." I smile. When he isn't being an incorrigible asshole, he's not so bad, I suppose.

"No need to thank me. Just keep practising to keep your shield up, and when we get back, we train."

I close my eyes. Something inside me settles at his promise, and I sink into my bedroll. Sink further beyond into what I think is going to be a blissful dream of—

"So, are we going to talk about it?" His words jerk me from my descent, and my body tenses.

"What?" I say with a weak voice, pressing my lids together tightly to prevent my eyes from betraying me.

"Are we ever going to talk about what the Eagles said? The curse, how to break it, and who. . ."

My heart takes off like hunted prey running for its life. The Eagles. The curse. The king. I cut him off abruptly. "You heard what they said, and until we can figure out what they meant, there is nothing to talk about." I swallow hard as that damn lump that lives in my throat starts to appear.

We haven't discussed any of it since Quentin left. The graveyard was the last time it was ever spoken about. I know Laz has written to Mhelodie about it, but not me. I have purposely avoided all conversations regarding it because once I talk about it aloud, once it's discussed, the reality isn't going to be something I will want to hear, and the responsibility of it is not something I will be able to evade.

"Paege, that is not exactly true. You are the only remaining Braxtion. You must have thought about what that means?"

My chest trembles, and the walls of the tent, of my life, of the kingdom, start caving in around me. Of course, I have thought about it. The thoughts infect every quiet moment. Every restless sleep. I may have to die to break the curse that plagues the kingdom. To unbind the Crescent Wolves from the moon. To free the fate of the Fae and return those who rightly rule the kingdom to the throne. I know exactly what it means.

"Did you know?" he asks, his voice cracking, breaking my chain of thoughts.

"Know what?" I reply, my breathing now short and sharp, none of it filling my lungs.

"Did you know about the bloodline? To break the curse?"

"No," I answer with so much conviction that I hope it deters him from more questions.

Lies.

"Paege?" he exhales. His breath is just a sigh against my lips. I open my eyes, and I am greeted with his dark amber eyes, transfixed on me. I didn't realise how close his face was to mine.

I take in a long breath, and the scent of leather and sweet cloves hugs me. "I assumed as much. I didn't truly know until the Eagles said it," I confess.

"And yet you gave up everything to travel to the end of the earth to find a way to free everyone, an entire kingdom, even knowing what it could mean?"

"Your point?" I choke on my words as warm, salty tears start to well in my eyes.

"Remarkable."

"Pardon?"

"You, Paege Vailenbyrg, are remarkable."

"I have not done anything that anyone else wouldn't do," I argue, and my face blushes with warmth, thawing my cheeks from the biting frosted air.

He scoffs and rolls his eyes. "That is not true." He draws a long breath in and exhales slowly "There are not many Beings out there who would do what you have done, and that, Paege, makes you remarkable."

I blink, releasing a deluge of warm tears that have puddled in my eyes. Laz lifts a hand and brushes my cheek with the back of a curled finger, catching the tears as they fall.

"Quentin. Sylas. They are both fools not to see that."

CHAPTER 43

The next three days are exactly like the last. Slow, cold, and treacherous. We don't cover much ground. We travel north, avoiding the Whispering Woods, which was the original path we would have taken had I not run off that evening.

I need to learn to keep my emotions in check, and I've tried. Gods, have I tried, but they keep simmering at the surface, and I am now certain that my damn Wolf keeps feeding off them, which is probably why I am having so much trouble keeping them under control. She doesn't want them shut away. She needs them, feeds off them like a succubus.

"Any luck with the journal?" Laz queries as we sit around the fire. Mhelodie has been researching the riddles these past few days, using her network of Witches to learn about any gaps or discrepancies in our history.

"Not yet." I stare at the journal in my lap. I haven't even brought myself to reread it yet. I think I have what those damn Eagles said to me scorched into my brain.

"When we get back to Ferinini, I will introduce you to one of the historians who helps out in the library, maybe one of them can help?"

I raise an eyebrow cocking my head to face him. "Historian? Library?"

"Paege, we are not all just brute strength. Some of us are quite intelligent as well." He chortles.

My cheeks warm. "I didn't mean—" His laughter cuts me off, and, damn, if it isn't one of the sweetest sounds I have heard in a long time. Everything has been so serious recently that I can't even remember the last time I laughed.

Back in Owenstown with Quentin and the gloves.

My heart stammers for a moment, and I shift my weight as if moving into a more comfortable position would ease the tension that just coiled itself around me.

Damn you, stupid memory.

Laz clears his throat. "The library is home to some ancient tomes and manuscripts. Even Star-Borne journals that detail accounts of wars, among other things. Maybe we will get lucky."

I raise two brows at that comment. "How? Didn't the king confiscate everything?"

"Ferinini is, as you know, concealed, but not only that, it's well guarded and warded. We have worked hard to protect what is ours."

It makes sense, now knowing what I do. The Guards were never meant to serve or protect the Wolves. They were meant to serve and protect the Fae. So, where do I stand in all of this? Why did Laz want to help and protect me when I am half Wolf and half Fae? Exhausted by all the questions, I rub my hand over the leather face of the journal. I then place it in the internal pocket of my jacket and stare idly into the flames burning brightly like the stars above.

"Are you going for a run tonight?" Out of the corner of my eyes, I see him stand and take a swig from his flask.

"Not tonight. I think I'm going to turn in shortly myself." Laz hands me the flask he just drank from, and he quietly slips away into the tent opening behind us.

Most nights, I have been unable to sleep. I've shifted into my Wolf and run through the woodlands, trying to tire myself out and heat myself up. Or that's what I have told Laz. In reality, my Wolf wants to hunt. Since our encounter with the Naga, she has wanted sweet revenge for all the wrongs done to me in my past. Its saccharine taste wreaks havoc on my senses, but for some reason, I have allowed it. I haven't fought her, but our efforts have been fruitless. The forest has been eerily empty every night, not a creature in sight. Tonight, though, Quentin's scent has been overwhelming my senses *and my emotions*, and shifting into my Wolf will only intensify things.

"Try not to keep me up with your *tossing and turning*." Laz yawns. "And don't drink too much of that stuff," he adds, motioning to the flask I am now holding. Marlow gave it to Laz before we left. He said, *"A couple of sips should warm you up and knock you out, even on the coldest of nights."* And as much as Laz says he isn't affected by the cold, he hasn't been sleeping too well without it, and it's showing. He's quieter than usual. Snappier too. In fact, he's acting very much like when I first met him. Cocky and selfish.

I stick my tongue out at him in response before sipping from the flask. I gag. "What exactly is this stuff?" I cough as the sickening liquid scalds my throat, unsettling in my stomach, and I gag again. He rolls his eyes at me and zips the tent shut. "Laz!"

"It's cold out, Paege. I'm not leaving the tent unzipped. You can unzip it when you come in," he yells through the canvas.

I stand, tucking the flask away, and I place my hands over the fire one last time, relishing the warmth it's providing, and make my way inside.

I stare at the dagger in my hands. Thick, sticky crimson liquid runs down from the blade, covering my skin, and it drips from my fingers. Blood, there is so much blood.

My eyes catch an object on the ground to my left. Not an object, a male. Guy. My brother. My twin. Blood seeps from a wound in his chest, pooling around him as he fails to breathe. I open my mouth to call for him, but nothing escapes my lips. I try to step toward him, but something snags me, and I can't move my legs. I look down and see a hand clenched around each ankle. I try to rip my legs free, but the grip is too tight, too strong. I'm pinned to the ground beneath me.

Twisting my body around, I try to see who has restrained me. The hands aren't attached to any Being. They are born from the soil, sprouting from the earth like seedlings. Old, decaying seedlings.

The earth trembles beneath me, and an unsettling force pushes through the earth. Four more hands emerge from the soil surrounding Guy, seizing his body, entwining his limbs, and securing him to the ground. I attempt to scream his name, yet my voice remains imprisoned, my pleas silenced in a surreal manifestation of helplessness.

The dagger.

I hold up the dagger into the night sky. The intricate wings around the hilt and the markings across the blade are illuminated by the reflection of the moon, and it hums as if it acknowledges my intentions. I swing the blade down, aiming for the hand wrapped around my ankle. . .

Paege.

A crack of blinding light appears in the inky darkness around me, tearing the seams apart as a gentle scratch scrapes my mind. Sharp as a talon, the scratches continue to rip into the emptying space that quickly fills my nightmare.

Paege, I need you to wake up right now. Wake up!

I stir, panting, my eyelids fluttering rapidly, unsure of what is the dream and reality.

Shh. Don't speak. I need you to open your senses up. Tell me what you feel, tell me in here.

In here? I find myself thinking in response.

Yes, in here. Open your senses now.

The panic in Laz's voice sends my heart into overdrive, and I find myself opening up. Searing heat fills my body as anger and hatred hit me like a tidal wave, flooding my soul with an oily darkness. A hunger I've only felt once before, but remember all too well, overwhelms me as a metallic taste coats my mouth, and my Wolf growls. Hunger for blood.

Can you feel them?

Yes, what's going on?

We're being surrounded. We have no time to grab our things. We need to get the horses and run. Do you understand me?

Yes.

We must flee now.

On Laz's words, I scrambled for the journal I tucked under my head and my daggers by my bedroll and crawl out of the tent. My heart is a war drum as I propel myself forward toward the horses. Lilith stomps her front feet, and Whisky jerks his head against the reins that have him tethered to the tree. The trunk groans with every pull he makes. I scoop up the saddle and hurl it across Whisky's body, frantically fastening the stirrups and buckles, ignoring the numbing pain that's slowly creeping into my fingers.

"We don't have much time!" he whisper-yells at me, doing the same. "Leave the duffel, and grab your pack and swords. That will have to do."

My stomach twists in disconcerting nausea as the metallic tang courses through my mouth. I grab my stuff per Laz's instructions. The emotions of whatever Beings are quickly approaching us seep into every corner of my mind. I clamp my mouth shut, swallowing hard and focusing on breathing through my nose.

The last time I experienced emotions like this, strong and wild, was at Lumeilia's art gallery. I was assaulted by the emotions of the Scorpions and their victims, and I could barely keep myself conscious. Quentin had to pull me to safety, but Quentin isn't here. I have to do this on my own. I have to push through, stay strong, and survive. Strangely, I never felt anything the night Guy died. I still don't understand how that is possible, but my gifts have been ever-changing and growing in recent months. If I had been comatose by the flood of emotions that night, there would have been more bodies to bury.

"Got it," I reply to Laz as I finish untethering Whisky, and I heave myself up, mounting him. He rears, and I squeeze my legs around his belly, keeping myself in the saddle.

"Let's move!"

Digging my heels into Whisky's side, we take off through the night. I reach for my Wolf, allowing my senses to shift, my sight, hearing, and smell bursting to life as she brushes against the tendril of life that connects us. The inky darkness before me transforms into a haunting palette of greys and greens, revealing intricate details of the looming trees, scattered rocks, and weathered logs. As we swiftly navigate through the woods, the once obscure shapes now emerge with newfound clarity.

I take the lead as Quentin's scent grazes my lips and gently teases my nostrils, weaving an ethereal path that guides me like a spectral whisper through the labyrinth of the night. Laz doesn't object. He must sense that I have partly shifted and now have the vision and the scent of the Wolves. Thank the Gods because we don't have time to argue. They are closing in on us. Their smell and emotions grow stronger with every moment that passes.

I try to urge Whisky to quicken his pace, but the forest floor proves slippery, and his hooves grapple to maintain steady contact. His body flinches beneath mine as he tenses his muscles, holding his ground as we manoeuvre our way through the trees. The air bites at my face as we gain speed.

He slips and neighs. Squeezing my thighs tightly, I soothe, "It's alright, boy," trying to keep him grounded, but also to keep him moving. We don't have time to falter. We are surrounded, and they are quickly gaining on us. "Laz?" I call out, my voice catching as I gasp for air.

"Keep moving, Paege. Just keep—shit!"

A cacophony of sounds grabs my attention, and I turn my head toward Laz, or where he should have been, for only a second, and that is all it takes. Whisky slides to the side, his front feet scrambling to maintain contact, but he tumbles over, and I'm thrown from the saddle. My skin stings, and my bones crack as I collide with something hard and cold.

I shake my head as I sit up, my body groaning out in pain. A rock. I landed on a rock. Lilith and Laz are still nowhere to be seen. "Laz?" I stand and limp over to Whisky, who is stomping his front foot but not galloping off. "What is it, boy?"

But then I see them, my Wolf sight honing in on two golden, marbled eyes staring at me through the trees, and my heart punches through my ribs.

Two more appear. And another two after that. Shit. Three Wolves.

I grab Whisky's reins and cautiously take an unsteady step backwards. *Shit, shit, shit.* I need to shift fully. I don't stand a chance in my Fae form against Wolves. Not against three Wolves. And I know there will be more. If I shift, I can't save my belongings, and I can't control Whisky. I need to secure him. I need to keep him safe.

I look behind me. I still can't see Laz or Lilith. Did they get attacked? Is that what I heard? No. I can't think about that. I need to keep Whisky safe. "Whisky." I gulp down the lump forming in my throat. "I love you, boy," I say, running my hand down his silken cheek. His head knocks back as he hooves the ground. He nudges me with his nose, rubbing his cheek against my chest before placing his forehead against mine. My heart bleeds. Whisky has been my best friend since I was a young child. He was gifted to me from Amerax, and we were inseparable growing up. I wish I had spent more time with him in recent years. When I left for the Neopolis, I left and didn't look back, barely visiting home, even during the holidays.

I place my hand on his cheek, closing my eyes, and breathe in his beautiful scent. Home. He smells like home. My best friend. My loyal steed. My childhood companion. Opening my eyes, I catch the Wolves slowly creeping forward, creeping toward us. They silently pad closer with eyes locked on me, and a thick oily substance slides down my spine.

"I need you to run, to save yourself," I whisper through the swollen form in my throat, my voice catching. I try to blink away the tears that fall from my eyes. I kiss his cheek and hold him closely for one more moment, but as the Wolves continue to stalk closer, I know I have no time to waste. I need to let go. I need to let *him* go. I draw in a long, unsteady breath and hold it for the longest moment. "Run!" I yell, and I push him away from me. I hit him on his rump as I leap back, and he rears again before bolting into the forest, running away from the Wolves. Running away from me.

A twig crunches behind me, and I pivot, coming face to face with three more wolves. Six fucking Wolves. I'm dead. This is no good, and Laz is still nowhere to be seen.

Snarls and snaps come from the Wolves behind me, and I pivot back to them, my heart still galloping away, chasing after Whisky. I watch as they shift their weight to their hind legs, and time seems to slow down.

Fuck. I'm dead.

Closing my eyes, I drop my pack and release my daggers to the ground. I can't take these where I am going. I will have to come back for them. Then I reach for my Wolf, and the dark shadows pounce. She takes hold of me, and I shift. Opening my eyes, I prepare myself for the assault, lowering my head to the ground, but it doesn't come. The Wolves leap straight over the top of me, and I turn to watch as they collide with the ground with such force that it pushes back the three Wolves behind me.

And time resumes.

What the fuck is going on?

The Wolves howl and snarl, canines flashing and jaws snapping. I step away from the carnage that's surely going to unfold. Flashes of Wolf bodies entwined, tumbling and rolling, clawing and shredding each other pepper my mind. I can't tell where one Wolf starts and another one ends. As the vision continues to assault me, I take another step backward, and I brush up against something warm.

Bones stiffening, I freeze like a Godsdamn statue. With twitching muscles, I slowly turn my head to face an exceptionally large white Wolf.

And its ocean blue eyes lock with mine.

Well, shit. This can't be good.

CHAPTER 44

The sheer size of the Wolf has my blood turning cold. Larger than the others, the white Wolf is at least the size Guy was. Shifting my weight to my hind legs, I attempt to run, darting to my left, but the Wolf moves at a speed I've rarely seen before and blocks me from my path. I pivot, changing my direction, but he blocks me again. No matter which way I turn, I can't pass, and I can't go back.

The Wolves behind me are still at a stand-off, snarling and snapping. Taking a couple of steps back, I prepare myself to lunge for the massive Wolf and fight my way out. It's my only option, but the Wolf surprises me when he lowers his head, bowing, and his deep ocean blue marbled eyes never leave mine. An act of submission?

"Paegence, we are not here to harm you," his deep, husky voice reverberates through my mind. "We are here to help you. Where is Lazarus?"

"Who, who are you?" I panic. Fully aware of the snaps and snarls still coming from behind me.

He raises his head, and his eyes meet mine. "My name is Keene."

"What's going on?"

"Come, we must run."

The barks and growls coming from the six Wolves behind me become more intense. Too scared to look back, I keep my focus on Keene and ask, "Are they with you?

"Yes."

"Should we help them?"

"They will be fine," he says firmly.

I don't know why, but something in the Wolf's eyes is so familiar and kind, unlike those of other Wolves. My Wolf doesn't warn me, and I take her silence as acceptance and trust. I nod in acknowledgement. "Lead the way," I say, accepting his help. "But we need to find Laz," I add.

"We will, but let's go." He steps around me. "Adriel?" he grumbles to one of the Wolves behind me.

"Take her and go!" one of the Wolves roars between snaps, and then he runs.

Following Keene, my vision adjusts to my surroundings, my movement rapidly accelerating as I turn and twist, dodging trees, jumping stumps, running to Gods know where. My torn and ratty clothing falls from my Wolf form as we move through the woodlands.

"How can I hear you talk to the other Wolves? I thought unless you're a member of the pack, you can't talk as a group," I query as we jump over a fallen tree. Landing, I notice just how slippery the forest floor is, and I am suddenly aware of what it must have been like for Whisky when we bolted. My heart pangs for having to let him go. There was no other option. It was the only way to keep him safe.

"It's different for different Wolves. It's all about intention." He jumps another fallen tree "This way," he adds as we veer to the right. "But some Wolves can communicate across packs. It's rare, but it happens."

"Where are we going?"

"Somewhere safe."

"What about Laz?" I glance around, searching for any signs of Wolves following us. For Whisky or Lilith or Laz, but there is nothing.

"I want to get you to safety first. We need to cross the stream," he says, barking another direction. "Then I'll go look for Laz, but hopefully he's there already."

"Already where?" I probe as we begin to climb out of the slushy stream and up the gulley edge. But he doesn't need to answer because as we reach the peak, the smell of burning wood envelopes my senses, and as I stare across the treetops, I spy a large clearing housing pitched tents, fire, and Wolves. Ten of them at least.

And Fae. Star-Borne.

"Who are. . ." My voice trails off softly as I gawk at the assembly in shock. Is Quentin here? Did he send for help?

"Friends. Come on," he urges, and he starts to descend.

We manoeuvre our way down the slippery slope, and when the ground flattens out, it only takes a matter of minutes to make it to the large campsite. Keene shifts to his humanoid form, and I follow his lead. He stands tall like the usual male Wolves, but his features appear softer than the others. Stubble hides his chiselled cheekbones, but I can tell they are more defined than most Wolves. His deep ocean blue eyes are soft and wise. He's older than the Wolves I have previously met.

A female with clothing draped over her arms pads over to us, flanked by three Wolves. The Wolves shift as they move. The rest remain as they were, carrying out what looks to be border patrol. The Star-Borne by the fire keep their distance, but not without throwing a few glances our way.

"What exactly is going on here? Who are you all?" I ask through chattering teeth as the cold starts seeping into my naked and exposed body. The female throws some winter leathers and boots my way before throwing clothes to the others, and I have never been more grateful.

"We are. . .friends."

"Friends," I chime in sync with Keene as I start dressing. "I know," I add. "You said that. But *who* are you?" I emphasise. They can't be Crescent Wolves as the moon is almost full.

Keene looks around at the others, running his hands over his shorn light brown hair before he starts getting changed. "We are the Shadow Walkers. Some from the alpha pack, some omegas, and back there, they were Scorpions, ordered to find and kill you."

Disappointment settles heavily in my gut as I realise Quentin isn't here to help us. Of course, he isn't. I swallow hard. "Ordered?" *By whom,* I don't ask. Keene nods. "And you're all Shadow Walkers?" I address the four Wolves who joined our huddle, who are now all fully clothed.

"We are. You also had the pleasure of meeting a couple of Dragon Hides earlier." The Wolves who held the Scorpions back while we escaped. Adriel, I had heard Keene call one of them. I hope they are safe. "I will introduce you properly when they return."

"How are you so sure they won't get hurt?" *Or killed,* I don't say.

"Paege, despite your experience with the Scorpions, we generally don't like to hurt or kill our own kind," Keene replies flatly, but his lips pull tightly, and I can't help but feel he is watching his words.

"Or others," the female mumbles.

"Ric was a loose cannon. I'm not concerned for their wellbeing." He speaks with such authority. Calm, confident, and an air of grace.

"Are you their alpha?" I enquire.

"Me?" He laughs. "Oh, no, I'm a nobody," Keene replies, shaking his head and walking over to his pack mates.

I find that hard to believe. He surely acts like one, and they all treat him like one, responding to his every command without hesitation.

The warrior-looking female with high cheekbones and a sharp nose whispers something to Keene and hands him a note. She stands proudly but not much taller than me. Dressed similarly in black leather pants and a jacket, I can tell she would be one mighty opponent in any combat, Wolf or humanoid form. Keene unfolds the note as he nods toward the group. "Paege, this is Camelia." The female who handed him the note bows her head in my direction, her long black hair falling around her face like a river of silk. "And Huntley, Tyrone, and Gunner. Shadow Walkers. The others I will introduce to you later." The three males, with similar features and hair to Camelia, bow their heads, but their dark, deep eyes, like pools of obsidian reflecting the night sky, remain laser-focused on me.

"Hi," I say awkwardly, bowing my head in response, and I am a little intimidated by all the Wolves surrounding me. I should be more than a *little* intimidated. I have been brought up to fear the Wolves, and after my past encounters with the Scorpions, I should be absolutely shitting myself. For whatever reason, I'm not. My heart rate is steady, and my Wolf is quiet.

"And the Guards?"

Keene finishes reading the note before he folds it in half and hands it back to Camelia, nodding. "Star-Borne, not Guards yet, but they are waiting for Amalyah, our only Guard, to return with Lazarus."

"You found Laz?" I ask, my voice rising a couple of octaves as excitement or happiness or something similar peaks within. Why is that name so familiar?

"Apparently so." He pivots, opening his arms as he starts to walk toward one of the large tents, gesturing for me to walk with him. "Come. You must be tired and hungry."

"Hungry? Won't the Wolves find us here? Shouldn't we be leaving?" I ask as I shuffle after him.

"It's safe here." He throws a look over his shoulder toward me, but he doesn't appear annoyed at my questions. He's more curious.

"Safe? How?"

Keene stops and pivots toward me, waiting for me to catch up. "It's safe because we are protected with concealment magic. Without a powerful Witch, no one can find us. Now, come eat."

The air wooshes out of me at that. Safe. I haven't truly felt safe in Gods knows how long. Something in Keene soothes my anxiety, and I feel an innate trust in him. He continues to the tent, and I follow. "I need to find Whisky, too," I add, falling into step beside him. Now that I know that Laz is on his way and we are safe, I need to track him and bring him back.

"I'll send one of the others out to find him. Right now, stay put. It is not safe out there for you." His gait is long, and I have to take two steps for every one of his to keep up. When we reach the tent, he opens the canvas door and turns to address the Wolf with thick tribal tattoos that I'm assuming cover a lot of his warm, earthy-hued skin, due to the markings on both his hands and neck up to his jawline. A Wolf who moved so stealthily that I didn't even realise he was following closely behind. "Huntley, can you track the horse?"

"On it, Thorn." The Wolf nods and runs off, shifting seamlessly into a massive golden-brown Wolf, one that would rival Keene's. His thick coat glistens under the moonlight with the same earthy hues of his skin as he pounces toward the end of the clearing. I will never get used to seeing that.

"Thorn? I thought your name was Keene?" I question, as I duck my head and enter an enormous space. Aromas of bread, spices, and herbs caress me, and my sandpaper mouth fills with saliva. It appears to be a magical tent that looks much smaller on the outside than on the inside. I still don't quite believe him that he is *no one*. These Wolves follow his commands without question as if he's their leader. But if he's not an alpha, then a leader of what?

Keene smiles, revealing a gold canine. "My name is Keene Thornsten, but my father called me Thorn, and it seems to have stuck." He ushers me toward the long table in the middle of the room that's topped with an array of foods, and I take a seat in front of a large bowl of meaty stew, some bread, and what appears to be a steaming pot of herbal tea.

Keene must think I haven't eaten in months with the way I inhale the food. He watches silently while I devour two bowls of stew and a few pieces of bread. After I finish, he pours me a cup of herbal tea, a blend that's oddly familiar and reminds me of home, of my mother, and we exit the tent and make our way over to the fire. The Star-Borne who were circling the pit are now nowhere to be seen. Keene sits on one of the camp chairs and crosses a leg over a knee while motioning to me to sit and join him.

Instead, I ask the one question I've been wanting an answer to since the moment I met him. "So, are you going to tell me what all this is?"

Keene opens his mouth to speak, but someone else answers for him.

"All what is?"

CHAPTER 45

Hearing his voice before I see him has my heart swelling like the ocean tide, filling my frigid body with a familiar warmth. I pivot to find myself facing one of my favourite Beings in the world. He stands a few steps away with a giant, amused smile on his beautiful face, hands on his hips, and his wings tucked away. His long, silvery hair is pulled back, and his dark violet eyes are wide and full of mischief.

Asheron.

And standing next to him is a female Guard who looks all too similar to him, but she has soft lavender streaks through her hair. My hands splay, the mug dropping from my grip, and I pounce at him, draping myself around his body as best I can.

"Whoa there, firecracker," Asheron chuckles as he wraps his arms around me, and I bury my head into his chest.

"What? How? What?" I ask, unable to string a coherent sentence together.

"All great questions," another familiar but rough voice from behind Asheron mocks, then chuckles, and my heart goes crazy in its cage. My Wolf howls in relief.

I peer around Asheron's giant body to see Laz standing there, dishevelled and muddy with a few scratches on his face but otherwise unharmed.

Thank the Gods.

Amber eyes lock with mine, and he smiles slightly. He holds my pack and my two daggers. *He went back for me.* My cheeks rise, tugging my lips upwards, and he holds my gaze with an unfaltering smile. After a long moment, Asheron clears his throat, pulling my attention away from Laz and back to him.

"I can't believe you're here," I squeal to Asheron as I bury my head in his chest once more. When I finally pull myself away, I realise Laz and Keene have joined our huddle. The female speaks, addressing me, her voice soft yet firm, a lot like her features. "I'm Amalyah Millenford, Asheron's cousin. You must be the infamous Paege I keep hearing about." She smiles warmly.

Now I know why her name was so familiar. She's Asheron's Star-Borne cousin, which explains the similarities. Their Star-Borne lineage comes from his father's side. Her mother and his father were siblings. Though she was activated many years before I met him.

"I've heard a lot about you, too. It's good to finally meet you," I softly reply with a smile.

"I wouldn't believe everything he tells you, unless of course it's about how amazing I am," she hoots, matching Asheron's ego, and winks, just like I have seen Asheron do on too many occasions. They could be twins.

Asheron rolls his eyes at her. "I'm sure you've got a hundred questions, but we still have quite a few hours before the sun comes up. How about you try to get some sleep, and we can catch up tomorrow. You're bunking with Amalyah tonight. Lazarus will bunk with us."

Us?

I open my mouth to object. I've gotten used to spending my nights with Laz, but snap my lips shut as I wonder how that might sound to Asheron. To Laz. To the rest. I certainly don't know how it sounds to me.

Friends.

I nod. Still, a gravitational pull has me slowly stepping toward Laz. At the very least, I have to make sure he's alright. Amalyah darts a look toward Laz, loops her arm through mine, smiling gracefully, and ushers me away before I can reach him. Our eyes connect once more, and he seems to say, *I'm alright, Paege. Go, I will see you in the morning.*

"Come on, let's get some sleep." Amalyah pulls me to a smaller tent than the one I was just in, but still larger than the ones I've been living in this past month.

"You're safe here, Paege," Keene calls out after me. "The Wolves will continue to patrol tonight. Try to rest, and we will sit down and talk in the morning."

I find Laz sitting by the fire, alone, when I rise. "Couldn't sleep either?" I murmur as I sit in the empty chair beside him.

I wasn't sure if I meant it as a question or a statement. Regardless, Laz replies as he leans back, stretching his legs and crossing an ankle over another. "No." And although he says he hasn't got much sleep, he looks refreshed. Rested. His face and hair are cleaned from the night before.

The moon still graces the night sky, but it won't be too long before the sun begins to show her face. Besides the five Wolves who are still patrolling the border, not another Being appears to be awake. "Do you know if Whisky or Lilith were found?" I whisper, unsure if I want the answer.

"Paege. . ." Laz breaks off, his voice cracking as he closes his eyes, "I'm sorry." I don't need to know his answer; it seeps from him. Even though he's shielding himself, the coppery metallic taste of death still fills my mouth. "She saved my life. She. . ."

"Lilith?" I interrupt as my chest collapses in relief. Not Whisky, but Lilith. Whisky could still be out there.

"Yes," he confirms softly.

An instinct to reach for him tugs at my insides, but I resist. "How? You could have just flown away?"

"I wasn't going to leave her, but she. . ." His throat bobs, "She sacrificed herself."

His words sting me like a scorpion's tail. He could have saved himself, but he stayed for her. Lilith, his loyal steed this past month alone, meant enough to him not to abandon her.

I, however, selfishly sent Whisky, my best friend since I was a young Fae, on his way. I tried to tell myself that it was to save his life. But was it really? Was it just to save my own?

Shame.

As if Laz is reading my mind, he adds, "You didn't have a choice but to set him free, Paege. You would have died if you didn't. You both would have. You probably saved his life."

But his words don't lift the heaviness that presses on my chest.

Dirty, muddy, shame.

I swallow down the thickness rising in my throat and try to push away the thought about Whisky roaming the woods alone, with the Scorpions out for blood.

"What *is* all this? And how does Asheron know the Wolves?"

"Asheron doesn't. Amalyah does. I'm guessing she told him." Laz doesn't look my way when he speaks. His eyes focus intently on the fire in front of us.

"And the Wolves?"

He turns to face me. "They are old friends of the Guards, but I didn't know they were looking for us, and I didn't know Amalyah would be with them."

"How did they find us?"

"I believe Marlow got word the Scorpions were looking for us, and he alerted the Wolves."

"Us? As in you and me?"

"I don't know—Shh," he hisses, sitting forward in his chair.

"Shh?" I retort.

"Bloody Hels, be quiet," he whisper-yells, looking around and reaching into his sheaths and pulling out two daggers. My two daggers. "Here," he says, handing them to me while still scanning the area.

I take them, and I glance my eyes around the border. The Wolves patrolling are nowhere to be seen, and a chill snakes down my spine. "Laz?" My voice shakes as a familiar discomfort washes over me, and my Wolf stirs. A tussle from behind makes me jump up and pivot around. Asheron and Amalyah are bounding towards us, weapons drawn.

"Laz, get Paege out of here now!" Asheron demands.

"I can—" Amalyah starts, but Laz interrupts.

"No, I got it. You stay with Asheron and the Wolves." Her eyes widen, and she opens her mouth as if she's going to object again, but I think something in Laz's glare has her closing her mouth, and she nods. She darts her eyes between the two of us and nods once more as if understanding something I can't quite tell.

My Wolf is alert and restless under my skin, and no matter what they think is going to happen, I know I'm not leaving without my friends. I dig my heels in and cross my arms "I'm staying. Whatever it is, I can handle it," I say to both Asheron and Laz.

"The wards are down. They found us." Out of breath, Keene rushes toward us with Huntley, Tyrone, and Gunner flanked at his sides, and my blood runs cold. They meet us with a few hurried strides, and Keene places a friendly hand on Laz's shoulder, the three wolves taking up a defensive stance around us. "Take her. We've got this," he adds, and Laz and Asheron nod as if not one of them heard me.

"I said I'm staying to fight," I repeat, clipping my words, annoyed at the blatant disregard of my offer to help, my need to help.

Huntly shoots a look my way with a raised brow and a smile that almost says, *"This should be good."* But Keene replies, "No, you're going home, Paegence. We came here to help you, but we also need to end this. We have this."

"But. . ." The drumming in my ears intensifies, and my fingernails dig into my sweating palms.

"No, listen. You need to get back home. You have other priorities to worry about. We need you to. . ."

"We will," Laz interrupts, grabbing my arm.

My head spins. Do they know? Do they know about the Eagles? The prophecy? The curse? How? How many others know?

How?

A roar, followed by a howl, interrupts all of us.

Close. . .So close.

"Come on." Laz grabs me by the arm. "Let's go."

A crash.

I inhale.

Another howl.

I hold it.

Then a pack of Wolves smash through the wooded area. Laz pulls me away from the pack careening for our group, and my body cries out as we tumble to the hard ground, and I drop my daggers in the fall. "I can shift. I can fight!" I scream at him, ignoring the pain shooting up my body as I twist and turn, trying to escape his strong hold as he tries to wrap his wings around me in protection.

"Let go of me," I demand. Partially shifting, I dig my claws into his arm.

"Fucking Hels," he bellows and releases me. "What the fuck was that?"

I retract my claws and crawl away from him. "I can fight," I pant as I try to regain my breath. Standing, my bones fill with lead, and the world slows down. I pin my feet to the ground and watch in horror as the three wolves I met in the forest, plus two others, stand off with Asheron, Amalyah, Huntly, Tyrone, and Keene.

Gunner has peeled off from the pack in a slow-motion sprint toward a large winding tree behind them to the left. I watch, my eyes widening, as he steps up the side of the thick trunk and twists his body. His muscles ripple as he pushes off from the trunk and shifts midair, his clothes ripping from his body to reveal the beast inside. Flying toward the Scorpions, he lands with precision on top of one of the Wolves, and time resumes.

And all Hels breaks loose.

Another roar, different from the others, has me spinning around again to see a group of large and muscular Lupa-Centaurs with coats of various colours galloping our way, led by none other than Perrin. All of them wear leather and metal armour and carry swords and daggers and shields. Every one of them has murder in their eyes.

Carnage unfolds from all angles. The Wolves that had been patrolling during the night barrel into the clearing after the Lupa-Centaurs. I blink, and Amalyah appears in front of me. She drops my pack and swords at my feet and winks. She nods at Laz and pivots to the Lupa-Centaurs, pulling her own sword from its sheath and shuffling her feet, preparing her stance, ready to fight. My Gods, she's a badass. Out of the corner of my eye, I see Keene and Camelia shift and lunge for us, also placing themselves between us and the five Lupa-Centaurs.

A hand gently grabs my shoulder, and I step back into it. Everything inside me says to stay—to shift and fight. But when I look for my Wolf, I can't see her. It's as if she's telling me we have more important things to do, and she's right. I may be the only hope at saving this kingdom, breaking it free from the curse that blinds it from the truth. If I stay and fight, I could die. Then what? All the species of Elyndria are doomed to live under the thumb of King Ishaan of the Crescent Wolf pack.

But I'm not going anywhere. So, if it's Braxtion blood it needs, then I have to survive this.

CHAPTER 46

Amalyah blinks again, disappearing and appearing behind the pack of Lupa-Centaurs. Their focus shifts, jolting and turning for a moment while they process what just happened, and it gives me enough time to reach and take hold of the ivory hilts by my feet, pulling my swords from their sheaths.

"We're staying?" Laz asks casually.

"We're staying," I confirm sharply, grabbing my daggers and swords. "Don't try—"

"I wasn't going to."

"Good. I have to survive, but I also have to fight. I have to help," I say with my daggers sheathed and my swords at the ready.

"I know you do, and you will." He smiles with that comment and then steps into the fray. The fact that the Lupa-Centaurs are here with the Scorpions solidifies everything I believe to be true.

The king wants me dead. Quentin's father wants me dead.

An odd satisfaction crawls its way through my body as I realise I was right all along, but that feeling is short-lived as the campsite erupts like a volcano coming to life—or really, bringing death.

The eerie Dead Forest is transformed into a battlefield, living up to its name in every sense of the word as the two sides clash in a fierce and bloody fight. Perrin and the Lupa-Centaurs charge at us, their swords gleaming in the moonlight. Time around us seems to slow once again as Laz and I meet them, flanked by Camelia and Keene. Amalyah takes them on from behind. The clashing of steel echoes through the forest. At a glance, I notice the other Star-borne and Shadow Walkers taking on the pack of Scorpions like a legion of graceful and loyal warriors.

I partially shift, hoping my Wolf strength, speed, and agility give me an advantage to survive this. And my canines? I don't know what venom I possess or what Wolf pack I belong to, but I suppose now is a good a time as any to learn. Every little bit of help counts.

Laz moves swiftly, as if he's defying the very essence of time, taking aim at Perrin with raised arms as he brings his sword down, and time resumes. Perrin shields, but not quickly enough, and Laz slices through his arm, staining the ground with blood. The Lupa-Centaur rears, kicking his front feet at Laz and forcing him to retreat a few steps. At the same time, I step forward, swinging my swords across my body, slicing through skin and muscle and tendon and bone of the Lupa-Centaur in front of me. Steel clangs, and my body jolts as the swords collide, separating its head from its body. My heart writhes and bile rises, burning the back of my throat as a warm sticky mist sprays at my face. Now isn't the time to let my emotions consume me, so I swallow it down, pushing aside my need to mourn for the life I just took. *Three.*

The air around us continues to fill with the sounds of metal clashing, snarls, and cries. To my right, the Scorpions and Shadow Walkers fight with pure ferocity. They have all shifted into their Wolf forms and are tearing through each other, their teeth and claws ripping flesh and bone. The Star-Borne use their Fae magics, strength, speed, and superior fighting skills to protect the Shadow Walkers at any cost. I turn to find myself facing a Scorpion in his humanoid form. His lip pulls upward, revealing an elongated canine, and my body shudders. I raise my sword, preparing myself for his attack.

Circling each other, I wait for an opening. I don't know my opponent, his strengths, or his weaknesses, but one thing Amerax always taught me when fighting is to be patient. *Watch and observe. They will always show you their flaws eventually. Just be patient.*

I draw in a long breath, trying to stop the hammering in my chest. He snarls, narrowing his eyes, but I don't taunt or tease him. I keep my face as neutral as I can. I focus solely on watching him, hunting my prey like the Wolf I am.

And just like Amerax said, he shows his cards. As if he were sick of waiting, he charges, dropping his arms and moving them sloppily as he runs for me. This is my moment. I pre-empt his attack, ducking out of the way and swinging my sword around to connect with his. The collision sends a jarring twinge up my arms, but I dig my feet into the ground, holding myself in place. My Wolf strength rivals his.

He pulls away, dropping my sword slightly, and he charges again. I meet his movement once more, and our swords clash with a deafening ring. Again, he lunges. I parry and riposte, my movements fast and precise. I keep my reflexes sharp and agile as he attacks again and again and again. Every attack is weaker than the last. He is tired, and each time I strike back with force and finesse, my silver blade flashing in the moonlight as it slices through the air.

Ducking his next swing, I slip. The world tilts around me as I tumble backward, tripping over a...I scramble to stand when a sticky wetness slicks under my legs. I pull my hand up, and my stomach churns violently and heaves into my chest.

I gasp. An arm. I tripped over an arm.

Discarding the body part and trying to keep the bile from making its way into my mouth, I grab for my fallen sword and move to stand.

"I wouldn't do that if I were you," the gravelly voice says. Fear, thick and oily, slides between my ribs, drowning me from the inside, and my lungs are rendered immobilised. "It'd be a damn shame for you to lose that pretty head." Slowly lifting said pretty head, my eyes meet those of my Scorpion opponent. He stands over me, glaring with disgust as if I'm nothing more than an insect that has infested his meal. "It's my lucky day, isn't it, darlin'?" He smiles, and his words crawl through me like a spider, his voice reminding me of Ric's.

The Wolf that killed Guy.

The Wolf that I killed.

He reaches for me, moving fast and precise, and I flinch, thinking he's going for my throat. Instead, he grabs my braid that's hanging over my shoulder and yanks me toward him, spinning me around and dragging me backwards. My scalp cries out in pain, and I thrash my legs to escape his strong hold, but it's no use. I strain my eyes to his face, and one side of his lips arcs upward in an evil wolfish grin, revealing an elongated canine. He swings his sword down, and my body squeezes itself in response. I close my eyes and wait for the impact.

I'm down.

I'm done.

And there is nothing I can do.

My body jolts as tears escape through my pressed lids. The sound of metal cuts through the air, and a brush of wind caresses my cheeks. The tension suddenly leaves my scalp, and I fall backwards, my body screaming as I hit the cold, hard ground. I hesitantly peel my eyes open, and he stands there holding my braid in his hand.

He cut my hair. My hair!

"Thanks for the souvenir, sweetheart," he sniggers.

Fire erupts in my belly, but it's short-lived. He lifts his sword once more, and this time, I'm sure he's going for a death blow. Frantically, I dart my eyes around, trying to see where Laz is. Where Keene is. Where anyone is. They are all busy fighting for their own lives.

This can't be it. This can't be how it ends.

My breathing quickens.

"They say revenge is sweet, and aren't you just the sweetest?" The Scorpion raises his sword for his final strike. I should have listened to them. I should have left when I had the chance. It's my blood that breaks the curse. I know that now. The king wouldn't be trying to kill me if it weren't. If I die here tonight, they are all doomed to live in this false reality for the False King, and it all would have been for nothing.

I have failed them all.

I should have left.

I draw in a ragged breath and hold it. Squeezing my eyes shut, I wait for the impact of his sword.

Please let it be quick. Let it be painless.

A cacophony of sounds snaps my eyes open just in time to witness one of the Shadow Walkers crashing into the Scorpion, hurling him meters out of the way from me and saving me from my end.

No. Not a Shadow Walker.

A Dragon Hide.

Its pewter armoured scales shimmer under the moonlight and pull me into a hypnotic state as it stares at me while pinning the Scorpion's thrashing humanoid body to the ground. The Wolf nods subtly to me before ripping the throat out of the Scorpion and pouncing off to join another fight, leaving the dying Wolf, eyes wide and unblinking, to gurgle and spit blood with every slowing beat of his heart. The sound of ripping and tearing flesh echoes through my ears, sending shivers across my body.

Breathe, Paege. Just fucking breathe.

Standing on wobbly legs, I notice two other lifeless bodies on the ground nearby, one Wolf and one Fae, as a thick pool of blood and gore expands around them. I can't focus on them. I don't want to know who it is, but my heart twinges as I think about the deaths that have already befallen because of me.

No. Not because of me. Because of the king.

My fury erupts deep inside, and I scream as I push forward, completely unleashed, careening into the carnage, blades swinging without regard. I lunge for another one of the Scorpion Wolves in his humanoid form that's joined the Lupa-Centaurs, my swords slashing through the air. The Wolf parries with a flicker of light. His movements are swift and fluid, and he swipes up a fallen sword from the ground. As he rises, he counters with a thrust of his own, aiming for my heart. His eyes narrow, glowing yellow with rage as my body moves, jumping backward, and I arc my torso to avoid being impaled by steel. A snarl escapes my lips as bloodlust rises, urging me to drop my swords and wholly shift into my Wolf form and tear the Wolf apart.

He thrusts again, swinging the sword, and I jump back again, but this time, I'm not fast enough. The sword rips through air and leather and skin, and the cold bite of metal slices through my torso.

Tears sting my eyes as the taste of copper coats my mouth. I look down, dropping my swords, before bringing my hands up to my belly, pressing against my jacket and now exposed skin. The burning spreads across my stomach and into my back. I pull my hands away to find them covered in blood.

Mine?

Others?

Both.

Shit, what do I do? What do I do?

Keene appears at my side, clothes torn and bloodied. He pushes me back, and I stumble a few steps behind him, jolting me out of my paralysed state. A wicked smile appears on his face, his golden canine glistening. He whispers a word to me, but it's one I can't decipher over the blood rushing through my ears. Pushing his hands forward, a blast of wind hits the Wolf, knocking him off balance and giving Keene time to lunge forward and shift mid-air and attack. I watch in horror and awe as Keene tears through the Wolf's humanoid body. He shreds skin and flesh and muscle, ripping him apart limb by limb. Bile rises in my throat with every bite he takes as the sounds of crunching bones fill my ears.

Searching for my friends, I scan the campsite that is now a graveyard with the stench of death filling the air. The heat in my belly grows as the warm liquid quietly falls from my open wound to the ground that's already heavily painted with blood and other bodily fluids. Asheron stands surrounded by three Wolves, and more are appearing. I open my mouth as a Wolf appears to lunge for him, but before I manage to get the scream out, time slows once more. I blink, and Amalyah appears next to him. She takes him by the hand, and they disappear. Time resumes as she appears with Laz next to me. Asheron is nowhere to be seen.

"Paege, we need to. . ." Laz pauses as he faces me. His eyes roam over my body, stopping on my stomach wound. "Paege?" He moves fast, scooping his arm behind me just as the world begins to tilt and turn around me.

Falling into him, tears escape my eyes. "Hi, friend," I whisper, my voice cracking as I try to force a smile.

"There are too many," Amalyah yells as Laz and I slowly descend to the slick crimson coloured ground.

"Where's Asheron? Is he alright?" I murmur as the burning intensifies, and dark clouds start to obstruct my vision.

"He's safe back in Ferinini." She turns to face Laz. "Laz, I can take her to a healer and come back for you." She reaches for him, but he rolls his shoulder out of her reach, not taking his inferno eyes off me, off my searing wound.

My breathing shallows as I fight the urge to fall into the lulling sleep that's drawing me in. Calling for me like a Water Siren in the Blethen sea. *Is this what it felt like for Guy when he died?* I thought when you die, your life was supposed to flash before your eyes, but I don't see anything. I don't even have a stray thought. I would have hoped to see Guy, but even he hasn't come to see me.

Well, this is disappointing.

"I've got her. She'll be alright. She'll heal. She's a. . ." He swallows. "They need you. You need to stay here and help. Get the others out." Amalyah nods.

"Laz?" I moan, the dark clouds growing darker and thicker.

"It's alright, little wolf." A warm smile crinkles his eyes, unlike one I've seen him wear, and my heart tries to swell in the tightening cage as I drift further toward the darkness.

Lifting my bloody, shaking hand up to his face, I run a curled index finger across his cheek. "Is that a tear?" I cough. "I thought you said I would be alright?"

"You are going to be alright. I will get you out of here. I promise."

Before the darkness wins, my heavy eyes snap wide open for just a moment. A shimmer of silver rips through the air. I blink, unleashing a deluge of tears that stream down my face. Tears not shed for myself or my own impending death.

The tears fall because I know that's a promise Laz won't be able to keep.

CHAPTER 47

Unknown

Lightning cracked across the sky, the creatures hot on his tail. Dusk was still upon him. This place between places never relented.

When he first saw them, they were tiny dots lined along the horizon. Tiny black specs that blotted his vision yet multiplied with every blink. At first, he was unsure what he was seeing. It was unreal. He was sure of it until they moved toward him. They moved fast, despite the distance between them, and it was only hours before they were upon him. But for some strange reason, they never fully gained on him. Regardless, they were close enough for him to see the horror that chased him through these lands. Their eyes were as crimson as blood. Their canines were longer and sharper than his own. Bones protruded through their scaly, grey skin, and, Gods, they stank. It was the stench of death that one could come back from. This would be a permanent, unending death.

Grunts and snarls filled his ears as he bound across the barren lands, but it was their rot that grew more rancid as they gained on him that made his stomach turn. Heavy thumping filled his chest. He knew his time was almost up. Hours, days, weeks, months. He pressed on and on, but these things, these creatures, they would catch him eventually. If he were lucky, they would kill him, but he had a feeling that what they would do to him if they ever caught him would be so much worse than death.

Distance and time moved differently here. That much he had figured out. Still, after Gods knows how long, he never made any progress on closing the distance between him and the mocking safety of the mountain ranges, no matter how fast or how long he ran.

So, he abandoned his plan to find refuge in the mountains and headed west, unsure if that was the best choice, but it was the only one. The creatures originally came at him from the east, but now trailed from the south, too. So, yes, west. He headed west.

One thing did change. Unlike before, no matter how much he ran from these creatures, the reset never came. He prayed to the Gods—if the Gods could hear him here—that he would be forced into that unconsciousness. Forced into that slumber that would usually reset this world and rest his body so he would be safe for another day. That reset never came, and exhaustion pressed against him. His body ached from attempting to sprint through the shifting sand beneath him. The wind whipped the sharp grains around him, and they bit into his skin like tiny shards of glass.

Run faster, run harder, he told himself over and over again. That voice inside his head was his only tether to sanity. But maybe it wasn't. He wasn't even sure whose it was. It was not his own. That much he knew.

Green eyes brimmed with silver tears.

A Wolf.

A sword.

A girl.

A scream.

The screech, like that of a banshee, carried across the winds. He had heard that sound before, but this time, it felt closer. Angrier. He wasn't sure what that sound truly was, but it usually accompanied the electrical storm that rolled through every so often.

The sound of war drums beat heavily around him. The sound encapsulated him as he moved through it, reverberating through his bones.

Then he saw it. No, it couldn't be. His eyes widened as he slowed his pace for a single step. He had to use all his willpower not to stop dead in his tracks because those creatures were still on his heels, but what he saw in the distance brought tears to his dry and tired eyes.

Trees. Shade. Safety. Where had it come from? He rubbed at his eyelids to erase the deception appearing before him. A cruel joke. The Gods heard him and were playing a cruel joke on him. He rubbed his eyes again, the grains of sand pulling tears as they scratched his corneas. When he opened them. . .it was still there.

Yes, he had finally gone insane.

The sparse woodland drew nearer. His lungs pumped more air the closer he got to it, as if breathing in the life he had been missing these last few months. The forest's edge was so close now, and he somehow knew this was his salvation. One hundred lengths. Eighty.

He was hurt. His body, his heart, and his soul were tired. But his body still moved, his heart still beat, and still, he pressed on. Fifty lengths. Not much further. The muscles in his legs burned as his blood pumped the adrenaline flooding his body to propel him forward. In some ways, he had never felt more alive than in that moment. Which was concerning because he knew he was. . .he plummeted into darkness as another screech filled his ears, his teeth watering from the sound.

Keep running, that voice urged.

Thirty lengths.

Then the world went bright as the summer sun, and an intense heat licked at his heels. His feet fumbled as he leapt forward. The heavy thumping of his heart thrummed harder. It drummed across the skies.

Across the skies. . .

He looked up, and his dreary eyes widened. The sky was blanketed with winged beasts. Oh, Gods, he knew he was so royally fucked. And he knew why as one of them breathed fire.

Shit, shit, shit.

He squeezed his eyes closed and drew every bit of life he had within him to find the power to make it.

Twenty lengths.

Ten.

He dove, unsure how the Hels these sparse trees would save him from the gnarly creatures or the flying beasts of fire. But he squeezed his burning eyes shut, gulped down air, and dove.

And when he landed, the world went black.

Chapter 48

"Hi, friend," I whisper, as I fall into his arms.

He sits next to the crimson-coloured river that flows past us, and he gently pulls me in his lap. "Paege, what happened?" The sky cracks and roars as it violently lights up around us.

"Did you see him? He's here." I cough. My eyes dart between the warping and twisting trees that seem to have eyes of their own.

"Who is?" he whispers as he brushes a sticky strand of hair off my face, a redundant thing to do, considering.

"He is." His name is right there on my tongue. Why can't I remember it? I cough again. My stomach itches. The drying scab is being picked apart by the insects' relentless sandpaper feet, scratching at my skin. Black and red fluid oozes from the opening wound.

"Shh, it's alright, little wolf. I'm going to get you out of here."

"What's happening? Why can't I remember his name?" My breathing shallows as I fight the urge to crawl into the crimson river, the rapids calling out my name with every clash of the swords echoing through the forest.

He answers. My brows furrow as I try to focus on the words coming out of his mouth, but someone turned down the volume.

"Don't leave me," I beg as tears start to fall from my eyes, and the sky opens above us.

"It's alright, Paege." He smiles. "I'm not going anywhere."

Lifting his hand, he runs a curled index finger across my cheek. "Is that a tear?" I cough. "I thought you said you would be alright?"

"I am going to be alright. You will get me out of here. You promised." He smiles.

A silver rips through the air, opening a rift between time and space. Laz's lips slowly curl upwards, and he calls my name again and again. And again.

"Paege?" He winks. "Paege?" Metal meets flesh. "Paege?"

Gasping for breath, I jolt upright, ripping my lids open to see Asheron's big violet eyes staring down at me. "Paege," he says. "You're alright. It was just a dream. You're safe."

My chest still heaving, I fall back into my pillows, squeezing my lids closed, and run my hands through my hair, my fingers weaving through strands for only a moment before falling through the air. I keep forgetting my damn hair was cut off.

"How are you feeling? Are you alright? Will you be ready for today?" He probes gently as he sits on the side of the bed next to me. Asheron has been sneaking into my room every night since we got back to check on me, sometimes falling asleep in the armchair by the fire. By the looks of things, last night was one of those nights.

"No," I answer meekly, forcing a fake smile to appear on my face. How can I ever be ready for this?

But he saved my life. They all did. The least I can do is honour them. No matter how hard it is. I was one of the lucky ones.

So much death.

So much carnage.

For what?

And Quentin sits idly by while his father recklessly and continually kills innocent Beings. Blood rushes to my ears.

"I know it's going to be tough, but we're all going to be there with you." He rests his hand on mine and squeezes it gently. "Can I get you anything? Coffee, breakfast?"

Nodding, I mouth, *"Coffee,"* and Asheron smiles widely and leaves the room. A male with a mission.

I'm back in Ferinini. The bedroom I'm staying in is below the one I stayed in with Quentin when we last visited here. It's a replica, and it brings back too many memories, but it's the only one available. I grab my scribe from the nightstand and peel myself from my warm bed, walking to the window that overlooks the ravine. I pull the blinds back to reveal a fresh dusting of snow from overnight. Snow has fallen every night in Ferinini since I got here, and it looks even more magical than when I was here last.

No new messages. My heart pangs. I haven't heard from Quentin since he left us in Owenstown. I don't know why I thought I would have. I don't know what I expected at all, but I suppose I expected more than absolute silence. Especially today. Surely, he would have heard of the attacks. The Guards have been talking about it nonstop. Likely because of Laz.

He wasn't supposed to be there.

He wasn't supposed to be with me.

Salty tears sting my eyes.

One, two, three knocks on the door pull my attention back to the present. I slide the scribe into my fleecy pant pocket and head for the door. Without asking who it is, I swing it open, and the chill of the winter air bites at my cheeks, but my heart swells, filling my body with warmth as I am greeted by a familiar face. I fall forward and wrap my arms around him, squeezing him tightly. Gods, I missed him so much.

"Pumpkin, how are you feeling today?"

"Hi, Dad. I'm alright. Better. Have you heard from Mum yet?" I ask eagerly.

"She is back at the academy, dealing with the twins. I am here, though."

"Can't she just leave the academy to deal with them?"

"I'm sure she will be here before you know it." He squeezes me tighter against his chest, his heart is beating so loud and fast that I can feel it underneath the layers of all his clothes.

"I know. I just haven't heard from her in so long. It's not like her." I pull myself away from him and look up to his face. His eyes are duller and darker than usual. I can tell he hasn't been sleeping. He misses Mum, too. They are used to spending a lot of time apart, with Amerax being a Guard, but it never gets easier for them.

"You're being paranoid, Paege. Too much adventure in one's life will do that to you. Trust me." He smiles and pats the top of my head as he strolls past me into the warm room. "I'm liking the new hair, by the way," Dad says as I close the door and follow him into the room. He nods at the armchair. "Did Asheron sleep here again last night?"

I nod. "Can you tell him I don't need a babysitter, please? He won't listen to me."

"He's just worried, Paege. We all are." Not worried enough for my mother to return. I'm starting to think she's avoiding me. Maybe the guilt of all the secrets and lies has been eating at her, and she can't stomach the idea of facing me. I thought our bond was stronger than that, but I also never thought she would hide something so tremendous.

"I'm fine. I promise" I place my hand on my heart and smile. "Plus, I'm all healed up."

When I first woke after being transported out by Amalyah, I was already healing. It was a deep wound, and according to the healer, if it were any other being, they would have died. Apparently, my Wolf managed to heal my body while I slept. All that remains is a slight scar across my stomach.

Another scar to add to the quickly growing list of them.

"It's not the physical injuries he's worried about, Pumpkin. It's the other ones. The ones you can't see." By the way my dad is looking at me, this isn't an argument I'm going to win with anyone.

I harrumph and fall back onto the bed. "Fine," I murmur sarcastically.

Amalyah blinks us all into the ceremonial amphitheatre nestled among the ancient trees of the forest. The pyre is a towering pile of wood adorned with carved pillars that hold the bodies of the fallen, and it stands in the centre surrounded by a ring of stones and crystals etched with intricate carvings. Standing by the pyre, watching the flames grow higher, I can't stop the tears that keep escaping from my eyes.

I scan the faces of friends and family as they gather closer for their farewell. We honour all the fallen today, but I feel like a traitor. An imposter. If it wasn't for me, none of them would have been in the Dead Forest, and Laz and the others would never have had to fight those dishonourable Beings. But that is who they are. They believed in the mission to free the kingdom so much that they died protecting me. They died heroes. They deserve this and more.

The air fills with silence as the incense and herbs are lit, removing the acrid smell of death and replacing it with something lighter. Something freeing. I take this opportunity to break away from the group to stand alone in my grief and gratitude, leaving my dad with the others. Placing my hand on my heart, I find my charm and zip around the chain in anxious movements. The electricity in the air today must be thick from all the power congregated in such a small space, as the static from the charm zaps me.

I haven't seen Keene. I half expected him to be officiating this thing. I'm sure he's around somewhere. I want to talk to him more. After the attack, he joined us in Ferinini, and we talked about what he knows. What they all know. I had no idea there was a whole group of Beings out there that knew the truth about the kingdom's curse. It feels nice to not be alone in this.

But I am alone in this. Because at the end of the day, I am the one who must die to end this all. Not them. I don't think any of them know that, though. I haven't shared what we learnt from the Eagles. Laz and I had decided not to tell anyone anything until we knew for sure what it all meant. Well, no one except for Mhelodie, which likely means Lumeilia and Sydney, too.

A familiar scent of leather and sweet clove snakes itself around me, gently caressing my senses, and my heart skips as warmth envelopes my hand. Tears sting my eyes as his arm brushes up against my shoulder, his bronze fingers lacing with mine. "I wasn't sure when I would see you again," I whisper hoarsely, my words catching as I try to hold back a sob. My eyes stay focused on the pyre as the chanting and blessings begin.

"You need to have more faith in me," he responds huskily, his voice hugging me like silk sheets.

"But you were taken by the Lupa-Centaurs, and Dad said you'd be charged with abandoning your post."

"I told you, little wolf. I do what I want when I want, and I answer to no one." The smirk in his voice triggers something inside me. I pivot and wrap myself around him, burying my head into his body. A sob cracks from my chest as the salty water breaks from the dams in my eyes.

Laz. It's only been a week, but his absence has left a gaping hole in my life. In my heart. "I thought you weren't coming back," I mumble into his chest.

"Paege, I . . ." He wraps his arms around me and squeezes me tightly as he pulls me into his body. "Oh shit, your wound. Are you alright?" he asks, pulling himself back from me, his amber eyes roving over every inch of me.

"I'm fine. I'm completely healed. See?" I lift my heavy knit jumper to show him my torso and my scar. His eyes flare, his amber irises dancing with the fire of the pyre, and my cheeks blush with warmth as I realise I just showed him my bare stomach.

Damn it, Paege!

I pull my knitted tunic back down and tilt my head so my eyes catch his. He reaches for my face, and I brace myself for his touch against my cheek, but instead, he pulls a piece of my chopped hair out from behind my ear, twisting it between his fingers. "I love it." He smiles. "So much more fitting for a badass hybrid warrior."

Warrior? I'm no warrior. I'm an emotionally charged female who acts without thinking and, more often than not, gets hurt in the process. Not a warrior. I drop my eyes to the ground. "I can't do this without you. I'm not strong enough. I wasn't born for this," I confess, tears threatening to escape my eyes once more, and I lean my head into the hand that's still cupping my jaw.

Laz sighs. "No, you weren't." His response surprises me. "But that's what makes you incredible. You weren't born for this, yet you are more than strong enough. Your strength has been forged from walking through the wildest of storms, weathering the fiercest tempests, and you've survived. You are made strong, and that, little wolf, makes you more powerful than any Being born strong."

Another rush of warmth blushes my cheeks, and my heart tries to jump out of my chest. I step away from him, unsure of what to say in response, and he drops his arm and turns back toward the ceremony. I follow suit. Laz doesn't take my hand again, but his fingers brush against mine, and he sighs.

After a few moments of silence, he says, "Kirin was a good male. A good friend. I'm going to miss him. Bloody Dragon Hides and their need to be a hero, thinking their scales make them invincible."

"He *was* a hero. He saved my life."

"I know. I mean. . ." He swallows thickly. "I saw. I should have been there." His fingers twitch, grazing against mine as they do. "I'm sorry I wasn't."

"Don't, Laz." I shake my head as the lump forms in my throat, restricting my ability to speak. I swallow it down and whisper, "You've saved me plenty."

A sigh of warmth brushes against the sensitive spot below my ear. "I will always save you, Paege. I hope you know that." A chill snakes around my arm, and I am suddenly aware of a vast emptiness beside me. I cock my head to face him, but I am greeted with an unoccupied space where he used to be.

And although I now stand here alone, I've never felt less alone in my entire life.

Chapter 49

"Are you ready to tell me what the Hels you and Cadieux were doing out there in the first place?" my dad asks as he takes the empty glass from my hands and places it on the desk.

I pinch my brows. "Who?"

He clears his throat. "Lazarus," he states firmly in his Guard's voice, clearly annoyed by this situation. His face softens when my face pulls tight, and I ground my molars together.

I've been evading this conversation for a week now, and I am not too sure how much longer I can keep side-stepping his questions. I don't even know how much information he truly knows about me or the curse. All that aside, how can I explain to him that his daughter may well have a target on her back, put there by the king, the male he serves? Or that her death might be the only way to free the kingdom from a curse put there by the Witches?

"Dad, it's not that simple," I supply on an exhale, rubbing my hands together to release some of the tension pooling in my palms.

"Pumpkin," he sighs. "I just need to know what you were doing. Why was Laz there? Do I need to be worried?"

"I told you Laz was there to help me. I was on a stupid mission with Quentin, and I got in over my head," I say, wrapping my scarf around my neck. Asheron and Amalyah are meeting Keene and the

Shadow Walkers in thirty minutes at the balcony bar downstairs, and I am thinking of joining them if I can ever get Dad off my back.

"Ah-huh." Dad nods as he walks to the fire and warms his hands above it. "And where is the prince now? Why wasn't he with you?" He clearly isn't buying any of this, and why would he? It's all lies.

Lies.

"Quentin, he. . ." Bringing my hands up to my temples, my fingers roll over the soft skin to ease away the ache that is blooming behind my eyes. "We got separated."

"What did he do?" Amerax storms me and puts his hands on mine, flattening his palm over the top. His forehead creases as he studies my face and body, searching for something. "Did he hurt you? That Wolf has a reputation." The way he spits the word *Wolf* is like it's some sort of dirty word, and I flinch. I, too, am a Wolf, or has he forgotten?

"No, he didn't hurt me." Well, not like that. Not the way I'm sure Amerax thinks. "We just won't be spending time together anymore, that's all." I pull my hands out from under his and step back, dropping my head, and I study my denim pants, wiping some invisible dirt from my legs.

The last thing I need is for Amerax to think Quentin laid a hand on me in any way. My dad, being who he is, was trained to interrogate and kill, and I do not doubt for one minute that if he thought Quentin had hurt me, it wouldn't matter that he serves the king. He would be dead.

"Uh-Huh. Can you tell me at least how you met Laz?"

Raising my eyes to meet his, I respond calmly, "I met him at home, actually, when I went to take the horses."

"For this secret trip with Quentin?" he asks flatly.

I nod.

"Pumpkin, does any of this have to do with Guy?"

His words pull my heart out of my chest through my mouth, and I choke. I take another step back, the soft skin behind my knees hitting the side of the bed. I drop down and land with a soft thump. With stinging eyes, I respond, "So, you do know."

Amerax sits next to me and wraps his arm around me, pulling me into him. "Of course, I do. And none of that changes how I feel about you. You will always be my Pumpkin."

I bury my head into his chest, and a sob cracks from my mouth. The conversation maybe over for now, but it's one that we'll be having again later.

Exiting my room, I pull a white knitted hat over the top of my head. I suppose that's one good thing about having my hair cut off: I no longer need to worry about doing anything with it. Not that I did much with it before, but somehow, it's freeing. The Fae usually keep their hair long, but these days, I am more Wolf than Fae, so maybe this change isn't that bad.

The icy air whips at my face as I walk across the balcony. The wind whistles as it blasts through the ravine below, and the sound has me pulling my wool jacket in and wrapping my arms around myself. Ferinini is an unusual place. Previously known as the Court of the Star-Borne, it was once home to a noble family and high-ranking Guards. Now, it's a place of refuge and respite for the Star-Borne, Fae, and their families. I haven't spent much time exploring, but I've done plenty of research. Asheron brought me ancient tomes and journals to peruse while holed up in bed, focusing on healing. Despite the wild weather setting in, Ferinini is full of life with Fae and Star-Borne everywhere.

The balcony is thrumming with laughter, and their casual ease calms my nerves. Music drowns out the sound of the wind and water blasting through the ravine. Naked jasmine and wisteria vines still knot around the balconies, their perfumes all but smothered by the wood smoke billowing out of the chimneys across the way. The various villas are lit up, and young Fae are playing amongst the now snow-laden paths and courtyards.

I make it halfway across the balcony when I see them. Asheron, Amalyah, and Laz sit at a long table with Keene, Tyrone, Camelia, and one other Wolf that I haven't met formally yet but know to be Adriel, one of the Dragon Hides from the Dead Forest. I don't know why, but when I see them, my feet glue themselves to the floor, and it seems as if time itself freezes for just an instant. Pausing, I watch them as they all laugh and talk among themselves, and for a moment, I think I could forget about all the death and pain from the last few weeks.

Then my eyes settle on him. Lazarus. Where the Hels did he come from? And how did he manage to sneak himself into my life, anchoring himself in my heart like the cunning viper he is? A month. One month ago, I felt so alone, so unsure if I would ever belong anywhere. My world was spinning out of control, and the only person I could trust was the one I didn't trust at all. Then I met him. He didn't coddle me. He saw me for who I was and told me the truth of my situation. He pushed me to be better. He saw strength in me when no one else did—when I didn't. He saw something that no one has ever seen before. Me. And standing next to him, I've never felt less alone. With Laz, I'm unjudged. Understood. Seen.

He smiles widely at something Keene says, his amber eyes sparkling with a mischievous joy that has my lips tugging upwards. I sigh. Maybe I should leave them. Maybe I could stay here in the crowd and just watch him, or maybe I could stop being such a creeper and just join them.

Laz's head flicks upward as though he heard every word of my internal diatribe. Amber eyes collide with mine, and my chest tightens, sending tiny prickles racing up my spine. He casually leans back in his seat. My eyes connect to his like a magnet to metal, and he gives me a wicked smirk as he raises his pierced brow. I can't help but roll my eyes at him as a little giggle escapes my lips, but I still can't move.

As if he read my mind, he rises from his seat and slowly weaves his way through the crowd, every step a slow-motion torture, until he stands before me. His eyes never leave mine, and the beat of my heart now plays through the lump in my throat.

"Are you going to stand over here all afternoon, or are you eventually going to come join us?"

I swallow.

For the first time, he isn't wearing his leathers. He's wearing black woven pants, boots, a grey knit tunic, and a black jacket vest. He looks good, not that he never looked good before, but since the first day I met him, he has only ever worn his Israykiel Guard uniform. Even during our time in Owenstown, he wore a more casual uniform, but it was a uniform just the same.

He has *always* been Lazarus the Israykiel Guard. Lazarus the warrior. But now? Now, the male standing before me is. . .just Laz. He feels different. Lighter. Freer.

"I, ah—" I stutter, unable to find my words as my mind empties into a puddle on the floor.

"Paege Vailenbyrg lost for words. I never thought I would see the day." He winks, and it steals my breath. "Come on." He takes my hand, and a tiny burst of energy explodes between our palms as they connect, but he doesn't react. "Let's get you a drink and see if we can't get that sassy mouth working again." He pulls me into the crowd, escorting me along the balcony. My body surrenders to the dance of his guidance, gliding effortlessly and moving without force or thought, until we arrive at the table graced with the presence of our friends.

"Look who I found," Laz supplies when we reach the group.

Amalyah throws a glance our way mid-sentence with Keene and pauses when she sees me. Her large lilac eyes drop, lingering for a drawn-out second at my hand cradled in Laz's. Her eyes narrow slightly, and her lips quiver, but then they arch into an unnerving grin, bringing her gaze back up to my eyes. "Come sit." She pushes Asheron in the shoulder, instructing him to sacrifice his seat for me.

"It's alright, I can..." A heavy thunk behind me has me turning my head. Tyron dips his head toward the chair suddenly behind me, which he procured from another table. "Thank you." I smile.

His silky black hair is pulled back in a tail tied at the nape of his neck, revealing what looks to be an ancient arrow tattoo. The fletching wraps around the back of his neck, and the arrow runs down his neck, disappearing under his heavy tan jacket. He doesn't speak. He merely goes back to his own seat, picks up his glass of clear liquid, and takes a sip.

I sink into softness, nestled between Keene and Laz, wriggling myself to get comfortable. Once I'm settled, I look up to the group only to find the entire table has fallen silent, watching me like I'm some peculiar object.

"How are you feeling?" Keene asks, breaking the uncomfortable silence.

"Like I keep telling everyone: I'm fine. I'm totally healed." I force a smile. "I'm sorry about Cruiz, Huntley, and Kirin." I dip my head in respect to the fallen warriors. "I would have stayed longer at the ceremony, but I was a bit overwhelmed by all the emotions, so I asked Amalyah to bring me back here. I hope the other Wolves weren't offended that I didn't stay longer."

"No need to apologise, Paegence." Keene runs his hands over his shorn head. "It can be tough, that's for sure. Wolves are slaves to their emotions. Their animal instincts are strong, and though we have a natural shield, only some have an affinity to do so. A lot of Wolves prefer not to. Thrill of the chase and all that." He shakes his head. "It's an old cultural habit, one we are trying to change." His lips form a straight line. "Puppy steps...But you're well within your rights to leave should it become too much for you."

Curious. I've always wondered why the emotions of the Wolves have always eluded me. There are times when I can feel the presence of Wolves and sense their emotions, and other times, it just slips away. I've chalked it up to my inconsistent gifts. But what if it's the Wolves themselves that ebb and flow in their connection to me? Wait, does that mean—

"Laz tells me you two will be training now that he's back and you are healed?" Amalyah questions casually, not looking at me.

"That's good, Paege. You need to train, and he's the best to help," Asheron interjects.

"Hm," I respond in agreement, my mind still hyper-fixated on Keene's comments and what it means about Quentin.

Time passes quickly as we all drink and chat, some more so than others. The Shadow Walkers are not big talkers, but Asheron and Amalyah more than make up for whatever conversation is missing, their cousinly banter inducing more fits of laughter than I have experienced in some time. Despite the lightness in the air, a heaviness spirals around me as tiredness takes hold, and I yawn.

"Are you still having nightmares?" Amalyah queries. Her lilac eyes, soft and full, find mine. Asheron must have told her or my dad. Both have witnessed my nightmares of late. The battle of the Dead Forest plagues my dreams every night, always ending the same way: Laz meeting a certain death.

"You're having nightmares?" Laz asks sharply, and he shoots me a concerned look, his silver arrow piercing arching once more. This time, no sinful smile accompanies it.

"It's nothing new," I respond dryly because it's not. I have been experiencing nightmares of some sort for months. Between the various Scorpions attacks, Sylas kidnapping me, Guy dying, finding out about my dad, Quentin, and the Curse, there has been no shortage of disturbing inspiration for the nightmares to fester and grow. Laz knows this. I don't know why this would be such surprising news to him now.

"She's barely slept since she got back," Asheron chimes in, not helping the situation at all.

Heat flushes my cheeks. "*She* is sitting right here, and she is fine," I reiterate, clipping my words.

"Sorry, Paege, we are all just worried about you," Asheron says with an apologetic smile.

"I know," I respond with a forced softness, trying to conceal the frustration setting into my bones. "But you don't need to be."

Nobody speaks, and the ensuing silence floods the air with an uneasy tension. Seizing the quiet moment and eager to evade the unexpected anxiety constricting my chest, I gracefully stand from my seat. Offering a smile to Amalyah, another yawn inadvertently slips from my lips. I couldn't have timed that better, even if I tried. "I'm rather tired, though. It's been a long day, so I think I'll turn in for the night."

As if answering for the entire group, Keene stands to meet me and nods. "Of course," he responds, a gentle smile gracing the Wolf's lips, his golden canine glistening from the soft glow of the balcony lights. He radiates an uncanny familiarity. Not in his appearance, but in the fluidity of his movements with an almost feline grace. An uncommon elegance I've rarely witnessed among Wolves, but one I know I've seen before. But how?

Pushing the thought aside, I say my goodbyes and make my way back to my room, surrendering to the beckoning embrace of sleep as if a dreamlike tether were gently drawing me forward with every heavy step I take.

Laz is back.

And I hope more than anything that his return acts as a calming remedy to lock down the unsettling nightmares that have plagued my sleep this week. For one night, at least.

CHAPTER 50

"Paege?" My name rolls off his tongue in a heavenly manner as my body prepares to cross over the threshold into my room, but I find myself ensnared in an invisible lasso, pinning my arms by my side and restricting my movement. "Do we need to talk?" he adds, his voice a deep resonance that courses through the very fibre of my being.

I close my eyes. "About what?" I don't turn to face him, but I hear his soft steps across the balcony as he approaches me.

"You. Your nightmares. Me?" His whispered voice tugs at something inside me.

My eyes snap open. "You?" I snort, his arrogance freeing me from my imaginary binds. I reach into my pocket to grab the room key. "Why would I need to talk about you?" I retort sardonically, trying to keep my emotions buried within the vault that has failed me so many times before, but somehow, I still trust. With shaky hands, I attempt to get the key into the tiny, tiny hole in the door.

He sighs. "I was gone. . .I was—"

"You were taken. It's not as if you died, and you are back now," I snip, trying to push all the strange and uncomfortable feelings back behind that door.

His hand covers mine, and I strain my eyes to my left to see him swallow hard. "You missed me," he declares softly with an air of jest in his voice.

I huff out a loud breath. "Good to see your ego is still intact." I jingle the key, and it opens the door, and I push it forward, his hand releasing mine as I do so.

"Paege?" he pleads. "Talk to me. We *are* friends, aren't we?"

There's that word again, friends. We are friends, but it also feels more deeper than that. He's become someone I explicitly trust. Someone I care for. Someone I worry about. "We are."

"Then talk to me."

Talk to him? About what? The persistent dream that haunts me, where I witness his head being severed from his body every night? About my irrational fear that he will be taken away again, and this time, not come home? Or my unreasonable need to have him stay close and not leave me again? None of these makes sense to me. How can I explain it to him?

"Sorry, I'm just tired, and. . .I don't need coddling," I retort brusquely, my voice rising an octave or two.

"I know," he replies in a hushed tone.

"I'm not some weak victim that needs looking after. I don't need rescuing."

"I'm aware," he says. I shoot him a surprised look. I wasn't expecting that. But why? Laz has never coddled me. "Paege, you are without a doubt one of the strongest and bravest Beings I have ever had the privilege of meeting. You have endured and survived more than most ever will, and you still walk this kingdom knowing all that you do with nothing but kindness and compassion in your heart and a smile on your face." My cheeks warm. "But you have *endured and survived* more than most. So, those who love you will always worry about you or try to protect you. You can't expect them not to."

A torrent of embarrassment surges through my veins, riding the rapid rhythm of my heart as it quickens, each beat echoing the vivid shade of my blushing cheeks. I step over the threshold, and my shoulders relax as I find solace in the room as if it were a haven from the traumas that have embraced my mind, body, and soul in recent months. It's the only place where I've genuinely felt at ease lately. A lingering doubt whispers within the darkened corners of my broken mind. After everything I have been through, will I even be safe when I return home? To the Neopolis. To my apartment.

Laz doesn't follow me in. He stands in the doorway, leaning against the frame. His pierced brow raised as if waiting for an invite to enter. He's never needed an invite to enter anywhere, even my mind. Why should tonight be any different? "Are you just going to stand there all evening?" I challenge him, sarcasm dripping from every word.

His lips tug widely. "Touché." He pushes off from the frame and saunters into the room. I sit on the end of the bed, pull my knitted cap off my head, and ruffle my shorter hair. *Still not used to that.*

Placing my hands in my lap, I look up to him through my lashes and sigh. "I don't understand," I blurt out before I have a chance to check my emotions. "You were—I saw. . ."

"You saw the Lupa-Centaur swing his blade. As did I." Something akin to awe flashes across his face. "In the reflection of your eyes," he whispers. I remain silent, my gaze burning into his, seeking more information, searching for a glimpse of clarity. "You gave me all the warning I needed in that moment, Paege. I was able to slow time just enough to avoid meeting my end, but unfortunately, not long enough to avoid being captured. I owe you my life."

My eyes widen at the news. "You can stop time?"

"In some situations, yes. It's one of my Star-Borne powers. Temporal magic. But unfortunately, with only Amalyah present, my—*our*—powers were limited." He pauses. "May I?" He points at the vacant spot next to me on my bed. I blink and nod, words still escaping me.

He sits, and my breath catches as the small space left between us transforms into an intense void, but he doesn't notice. "Star-Borne gifts are linked. We are warriors. A legion. A unit. We always have our gifts, but we are not *whole* unless we are with a complete unit. As a unit, we are powerful. United as one."

Letting my gaze drift from his to the door, I ask, "How many in a unit?

"Five. One of each elemental power gifted to us by the Gods Isra and Aesther."

"Five," I echo, my mind hastily assembling all the information I possess about the Star-Borne. Five elements. Five ranks in training. The five-pointed star.

How had I not known this? Surely Amerax, the twins, and Hels, even Asheron would have mentioned this at some stage. As if he was delving into my thoughts, he adds, "Don't be upset they never told you. It's not a detail we're keen on sharing, considering it's a vulnerability."

I reflect on the battlefield. There were instances when I could swear time itself had slowed. Laz orchestrated that, manipulating time to secure an advantage for us. "So, you *can* stop time?" I finally ask, bringing my eyes back to his. Amber eyes meet mine, and there's a softness in them I rarely see. I see it for what it is. He is opening up to me, trying to be vulnerable.

"Yes, and no. It's more complicated than that," Laz supplies.

"And what about Amalyah?" I remember her moving between places in an instant. Was that Laz's gift of slowing time for her to move quickly, or can she slow time, too?

"She can manipulate energy to move through time and space. It's called planar travelling."

Mortification floods my veins, my neck flushing with heat, and I bury my face in my hands. "So, it's not blinking? I've been calling it blinking."

"I'm aware." Laz tugs at my hands, exposing my embarrassment. "But I suppose it's almost like a blink. We call it travelling," he chortles.

"And Amerax?" I ask as it suddenly dawns on me that I don't have any idea what his special gift is either. I know he can form portals, but that is standard Fae magic. I wait for what feels like an eternity for him to answer.

"You need to speak to him, Paege," he sighs.

I nod in understanding. It's not his place to tell. "And I suppose Asheron or the twins won't know theirs until they are activated?"

"Yes, but it wouldn't be too hard to speculate. Gifts tend to travel through bloodlines, being passed down through each generation. On the rare occasion it isn't, it's generally due to some sort of throwback to when two bloodlines crossed."

As Laz fills me in on bloodlines and magic, I realise how little I know about the Star-Borne, considering the sheer number of them I have close to me in my life. Leaning over, I bring my hands to my temples and press hard. I roll my fingers over the tense muscles, and they twitch under the pressure as a faint ache begins to bloom. "And as a unit, all your powers are?"

"Unstoppable."

I laugh, dropping my hands back to the bed. "Seriously, Laz, I want to know."

"I'm not joking, Paege. As a complete unit, we are unstoppable. But that's something we can talk about another time. It's late, and I should let you get some sleep."

I nod, and another dilemma surfaces within me. Do I want him to leave? I've missed him so much this past week. The Gods know I haven't been sleeping well without having him close. Without dwelling on the thought too much, I extend my hand, gently halting his attempt to rise. "Can you stay with me tonight?" I ask.

"Paege," his voice softens, barely above a whisper.

"I haven't been sleeping well. You know, the nightmares," I state expectantly.

"About?" he drawls.

"The battle, being stabbed, everything." I swallow. "You." I cock my head to face him, and a rogue tear rolls down my face.

"I'm back now, Paege, and like you said earlier, it's not as if I died. I'm alive. And you're healed."

"I know that. I mean, I've always known you were alive, but I've still had nightmares of you dying every single night." I shuffle back on the bed and lean against the headrest without taking my eyes off him, hoping, praying he will stay, just for tonight.

Pushing off the bed, Laz makes to leave. "I don't think it's a good idea."

"I know, I know," I say, nodding. It sounds so childish, but maybe I won't worry so much if he is near. I slip down the bed, lying my head gently on the pillow. Rolling onto my side, I find myself facing the vacant expanse beside me. "I only just got you back."

I close my eyes, and then the bed groans beneath me, and I loosen a breath. "Just one night," he murmurs, his fingers delicately tucking a strand of my hair behind my ear, prompting a swell of warmth in my chest.

"You're back," I sigh.

"I'm back."

"You'll stay?" I whisper into the darkness.

"I'll stay." His hushed voice is nothing more than a vibration that ripples through the space between with a soft cadence, and my body starts to relax.

And as the darkness pulls me under, I whisper in response, "Just one night."

CHAPTER 51

Of course, it isn't just one night. Night after night, the ritual repeats itself. After dinner, he escorts me to my room, and the familiar conversation ensues: I ask him to stay, he questions whether he should, and eventually, he relents and stays.

The landscape of my nightmares has shifted. I no longer dream of Laz's death; instead, the haunting scenes depict my own death or Guy's. Fortunately, Laz sleeps so heavily, he's rarely disturbed by my body's restlessness, tossing and turning, and my arms and legs thrashing about.

At least one of us is getting a full night of sleep.

Asheron stopped frequenting my room the night Laz returned, clearly acknowledging that with him back, I no longer need protection—not that I ever needed protection here. Nonetheless, I've come to realise my life is easier when I no longer fight them on these things. After all, their worry stems from love. Although Amalyah has stealthily entered on a night or two. I've woken to discover new clothes, shoes, or other feminine essentials placed in the room. The Star-Borne, I've come to realise, aren't particularly big on personal boundaries, but it warms my heart to accept the depth of their care and concern.

Pulling the curtains open, I smile. No new snow fell overnight. That's four nights now. Whisky is still out there somewhere, and every night without snowfall gives him a greater chance of survival. If he has survived this long at all. I've still not spent time exploring. Laz has been bringing me tomes and journals to read and keep me busy to help me research the curse and try to figure out these damn riddles. But today, Laz finally agreed to bring me to what I think will be my favourite place—the archives.

I need to be certain without a doubt whose bloodline must be ended. I need to find this weapon. Although, for the most part, this curse conceals the specifics related to its nature and the method to undo it, I am certain there must be some details in history that can help guide the way. A document somewhere itemising a unique blade. An account of something. A conversation. Surely someone, somewhere, knows something. Anything. I'm getting desperate. My birthday, my Unification, is less than two weeks away. I'm running out of time.

After lunch, Laz escorts me down endless hallways lined with tapestries and paintings and private courtyards overlooking the ravines. Ferinini is almost castle-like. We pass grand rooms filled with looming artwork, and Star-Borne and Fae bustle about, throwing glances at us as we pass them by.

"Good afternoon, Selene," Laz greets the archivist as we enter a vast room filled wall to wall with hundreds of full bookcases, and my mouth drops open. The collection of books here rivals that of the Neopolis Museum. It's impressive. "Selene likes to hide out in this room. She is a historian. She documents and maintains official records related to the Guard and their activities," Laz explains. Apparently, she has a perfect memory," he adds with a flirtatious grin to Selene.

"Hello, Selene," I greet the dark-skinned female behind the desk, trying to bury the sudden surge of fury brewing in my belly as she throws Laz an equally flirtatious smile.

"'Ello, Paege. More researching today, Laz?" She drops a book on the desk, and I can't help but notice the black bands tattooed around her wrists, weaving among gold tattoos that snake around her fingers and up her beautiful skin. A Siren.

"Perfect memory? So, do you remember—" I start to ask.

Laz cuts me off. "No, she doesn't." *Well, not perfect enough if she remembers nothing of the curse.* That's not fair. The curse is crafted to precisely achieve that—hide all information pertaining to it.

"I'll be escorting Paege today," he says to Selene. He throws his hands forward, gesturing to the walls of books. "Selene has helped me out a lot the past week, pulling me old texts that relate to any sort of war," he says to me. "Which is when I think the curse was made. Although the riddles were ominous, Arnrun mentioned a war forgotten. So, I figured researching the past wars of the kingdom may lead us closer to the information you seek," Laz explains.

"Yes. I was particularly interested in that tome from yesterday that documented a war between kingdoms five hundred years ago. Would you mind locating it for me again?" I ask eagerly.

"O' course. I um, didn't shelve it, so I still 'ave it 'ere."

She leans down, and her burgundy braids fall across her shoulders, chattering as the rubies and other gems she has woven into her hair clang together. She moves effortlessly, as if underwater. She reaches to the floor, picks up a large pile of books, and dumps them with a thunk on the table. She lifts a few texts up and motions for me to take the top text on the remaining pile.

I take the book but pause when the title of the book underneath has me catching my breath. "What's that?" I ask as my eyes rove over the familiar cover. The same but *different.*

"Laz was looking at it the other day." She darts her caramel eyes to Laz. He nods. "Are you interested in looking at this 'eries too. I believe there are a few of 'em. I would 'ave to find 'em for you."

"Yes, please." My hand reaches out and runs over the soft red leather. *Origin Series: The Crescent Moon Curse.* "May I?"

"Please." Selene nods, her braids chattering together again, and I take the book. It feels heavier than before.

"'Appy reading, and, um, don't 'esitate to let me know if you need anything else, yes?" she chimes as she puts her earmuffs on and returns to whatever she is documenting.

Laz takes the book from my hands and silently leads me through the library, weaving through aisles of books to a dark and secluded nook. Private.

"She's a Siren?" I ask when we are out of earshot.

"They aren't all bad," Laz answers with a shortness that tells me I offended him.

"I never said they—"

"No, but you are thinking it. I understand after your experiences, but trust me, they don't all walk around trying to compel innocent Beings for fun. They were once highly respected and loved by all. Their ability to ease minds and comfort others was a cherished gift, especially in war. Like any species, some are bad, but most are just like you and me, trying to figure where they fit in a world that rejected them."

He's right. How is he always right? "Sorry," I apologise.

"It's fine. Sit." He plonks the books on the seat and waits for me to obey his command.

I do. Glancing at the books beside me, I catch Laz out the corner of my eye hovering around. "You can go, you know."

Laz straightens his spine. "I can't leave you to roam around this place by yourself. You are not supposed to be here."

"Well, why did you agree to bring me here?" I pull the red leather book into my lap and run my hands over the soft leather. Its scent, musty and leathery, drifts up my nose.

"Selene owes me a favour," he says nonchalantly, but everything in his demeanour tells me it's a big deal that I am here.

"I know you have more important things to do. I promise I won't leave this spot," I say, reassuring him.

Laz lifts a brow, contemplating me closely, as if not believing a word I just said. I suppose he's right. There are so many books, tomes, and journals. I could spend an eternity in here. "You won't go anywhere?" he finally asks.

"I promise," I pledge, placing my hand on my heart.

He hums. "Why do I find it hard to believe you?"

Oh, I don't know, I think. Because when have I ever done anything I was told to? I don't reply. Silence pulses between my ears while I wait for him to agree. Every breath, every rise and fall of his chest, is a slow torture while waiting for him to leave. Which I know he will.

"Fine," he finally relents. "But, little wolf, do not go anywhere. I mean it. Stay here, read those, and I will be back for you before dusk. If you need anything else, anything, Selene will check in on you regularly, and you can ask her." I nod, trying to conceal my grin of victory. He turns to leave me with my tomes and journals but pauses briefly. "Paege, I'm trusting you."

"I know you are," I respond more earnestly because I will try, I will absolutely try not to defy his wishes. After all, he's just trying to help me. They all are.

When Laz is finally out of sight, I pull my legs up, crossing them over each other, and focus on the red leather book I hold. It is heavier than before. What is Laz doing with this book? How did they get this here? Do they have the rest of them?

A light tapping breaks my chain of thoughts. I look up from the book, but I don't see anyone nearby. Hm. My Wolf growls as I draw my attention back to the book. *Calm down. We've got this.*

I open the book at a random place, and the words swirl around on the pages in a nauseating manner. My eyes are dizzy from tracing their movements. Not again. . .

Tap, tap, tap.

My heart jerks, and I slam the book closed, jumping to my feet and looking for where the sound came from. The tapestries along the wall are old and regal-looking. There is one positioned after every bench nook in this part of the library. There is nothing there. But as I twirl to return to my nook, one of the tapestries suddenly flows away from the wall and rests back in its place with a few light taps.

Taps.

My body stills, eyeing the tapestry for a moment, silent, waiting for it to move again. But nothing. I walk back to my nook, pick up the book, and fall back into the bench. I fling it open to another random section, and the words continue to swirl at me in a dizzying effect, whirling around the pages. My eyes, heavier with every breath I take, continue to trace their movements, and as if time itself were draping a heavy curtain over my lids, they begin to close.

Tap, tap, tap.

My body jerks and lurches as a heavy thud echoes through the darkened room. I lean down and pick up the red leather book and place it on the bench next to me. I rub the back of my neck where an ache at the base of my skull is beginning to form, where I must have been uncomfortably resting my head. How long was I asleep for? The last thing I remember is the words spinning on the pages. Damn curses and cursed objects.

Tap, tap, tap.

There's that tapping sound again. Only this time, it continues to tap away. A rhythmic cadence akin to a solo musician, tapping his feet to a beat he hears in his head. I stand, looking around. The library is much darker now. The afternoon sun must be starting to set, and Laz will be back soon. I stare hazily at the tapestries for a moment, sure that the one that moved earlier created an echo of this exact sound.

One of them is moving. But how? I watch the tapestries closely as I walk alongside them, searching for the movement that's creating the song. It must be the smallest of airflow because none of the tapestries show any signs of life. As I further myself along the wall, the taps become quieter. I turn on my heel and lower myself to the floor. Placing my palms on the cold wooden floorboards, I begin a slow and steady crawl, running my left hand along the bottom of the tapestries, feeling for any sign of activity.

I gasp as I feel something unexpected brush over my hand. A cool breeze. A faint, cool breeze. Standing, I stare at the wall hanging. Adorning the tapestry is a tableau of heraldry, where two avian-like beings, that also somewhat resemble Wolves, clad in a vibrant array of royal green and red feathers, stand face-to-face atop an embossed golden shield. Flanked by a pair of golden swords, they create an intricate and regal coat of arms.

Retreating to the floor, I run my fingers along the base of the tapestry, and the cool air bites at my fingertips. There's something back here. I pull the tapestry from the wall and study the mahogany panel. It looks just like the rest of the walls around here, except for one minor detail. The panel moulding is recessed, where the rest of the walls of the manor are flat with a decorative crown moulding used to give the illusion of a recessed panel. I run my hands along the recessed edge, and cool air kisses my fingers.

Kneeling, I press both palms against the panel and push gently. The panel shifts beneath my weight ever so slightly, but nothing else happens.

Hm.

I bring myself back to my feet and place my hands against the panel once more and push again, this time putting a little bit more power into it, and the wall clicks forward and then releases back. I jump out of the way as the door swings back into the library, pushing the tapestry away from the wall as it does so and revealing what looks to be a secret passageway behind it.

CHAPTER 52

*D*on't *do it, Paege!* The tiny voice of reason screams at me to turn around as I step forward through the concealed entrance into the infinite darkness, and a palpable sense of anxiety fills the air. I close my eyes and see her there, my Wolf, urging me to proceed.

Conflicted by the opposing feelings, I bite down on my lower lip, considering things. My Wolf has never led me astray. In fact, before I merged with my Wolf, I more often than not found myself in a heap of trouble. I trust my Wolf. The bond I share with her is a tether woven from life and death. A union that transcends mere companionship. She's my intuition. So, despite the scorching embers of unease flickering in my mind, I choose to ignore their warning and continue along the shadowed corridor opening before me. That cool air I felt through the cracks of the panel thickens as it continues to curl around my fingers and neck as I pass into the narrow passageway, sending tiny bumps to scatter across my skin.

The musty smell of earth coats my mouth and nose with every silent breath I take. The stone ceiling hangs low, and even though I don't stand tall, I still have to crook my neck to the side to avoid knocking my head. Surely this wasn't made for the Fae. They would have to crawl through here. If it wasn't made for the Fae, then who in the Hels was it made for?

My footsteps softly echo against the uneven floor as I step further into the darkness and deeper into the unknown. The subtle light from the library quickly dims, and the shadows come alive around me, encasing me in their eerie silence. Something creeps across my bones, and my body shudders in response.

Go back, Paege.

For a quick moment, I contemplate it. Should I? Maybe. Or I should partially shift into my Wolf to awaken my senses and calm my heart that thrums so loudly in my ears? As if responding to my thought, torches lining the walls spontaneously ignite with fire. The soft illumination dances across the stone, revealing intricate carvings along the walls and low moss-covered archways ahead.

"What is this place?" I whisper to myself, my words bouncing off the walls like music while I run my fingers over the carvings. The chill from the rock sets into my bones, and I stiffen as the walls groan around me, as if the manor itself is coming to life. While the presence of the flames guides my way with an almost sentient understanding of my existence, the light does nothing to calm my gradually swelling nerves. Each step I take feels like a deliberate move through a living, breathing history, where the very soul of the manor responds to my uninvited meanderings.

Go back, Paege.

Am I going to? No.

The narrow passage winds its way beneath the court, beneath Ferinini, occasionally opening into hidden chambers or branching into labyrinthine paths. I can't say how long I've been down here for exactly, but I stay on track, honed in like an ethereal torch directing me somewhere I need to be.

Directing me home, perhaps?

I bend down and pass under an archway and arrive at another crossroads. A gravitational pull from the centre of my core guides me toward a large chamber door to my left.

Don't do it, Paege.

Another groan and a tumbling clatter have my bones stiffening once more, and my breath catches. I turn around, but the echo fades into the distance, and the tunnels remain silent for a long moment. The large iron door bears the scars of its time. The lock above the rusted handle is unclasped, and the door is slightly ajar, revealing a flickering light coming from within. I rest my hand on the cold metal, and the door creaks open with little protest. As the door begins to move, an unusual metallic tang subtly lingers in the air, causing my mouth to dry. I press my tongue against the back of my teeth, and the sensation is like the abrasive bite of sandpaper.

My breath quickens as I push the door some more, yawning open with ease. The room is empty save for one thing. Standing in the middle of the room is a long wooden crate, sitting on a support structure of some sort. It's rectangular in shape.

Don't do it, Paege.

I close my eyes and swallow, and when I open them, I take an uneasy step into the chamber.

Something inside my mind screams at me to run away, leave this room, and never come back. But like the masochist I am, I can't help but take another nervous step forward. It's that same invisible rope that keeps pulling me down into my nightmares. Its darkness snakes around me, heaving me into the chamber. My chest tightens, restricting my already sharpened breath, and a growl rolls through the pit of my stomach. I pause, and my breath catches.

It's not a crate.

It's not a crate.

And it's not empty. I'm standing a few meters away, but I can already see her platinum hair curtaining her restful face. Her eyes are closed.

Peaceful. She looks so peaceful.

A blink interrupts the world around me. My arms are heavy as though anvils hang from them, resisting any attempt to defy gravity's relentless pull. My chest constricts further, extracting an ache from my heart that mirrors its incessant pace.

It's a coffin.

"Mum?" I choke out.

No.

Maybe a short moment passes. Maybe a day.

"Mum?" I whisper again.

It can't be.

It's a dream. Another nightmare.

"Mum?" My plea sounds louder but distant. It's as if I'm no longer inside my own body, and instead, I'm floating above, watching myself and listening to the echo of my own words.

It's a dream. Another nightmare. Surely, I'm still in the library, asleep.

"Mum?" I repeat, my voice box finding its volume, raising another octave. I try to move my shaking legs, but my knees buckle beneath my weight, and I fall to the hard, cold floor. My fingernails bite into the solid rock, my breath catches in my lungs, and the world blurs in a disorienting haze. Tears sting my eyes, and a sound I've never heard before escapes my lips and ricochets off the stone walls, throughout the room. It's not a cry nor a scream. It's as if the actual cracking of my heart is reverberating out of my body through my mouth.

"Paege?"

It's not real. It's a dream. Another nightmare.

"Paege?"

It can't be. My eyes are deceiving me. It's a dream. Another nightmare.

"Paege?"

I'm still back in the library with that book. Sleeping. It's a dream. Another nightmare.

"Mum!" I erupt, a primal scream breaking free from deep within the darkness that consumes me, and violent sobs explode out of me like a volcano spewing lava. Every fibre of my being urges me to move, to try and reach her. But it's as if time stands still, and no matter how hard I try to push forward, I hit an invisible wall preventing me from getting to her.

"Paege?"

A silkiness envelops me, pulling me back into warmth. It's not the embrace I want to feel.

I want to feel my mother's arms around me.

"I've got you. You're safe now. I've got you," he hushes into my ear.

"No!" I push back, but his grip tightens, pulling me in closer, his heart beating erratically against my cheek. It's not the heartbeat I want to hear.

I want to hear my mother's heartbeat in my ear.

"Mum!" My voice cracks.

"Sh, Paege," he whispers and kisses the crown of my head. It's not the kiss I want to feel.

I want to feel my mother's soft lips gently kissing away my tears.

"Paege, I'm going to get you out of here. I'm going to take you home," Laz utters urgently as he scoops me up in his arms, and my body becomes weightless against the cold, dead air of the chamber.

My mother is dead.

Breathe, breathe, breathe.

The weight of the truth is a tidal wave crashing over me, and tears sting my eyes again as another sob breaks free from my chest. I thought she was just. . .How could I not have known?

Bang, bang, bang.

"Paege? Open up. We need to talk," Laz calls out, concern lacing his tone. Why would he be concerned? He did this to me.

"Do we think she is still in there?" Amerax asks with a hushed voice.

"I brought her home. . ." Laz's voice trails off as a new wave of anger surges, their betrayal slipping between my ribs like a blade and twisting into my heart. I may be back in my room, but it's far from being my home. I don't want to be here, but where else can I go?

I bury my face into my hands, and I gently rock myself back and forth, back and forth, as I sit crouched in the corner, wishing for any sort of relief from *this*. Home? Where is home exactly?

It's not here in Ferinini.

It's not my apartment in the Neopolis.

It's no longer in my family home in Orphelious.

Home.

My mother is dead.

Laz's words keep replaying in my head.

Home.

My mother is dead.

My dad is a liar, just like everyone else. Amerax knew.

So did *he.*

Why would he lie about such a thing? Why would he hide it? Why would any of them?

Bang, bang, bang.

"Go away," I cry out through a cracking sob.

The relief in the sigh of my father's voice is thick with remorse. "Pumpkin?" A gentle thump against the wood has me peeling my face from my palms. "Please, I need to make sure you are alright?"

"Go. Away. Amerax. I don't want to see you or talk to you."

Silence.

Calling him Amerax instead of Dad would have stung, but I don't care. He lied to me. Oh, Gods, it hurts. It hurts so much. My mum is dead.

She was my only living parent, the one person who understood me completely, and now she's gone, and I don't know how to do this, any of this, without her. The anguish courses through every fibre of my being like an unrestrained tempest, an excruciating symphony of heartache that threatens to drown me in its unforgiving depths as I gasp for air to fill my lungs. How do I live without her?

Bang, bang, bang.

"Paege, please open up," Laz calls out with desperation in his tone.

I ignore the desperate pleas that cling to hope in the air and bury my face in my pillow, unleashing the torrent of my grief. My sobs reverberate through the hollow chamber in my chest, and my tears spill out of me like a deluge breaking free from the restraints of a besieged dam. I haven't talked to anyone since I returned to my rooms. I pushed Laz out as soon as he brought me back, and I locked the door and barricaded it with as much furniture as I could. No one is coming in, and I am not leaving, not until I can figure out where to go.

"Please, little wolf." Laz's plea echoes through the refuge of my consciousness, and an inferno of fury violently courses through my veins.

"Go. The. Fuck. Away!" I warn, clipping my words and baring teeth, although no one can bear witness to it.

"Don't make me kick this door in, Paege."

He wouldn't.

"Laz, maybe we should leave her for a little bit and come back?" I barely hear the whispered plea of Amerax through the locked door, and I let out a sigh in relief. Finally, they are going to leave me alone.

But my relief is short-lived when I hear the jingle of keys.

They won't.

And the click of a lock.

Of course, they would.

After everything they have done, there's little reason to believe they'd suddenly adopt a set of morals and values now. The bed starts to quake and grumble, moving beneath me as the door is pushed open through my apparently useless defence. Guard strength. I jump from the bed and storm over to the other side of the room, giving myself a wide berth between me and whoever my intruder is going to be. When enough space is cleared for an opening, Laz steps into the room.

"Paege?"

"Get out!" I spit, folding my arms across my body, my legs shaking in the spot they stand.

"I can't do that. I need to make sure you are alright," Laz says calmly as he takes a cautious step toward me, raising his hands in an act of peace.

"Get. Out," I growl.

"I just want to talk," he says, not reacting in the slightest to my actions or words.

A spasm of angst deepens within me at the mere notion that he might have been withholding the truth about my mum from me. I tap my foot against the ground, and my teeth clench together tightly, an ache blossoming in my jaw. Maybe I'm overthinking it. Maybe my grief is clouding my judgement, and Laz has nothing to do with any of this.

Laz wouldn't betray me like that. There must be a reason. The uncertainty gnaws at me, and every unanswered question from the last month feels like it's revealing a crack in the foundation of our friendship.

"Talk to me, Paege, please?" he pleads again.

"Trust is everything, right?" I ask with a shaky voice, needing to remind him that that's what he said to me when we finally started to become friends. So, if he can't be honest about this now, then I suppose we never were friends.

"Yes," he replies softly, lowering his hands and taking another step toward me. His face is expressionless, just like he gets when he's wearing his Guard mask.

"Did you know?" I ask bluntly.

"What?" He steps back and shakes his head as if my question's a surprise to him.

"Did. You. Know?"

"Paege?" he pleads.

"Answer the question, Lazarus. Yes or no?" I stop tapping my foot in anticipation of his response, and the silence becomes a deafening scream.

"Yes."

As the word spills from his lips, an insurmountable storm unfurls within. I clench my jaw, attempting to stifle another sob, while the salty puddles of emotion well up in my eyes. *He knew.* "When?"

I say through gritted teeth. With each suppressed sob, I am pulled beneath waves of betrayal.

"When what?

"When exactly did you know?"

Silence again.

"When I met you at the house."

"At the. . .At the house?"

His confession sucker punches me. Another stifled sob escapes me, and I gasp for breath. My chest burns as I inhale the drowning waters of his deception, my lungs submerging in the bitter sea of duplicity. A torment of memories hits me like a hurricane, surging forward from the darkest recesses of my mind. *The house.* It's worse than I ever imagined. He knew from before I met him, and everything since then has been lies. It was all lies.

The vision.

"You. . ." I choke on my words as I crumble to the ground beneath me.

Laz is here in an instant, grabbing for me. "It's not what you think, Paege. I didn't have a choice."

The vision of Mum lying in her bed suddenly bursts through my mind's eye. "You, you compelled me?" I manage to spit out. He changed my memories. After what Sylas did with all the compulsion, I can't see past the betrayal burning through my soul. Fury balls like a wildfire in my gut. A violation of my mind. That's what it is. Another violation.

"No." Laz lurches forward a moment before shaking his head, as if trying to erase the truth of his actions. "I didn't compel you. I just changed—"

"Semantics," I scream. His visions. He changed what I could see when I entered the room. She was there. She was always there, dead in her bed, when we were. . .Oh, Gods.

"No, Paege, just listen to me, please."

In that fleeting moment, his voice becomes a trigger, an unwelcome accomplice to the storm of anger that whirls within the confines of my wounded spirit. The air crackles with the intensity of my fury, and each syllable he utters is a catalyst for the smouldering resentment that festers beneath the surface. "You knew, and you lied to me for weeks. You've been lying to me this entire time."

"I wasn't. I . . ."

"I hate you!" I roar. I push him off me and close my eyes, shifting into my Wolf.

"Paege, play nice," Laz pleads as he stands and steps back away from me. The first smart thing he has done since he entered this room. Since he entered my life. Baring my teeth, I snarl at him. The anguish of everything is lessened by my beautiful Wolf as she absorbs my pain, my hurt, my anger. Slowly, I pad toward him, my presence pushing him back to the door until he reaches the opening and silently slides back behind the barrier like the slimy snake he is, disappearing into the cold night, out of sight *and out of mind*, closing the door behind him.

The moment the door locks, I release a howl, my voice morphing into a scream. No longer encased in my Wolf's body, I seamlessly shift back to my Fae form and collapse to the cold, hard ground, and the world shatters around me.

"Paege?" Her angelic voice sings through my wounded soul, breathing life back into its lifeless cage, and my heart starts beating.

"Mum?" I call out into the darkness.

"Paege, it's us."

I sit up from the floor and crawl across the room to the door. I never pushed the bed and armoire back across the door earlier.

I just let the tears of grief wash me away to a slumber. "Khollan? Nassurah?" A cry breaks from my heart as I scramble to my feet and unlock the door to see the twins standing on the balcony outside my room.

"Paege. . ." Nassurah cries as she hurls herself into my arms, and Khollan follows a moment behind her. I grab onto them for dear life, pulling them into me and vow to the Gods above I will never let them go.

"I've missed you so much, little twiblings. Are you alright?" Stupid question. Their mum is dead. Our mum is dead. I pull back from them and study them up and down.

"We're not so little anymore, Pance," Khollan mocks as he walks inside my room while Nassurah leans in for another hug. He's right. They aren't so little anymore. Although they are only fourteen, they both stand as tall as me, but they still wear the face of little ones.

"You know you've been able to say my name properly for nearly ten years now, Khollan," I retort to his name mocking as I guide Nassurah into my room and close the door behind us.

"I'll start using your proper name when you stop calling us twiblings. We're fourteen now," Khollan chides as he sits on the end of the bed. "Redecorating?" Although he's trying to be witty, there is nothing joyous in the features of his face. His golden eyes are lifeless, swollen and red; his lips pale and cracked; and the tone in his voice carries less weight than a feather. Nassurah isn't looking much better.

"Something like that," I reply as I sit Nassurah on the side of the bed, and I try to stifle the tears that want to rise their ugly head, while wiping hers away.

Damn it, Paege, keep your shit together in front of the twiblings.

"Khollan, can you sit with me, please?" Nassurah sniffs as she holds out her arms for her brother, and he slides across the bed without a word and wraps his arm around her. A sob escapes my lips as I watch them. Twins. That should have been me. With Guy.

This world, this life has taken so much from me.

Not anymore.

I sit next to them and sigh. With the weight of our mother's death settling upon my shoulders, I find myself teetering on the edge of a grief-stricken cliff. The news that Dad hid her death from us for months is a cruel echo in the hallows of my soul, threatening to unravel the threads that bind our family together. Salty tears well in the corners of my eyes once more. My heart, already burdened by the weight of my own sorrow, now bears the heavy responsibility of breaking this shattering truth to the twiblings.

"I have something I need to share with you," I say, my words barely a whisper as they leave my dry, cracked mouth. A sense of helplessness washes over me as I grapple with the enormity of the task.

"What?" Khollan answers for them.

Dad hid Mum's death from us. How do I explain that to them? How do I find the strength to utter the sentence that will forever alter our very lives even more? Mum's death is enough. Should I burden them with this truth, too? "I don't even know how to say this. . ."

Dad is a liar.

"Just say it, Paege. Gods, you've always been so dramatic." His words slap my face with a sting that resonates far beyond the physical, leaving behind a mark of disbelief and hurt, and my eyes well with tears once more.

"I know you're grieving, Khollan, but that wasn't necessary," I retort, my tone laced with a subtle hint of disapproval.

"Sorry, Paege," Nassurah replies on Khollan's behalf. "What he meant to say was, you can tell us anything."

I lean in and kiss her cheek. "When did you become so smart and level-headed?"

"Right around the time Khollan became an emotional roller-coaster I am forced to ride," she quips.

"What? You're an Empath?" The words fly out of my mouth before I even get to process the information.

"Lucky me," he teases. "Looks like we have more in common than I thought."

I would never wish the burden of empathy on anyone. It's hard enough having to control your own emotions, but when you start adding the unregulated emotions of others into the mix, that shit can drive you insane. "Khollan, I'm sure you'll be much better than me at controlling it. I have no doubt."

"I'm not worried. I have Nassurah, and she'll control it for me." He shrugs, and Nassurah pulls him in closer.

Brows pulling together, I ask, confused, "Nassurah will control it?"

"You know, the twin thing?" Nassurah answers casually as if this is some sort of common knowledge.

I shake my head. With absolute certainty, I have no idea what they are talking about.

"Ying and yang. . ." she continues.

"Light and dark," Khollan adds.

"Sorry, twibs, but you're going to have to fill me in. I don't understand."

"Every set of twins is one of two sides. With us, Khollan is the empath, and I am his shield. I can shield him from others. I can absorb his emotions and calm him when it all gets too much for him. I am his other half."

Khollan takes Nassurah's hand and forces a smile.

"Together we are whole."

Chapter 54

The twins left hours ago to get some sleep, but I haven't been able to close my eyes since they left. They hadn't reacted the way I expected. What I thought would be a harrowing experience telling the twibs about our dad turned out to be nothing more than an emotionless discussion—on their part—about the theories of why he would have done what he did.

It was more emotional for me than anyone else.

Of course it was. It always is.

I can't understand how no one is angry that he hid her death. Not just perturbed as to *why* he didn't tell us. There is no amount of justification and reasoning or pledging to one's service that can change my mind to think otherwise.

Mum's death isn't the only thing keeping me from my sleep tonight. It's what Nassurah said about the twin thing.

She is his shield.

All the times I felt no one else's emotions in Guy's presence, all the times my own emotions inexplicably found calmness, and the inability to shield during training with *Captain Leather Pants*—I attributed these anomalies to my wonky gifts and convinced myself something was fundamentally wrong with me. Is it possible that, all along, Guy was my shield? My heart rips at the seams as the knife of betrayal digs a little deeper, the ache threatening to consume me.

Right now, if I could, I would be talking to the one person whom I somehow trusted more than any of them. And, it turns out, he was the worst of them all. I pick up my scribe, unsure if I should send a message past midnight, but ignoring my better judgment, I type out what I need to say.

Me: I know we haven't spoken in a while. But I thought I should let you know that my mother is dead.

I hit send before I rethink my decision. I'm probably crazy for sending him anything. I haven't heard from him since he left us in Owenstown, and I don't expect a reply. But in the not-too-distant past, he would have been the one person I wanted with me.

I place the scribe back on the nightstand and roll over onto my side. Mum, Guy, and my real dad were all taken from me, and I'm certain, without a kernel of doubt, it was by the same person. He may not have wielded the sword, but I'm sure he ordered the word.

Quentin's father, the king.

Rolling onto my side, I'm greeted by a cascade of hair that tickles my face. *So much hair.* My attempts to brush away the strands result in my fingers becoming entangled. Peeling my sandpaper lids from my eyes, I'm met with a mass of golden curls, the morning sun gilding her strands.

"Paege, can you please stop running your fingers through my hair? Lu-Lu might get jealous."

My heart skips a beat as Mhelodie rolls over and smiles. She reaches out and pulls me into her. It's the first real hug I've had since Mum died. Suddenly, I'm enveloped from behind by a long, elegant arm wrapping around my waist, and a sob cracks from my chest. Lumeilia.

Their presence pushes me over the edge I've been teetering on, and the tears start to come again, fierce and wild like a rainstorm. Minutes pass, maybe hours as they hold me in their warmth, anchoring me in the storm so I don't get lost in the sea of emotions. When I finally manage to catch my breath, it's almost as if I feel nothing at all. My mind is numb, no fleeting thoughts passing through, and inky shadows fill the cavernous space beneath my ribs.

Sniffing, I peel myself out of their embrace and sit up between them. "I just want to stop crying. Why can't I stop crying? I'm always fucking crying." Two sets of eyes, one honey and one mahogany, stare at me with gentle concern. Or is that pity? It's hard to tell since Mhelodie can now shield, and Lumeilia, well, I can't feel anything. Strange.

Mhelodie sighs as if expecting this. "You've been through a lot, Paege."

Pity.

"Even before all this," Lumeilia adds, squeezing my hand gently. I tug it from her grip.

Definitely pity.

"I don't want to feel like this anymore," I admit sheepishly, but the numbness calls to me, a sweet lullaby with promises of peace beckons.

"Paege," Lumeilia sighs. "It's perfectly normal to feel this way."

"You're an empath. You not only have your own emotions to deal with, but you've got everyone else's to feel, too," Mhelodie says. "That has to be hard."

Lumeilia nods in agreement. "It's meant to be difficult. Do you not think we aren't given these gifts if we aren't able to handle them?"

Their words hang in the air between us, waiting for me to accept them. Hard, difficult, handle. Enough is enough. "What if I don't want to be an empath anymore?" The second the words leave my lips, guilt whips through me, and as if lancing me with pain, I wince. Is it true? I don't know. Maybe it is.

Mhelodie's golden eyes line with silver. "I don't think it works like that."

"I'm just so exhausted." I crawl over Mhelodie and push off the bed. Standing, I rub my swollen eyes and pad over to the fire that's almost extinguished. Tilting my head, I get lost in the glow of the embers, almost hypnotised by its calmness. No flames violently lick at the edges. No fire fiercely escapes or consumes.

"Of course you are," Lumeilia whispers from behind me. I pivot to face the bed where she and Mhelodie now sit at the edge, sorrow painting their beautiful faces. Neither of them makes to move, though.

"It's alright to feel that way," Mhelodie says with a sad-looking smile.

The two of them interlace their hands, neither taking their gaze off me, and still, no emotions radiate off either of them. "But things will be better soon," Lumeilia says, tilting her head to the side as if trying to coax an agreement out of me.

I am not too sure I can agree. How can I when I don't truly know if that is the truth? It's not just my mother's death, it's Guy's, too. It's also so much more than all of this. I'm not going to complain about this brief reprieve from pity I know they are feeling, but to agree that things will be better soon is like a lie I'm being forced to say.

Unsure what to say, I open my mouth and close it again, then silently walk to the bathroom. When I reach the door, I look back over my shoulder at my friends. "I don't want—"

"Paege?" Lumeilia starts, standing.

"I'm going to shower," I say, cutting Lumeilia off and closing the door behind me.

Once showered, I return to the room to find my two best friends curled into each other on the bed. They hesitantly move toward me but stop, like I'm a spooked animal that would bolt at the slightest movement. While getting changed, they listen with sympathy as I reiterate the events that occurred over the last few days. Asheron messaged them in a panic, and Amalyah travelled to collect them, and Asheron let them into my room. He didn't stay. I'm starting to wonder if he's trying to avoid me. I truly believe he didn't know anything, but I know his loyalty lies with the Guards, and if my conversation with Khollan and Nassurah is any indication, their loyalties and support of their Star-Borne ways are unwavering, even in the most immoral of circumstances. Still, it's upsetting that even though we probably won't see eye to eye on the morals of the situation, Asheron hasn't come to see me or been here for me.

"I still can't believe he did that. I mean, he's your dad," Mhelodie says as she paces back and forth across the room, her fingers wringing together.

"I *still* can't believe you're a Wolf and neither of you told me," Lumeilia jibes from where she sits on the bed. I scrunch my nose up at Lumeilia's comment.

Mhelodie changes route and sits next to Lumeilia, taking her hand. "I'm so sorry Lu-Lu. It wasn't my place to say anything."

"She's right. Don't be mad at Mhelodie. If anyone, be mad at me," I reply to the girls as I throw another log into the fireplace.

"Oh, I'm not mad at anyone. I just can't believe either of you two was able to keep a secret that long," Lumeilia chides as she gets up and heads for the door.

"What are you doing?" I ask as I jump to my feet and quickly walk to the bathroom, the irrational urge to hide away from the world outside of this room overtaking my rational mind.

Lumeilia pauses, her eyes knitting as she takes in my actions. "I was just going to see if breakfast and coffee have been delivered. Mhel ordered us something to eat when we arrived. I asked for them to deliver it mid-morning," she muses. "What are *you* doing?"

"Nothing," I reply casually as I cautiously re-enter the bedroom.

"Were you seriously going to hide in the bathroom if I opened the door?" Lumeilia teases, a giggle bubbling from her lips as she purses them together.

"I was not," I reply curtly, trying to hide the shame that's slowly creeping into my cheeks.

"She was," Mhelodie chimes in. "This Lazarus has you rattled, doesn't he?"

I don't answer. I just curl back into bed next to Mhelodie and lay my head on her lap while Lumeilia slips out, returning a moment later with a tray of coffees. She repeats the same process two more times with trays of food. I don't eat, though. My stomach has no appetite, even less so at the sight of gridcakes. Too many memories. Too many feelings. Must push them down.

But coffee, that's a different story. Three cups later, and I'm slightly buzzed on caffeine and Mhelodie's *special remedy*. A little bit of Psyloxin and a dash of AmberFyre mixed in with the coffee. I'm not buzzed enough to forget everything, though.

My scribe chimes. I reach for it and see that it's Laz. Disappointment burns inside my core.

Delete.

"You're not even going to read it?" Lumeilia queries. Her keen Fae and friend sense knows exactly who messaged. I expect Laz to message. I expect him to keep on messaging, but I hoped it would be Quentin responding to my message from last night. Any acknowledgment that he cares or even cared. Hope is a fickle thing, and ultimately, all it does is lead to disappointment.

"Nope." I place the scribe down and lie back in the bed.

"Should we get Asheron?" Mhelodie sits up. "It's weird that he isn't with us."

"Agreed," Lumeilia says as she runs her hands through her hair, a gesture similar to what a mother would do with her young child. It's oddly comforting yet equally upsetting.

"I don't know," I answer, trying to suppress yet another burst of hysterical sobs. "I mean, yes, I want him here, but I don't know if he will come."

"I'm going to message him." Mhelodie jumps up. "And tell him to get his pretty ass down here."

Asheron doesn't come.

Night falls, and the three of us still haven't left my room. Lumeilia organised lunch and dinner for us, but I still haven't been able to eat. Mhelodie's special remedy has managed to give me legs all day. The twins haven't visited again either, and I dare say I won't see them while the girls are here. Which I don't think will be long. They haven't said. I haven't asked.

Laz keeps messaging, and Amerax tried to visit once. Mhelodie went out and saw him. I have no idea what she said to him, but he hasn't been back since. I asked her to weave that same black magic on Laz, but she just laughed me off. I wasn't joking.

"I love you girls. Thank you for coming here," I say, around a yawn.

"We love you, too, Paege. Please, let's not go so long without catch-ups again. This is the longest we've ever been without seeing each other," Lumeilia says.

"It *has* been the longest. Two months, I think?" Mhelodie muses.

"No," I sit up, knocking someone's feet out of my face. Somehow, I ended up being the tail between the two beauties, their feet wiggling away joyously in my headspace.

"Yes," Lumeilia responds. Her and Mhelodie's eyes are closed, their fingers laced together, and their faces both wear the biggest smiles. Once upon a time, I would have thought that was the most beautiful thing I had ever seen. Now all I can see is the inevitable heartbreak that one, or both of them, is going to feel one day. A tear creeps down my face. I swipe it away before either of them opens their eyes. Because, Gods, do I hate that. I hate that all this trauma, all the lies and betrayal, has taken the light inside of me and snuffed it out, leaving nothing but an empty void of darkness. Yet at the same time, it's the most peace I've felt in years.

"A pact," I blurt out.

"What?" Mhelodie asks, opening one eye.

"We need to make a pact," I repeat, knocking both their feet, urging them to wake up.

Mhelodie sits up, Lumeilia following suit. "For?" Mhelodie drawls as she studies me closely.

I roll my eyes. "For us, silly."

"That's a great idea," Lumeilia says, knocking Mhelodie's arm. "Mhel, do you know of any white spell pacts we can do that bind the three of us?" she asks, batting her beautiful, long lashes over her dark mahogany eyes.

"I don't know, Lu-Lu. It might not be safe," Mhelodie supplies, but her brows pinching tells me she is considering it, and I try to hold back my premature smile.

"Come on, Mhel, it's for Paege. Surely there is something we can do," Lumeilia sings with enthusiasm.

I sit and watch the two discuss our options for a moment, hope unfurling inside my chest. This pact might be the only chance I have left to tether myself to some goodness. To some light. These two are my light.

"Alright," Mhelodie finally answers.

"Whoop!" Lumeilia cries over a sigh of relief that pushes from my chest.

It's not long before we are sitting on the floor in a circle, the room dark save for three burning candles positioned in front of us. The necklace and charm my mother gifted to me are coiled in a circle in the centre. Apparently, the pointy end of the charm is what we are going to use to prick our skin with for this blood bond.

With eyes closed, Mhelodie starts to chant, "Mother of the earth, Mother of the light, Mother of the day, and Mother of the night. We ask for your blessing to protect our hearts. Bind us three together, so we never feel apart. Bless us with your truth, and bless us with your love. Shower us with blessings from the stars above."

We all reach for our candles and pour the melting wax into a puddle in the centre of the circle. Mhelodie then takes the pointy end of the charm and pricks her index finger and hands it to Lumeilia with a smile. Lumeilia does the same and winces as the charm pierces through her delicate skin, blood bubbling into a small pool on her index finger.

She hands it to me, my hands warm and damp as tightness twines around my core. I press the tip of the blade into my middle finger and puncture through the skin, also wincing from the pain. My heart thrums like a symphony within my chest as I hover my finger to the centre of the circle, and the other girls do the same, our blood pooling on our fingertips. United, we turn our hands over, gently releasing the essence of our lives, and our blood mingles with the wax, seamlessly blending and forming a fluid connection. Bonding us. Solidifying us as friends for life.

A sudden burst of energy whips through the room, electricity crackling around us like a lightning storm. "What in the Hels, Mhel," Lumeilia squeals as the candle flames all burst from their wicks, burning brighter. Their intensified glow casts ethereal shadows dancing across the room before returning to normal.

"Damn, that was intense." I let loose a laugh as the energy starts to subside.

I reach out to pick up my charm. "Ouch," I yelp as I drop it back into the circle, the damn thing zapping me from the electricity-fuelled air that surrounds us.

"Mhel?" Lumeilia asks.

I turn toward Mhelodie, and she sits still in her place, her golden eyes wide open, not blinking, but moving erratically around the room, not focusing on any one thing. *What in the Hels?* Before either of us can help her, Mhelodie's chest collapses, and she blinks. Her lips arc up in such a wicked way, a way I've only ever seen once before. Then her eyes connect fiercely with mine. She picks up my charm and holds it in her palm for a moment before holding it out for me to take.

"Hidden in plain sight," she sings as I take it from her.

"What is?" I ask, unable to place what she's saying.

Mhelodie doesn't answer, she just winks at me. "Girls," she addresses the room. "We have some dancing to do." She jumps up, pulls three little red pills out of her pocket, and takes one. She hands one to Lumeilia, who takes it without question, and then she holds the last remaining one out to me.

As I take it from her hand, she grabs me and pulls herself close to me, leaning in, her breath just a sigh against my cheek. "Paege," she whispers. "Hidden in plain sight," she repeats. "Everything is going to work out."

In a graceful whirl, she takes off, seizing Lumeilia's hand, twirling her in a dance of spontaneous joy and laughter, spinning her around and around and around.

CHAPTER 55

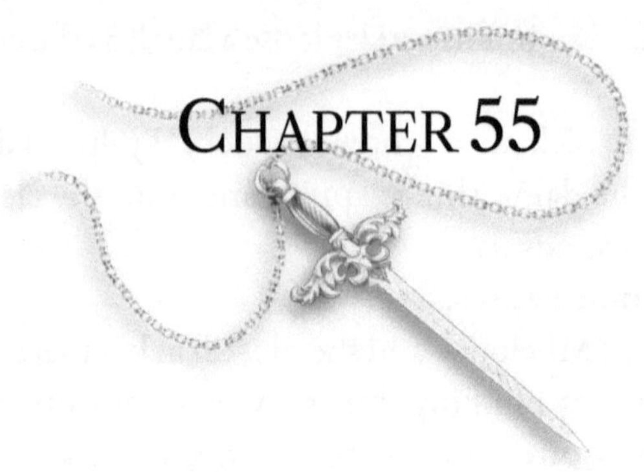

I wake to an emptiness in my chest and an even emptier bed. Sometime during the night, the girls slipped out. They stayed for two days, which was longer than I expected, but still not long enough. Even though their presence managed to kickstart a tiny bit of life back into my unbeating heart, their departure has left a hole in my soul.

The note left on my pillow says they will be back in a week for my birthday and Unification. And, of course, for the ceremony that will be held for my mum. Whenever that will be. If at all. I still don't know exactly how she died or what happened to her, but sifting through my hazy memories over the past couple of days, I've managed to piece together a few things myself. I know she was murdered at the house. Bitten by a Wolf.

Grabbing my scribe, I send another text message, but I don't expect a reply. He never replied to the first message, and of all the messages one would respond to, that would be the one. Still, I remain somewhat optimistic that he will.

Me: Can we meet?

Throwing the scribe down on my bed, I lie back and stifle a mock scream into my pillow. Frustration and fury unfurl in my stomach like a wild storm, and no matter how hard I look, I can't see my way through it.

My scribe beeps, and my body jerks up, the tension in my head tightening like it's in a vice, and my heart throws itself against the cage in my chest. *That was fast.* With shaking hands, I pick up the scribe and read the name flashing across the screen. My chest collapses.

Asheron: Can you meet me in the library?

The library? Is he crazy? I haven't left my room since discovering my mum's body, and he wants me to leave and go see him in the place where this all started. It's been three days since the event, and I hadn't seen or heard from Asheron until last night when he asked to catch up with me today. Now, it's hardly going to be a social visit.

The event.

The moment that I found my mother's dead body being kept in a hidden chamber underneath a Star-Borne court and learnt everyone was lying to me.

The event.

Blood rushes to my ears, and the vice that's been constantly applying pressure tightens, constricting around my mind like a python squeezing the life out of its prey, and my eyes begin to haze.

Me: No.

Minutes pass as I regret my short message. I do want to see him.

Me: Can you please come to my room? I've missed you.
Asheron: I'm coming. Be there shortly.
Asheron: I know, and I'm sorry. I've missed you, too.

Walking back to the library is surreal. It's as if I'm travelling through my own personal nightmare. But I'm awake. I know I'm awake. Somehow, after an uncomfortable reunion, more so on his part, Asheron convinced me to come with him on this little adventure. He's been keeping his distance from me. He won't tell me why the library, but he's promised it's not to see my mum. I am not so sure I believe him, but if I am to find out what the Hels is going on, I need to go with him. While he never said the words out loud, I know he's taking me back to the hidden tunnels.

Sweat beads on his brow. He's nervous. I don't think I've ever seen Asheron nervous before. Standing at the entrance of the secret door, visions of my mum hammer at my mind, climbing out from the darkest corners as I continue towards my own personal Hels, hand in hand with Asheron. His touch, his skin on mine, is my only tether to reality.

"I thought you said you weren't bringing me back to see my mum," I say with a trembling voice as he pulls the door open. The frigid air brushes against my skin, pulling a shuddering gasp from my lips. He gestures for me to go inside. My breathing quickens, and I can't step through the opening, my body hitting an invisible wall refusing to let me pass into the darkness.

"I'm not. I'm taking you somewhere else."

Looking down the shadowed tunnels where I know my mum's cold body still lies lifeless and alone, tears pool in the corners of my eyes. It's like staring down the barrel of a cannon. My body becomes heavy, and I shake my head at Asheron. Nope. I'm not ready for this. Asheron steps in front of me and holds his hand out. A simple gesture, but one that holds so much meaning. He is trying to show me I am not alone in this and that I can trust him, but can I?

You don't know who you can trust, Paege.

I gently close my lids and swallow the lump forming in my throat, taking a few long, slow breaths to release the pressure coiling around me. I've known Asheron for years. Aside from him keeping the information about my dad being a Wolf from me, he has never done a single thing to harm me or give me any reason not to trust him. I suppose there is no reason to stop trusting him now. Lifting a shaky hand, I take his and let him guide me into the emptiness.

We silently traverse deeper into the hidden passageways with Asheron hunched over like he's folding himself in half, and the lanterns magically light the way. We take an early turn to the right, and my chest collapses as relief sweeps through me. He isn't taking me to Mum. "What is this place, Asheron?" I ask, my voice ricocheting across the hollow tunnel in a dance of whispered echoes.

"It's where the Star-Borne bury their secrets," Asheron replies in a hushed voice, not turning to face me. The way he says it has the knot in my stomach twisting tighter.

"Secrets?" I choke out as my breath catches.

"I'll explain everything when we get there. It's not that much further."

I stop. "Asheron," I command. As if my words have fallen on deaf ears, he carries on traipsing down the passageway, unaware I'm not following him. "Asheron," I call out, crossing my arms over myself. "Will you just stop and tell me where the Hels we're going?" A wildfire rolls through me in tidal waves, a fury ready to spill over the edge.

Asheron stills, slowly pivoting to face me. The shadows dance across his gentle features like Daemons of the night weaving their magic, but I'm not falling under their spells. "Paege." He steps forward, arm reaching out to me. That familiar and comforting gesture, now nothing more than an annoying habit I'm trying to kick. "I need you to trust me," he adds.

"I'm so sick of everyone and their secrets," I mumble under my breath, but the acoustics of the tunnels carry my voice further than I anticipated. The way Asheron drops his hand and his throat bobs has my heartstrings panging.

"I know, and I'm trying to rectify that. Please, I promise it's just a little further," he pleads, holding his hand out again.

I drop my hands and slowly tread toward him, pushing through the wariness snaking around me with every step. Stopping in front of him, I force a smile, trying to conceal the suspicion that's now slithering over my bones. I don't take his hand. "Come on then," I say, rather defeated. I step past him and continue down the shadowy passage to only Gods knows where because it's clear Asheron has no intention of telling me anything until we get there.

A moment later, my heart sinks to the depths of the Hels below, stealing my breath as we stand outside a familiar-looking door at a familiar-looking cross-section. My mother's chamber. How? Why? "Asheron," I choke on his name as I try to smother a cry that violently escapes my lips, breath nothing more than an elusive fugitive, avoiding being caught.

Breathe, Paege. Just breathe.

He promised. How are we in my mother's chamber? Did we somehow travel around in circles? Asheron's eyes widen, and he grabs me as the world tilts around me. My legs buckle and send me to the ground. I reach my hand out to Asheron's shoulder to support my unstable body from colliding with the ground.

"You promised," I manage to mutter as my surroundings start to turn hazy.

"Paege, it's not your mum's chamber. It's Guy's."

No words I've heard in my entire life have me jolting back to life like the ones Asheron just spoke. Guy? What does he mean, *it's*

Guy's? The Wolves took Guy's body. In fact, I believed, for all this time, that it was the king who stole his body. It was the Star-Borne?

"Asheron? Did you say Guy?"

"Come on." Asheron stabilises me with one hand as he pushes the iron door open with the other. It gradually creaks open, groaning as it shudders across the uneven ground to reveal its hidden truth. I tumble to the ground, with my barely beating heart, and hit the solid, cold stone with a thunk. My hands slap the surface, the sting violently ripping me back to the insane reality before me.

Guy lies on an altar in the middle of the room, adorned with candles and flowers, a scene that eerily mirrors that of my mum's. *"Guy."* The words are barely a whisper as they cross over my lips.

Thousands of questions pepper my mind like a swarm of agitated insects, and blood rushes to my ears. Asheron is in front of me. I can see his lips moving, but the sound of my pounding heart drowns out his words.

It can't be.

Not again.

My chest collapses under the heavy weight of this nightmare, and tears sting my eyes as fear engulfs me in a suffocating shroud. But in sweet relief, a hazy fog starts to coil around my mind, erasing the terror that stands before me, until I finally see nothing.

Hear nothing.

Feel nothing.

Until. . .nothing.

A scream shocks a rhythm back into my lifeless heart, jerking me back to life. I don't know how or when it happened, but I'm standing in the chamber next to Guy, a new fury brewing in the depths of my darkened soul. Asheron takes a tense step toward me, and my Wolf howls as grief succumbs her, pushing herself to the surface. Urging me to shift, a primal instinct kicks in to protect me, to protect Guy at all costs.

I resist. "Asheron, I need you to explain to me what in the Hels is going on right now," I demand through gritted teeth, salty tears threatening to seep from my eyes.

"Synthony had his body stolen after that weekend you and Quentin went and saw her. The weekend she told you the truth."

Mum. I swallow the lump growing in my throat as I place a hand on Guy's chest over the wound I know is hidden under layers wrapped around him. He looks as if he's sleeping. How is that possible? *Magic, most likely.*

He's been here for months.

He's been here all along.

"She wasn't going to let the Wolves keep him after everything they did. She wanted to give her son a proper ceremony. With you."

"Mum did this?" My shoulders sink, and a tear finally escapes. "How do you know about this?"

"She told me."

My chest tightens, a viper coiling itself around my lungs. "She told you?" I choke, looking up to him. Asheron stands next to me now, and he nods. I didn't even sense him walk toward me.

"She told Laz, but I was there." Asheron dips his head, his eyes not meeting mine, as he tucks his hair behind his ears.

"Right, Laz," I murmur, redirecting my focus back to Guy.

My eyes roam over his face. He looks like me. Our eyes are the same colour, same shape. His nose. Even his lips, full bottom lip and thinner top, are the same. But lying here, his features appear less harsh, less Wolf and more Fae. Even his ears are a little pointed. How had I never noticed that before? "He looks. . ."

Before I can finish, Asheron interrupts, "That's his natural state. After he died, whatever glamour had been put on him to conceal his Fae features must have lifted."

More magic.

Pivoting to face Asheron, I ask pointedly, "How did Laz know my mother?" Confusion around their relationship settles deep within. She never mentioned him to me ever, but it's obvious they were close. He was at the house. She confided in him. Trusted him. Who was he to her. . .Or her to him?

"That's a question for Laz," Asheron's voice drops, and he shifts his gaze from me to Guy.

"So, you don't know?"

Asheron doesn't respond; his face tightens as if he swallowed a bitter pill.

I nod in disappointment. "You know, you just can't tell me."

"It's not like that—" he starts.

"It's fine, I get it," I interrupt, turning back to Guy and taking his hand in mine.

Lies.

It's not fine. I don't understand how they all keep so many secrets. All. Of. Them. How do they sleep at night with the weight of their lies resting on their shoulders? How do they reconcile lying to their loved ones over and over again? Heat rises inside my belly.

Breathe, Paege. Just breathe.

"Is there anyone in my life who hasn't lied to me or kept secrets from me? You, Laz, Quentin, Amerax, Hels, even my mum," I sigh, defeated by all the betrayal.

"That's not fair, Paege."

I pivot, taking my hands from Guy's body and crossing them across my body. "How is it not fair? You lied to me, Asheron." My jaw tenses. "You kept information about my life a secret. You saw what Guy's death and his missing body did to me. Yet you kept all this quiet. You all did." A sob pops out of my mouth before I have a chance to clench it shut. Asheron says nothing. The bloody Star-Borne. Always keeping their secrets. All this makes me wonder if Asheron knew more about my mum's death all along. I gave him the benefit of the doubt until this moment, until right now, but everything's so surreal, and no one is who they seemed to be. "Did you know?" I step back from Asheron, trying to give myself some space as the chamber walls start to enclose in on me.

His brows leap to his hairline. "Know what?"

"About my mother. Did you know?"

"Her—her death?" he stutters.

I don't respond. My eyes burn into his with a steely resolve, and I place my feet wide, preparing myself for the onslaught of emotions after the truth is finally revealed.

"No, I didn't know." A breath leaves my body, pressure releasing from within. "Laz nor Amerax told me, but we have spoken about it since."

That's something, at least. Asheron wasn't keeping that from me, too. I still don't know how I feel about all this, though. "How can they all go on with their lives like nothing happened? She died, Asheron. Mum died, and no one seems to be affected but me."

"It's different for Guards, Paege. We are trained not to let death affect us. We are told emotions make us weak. We are exposed to so much death. We deal with loss differently." He shrugs.

"You're telling me that Guards don't feel death? I call bullshit! You lost your shit when Remi died. You went missing for days. I still don't know exactly what happened, but that wasn't the actions of someone who had been trained not to let death affect them."

Asheron argues, "Remi was different."

"Why?" I challenge.

"Because she was my FaeMate. Synthony and Amerax aren't, *weren't*, FaeMates." He states it as a matter of fact, and I see red.

"Don't you dare suggest they didn't love each other."

He shakes his head. "I wouldn't. I wasn't. They did love each other. They loved each other a lot, as much as any non-mated pair could, but they weren't FaeMates, Paege. They weren't bonded."

"You're saying that unless your FaeMates, you can just brush death off like any other non-important event?"

"Paege," he breathes. "You need to speak to Amerax. Speak to Laz."

"No way," I spit, crossing my arms across my heart as it picks up speed at Laz's name.

"Why?" he gently presses.

"Because he lied to me. He kept her death a secret. I was there, in the house with her, when she was dead. He. . .he. . ."

"He what?" Suddenly, he sounds frustrated. Annoyed at me. I roll my eyes, but he continues. "He concealed her dead body from you. He shielded you from more pain and trauma after everything you had already been through." My chest collapses, and my cheeks warm, a subtle blush painting the canvas of my face. The weight of my surprising emotions pulls my eyes to the floor. "You need to give him a break. Yes, his methods were less than ideal, but his intentions were good, which is rare for him. And he had no choice." I dart my eyes back up to meet his, in another challenge. "Look, I know Lazarus can be. . ." He digs his hands deep into his pockets and rocks back on his heels.

"Selfish and arrogant," I interrupt.

"Selfish." Asheron shakes his head and rolls his eyes at me. "But I honestly believe that he was trying to do the right thing."

"The right thing for him," I murmur under my breath, my words dripping in sarcasm as the words spill out of my mouth.

He huffs. "I don't believe that for a second, and I know deep down, neither do you. He cares for you, Paege."

"The only thing he cares about is himself. . .Oh, and *Amalyah*," I scoff.

"Amalyah? What has she got to do with any of this?"

"Surely you've seen the way she looks at him." I uncross my arms, my fingers finding my charm, also unsure why I mentioned Amalyah. "There's something clearly going on there."

Why does that matter, Paege?

"I don't. . .I don't know about that, but I do know that he didn't have to help you and Quentin."

And there it is. The truth. Laid out bare for all to see. "Oh, no. He made it clear that he didn't want to be there. He looked me dead in the eyes and told me he was there because it was his duty to help me, not because he wanted to."

"Do you honestly believe that? Think about it. If you were just part of his duty as a Guard, he would have flown you out of there the second there was trouble. He would have brought you home. Instead, he risked his job and his life to ensure you could carry out that ridiculous journey. Do you know how much trouble he got in when he was arrested?" he snarls at me. My heart stops, and I drop my charm, taking a step back. In a much softer voice, Asheron pleads, "Just think about it, alright?"

Laz did risk himself for me, but that doesn't change the fact that he lied to me. He manipulated my memories after what Sylas had done to me. He violated my mind. I just don't know if I can ever get over that.

"When did you become so wise?" I toy with Asheron, trying to show some mercy. I don't like fighting with him. He's one of my best friends, and we have never fought in the past. I know his loyalty to Laz lies beyond the Guards. It's with Remi. Remi was Laz's friend. Laz is most likely the only connection he has to Remi left. How can I deny him that?

"I've always been wise. You just usually see the other Asheron. The fun Asheron." He winks.

"Well, I like this Asheron, too," I say kindly, taking his hands and leaning in, kissing him on the cheek. A rogue tear falls down his cheek.

"So do I," he smiles softly. "So, is all forgiven?"

"Not yet, but I am working towards it. I promise." My hand reaches my heart, and it pangs.

"I am sorry," Asheron whispers as he turns to leave the chamber.

"I know," I respond, "I am, too."

And as I let him guide me back to my room, a new revelation strikes me with the force of an unexpected slap, jolting me alert with a new realisation.

Guy is here.

And Quentin doesn't know.

CHAPTER 56

Today is supposed to be a day of happiness, new beginnings, and transformations. One of the most important and joyous days of my life. Instead, it's a day filled with nothing but dread, emptiness, and sadness.

My Unification.

Sitting on the edge of the bed, I run my hands down the soft, grey, velvety fabric cascading down my body to the floor and let out a breath. Amalyah left the dress in my room overnight, a gift for my Unification, and it's beautiful: form-fitting, plunging neckline, and long sleeves. Of course, it won't be worn during my actual Unification, but before and after during the celebrations. I don't even know if I will stay for the after-party, but for all intents and purposes, it's what I would be wearing.

I pick up my scribe: no new messages.

Mhelodie and Lumeilia will be arriving any moment with Asheron, and Amalyah is going to transport us to the Sacred Lakes when they get here. Then the ceremony will begin.

Me: Are you getting my messages? Just thought I would let you know it's my birthday today. I suppose you know that, though. It's also Guy's.

Me: My Unification is soon. I'm nervous.

I consider whether I should tell him about Guy, but I decide against it and hit send, then toss the scribe on the bed behind me and sigh. He still hasn't replied. I'm not sure what I was expecting.

I spent most of the last week sitting with Guy in the chamber. I haven't been able to bring myself to visit Mum. I'm not even sure if she's still down there. I'm avoiding Laz and Amerax like the plague, and I haven't seen much of the twins. I don't want to put that burden on them. They are too young. They shouldn't be dealing with this at such a young age. But the avoidance will end today. They will all be at my ceremony. Every. Single. One of them.

The door gently creaks open, and I hear Asheron's voice from the balcony. "Paege, can I come in?" Even Asheron has been more cordial than usual. I don't know why. Nothing about him is polite. Usually, he would saunter in as if he owned the place. Now, he is courteously asking to enter.

"Only if you brought gifts," I call back, a smile breaking free from my lips.

"I did one better," he responds, swinging the door open wide. "I brought two."

Mhelodie, Asheron, and Lumeilia come falling through the door at once, and my smile turns into a bubbling laugh. The girls rush me, squealing like birds, and pounce on me. I wrap my arms around them as we all fall back on the bed in a huddle. Their sweet laughter fills my ears and the empty cage in my chest with warmth. The sound of throat-clearing has us composing ourselves, and we sit up. Asheron is standing in front of us, a sullen and sad look washing over his face, his explosive violet eyes now nothing more than a dull purple. He smiles awkwardly.

He's my best friend. I've missed him so much, and this distance between us pulls an ache from my chest. In this moment, I want nothing more than to be in his embrace and for him to call me one of his weird nicknames. I stand, taking a step toward him and closing the gap between us, but it is still a giant abyss. He starts to step back, but I smile and reach for him before he steps away and yank him toward me with all my might. Asheron doesn't resist, and he moves effortlessly with me backwards. He tumbles forward into my arms as we land between the girls in an almighty hug, and then the girls jump us. The four of us become a tangled mess of arms and legs while dressed in our finest. The four of us together. The four of us forever.

Just like that, stitch by stitch, my heart starts to repair, and I know I'm going to survive this, even if I don't.

"Stop fidgeting." Mhelodie swipes my hands down to my side.

"I can't help it. I'm nervous," I drawl out in a shaky voice.

"We can tell," Asheron mocks as he takes my clammy hand in his and squeezes it gently. "You are going to be fine."

Laughter filters through the air to us, and I cast my eyes over towards the community surrounding the dais by the glistening Sacred lake. My family, my new friends, and Laz. There are some other guests I don't know, but I presume are Star-Borne. Even Keene and the Wolves came. A high priestess of the Fae is standing by an altar to their right. Everyone is enjoying themselves, talking and chatting. Yet here we stand between two of the lakes, under a canopy of trees, because I am too scared to enter the ceremonial area.

"I just. . .Is it going to hurt?" I blurt out, unsure where the idea of it hurting came from in the first place. In all my years alive, I've never once heard any of the Fae ever refer to their Unification as a painful experience. More so blissful.

"It's different," Asheron answers.

"It won't hurt, Paege," Mhelodie clarifies. "I don't know what it's like for Fae, but for Witches, it's scary, yes, but not painful." Mhelodie told me what her ascension entailed, and I find it hard to believe it wasn't painful. Arms sliced open, bleeding out in a warm, magical cauldron bath until your heart stops beating and you submerge beneath the murky waters. She woke later, fully healed, alive, and Ascended. Apparently, the longer you take to wake, the stronger your powers are. Most only take a few hours. Mhelodie took two days to wake. "It's peaceful," she continues.

The Fae Unification doesn't entail us to bleed out, only to submerge under the lake waters and drown.

"I can't give you any advice, because I haven't been through it yet, but I've never heard anyone say anything other than it being euphoric, a Gods-like experience," Lumeilia adds.

"It's definitely different," Asheron repeats and squeezes my hand again before letting go.

"But I'm also Wolf, only half Fae. What if I submerge beneath the lake's icy waters and Zephyra rejects me? What if I die?" My breathing begins to quicken. "Oh, Gods, what if I die?" Until right now, I hadn't even considered if being Wolf would affect my Unification. Could the Goddess of Wind reject me? I don't even know if any hybrid existed before me. And if so, did they even unify with their gifts?

"Breathe, Paege," Lumeilia says softly as she takes my other hand. "Breathe."

Breathe in, breathe out. Breathe in, breathe out.

I repeat the process, my face now locked with hers, trying to calm myself down from the quickly escalating worry that's wrapping itself around my mind.

"I don't think your Wolf is going to affect your Unification because you possess Fae gifts. You have been blessed by the Gods already, Paege," Mhelodie adds calmly.

Paege. . . I know it's hard not to focus on the lake or what's going to happen when you're down there. Just remember you are strong. You are powerful. You are remarkable. I won't let anything happen to you. You're going to be fine. Breathe, just breathe.

"Yes, breathe." I nod. "I'm going to be fine. You won't let anything happen to me. Thanks," I repeat between long breaths.

The group shares a glance between them and then smile at me, nodding. "Alright," they repeat in unison.

"Asheron, what's going to happen?" I ask again.

"I told you already, I don't remember. I wish I did, but I don't. Most don't, but I don't remember any pain. It's like Mhelodie said, peaceful."

"Peaceful, right?" I sigh. "Peaceful," I repeat, trying to manipulate my mind into believing the words I spew from my lips.

"I hate to do this, Paege, but your dad noticed us and is waving us over to join them." I snap my eyes up to meet Mhelodie, a small fury rising within the at word she just used. *Dad.* She swallows. "Amerax is waving us over," she says, correcting herself.

I nod and smile, extinguishing the fire within. My focus returns solely to the task at hand. "I don't know if I can just yet. . .I'm just going to go for a quick walk. I will be down in a moment." Asheron stares down at me, brows raised in a questioning manner. "I promise." Forcing a smile, I place my hand on my heart, and its beat shudders beneath my skin.

"Don't make me come back to get you." He winks, and I reach for his hand, pulling him in for a hug.

"Thank you," I whisper into his ear. "I'll be right behind you"

"Alright, bond sisters, let's liven this place up and get ourselves a drink," Asheron hollers as he heads off toward the crowd.

They silently make their way through the trees toward the colourful lake, and when they reach the crowd, I turn and walk to the bank of the lake, humming the little tune of the old Fae song I sang for Guy, one Mum used to sing when I was young and nervous. The sun beams down on me, my skin prickling from the subtle warmth of its winter rays. The chatter from the ceremony falls further away, and I can't help but tune into a flock of birds singing a melody high up in the treetops. I'm glad some of us are enjoying ourselves today. The birds' chorus comes to an abrupt end, and I tilt my head to watch them scatter through the sky in chaos as they disappear over the trees. The sudden silence pierces my soul's darkness, and a shudder crawls down my spine.

I jump as my scribe beeps. *Shit, Paege.* I pull my scribe out of my pocket and open the message.

Q: Books, I'm sorry. But I'm here now. Where are you?
I'll come to you.

My heart bolts like a startled wild horse, blood rushing in my ears. He messaged.

Me: I'm about to have my Unification. Can I come
meet you after?"
Q: Where are you? I can come to you.
Me: At the Sacred Lakes.
Q: I know where that is. Which one? I can be there soon.
Me: The first one.

I stare intently at the scribe for a long moment. Stupid, this is stupid. He will never make it here. Even if he shifted, it would take him all day to get here. Drums start pounding, and I know I have to go. The ceremony is starting, and I promised Asheron I wouldn't be long. It's already been a lot longer than I promised.

Me: I have to go. I'll meet you after.

"Or you could just meet me now."

The world stops for the briefest of moments, and my body lurches as I suck in a quick breath, barely filling my tightening chest. My scribe flies from my hand to the ground as I pull my hand to my chest to help ease the pain his voice pulled from my body.

Breathe, breathe, breathe.

I slowly turn to find Quentin standing there. Dressed in. . . Well, this is new. He's wearing his leather combat pants and a jacket that is adorned with the royal crest, the Crescent Pack badge, and his family crest. A sword is sheathed at his side, hanging from his belt.

He looks like a prince, like the Prince of Elyndria.

He looks different. Harsher. Older.

"What? How?" Oh, my Gods." I move to run for him, but he laughs, throwing his head back in an unnatural manner and baring his canines, and it pauses me. The lines in his face deepen as he does. My pulse quickens, and I try again. "How did you get here so fast?"

He shrugs. "I have my methods, and it wasn't hard to find you once you told me where you were."

I look around, searching for what, I don't know. An explanation, maybe? "But it was only a moment ago—" Even if he shifted, he would never have made it in that time.

"That's not important. What's important is I'm here." He starts padding softly toward me.

"You're here," I agree. I didn't expect him to come. I didn't know how I would feel if he did. Now that he's here, something in my chest settles. But my Wolf, she stirs.

"You wrote." Quentin flashes me a wolfish grin, his eyes fixating on mine, filled with something that resembles desire as he licks his lips.

"I wrote a lot, but I never heard from you. I thought. . ."

"I know." He swallows, wiping the hair from his brow. "Saw your message about your mum, though. I'm sorry, Paege. I should have come sooner."

"But you're here now?" It wasn't meant to be a question, but I can't help but wonder why.

"I am." When he's standing a mere arm's length from me, he reaches his hand out for mine.

I don't take it. His eyes narrow for the smallest of moments, then his face becomes emotionless once again. It was just a flicker, but I saw it. "What's with the. . . ?" He motions to his own hair, a question about my own.

An agonising knot twists in my stomach. "It was cut. Not by me. You would know if you ever answered my messages."

"I think I prefer it the other way," he gleans.

That's what he has to say? Not, "Are you alright?" Not, "By who?" Just an insult about how he prefers it longer. The calmness dissolves as a wave of rage surges through me. "Good thing I didn't do it for you then. How did you get here?" I ask because I don't understand exactly what is happening.

My Wolf sits up, and a cloud of unease rolls through the pit of my stomach. Where has he been these last few weeks? I know things were tense when he left Owenstown, even in the past and into the weeks leading up to it, but what was so important, so time-consuming that he hasn't been able to reply to a simple message? To acknowledge my mum. And why is he here now, today of all days? "Quentin, how did you get here?" I ask again as my eyes dart around the embankment. Panic starts burning in my chest. I take an uneasy step back toward the bank of the lake, putting some space between us.

"I told you it's not important. What matters is I'm here." He steps toward me again with his hand still reaching out and his eyes still glued to mine with an intensity I've barely seen in the past. But it's not desire.

"Hm," I muse and step away from him once more. It doesn't make any sense. "Where have you been?"

"I've been busy, Paege, but I came as soon as I could."

"Uh huh." My Wolf releases a low grumble in my chest, and I swallow, closing my eyes for a moment. She's here, like she always is, waiting, watching, but this time, she bares her teeth, sending me a clear warning. A warning about what? A chill slithers across my skin, and I open my eyes.

"Paege!" I hear my name called out through the clearing. Laz is coming for me, not Asheron, like he said.

"I, ah, I have to go," I stutter. I don't want to see Laz, but something is screaming at me that his timing couldn't have been better. I turn my attention from Quentin to face where Laz's voice is travelling from to call out in response, but instead, a gasp is pulled from my chest as a bitter cold bites against my skin, wrapping around my wrist. I turn back to face Quentin and yank my hand back, but I meet solid resistance as the metal clasps shut.

"What the fuck, Quentin?" My heart slams against my chest as I take in what just happened. Shackles. He shackled me.

"Sorry, Books," he replies as he tugs me in close to him and brings his hand up, moving unnaturally fast, even for a Wolf, and he blows something into my face.

I cough.

He wraps his arms around me. My body goes limp beneath his hold, and the world starts closing in around me, dragging me into the darkness. I try to struggle. Nothing. I try to call out for help, but my body is incapacitated. My mind screams as I fight to stay awake, to keep some sort of control. My Wolf thrashes deep within and howls in grief, but it's no use. I'm paralysed.

"Why?" I manage murmur as I resist the urge to slip under, disappearing into the shadows.

"I didn't have a choice," he whispers into my ear, and he lays a gentle kiss on my cheek, just as the world goes completely black.

CHAPTER 57

"Hidden in plain sight, broken by the light, hidden in plain sight, your wings can take flight," Mhelodie sings again and again as she skips and twirls around me in a hazy shade of silver. She holds a ribbon of fire in her hands that swirls through the air, trailing her like an obedient pet and leaving nothing but ash in its wake.

Lost in time, I can't move. The thick, smoky air chokes the breath from me as I crumble to the ember-covered floor beneath me.

I cough.

"Hidden in plain sight, broken by the light, hidden in plain sight," she sings again before coming to an abrupt stop in front of me. She bends down and leans toward me. The fire slithers like a serpent toward me, reaching my hands. Restricted by the darkness that holds my soul, I remain still as it wraps itself around my wrists, binding my hands together within its snare.

"You are a lost, little winged one, aren't you?" she coos quietly in my ear as the binds pull tighter around my skin, the searing pain of the flames yanking a gasp from me.

"You can free him, though, but you need Ardronis. When you die, he will rise."

She lurches back, the fire releasing me from its grip, but it doesn't recede. It playfully slinks around my hands.

I need Ardronis? What does she mean? Who's Ardronis? I look at my fists, and my eyes widen as I watch the flames dance around my skin. No longer do I feel the burn or the pain. Only gentle, cool air thins out around me. I open my hands, facing up, and the fire stops, pooling above the delicate skin in my palms. Studying, I watch it carefully as it pulsates from me, completely in rhythm to my beating heart.

"Paege, don't play with your fire. It's not the time to burn," Mhelodie taunts as she stands and starts skipping around me again. Her golden locks dance around her like tendrils of sunshine.

I open my mouth to take in a strangled breath, but the fire pulses, and before I have a chance to retreat, it spurts from my hands, leaping for my face. I jerk back, closing my eyes, and I scream. My mouth heats as the stream of flames pours itself straight down my throat, choking the fresh air from my lungs.

I gasp.

Again and again and again. . .

"Paege, it's time."

The back of my head throbs in time with my heavily pounding heart. My breaths are ragged, and the thick, musty air coats my mouth with an acrid taste. I swallow hard, and a sting bites at my cheek as I squeeze my eyes before peeling my lids open, scrambling to reconcile my memories.

The last thing I remember was. . .I was by the lake with. . . He came for me.

"Welcome back." His harsh voice spider-crawls through me, and it pulls a shiver from deep within my core. Quentin.

"What happened?" I choke as I peel myself up off the damp floor. I try to inch toward his voice, but I can't move far, my body meeting a solid resistance. I blink quickly, trying to bring my eyes into focus. The room is inky black except for a flicker of light by Quentin's face. He kneels before me, holding a single torch, and the flames dance across his wolfish face. His features morph into a Daemonic visage, casting shadows that twist and contort with each flicker of the light.

"You're safe, for now." A wicked smile crosses his face, and it sends the hair across my body on end.

"Quentin, what's going on?" I try to move again but am met with a hard, sharp tightness around my waist. The sound of clanking metal pauses my heart, and my breath catches in my throat as I try to swallow.

What in the Hels?

"Quentin?" I plead with a shaky voice. My hands find my neck, where a metal collar is shackled around it. Tears pool rapidly as I find yet another shackle belted around my body, snugly secured. I try to stifle a sob as the reality of the situation hits me with the force of a hurricane. "What's going on?" This is all too familiar. I've been here before. Last time, it was Quentin who saved me. This isn't happening. I've got it all wrong. This isn't happening.

He leans forward. "You and I have some things to discuss, Paege," he croons into my ear, before falling back from me again.

My breathing speeds, my chest rising and falling in a violent rhythm, short and sharp. "You could have messaged. We could have met to talk," I manage to say through the tight collar around my neck, my arms stretching out for him, but he's just. Out. Of. Reach.

"We needed to meet alone without *him*." He rubs at his forehead and then wipes his hair out of his eyes. *"Without her."*

"So, you drugged and locked me up?" I ask through gritted teeth as I stand on shaking legs and yank at the shorter chain secured to my waist, trying to rip it from the wall I'm tethered to. It's no use.

"I did what I needed to do."

"Wait, without—" I drop to my knees again and close my eyes, searching for my Wolf. She isn't there. A void of emptiness fills the space where she usually resides. Oh, Gods. "What did you do?" I cry. "Where is she?" I demand, pushing down the panic rising from within.

"She's fine. Just on a little vacation. Can't have you shifting into your Wolf." Amusement curls around me, slicing at me like millions of razor blades. A sour taste fills my mouth. I swallow it down and gag. I can feel his emotions. He is taunting me.

"Oh, I forgot." He holds up his hand. The iron ring Mhelodie made him sits like a little crown on a throne in the palm of his hand. "I figured I won't be needing this anymore. Not that I ever needed it." He throws it casually into the air, catching it in his palm. He hurls the ring into the darkness. It clangs as it hops and rolls along the rocky ground, coming to a gradual stop on the other side of the chamber.

"Quentin?" He doesn't answer me. He stands, his deadpan eyes never leaving mine. Holding the torch, he walks a few steps to my right before kneeling again next to—Oh, Gods. "Is that?"

"Guy." He places the torch next to his body and stands again. Wiping the dirt off his pants, he silently pads toward the opening on the other side of the room. He stills as he reaches the chamber door. Not looking back at me, he finally speaks again, "Surely you can figure it out."

My mind rapidly scans all the information I have gathered over the past few months. There is only one reason why Quentin would have me held captive. One reason he would need me. "You're going to break the curse," I mutter into the darkness.

"And you're going to help me do it," he confirms as he closes the door behind him, the clasp locking into place.

CHAPTER 58

The air in the chamber is thick and uncomfortable. Or is that the chains around my neck restricting my breath? It's hard to tell. My chest tightens with every inhale of the rusty air, and my lungs burn as they barely fill. I twist my neck trying to relieve the pressure against my throat, but all that does is dig the cold metal into my skin further.

Tremors quake through my body, unrelenting and wild. My tears fall from the dark cloud that looms above my heart. I stare at the door. Even if I weren't shackled to the wall, I don't think I could move. Again, I close my eyes, searching for my Wolf, but I know it's no use. Whatever Quentin gave me not only knocked me out, but it also severed my connection to my Wolf. Hopefully, not forever.

Quentin. My Quentin. *"There isn't anything I wouldn't do,"* his words ring through the vastness of my mind like a piercing cry. Quentin did this. He did this to me. I know we had our issues lately, but those were because of what his father had done. My accusations, he said, were unfounded. He constantly defended his father and swore he wouldn't be involved. He tried to make me feel like I was paranoid and prejudiced towards his father, towards the Wolves. I should have seen this coming.

"Quentin?" I call out into the darkness. "Quentin?" My voice ricochets off the chamber walls, filling my cage with the sounds of my captor's name as it burrows like a jackhammer into my chest. When it finally stops, the silent reply is deafening. Did I do this? Did I push him to this? I shouldn't have brought him with me. I should have left him out of it. We still would have had our issues, but those issues were nothing like this.

"You better not come for me or my family," his parting words to me—nothing more than a hypocritical warning. Is this what he has been doing since he left me in Owenstown? Learning about the curse. Figuring out how to break it? Did he speak to his father and decide to help him?

I grab the chains and yank them. Without my Wolf strength, it's no use. Even with her strength helping me, I doubt I could free myself. They are bolted. I lean against the shackle belted around my waist, my weight dropping forward. The collar around my neck presses into my throat, choking the breath out of me, and the chain groans under the tension. I pull back, coughing as the air fills my lungs in sweet relief. I run my hands over the collar and belt again. They are made of a thick, heavy metal of some sort. My fingers catch on a sharp divot in the belt. I look down, and in the subtle warm light, I can make out etchings engraved across the belt. They're enchanted, no doubt, to suppress my Wolf and other magics. Not that I have any active magic. I didn't get to have my Unification.

Oh, Gods.

My Unification.

My family.

Asheron was there. Laz was there, and he was coming for me. What does he think happened? My friends, my father? Where do they think I went? Where do they think I am? Tears threaten to build in the corners of my eyes as an unpredictable storm starts building within. I try to take a breath, but it catches as the pressure in my chest tightens some more.

Come on, Paege. Breathe.

Regardless of my fight, I can't seem to fill my lungs, and the corners of my vision begin to morph into the darkness as I sink to the wet, cold ground beneath me. An animalistic sound leaves my body. I repeatedly yank at the chains, and the clanging pierces through the eerie silence with every tug. The stillness of the chamber fills my bones in a way I'm becoming all too accustomed to. I'm alone.

Pulling enough strength from deep within my core and ignoring the empty void that lies inside, I finally allow myself to glance over to where the torch was left by Quentin. Next to Guy's body. My stuttering heart dives as I take in the scene before me. Guy. He lies like he did on the altar, peaceful and flat on his back with his hands neatly placed across his chest. As my eyes adjust to the darkness, strange symbols etched into the stone floor around him become clear. My heart stammers. He wasn't dumped there. He wasn't discarded. He was carefully positioned.

When did Quentin manage to take Guy's body? How did he even find him? How did he find me? I never told Quentin about Guy being in the chamber under the court. There is no way he could have known. And how did he get in? Someone must have told him. Someone let him in. But who? No one knew. Mhelodie and Lumeilia, Mum, Amerax, Laz, and Asheron are the only ones who knew. Mum is dead, and there is no way in Hels Amerax, Laz, or Asheron would have told him. Mhelodie and Lumeilia—I won't even allow myself to go there. They aren't working with him. That I know without a kernel of doubt. So, who?

I sink back to the ground and bring my knees to my chest, wrapping my arms around my legs. The long velvet sleeves on my dress do nothing to relieve the chill that's in the air. I can't survive down here for too long. I don't even know where down here is. I'm in an underground chamber, and it's safe to say it's connected to the tunnels under Ferinini, but where? Am I still in Ferinini? How long was I out? I don't even know how long I've been gone for.

My stomach grumbles, and a gnawing emptiness in my stomach begins to consume my thoughts. Hunger. I'm starving. I haven't eaten in. . .I have no idea. Standing again, I yank at the chain. "Argh." I fall back to the ground, crawling over to Guy's body, and I grab the torch from beside him. Curling myself up again, I hold my hand above the tiny flame, hoping for a nugget of warmth. I feel nothing. It's too cold.

A sob breaks from my aching chest, bringing forth a tsunami of tears as the terror rises within. I wrap my arms back around my knees and rock myself back and forth, back and forth, humming that same little tune my mother used to sing to me when I was nervous, allowing the plethora of emotions to swarm me until I finally drift off in the cold, harsh nothingness.

Laz stands shirtless before me with his black hair in disarray. He's not wearing his combat leathers, but he still looks every bit the warrior I know him to be. His eyes glisten with desire as he drinks me in.

I look down and gasp. "What am I wearing?" My silver gown is now almost see-through with a plunging neckline and two splits up each side of my legs. I've worn undergarments more modest than this. My hair is long, flowing like it never saw the battle.

"You don't like it, little wolf? I thought your silver gown needed. . .fixing." He pushes his lips into a mischievous grin, but it's not right, none of this is right.

Is this some kind of dream? Is my mind so completely fractured that I'm conjuring thoughts of Laz now? Wearing a ridiculous see-through dress? "What is this?"

As if he didn't hear me, he asks, "Where are you?"

I blink. "You mean, where are *we?*" It's the woods or a forest, but I hear the faint trickle of a river of water flowing somewhere nearby. It's not the Dead Forest nor the White Forest. It's beautiful, luscious, and green. Birds chirp cheerily, and the sun is high and bright, peeking through the canopy above.

"We are somewhere safe. I need to know where you are."

Where am I? How can he not know? I'm here with him. Or am I? "Am I dreaming?"

His face shifts when he answers, "Yes, and no."

Well, that wasn't an answer at all. I must be dreaming, having a hallucination, a cruel trick of the mind. I'm finally losing it. Cracking at seams, my reality slowly slipping away. "Tell me where you are?" He asks again, his eyes wide with hope but also with something else. Fear. Laz is fearful. I've never seen him afraid of anything. *Yes, a dream,* I tell myself.

I must have said the words out loud because Laz answers. "No, little wolf, it's not a dream, but no, none of this is real." His expression turns taut. "I need you to tell me where you are."

I shake my head to anchor myself, to pull myself back out of this insanity, but memories slip between my fingers like water, and I am getting swept away. Laz reaches out a hand, as if he's going to cup my face, and I step back. My body hits a tree, and I stand firmly against it. Why did I move away from his touch? I know I'm not scared of him, but. . .

"Where are you, Paege? Think."

Think. Think. Think. Where am I? The last thing I remember is. . .my Unification, yes.

"That's it, little wolf, remember." He gently coaxes my memories to the surface.

Images of Asheron, Lumeilia, Mhelodie, Laz, and Quentin at the lakes flash before my eyes, then another with Quentin in the chamber with Guy. Then the shackles. They move like a fast-playing movie. I can't grab any particular moment. All of them flip forward and backward too fast, too violently for me to hold onto. "Laz, what's happening?" I sob. I didn't even know I was crying.

"Sh," Laz starts, and with soft fingers, he lifts his hand. This time, I don't move out of his reach, and he wipes away a tear that is slowly rolling down my cheek. His touch soothes something inside of me. The panic slowly disappears, dissolving like clouds after a wild storm. I try to lean into him, to cherish his touch. More. I need more of him. Oh, how I missed him these last few weeks, but with a violent tug, I'm ripped from my dream. From Laz.

"I'm coming for you. . ." His voice echoes around me as it fades into nothing. "Coming for you. . . For you. . . You. . ."

Blinking, I bring myself back to the present. My dreary eyes remain unfocused. My dress is soaked through, the freezing air numbing my body. Ice bites at my skin as I lie curled in a ball in the dirty cell. I swallow as I roll myself over, the weight of my chains serving as a constant reminder that I'm being held captive. How long has it been? I still don't know.

"Laz," I whisper into the darkness. "I forgive you."

I close my eyes again and let the darkness pull me back under.

Grating metal across stone violently pulls me from my stupor.

"Get up." The harshness of his voice equals that of my reality. Something slaps at my wet dress, and the sting against my skin is a rude awakening, even in these conditions. "Put that on," he demands.

I groan as I roll over and push myself into a seated position. The light went out days ago—was it days, or is that just how it feels—but when I drag my eyes open, I realise he brought another torch with him. I don't speak. I won't give him the satisfaction of hearing my cries or pleas.

"I'll be back shortly. Then you and I are going to have a little chat."

He places the torch by the exit and steps back, heaving the chamber door shut. The lock clasps once again. Tears sting the back of my nose. I look down and see he has thrown leather pants, a button-up shirt, a jacket, socks, and boots at me. And gloves. Gloves just like the ones he gave me before. Without any thought, I tear at my wet dress, ripping it from my sodden body, and pull the clothes that Quentin threw at me on. The cold metal of the belt shackle bites into my skin as it rubs against my bare stomach and back while I pull the shirt and jacket over the top of it. It's too tight to slide the material underneath it, so I grit my teeth and bear the pain, hoping that eventually, he will release me, or at least, release the chains at least.

The constant drumming in my ears becomes insufferable in the silence as I wait for Quentin to return. I continue to rock myself back and forth. It's become a somewhat soothing rhythm in the stillness and chaos that's been unfolding around me.

The door groans open again, and Quentin enters my cage. He doesn't close the door behind him; he just takes a few steps toward me but stops where the end of my tether allows me to reach. He's keeping his distance. Smart. He holds a bottle of water and a paper plate with bread and some sort of spread. He sits down in front of me, folding his legs, and places the water and plate down, sliding them across the ground. "Eat," is all he says.

I don't take the plate or the water. I just stare at him in utter disbelief. After minutes of silence, I finally ask, "Why?"

"Why what?" he replies coolly, like he honestly has no idea what I am referring to.

"Why all of it, Quentin? Why me?"

"Where is the blade, Paege?"

I flinch. I wasn't expecting that. "I don't know," I answer, trying to understand what he's referring to.

"I know you have it. The Seer has been tracking it for months."

"The Seer?" I repeat.

"Yes, the Seer. You knew I had her," he replies sardonically.

"I thought your dad. . ."

"My dad. Me. It was *our* plan, Paege."

My chest clenches violently, this revelation sending me into a chaotic spin. "How? When?" I can't believe for one second Quentin was smart enough to pull this off. His father, absolutely. He's a snake, a viper. But Quentin? No.

"After the night I met you in the street, all sad and weepy, after your boyfriend broke your heart. You kind of made it too easy for me. I followed your scent there. I was not expecting to find such treasure, that's for sure." Quentin was the one who kidnapped the Seer all along. But. . .why? I don't understand. She's a gimmicky Seer who told me about Sylas. Maybe she saw Guy, too, but what on earth would she have known about any of this?

He snaps his fingers twice in the space between us, bringing me back to our conversation. "Now, the athame, where is it?" he repeats.

"I don't have it." I shake my head, a zap between my breasts yanks a gasp from me.

"Paege," he drawls, frustration dripping from his voice, "where is it? Tell me!"

"Quentin, I don't have it," I reply, clipping my words. "I have no idea where it is. I've been trying to figure it out, but I swear to you, I. Do. Not. Have. It."

He stands, taking a step closer and towering over me like I'm some insignificant insect. "I. Don't. Believe. You. Where is it?" he snarls.

Feeling so small under his shadow, I push myself up to my unstable feet. Closing my eyes for a moment, I attempt to steady myself, breathing deeply into the dizziness, thoughts, and visions swirling around in my head. "Why are you doing this? I thought you. . ." I say, bringing my hands to my temples and rolling my fingers over the soft skin to ease the pressure that's building beneath my touch.

"You thought what? That I loved you?" He laughs. It's such an evil thing, and something inside me cracks apart at the sound of it.

I snap my eyes open, my gaze meeting his. "You told me," I whimper, remembering his words he said to me the night Guy died. Why would he say that in that moment if it wasn't true? There was absolutely nothing he stood to gain from saying that in that moment. *Except for my trust,* that niggling voice inside my head reminds me.

"I told you what you needed me to say for you to trust me."

And there it is. The ugly truth I had been so desperate for, but also hoped wasn't true. "I don't believe you," I croak, trying to ease some of the shame rippling over me. How could I be so stupid as to think anything had changed? To think he truly cared.

"Fine, maybe there was a time when I thought I might have been falling for you. . .But that was before I knew what I know now," he begrudgingly admits. Hearing it doesn't dissolve the bitterness coating my bones, nor does it ease the storm brewing inside me. In fact, it just makes everything that much worse.

"Don't act so innocent, Paege. You took me on that whole journey without telling me. And if the tables were turned, you would be killing me. Or my father. You. . ."

"That's a lie, and you know it," I interrupt him. "I would have found another way. I was trying to find another way. I have spent every minute of every day researching in the library, pulling old archives and reading the journal pages, trying to find another way. Trying to find anything that could help us." Quentin swipes the hair out of his eyes and raises both his brows, but he doesn't speak. His cold blue eyes burn into me. "And what about Guy?" I probe. "What about the Scorpions?" A fire ignites in my core. Every moment with him was a lie. Lies. It was all planned and preconceived. I was nothing but a pawn in his game to free himself from a curse that he knows absolutely nothing about.

"Guy was not supposed to die. You, maybe, but not him. You got him killed. He died because of you, and I have barely been able to stomach looking at you since. But in the end, I learnt a lot from you, too. And after the Eagles, I had my escape planned, and I no longer had to pretend."

"You. . ." The walls around me start caving in, pulling the air out of the room, suffocating me with every inch they creep. "Was any of it real?"

"Not really. Gods, Paege, you are divine. I wished it didn't have to end this way, and for a while, I thought maybe there might be another way. But the truth of the matter is that you are the key to breaking the curse. There is, unfortunately, no other way. I wish I could have another taste of you, but your damn ex and the bloody branding. . ." he muses out loud.

My stomach rolls. "You're disgusting!" I spit.

"That's not what you said when I had my fingers inside you."

"Go to fucking Hels, you pig."

"I'm afraid, Books, that's where you're going. Not me."

"You're worse than Sylas. I hate you." I suppress a sob. I won't let him see me cry again. He doesn't deserve my tears.

"Now, now, don't be like that. If things were different, maybe we could have had a chance."

"You're delusional," I snort.

"Hm. . ." He steps forward and swiftly grabs my wrists, pulling me closer to him. The chains creak under the tension as he holds my arms to my sides and brings his face to mine. I hitch a breath as his lips skate across the delicate skin under my ears. My traitorous heart skips a beat as the soft scent of fresh pine coils itself around me. "Not that delusional," he laughs cocking a brow. *Asshole.* "Now tell me, where is the athame?" he whispers into my ear.

"I don't have it!" I scream in his face. At my outburst, he pushes me back with brute force and steps away from me. I lose my footing and trip, violently hitting the ground, and my body barks in pain as I smack into the rock.

"That's fine. We have time. I'll be back."

"Are you going to kill me?" I whimper as he heads toward the exit.

"Not yet. . . Eat." He motions to the food he left on the floor.

"No, don't leave me down here, Quentin, please." He doesn't turn back. He doesn't even flinch as I cry out to him, begging him not to leave me alone in the dark again.

"Don't leave me," I cry again and again and again. But the door closes and the lock snaps.

Once again, I'm left in my solitary confinement with nothing but my delusions and fears to keep me company.

Chapter 59

How does he know? How does he remember? He said he's known since before I knew, before I knew him, but how? And why are they all so sure I have this blade? He has been with me for months. If I had it, I would have told him. He would have known. How can he possibly think that I have it and am hiding it from him?

I pull my knees in closer, curling myself into the smallest ball I possibly can. "Help me," I whisper into the cage I'm trapped in. "Please."

A golden talon rips through the inkiness of my mind, the blinding light instigating a thunderous ache from behind my eyes.

Paege. Where are you? He whispers it gently into the night, and his voice is a sweet symphony, caressing my shattering mind. I blink. There's no one there. The darkness has been playing games with me for days, taunting and teasing me like a predator playing with its food. I close my eyes again.

Paege, tell me where you are, the emptiness whispers into my ear.

"Laz?" I sigh into the dark.

I'm coming, Paege, the darkness seems to answer back. I haven't eaten in days. I'm delirious. I've seen him standing in my chamber when I'm in that haunting place between sleep and awake. My mind is playing cruel, twisted jokes on me.

I'm coming, Paege, it whispers again.

Salty tears sting the back of my throat. No one is coming. The realisation of everything comes crashing down on me like a crumbling building.

I'm trapped.

I'm alone.

No one is coming to save me.

Quentin is going to kill me.

Closing my eyes, I rock myself back and forth. . .back into the nothingness, and just like a tightly wound music box, that sweet little melody begins to play again in my mind, bringing me the only peace of mind I can hold onto.

A clash disrupts my slumber. "You haven't eaten," he growls. "Do I need to force you?"

I peel my sandpaper lids open. Quentin's face, a face I used to think was so handsome and beautiful, so misunderstood, is mere inches from mine. I open my mouth to speak but close it again, and instead, I swallow. What's the point in eating when he's just going to kill me? What's the point in begging when he's just going to ignore me?

"If you've got something to say," he muses, as he taps his boot on my cage floor, "then by all means, speak."

I shake my heavy head, the ache behind my eyes intensifying as I move.

"Eat, Paege," he says softly. "You need to eat," his words softly dance across my skin in a blissful rhythm, cocooning me in a symphony of concern. It's a sound that resembles the Wolf I thought once knew.

"Don't pretend to care," I finally bite. "If you're going to kill me, just do it, Quentin," I rasp.

"I can't yet. We need the blade. The blade you're hiding." He stands and starts pacing the chamber. Despite the darkness, I see a muscle feather in his jaw. "I know you have it. I just wish you would tell me. We could end all this right now. Don't think I enjoy this, hurting you. I'd rather not. I just want all of this to end." He leans against the wall, crossing his arms across his chest and swinging an ankle over the other. "Don't you?" he asks, his lips pulling down and his eyes narrowing.

He pushes off the wall and lightly treads over to Guy and kneels beside him. A possessiveness I've never felt before burns through my darkened soul as he places his hand on Guy's shoulder. I don't want Quentin to touch him. I don't want him anywhere near Guy, but even though he's not who I thought he was, even though he's the evil, conniving psychopath he has turned out to be, he loved Guy like a brother. I know that without a nugget of doubt, and the small part of me that hasn't died can still somehow feel compassion for this monster.

How can I feel anything but hatred and disgust for him after everything he has done? Everything he's doing. After discovering who he really is. Disappointment settles deep in my core. Even broken, I can't hate my captor.

Pathetic, Paege. You're pathetic.

A tear rolls down his cheek as he brings his gaze back to me.

"I know you hate me, but everything I'm doing is for him."

"Bullshit," I spit. "It's for you and your dad. You don't give a shit about him or anyone else."

"You have me all wrong. You have us both all wrong. Yes, it's for us, but it was also for him."

My eyes widen in disbelief at what he's saying. How can he possibly say that it was for Guy? His lifeless body lies feet from me, and it's all because of his father, the False King.

Quentin's face briefly flinches, and I see a flash of the Quentin I knew. The lines of his face soften, and he shakes his head. Is he pretending now? Was he pretending before? It doesn't matter. After everything he has done, I don't want to feel anything but hatred for him. I swallow every emotion. I refuse to give him anything.

I pull my gaze from his, and with every bit of energy I can muster, I stand. "Kill me!" I demand. "You've got a sword; you've got a blade. Who's to say that it won't work? Just kill me, and be done with it."

He pushes himself off his knees and approaches me with determined steps. "I told you, I can't without the athame."

Pulling my lips into a straight line, I don't answer. I just watch him as intensely as he's been watching me. He turns away, and I see his dagger sheathed at his side. Seizing my opportunity, I reach out and grab the hilt and pull it. He pivots fast, but I'm faster. As I draw the blade from its sheath, I whip it back, holding it up to my throat. Quentin stills, holding his hands up in a mock surrender.

"Let me go, Quentin, or I'll kill myself now, and no one will be saved."

He laughs. He fucking laughs. "I know you, Paege. You don't have the courage to do it." That would have been true at one point in my life, but since I met him, everything has changed. I have been pushed and pulled, stabbed and branded, played and betrayed. I've seen more death than I care to admit, and whatever light I once had burning inside has long been extinguished. Nothing remains of my heart except for a pile of blackened ashes.

"Don't test me, Quentin. I will. I swear I will." With shaking hands, I press the blade into my throat, and the cool metal bites against the soft skin under my jaw. When it lightly nicks the flesh, it catches my breath, and I smile mockingly.

"Paege. . ." he pleads as a flicker of doubt flashes in his eyes.

Stepping back, I hit the wall. I'm trapped. If I'm going to do it, I have to do it now. I can't let him win. I can't let this pathetic excuse of a male take away my dignity. If I'm going to die, I'm going to do it at my own hands. Not his. That was a decision I made long before we ever got here.

I dive deep inside myself, searching for the strength I need to do what I need to do. I tunnel until I see that little nugget of mettle.

And when I grasp it, I hold on tight, refusing to let it go, just like the grudge I hold for what Quentin has done. Visions of the twins, Amerax, my friends, and even Laz assault my mind. A tear slowly leaks from my eye and falls down my face.

Do it, Paege, just do it.

My hand tightens around the hilt, nails biting into my palm, and I swallow hard, trying to kill the lump that's growing where the blade touches my throat.

Do it, Paege!

Lifting my lids, I stare into his icy blues through my lashes. Quentin takes another step and slowly raises his hand to me. My muscles stiffen as his hand wraps around mine, and he gently pulls my arm away from my body. I shudder a long breath, and my chest collapses as he yanks the blade from my hand and steps back. His eyes roll with sheer disappointment and amusement at my actions. Or lack thereof.

A painstakingly primal sound releases from my body right before I fall to the ground, and I bring my clenched hands down into my thighs over and over and over again. Through hazy eyes, I watch Quentin turn around and walk off toward the exit, looking like he doesn't have a care in the world.

And as he closes the door to my cage, he huffs with amusement, "I knew you wouldn't have the guts to do it. I'll be back."

Peeling my tongue off the roof of my mouth is like trying to unglue two pieces of paper. The tender muscle cries out in pain as I finally release it. With the constant darkness, I have no idea how long I've been down here or how long it's been since I have eaten or drunk anything. It could be days, weeks, maybe longer. The water bottle remains by the wall, untouched, and fresh bread appears every so often when I wake.

I try to stand, but the weak muscles in my legs tense again, a pain shoots up my right calf, the tendons stretch thin and the muscle twitches. I yelp, and my legs give up, and I fall back into the ground. Another cramp. I don't know how much longer I can hold out. My body aches in places I didn't know it could. My insides are shrivelling up like a prune. Even the smallest of movements, like opening my eyes, uses energy I just don't have.

Maybe just one sip?

Like a wounded animal, I slowly drag my carcass across the filthy floor to the water bottle, each movement a struggle against the weight of my exhaustion, and with trembling hands, I release the lid. I didn't even think it was possible, but I swear I can smell the freshness of the chilled water as I open the bottle. The simple act of carefully bringing the water bottle to my mouth is a failure and a success, the betrayal of my actions nestling against my very soul. It disappears as I tip the cool, silky liquid into my mouth, and it washes over my tongue and gums, filling my body with a refreshing burst of life. Like a wild beast, I open my throat and start pouring the liquid life down, gulping ferociously while I become aware that my life depends on it.

The water bottle is ripped from my hands before I even manage to get more than a few large gulps down. "Whoa, whoa, whoa," Quentin hurriedly says as he pulls the bottle from my mouth.

I didn't hear the door creak open or see him walk into the chamber. I didn't feel his presence as he knelt in front of me. I was so focused on filling my body that I didn't notice anything else. Water spills from my mouth, and I blink, my stomach rolling without warning. I twist to the side as the water I just swallowed rises back up and dribbles out of my mouth. I cough and cough and cough, the bile and water choking my breath and stinging my raw throat as it leaves my body.

Once I stop vomiting, Quentin gently wipes the damp hair that's stuck across my cheek away, like a mother would her child. "Books, you haven't eaten or drunk in days." He caresses my cheek, "You need to take it slowly." He offers the water bottle back to me.

I nod, understanding what he's just revealed. Days. I'm sure being kept underground in the dark, with no sense of time, is designed to confuse me, make me believe I've been gone longer than I have, but it's only been days.

He brings the bottle to my mouth and gently tips it, and I accept it, my mouth opening wide like a baby bird. A few small mouthfuls later, he pulls the bottle back. "That's enough for now. In a little while, have a couple more sips, alright?" I nod again. Why is he being so kind to me now? He's going to kill me anyway. What's the point of this? "I'll be back with some fresh food soon, Books."

"Don't." I cough. "Call me that," I rasp, coughing again, the disgust at hearing that name threatening to bring the water I just drank back up.

He turns with an arched brow. "Huh?"

Digging the tips of my fingers into the dirt floor, I repeat myself. "Don't call me Books."

He doesn't acknowledge my request. "Another couple of sips in a little while. I'll be back." He pivots and exits the room.

I'm alone. Again.

"Stop it, Quentin, there has to be another way," I beg as he paces the chamber. Quentin isn't wearing any of his weapons. Every time he enters my cage, he disarms, leaving them at the door, obviously not wanting to take any more chances., but I don't even have the energy to try.

He pivots to face me. "There is none."

"I don't believe that. *You* don't believe that."

"You heard what the Eagles said." He leans in and whispers in my ear, "With blood it's bound, with blood it breaks. The curse needs blood to break it free, and only blood will satisfy thee."

He stands tall, resolve settling in his shoulders. "It's pretty damn clear."

"We don't even know if it's my blood it needs," I beg again. I've had the suspicion all along that it was my blood. I don't know if I would ever be able to go through with it, but I thought I would be doing it on my terms. I wanted to have all the information, understand exactly what was at stake, and at least be able to say my goodbyes, even if no one understood or knew what I was doing. I would do it when I was at peace with the decision.

"You would like that, wouldn't you? For it to be mine? I am sorry, Paege. I've read the pages over and over again. They are not of light; they do not renew. The Crescent Pack are bound by the moon and immune to venom. We renew when we are bitten. It's not my bloodline, Paege. It's yours."

You wear the blood of the cursed. Use it to set them all free.

That's what he was doing with the journal in Owenstown. He was taking copies of our notes.

"Now, if you would just tell me where the blade is."

I am a bloody broken record. No matter what I say, he doesn't believe me. "I swear, Quentin, I don't know." A jolt of energy in my chest shudders a gasp from my broken body. I ache from the manacles binding me to the wall and the little space I have to move. If I knew where the damned thing was, I would tell him.

"That's fine, Paege. We still have time. We have all the time." He stands and heads toward the door.

"No. Please, Quentin, don't leave me again. Please," I beg, I plead, I cry out.

"Oh, I'm not. I'm sending in someone else. If you won't talk to me, then maybe you'll talk to her."

Her? "No, wait, don't leave me in here. . ." I scream again and again and again. My pleas fall on deaf ears. He doesn't even look back another time as he exits the chamber and closes the door behind him, leaving me alone again in the cold, dark room.

Alone.

Her? His sister? No, she's a baby. Juno? It can't possibly be Juno. He hates her after what happened with Ric. I know he does. I felt the hurt and disgust roll off him in thick, muddy waves when we met them at The Pit. You can't fake emotions like that. But then again, I also felt his desire for me. No, I refuse to believe that was a lie. It couldn't all have been lies. No matter how far I dig into the depths of my murky mind, searching for some sort of clarity, I can't think of who else he's referring to. There just isn't anyone.

My intrigue doesn't last long. The second I hear her voice, it all comes crashing down around me.

"Hello, Princess," she drawls in her heavily rounded accent. "I'm so sorry I kept you waiting, but I believe you and I need to have a little chat."

Chapter 60

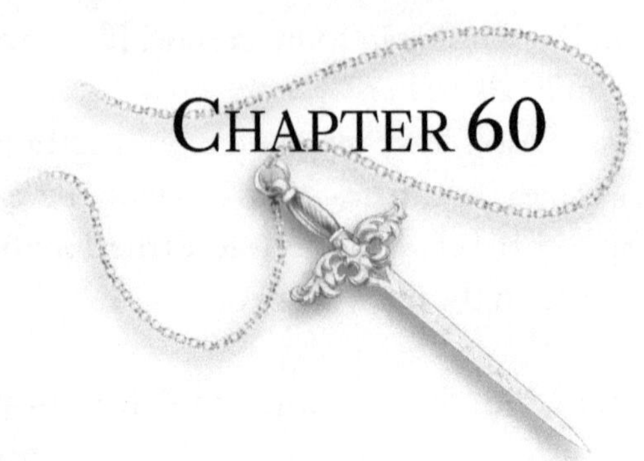

Disbelief coils itself around my fracturing mind as I stare at her through glassy eyes, trying to reconcile who I'm seeing before me. Her auburn hair falls around her ivory cheeks in cascading waves as she hitches her flowing plum skirt up and gracefully makes her way through the chamber. Shadows dance across her face from the reflection of the lantern she carries, and her auburn hair sparkles with golds like stars burning bright in the darkness.

Sydney.

Kneeling, she extends her arm slowly to my face. I flinch back in horror, and my breath hitches when her cold fingers curl against my cheek. Gently, she wipes my skin, smearing the wetness from my tears across my face. "It's fine, Princess. I won't hurt you. I promise," she reassures me with a gentle smile.

"What are you doing here?" I manage to muster enough strength to respond to her as I push myself back into the stone wall behind me, willing my body to morph into the rocks and out of her touch as emotions roll through me. How did this possibly happen? And why would she be working with the Ishaans? She is Mhelodie's mentor. A Witch. *Why* would she be working with the Ishaans?

"We need to have a little talk."

"Is Mhelodie alright?" I blurt out.

Her chestnut eyes widen, and she shoots back, straightening her body. Is that surprise or hurt I can see on her face? "Mhelodie?"

"Yes, Mhelodie. Is she safe?"

"Of course, she is. Why would you ask such a thing?" Her shoulders drop, and her voice lowers to its usual slow, rounded tone.

Is she really asking me why? As if she hadn't befriended her while conspiring with that monster all along. She says she won't hurt me, but at this stage, I trust no one, and I don't want to give her any reason to lash out. Biting my tongue, I respond through gritted teeth, "Because you were her mentor, her friend."

"*Am*, Princess. I *am* her mentor and friend, which is why she is perfectly safe. They all are." A feline smile appears on her face, and I can't tell if she's taunting me or if she's genuine. Does she care at all for Mhelodie, or is this another part of their vicious game?

I'm relieved Mhelodie is safe and not in trouble. I couldn't handle the guilt of being responsible for her being in danger a second time. But what does that mean for me? "Why are you here?"

"I need you to tell me where the athame is, dear," she says, unclasping the cloak that's secured around her neck.

"Like I told him, I don't know."

Once the cloak is unfastened, she drops it from her shoulders and catches it across her arm. She kneels, swirling the cape around me and draping it over my shoulders. I shudder. The warmth of her body heat still in the fabric saturates my freezing body. I remain silent and still as she works to clasp the fabric.

Once the cape is secured around my neck, she reaches out and snaps her hand around my wrist in a bruising grip. She closes her eyes and hums, as if my body is speaking to her, exposing my secrets and betraying me in every way possible. "Hmm, interesting. You don't know, do you?" Her fingers loosen their hold.

"That's what I've been trying to tell him." I rip my hand out of her grip, wrapping my arms around my curled-up knees. "Now get away from me!" I scream, but my outburst doesn't elicit a response from her.

Quentin snickers from a distance. I tilt my head up and find him standing at the door to my chamber, an evil sneer forming across his face. Sydney's eyes follow my gaze over her shoulder. She stands, wiping her hands down her plum-berry skirt, and approaches him. He hands her a small glass vial. She unsheathes a dagger from Quentin's thigh and gestures for his palm. He obliges without any questions. "Your Highness, would you please give us a moment?" she respectfully asks as she drags the blade across his palm, then forces his hand into a fist and squeezes. Blood drips from his hand, and she catches it in the glass vial, slowly filling it.

He doesn't move, nor does he flinch. He also doesn't answer.

"I know you're eager to get her to speak, but I think it's clear by now that she won't with you standing there."

He nods. "Fine," he finally says, pulling his hand back. "But you had better get her to tell you where the Hels it is. I trust you remember our deal." A shiver spider-crawls its way across my body. Deal? She made a deal with Quentin.

"How could I possibly forget?" Her lips curl, and a saccharine smile graces her face.

Quentin swipes the hair that's fallen across his forehead. "I'll be back soon." His hand lands on the chamber door handle. "I don't care what you have to do, just get her to tell you where it is." He drags the giant chamber door closed, disappearing out of sight as it closes, but the latch never secures. He trusts her enough to leave the door unlocked. What sort of deal could she have possibly made to justify all of this?

She pivots back to face me, and she walks across the room with the dagger still in one hand and the blood vial in the other. Her eyes soften, and she kneels beside me. "Princess, we don't have much time before he comes back," she whispers. "I need your palm. I don't want to force you, but I will if I have to. I know you don't trust me right now, but please, if you follow my instructions and hear me out, I can explain everything. I am not your enemy."

My eyes widen. Like I have a choice. I'm chained to the wall. I can't go anywhere. What could she say that could justify any of this? That could make me think, *Gee, alright, I don't hold it against you that you conspired to kidnap and kill me.* I hold out my palm, not the one with my bond with the girls, but the other empty one. She takes the blade and cuts through my skin. When the blood pools, she pours the vial of what I'm assuming is Quentin's blood into my palm and starts to paint markings on my palm and wrist. "It wasn't supposed to happen like this," she starts. "It all began before I met you, before I knew who you were. You see, when you've lived as long as I have, with the knowledge of truth running through your veins, there comes a time when one must no longer sit idly by. When one must act. Twelve months ago, I decided to act. I decided to set the wheels in motion to free us all."

My eyes narrow with that nugget of information. Just like my mother, she too has been living with the truth for years.

"You see, the secret to breaking the curse lies within Ardronis."

"Ardonis?" I murmur to myself. Why is that name so familiar? "Who is Ardronis, and. . ."

"Not a who, Princess," she interrupts my idle thoughts, "a what." Her eyes drop to my chest, and the familiar burn presses against my skin before she stands and walks over to Guy's body. She kneels beside him, her hand gently stroking his cheek. "Ardronis is an athame that once belonged to King Vharkus Braxtion. It was handed down to him by King Tiergan Braxtion, your grandfather. It was originally gifted to him by his dear friend, Halexander, also known as the Fae King of Elyndria."

I gasp, my spine lengthening against the stone wall. King Grynderwall was a friend of my grandfather.

She throws a glance back at me over her shoulder. "I assumed after King Vharkus Braxtion had passed, and Ishaan took the throne, Ruhaul had it. Or his son."

"Guy," I muse out loud.

"Yes, *Princess*, Guygar." Sydney takes Guy's palm and turns it up. She starts idly tracing lines and circles along Guy's palm. "I approached the king under the guise that I could cure the Crescent Pack's curse, which wasn't entirely untrue. As you know, by breaking the kingdom's curse, the Crescent Wolves will also be unbound from the moon." She purses her lips for a moment, as if contemplating what to tell me before continuing, "So, I told King Ishaan about the curse, and we made a deal."

My stomach twists as suspicion unfurls within my core. "You made a deal with the devil," I spit.

"I did what I had to do. I promised, in exchange for his help with locating the lost athame, that I wouldn't kill or harm any of his family, no matter what I discovered. Obviously, I originally thought it was Ishaan's blood that was going to be needed to break the curse, but I never told him that." Sydney stands again and wipes her hands down her dress, straightening out creases in its skirt. Her chestnut brown eyes collide with mine. "I figured once the athame was found, it wouldn't need me to kill him. That deed would fall on someone else's shoulders."

Heart racing like a wild horse, I push myself up off the ground. My weak legs tremble, but I fight through the discomfort and take a few unsteady steps toward where she now paces across the chamber. She stills and takes a cautious step back out of reach. Smart.

"I needed the Ishaans to instigate the investigation, so yes, I made a deal. Our deal was sealed by blood, initiating the Blood Accord." Sydney pulls her long sleeve up to her elbow, and on her left forearm lie three red lines. The Blood Accord marking. Two lines represent each party in the Accord, and the third line represents the promise. It's rare for anyone to initiate such a deal. "When Ishaan couldn't locate Ardronis, I did some research and discovered a secret."

"A secret?" I whisper, my brows pulling together. I tilt my head, waiting in anticipation for her to keep talking.

"You see, Ardronis would have been passed down through the family. It would have to be with either the king or one of his children." Sydney's eyes don't shift from mine, her gaze burning through me like a thousand shooting stars. And then one hits. The secret my mother had been keeping all this time. The only secret that would ultimately link me to all of this. I bring my hand up to my chest, and a warm hum reverberates across my ribs.

"Me," I croak. My chest collapses, and tears threaten to erupt from my eyes. "Me."

"Yes, Princess. I discovered that King Braxtion had another child."

"So, you sold me out," I howl, full of fury, at what Sydney set in motion. I close my eyes and look for my Wolf. It's moments like this where I need her to be my calm, my reason, my guide. All I find is the emptiness that's been eating at my soul without her.

"I told the king you existed, yes." Sydney's voice, now softer, pulls me out of my inner fury as she admits how she set the wheels in motion for my ultimate death.

I swallow hard, pushing it all down. "And the king sent Quentin to track me down," I seethe.

"It was not supposed to happen this way. They were to find Ardronis only, but the king and his prince went rogue, sending the Scorpions to cause chaos in the city. Killing innocent beings was not part of the plan."

"No, the plan was to use me, to make me trust them. . ." I swallow. "To kill me."

"No, Princess, you were not supposed to die, just lead us to the athame. When I discovered what they were doing, I wanted no part of it. I tried to fix what I started, which was why I approached Mhelodie, why I approached you."

"You involved my best friend in a plan that was meant to kill me," I bite. "You're just as bad as them." I stumble back toward the wall and let myself slide down to the floor, pulling my knees into my chest. The weight of the truth on my shoulders pushes my body into the grave Sydney dug for me when she set all of this in motion.

Sydney comes closer and once again kneels in front of me, her hand brushing a piece of hair off my sodden face and tucking it behind my ear. "I am truly sorry for what Quentin has done, especially to your mother."

Her words sucker punch me, winding me like a wounded animal. "Mum?" Sydney drops her hand and falls back. "Mum?" I roar. "What did he do to my mum?"

"Paege, I'm sorry, I thought you knew. . ."

Scrambling, I push myself forward, pure loathing exploding like lava from my veins, and I reach for Sydney, my hand clenching in the material of her dress, and I yank her into me. "What do you mean?" I growl.

"He. . ." She trembles, and cocks her head in pity. "He sent the Scorpions to her."

I violently push Sydney from me, and I turn myself away from her as my body heaves and heaves and heaves.

It wasn't the king.

It was Quentin.

Quentin killed my mother.

"Breathe, Princess, just breathe," Sydney croons as she runs her hands up and down my back in soothing motions while my body continues to heave. Endless sobs break from my shattered heart. Sydney offers me some water and pulls me in close to her, her arms wrapping around me. Although every part of my mind knows this woman betrayed me and my family, I still let the warmth of her embrace comfort me. I still let her touch soothe me.

Gods know how long I stay there in her arms, but when I finally muster up the energy to move, I also find the courage to speak once more. I bring my hands to my neck, curl my fingers under the chain, and slide my necklace out from under my jacket. Holding the athame charm in my hands, it zaps my fingers, the truth of everything setting over my bones like the aftermath of a chilling tempest. "Sydney, I think it's my blood that breaks the curse," I mutter as she continues to hold me close like a mother would her child. But I'm not her child. And she is not my mother.

My mother is dead.

"I think it is, too. And now, your blood is bound to his."

"What?" I spit out.

"I just bound your life to his. And his to yours," is her only reply.

CHAPTER 61

Waking, I find Sydney has left my chamber. Frantically, I lift my hands to my neck, and a sigh escapes my lips as my fingers run down the length of my chain, settling on the charm that lies between my breasts.

Ardronis.

The charm my father gave my mother.

The charm my mother gave to me.

And according to Sydney, the athame that is going to break the curse and free the kingdom.

Sydney believes it will reveal itself to me when I need it and not a moment before. Its magic keeps it hidden and safe from those who want to destroy it. Wrapping my hands around the charm, I close my eyes and say the name "Ardronis" to myself. I open one eye, pulling my lips straight, I wait for the charm to morph into a dagger. . .Nothing.

Closing my eyes, I try again, "Ardronis, reveal yourself to me."

I wait some more. Nothing.

Urgh.

"Ardronis, I call you forth." Again, opening one eye, I suck in a breath and pray to the Gods it works.

Still nothing. Shoulders rolling forward, I sigh and let go of the charm. *Fuck.*

I run my hands down the cloak Sydney wrapped around my shoulders. My hand snags on something sharp buried in the fabric. A pocket. I slide my hand in, and my fingers wrap around cool metal. When I pull the object out of the pocket, a tear slides from my eyes. In my hand is Guy's silver ring. He must have stolen it when he was at the apartment, and now *she* is returning it.

The last thing I remember before I fell asleep is Sydney promising me that she wouldn't tell Quentin where Ardronis is. I won't allow him to be the one to take my life. I won't give him that satisfaction. While Sydney put all of this in motion, I can't help but believe her when she says none of it was supposed to play out like this. Though, I don't entirely know what she thought would happen. With the king evoking the Blood Accord, I keep wondering how much of the curse he knew about before all of this. Why bind himself to her service for the promise of keeping his family safe if he didn't think it was Ishaan Blood that broke the curse?

The ground shudders, and I drop the charm. I frantically fumble for it, attempting to hide it down my jacket. Before I can, Quentin storms into my chamber with an unimpressed look on his face and a dagger in his hand.

Oh, fuck.

I quickly step back but hit the wall, and Quentin stomps up to me, slamming his hands on either side of my head. The blade angles toward my eye. Turning away from the dagger that's pointing my way, I squeeze my eyes shut. Quentin's breath lands heavily against my cheek, and a shudder crawls down my spine. "I know I said I couldn't kill you before I find that athame, but I never said I wouldn't hurt you. Seems sending the Witch in did no good. It's time to resort to other means."

I squeeze my eyes tighter as the cold from the metal blade gently touches the skin under my chin. I try to take another breath, but it catches, my lungs constricted by the fear coiling around my chest. With the little strength I can grab onto, I open my eyes to look into his cold, steel eyes, now dark and filled with disgust. A thick, coppery tang rolls through my stomach, his darkened hatred seeping into my body with every breath he takes. "Just kill me," I rasp as the blade pinches at my skin.

"I can't without the blade, so just tell me where it is."

"I don't have it," I snarl at him through gritted teeth, hoping he doesn't notice the charm hanging around my neck and put all the pieces together. I still can't believe I had it all along. Ardronis, the cursed athame, has hung around my neck all my life. Did my mum know what she gave me? Did my dad?

"Please," I beg stupidly because I know he won't. His selfish desire to break the curse will outweigh any tendency to lash out in frustration. He has played the part so well these last six months. He has sat idly by while I was attacked over and over again. He played the doting boyfriend. The caring friend. The loyal companion.

"Why would I not tell you? I've got nothing left to live for now. My brother, my mum, my dad. They are all gone. You've taken everything from me. Everyone. So, just do it. Just kill me."

"That's not entirely true." His angelic voice startles us both. Quentin lets me go and steps back, pivoting quickly. I slide down the wall, sinking onto the floor with a solid thunk. "You still have me."

Lifting groggy, hazy eyes, I see him, and my dying heart stutters. I struggle to focus, but even in the darkness, I see his outline clear as day. His lethal wings flared like the dangerous winged warrior he is, and with every step he takes toward us, the clearer his image becomes.

My Gods, he is utterly, viciously, beautiful.

But is he here? I'm so exhausted, so broken that I must be imagining him here. I've seen him before in my dream. Is my mind playing tricks on me again? Have I finally cracked?

"Laz?" I rasp, choking on his name.

"I'm here," he answers softly, a strange contradiction from the warrior I see standing before me.

"You found me." A sob erupts from my chest. "You came."

"I came."

"But how?" I push myself off the ground. Standing, I exhale the longest breath and try to run for him, but the force of the shackles wrapped around my waist and neck yanks me back mid-step, my bindings not allowing me to close the space between us. I fall back, crashing hard to the ground. Pain roars through my body as I try to take a strangled breath.

"I told you, little wolf, I will always find you." I look up. Laz winks at me as he stalks calmly into the chamber. A crimson fire flashes across his amber eyes as he takes in the shackles around my body. Tall and proud, he prowls toward me. His movements are slow and steady with a preternatural grace, and a shudder creeps through my body.

"And you. . ." he growls, his eyes darting to Quentin. "What am I going to do with you?"

"How did you—" Quentin starts, but Laz interrupts.

"Perrin told me your plan. It didn't take much for him to turn in the end. I must admit, I didn't see this coming. I always knew you couldn't be trusted. But this. . ." He rubs his chin as he continues to pad toward Quentin. "This was unexpected."

Quentin lunges for Laz, dagger drawn. Laz moves so fast, I barely see him move at all. Quentin stumbles forward but corrects himself. Before I can blink, Laz has his sword drawn and is standing between Quentin and me.

"Don't kill him!" I call out into the chamber, and Laz stills.

"Don't kill him?" he queries, not looking back at me, his eyes still firmly glued on Quentin as he circles him like prey. "He would have killed you, Paege. He killed your mother, got your brother killed. He deserves to die." I couldn't agree more with Laz, but death is an easy out for him. I want him hurt like he hurt me. I want to make him pay.

"No," I cry out again as Laz looks like he's about to lunge forward. "He bound my life to his."

Laz falls still. He glances my way, and I swear a look of pain flashes across his face. Quentin drops his dagger briefly, his jaw following suit as if shocked at what I said.

Laz nods as if taking in the situation, then casually replies, "Alright." He quickly turns to face me. "Give me five minutes, and I promise I will get you out of those things."

I nod in return, and Laz turns back to Quentin, who has regained his composure and has his dagger at the ready. Drawing his sword, Laz resumes circling the Wolf, Quentin matching the moves of this dance, step for step.

"When I free her, Wolf," Laz says, "you will suffer. Death, it seems, is too easy of a punishment." Laz raises his sword and pounces toward Quentin. Quentin lifts his dagger, blocking the swing from Laz and pivots fast, swiping a foot out. Laz jumps and swings his sword again and again and again. The piercing sound of their weapons clashing rings through the chamber like fortress bells sounding a warning. It must not be a crescent moon because Quentin doesn't shift. And thank the Gods because I know Laz is good, but I don't know if he could survive a Wolf attack on his own. Not if he was bitten anyway.

Watching the two of them dance around each other, my eyes momentarily shift to Guy.

Is he closer?

I rise and take an unsteady step toward him, not wanting to put any pressure on my shackles. My neck still cries out in pain from when I tried to run to Laz. But in only a few short steps, I am standing by Guy's side. What in the Hels? I study the ground. The etchings that were surrounding his body are smudged away, and there is a drag trail, clearly defining the path by which he was moved.

Sydney.

She gave me back my brother.

I kneel beside him and reach my arm out to touch his face, to run a finger down his cheek, but my chest heats, burning me with a searing pain as my skin touches Guy's. Looking down, the chain around my chest starts glowing. It's a faint yellow at first, then brighter, then orange, and then red. Red like the crimson fires that burn in the depths of my soul.

Confused, I look up, and neither Quentin nor Laz has noticed anything. They are both holding their own, continuing to defend against each other's strikes, each clash as deafening as the last. Neither of them seems to gain on the other.

Inhaling slowly, I place my hand over the charm, trying to shield the glow from Quentin. If he sees it, only the Gods know what he would do. It jolts beneath my touch, and before I realise what's happening, I am holding against my chest a beautiful golden athame with a bluey ash stone in the hilt. It's a perfect replica of the charm that still hangs between my breasts.

Staring at Ardronis in my hand, I don't notice when time seems to slow down until Laz steps toward me. "I will get you out of those, little wolf, I just need one more. . ." Snapping my eyes up to him, his eyes widen as they land on the athame in my hand. I drop the dagger by my side.

"Is that?" he asks.

I nod.

"Shit."

I nod again.

"Just give me a moment, and we can. . ."

Quentin howls as he bursts through the time warp at Wolf speed, and Laz pivots to face him again. I pick up the athame, and its energy buzzes through every inch of my being. I've been feeling it for months, zapping and warning me. It calls my name, beckoning me home.

Watching the Wolf and the Guard fight, I realise what I must do. I need to end it all now. There has been enough fighting and blood spilled. It is *all* enough.

"You don't even know if it will work, Paege," I say to myself. I'm risking everything based on what the book says. What the Eagles said. What Sydney says. . .What he says. Swallowing down the lump forming in my throat, I watch Laz land a blow to Quentin's face. They abandoned their blades and now fight like two males in a bar fight. Godsdamn them both. I know I told Laz not to kill him, but this is ridiculous.

I can end it all right now.

Quentin swings a hook, and Laz ducks, but Quentin kicks out in front of him low, landing a clear blow in Laz's shin. Quentin doesn't realise the extent of the curse. He just stupidly thinks it's going to free him from the crescent moon. Little does he know, the curse is more than just the Wolves being bound to the moon. It's the entire history of our kingdom erased.

Laz plants an elbow into the side of Quentin's head. Tears start flowing down my face, gushing from my eyes like a dam bursting open from the pressure of my fate. Laz being here makes it that much harder to fulfil my destiny, but it doesn't change the fact that I need to die. It can't.

Holding up the dagger, I stare at the golden blade. The vice in my chest tightens. I look down at Guy, pressing my lips together, and I strangle a sob. I have to do it now. Leaning down, I plant a kiss on Guy's cheek. "I love you," I whisper to him. "I'll see you soon."

"What about me?" I look up. Laz stands above me. Cocking my head, I see Quentin behind him on the ground, unconscious. "You're just going to give up without a fight, without saying good-bye, without talking this through with me?"

And that's the thing about the dark. There are no shadows to show you who stands beside you. If you're not looking, you won't see anything.

CHAPTER 62

"You are a terrible liar, by the way," Laz mutters as he reaches for me. His arm loops beneath mine, and he pulls me to my feet. Turning me around, he inspects the collar around my neck.

My mouth falls open, but before I can ask, he answers as if he can see the bewilderment brewing in my mind. "You hate me?" His hands continue to work on the collar around my neck as I scoff. I told Laz I hate him, but we both knew then that was not true, just as we both know it now. Why is he bringing this up? I start to turn to face him, but he places his hands on my shoulders. "Hold that thought, little wolf. I need to get Sydney to free you. These are magical cuffs."

"Sydney? Is she. . ." I swallow. Does Laz even know she's involved?

"She is. . .indisposed, but I can fix that." He steps back. "Don't do anything stupid until I get back," he chides.

"Stupid?"

His gaze drops to Ardronis, still clamped in my hand. Laz hasn't tried to take it from me, but I wouldn't even know what it would do if I let go of it. Would it disappear? Would it let someone else hold it? Sydney said it was meant for me.

Laz rushes from the chamber, leaving me alone with Quentin and Guy.

"Now," a voice whispers to me from the darkness. Spinning, I see no one, just the two lifeless bodies on the ground, but I can't help but feel I'm not alone here. Looking at the dagger still gripped tightly in my hand, the voice whispers again, *"Now."*

"Now what?" I ask into the emptiness. Insane. I'm going fucking insane. There is no one there, but the word presses into me as if trying to spark some lost memory buried beneath the trauma.

With blood it's bound, with blood it breaks.

"NOW," it demands. I look down to Guy's lifeless body.

Do not fear death. For those who bleed, shall repay their debt.

The realisation smashes into me.

I just bound your life to his. And his to yours.

"Now, now, now, now."

I know what I must do. I suppose I have always known. *With blood it is bound, with blood it breaks.* But the hard truth of the matter is, I won't survive this, no matter what. I was never meant to survive this. That was not my destiny. *A bloodline shall live; a bloodline shall fall.* This is my destiny.

Kneeling, I place a single kiss on his cheek. "I love you. We'll be together soon," I whisper, and a single tear falls from my chin to his.

Heavy footfalls echo through the tunnel system. My heart hammers. I need to do this before he comes back and stops me. I flick my eyes up to see Laz walking back into the chamber. He stills, as if time has paused.

I smile. Without taking my eyes off his, I twirl the hilt of the athame in my right hand, angling it toward my middle. His eyes widen with realisation. But before Laz can move, I plunge the athame into my stomach. Ardronis slides deeply into my belly, the pain instantly searing through my body, and I let out a guttural sound as it slides through skin and flesh and muscle and organs, and frees the kingdom from its curse.

We twirl around each other, the sun beating down on us as our wooden swords smack together in unison—clank, clank, clank. I gobble down air and take a small step back, lowering my sword for a moment as I regain my strength. We've been playing this game all afternoon, and the weight of the wooden sword is becoming heavy in my little hands.

"Are you too tired to continue, Princess?" he taunts, his single dimple just like mine, appearing with his grin.

I hold my sword back up, using both hands just like Amerax had taught me. "Never, Prince! I will fight you until my last breath." I lunge for him, and he jumps out of the way, bringing his sword up to meet mine again with a clank.

"When I best you, I will lock you in the dungeons to be forgotten about forever," he laughs.

"You will never be able to best me, Prince," I reply with a giggle. "I am too fast." I swing at him again, and our wooden swords smack. "I am too skilled." Another smack. "Too smart." Smack.

We still, our swords kissing. Neither one of us moves. His emerald-green eyes glisten in the sunlight, and a small bead of sweat drops to his brow.

"Honey, it's time to go."

We relax our swords to our sides as the summer song in my mother's voice carries softly across the garden like petals floating through the air. We both look up, and I see Mum standing with the silver-haired female, one of the two who comes with him every year.

"I'll see you next year?" he asks as he drops his sword to the ground and runs off to the tall dark-haired male, who always watches us play from the balcony while my mum and the other one talk.

"Guy?" I call out after him, as something in my chest pulls tight.

He stops and pivots to face me "Yes, Paege?"

"Happy birthday."

Guy runs back to me and when he reaches me, he wraps his arms around, pulling me in for a hug. "You, too, little sis."

And then he takes off running back to the male and female, who, it seems, have known me my entire life. Guy pounds the dirt to reach his companions. She stands there, her silver and purple hair shimmering like glitter. And the male, his amber eyes shine brightly in the afternoon sun. The male looks up, his eyes connecting with mine. They flash, glowing red irises burn into me, as his face contorts with what appears to be pain and fear.

I open my mouth and scream.

Laz.

"What did you do?" Laz's cry breaks through the memory. It was him. It was always him. There.

"Huh?" I tilt my head, confusion curling itself around my broken mind. I can't seem to follow the conversations, and my body burns.

"I've got you, little hybrid." The art gallery.

He grabs my arms in a bruising grip, his eyes wide with horror. "Paege," he says again. "What did you do?"

I don't answer. Confusion still burrows into the recesses of my mind.

The male Guard pivots, his amber eyes colliding with mine, and he raises a pierced brow. "Can I help you?" he chides. The gym.

He brings a hand up to my face, and I flinch back. Why didn't he ever tell me? He slowly drops his gaze to my belly. Tracing his line of sight, I see the golden hilt of the pretty blade protruding from my flesh. Then I see the blood.

Mum and Dad stand with a tall male Guard. His onyx hair bounces hues of blue in the afternoon sun, and his bronzed skin glistens. My apartment.

"You stupid, selfless. . ." he scolds me. "Why did you do that?"

"It was you," I choke out, trying to reconcile everything. His brows furrow. "I remember, Laz. I remember. It was always you." The pain in Laz's face mirrors that of my body: unbearable. Everything turns black. Releasing the hilt, the blade still deep in my stomach, my resolve crumbles. A moan fills the chamber. Mine, his? I don't know. But his hand finds mine, and he pulls me into him before I hit the ground.

"Paege, I thought. . ." His throat bobs. "I thought we would have more time. To explain things. To fix this. To fix us."

Pushing through, I peel my eyes open and see the pain of a thousand hurtful words burning in Laz's eyes. The words I said to him in my time of anger. In my time of pain. "There's nothing to fix," I whisper. I try to take in a breath, but instead, I gasp. The pain stabs through my ribs as my lungs fail to expand.

"But there is."

"No. There isn't." I cough. The sting of the dagger in my torso crawls through my body, pulling me to fulfil my destiny. I can feel it, but I need to hold on, just a little longer. I don't know what it means, what any of it means, but I know that Laz has always been there in my life, watching over me, over us. He knew my mum. He knew my dad. My real dad. He knew Guy. It wasn't some duty to the kingdom. Whatever he did for my family, it was personal.

"Don't say that, Paege. You can't mean that."

Murkiness fills the remaining light inside, making it hard for me to say what I need to say. I swallow the regret building and pushing through all the discomfort and the pain. My throat is still restrained by the collar around my neck, and the protruding blade makes it awfully difficult to find the words. "I do because there is nothing to fix. We are alright." With bloody hands, I take Laz's hand and place it over my heart. "I forgive you, but you need to let me go," I mutter.

A tear pearls in his eyes as he brings his brow to mine, and his nose brushes against the tip of my own. His breath is just a sigh along my lips as he whispers, "I don't know if I can do that, little wolf.

There is so much left to say. There is so much more to—" He sucks in a sudden sharp breath, and the remains of my broken heart fly from my chest.

I know what he's saying. I know because I feel it, too. What it is, I have no idea, but our bond, our connection, goes beyond any friendship I've ever had with anyone. Still, he hurt me. He lied to me. That is probably why it hurt me so much because I think I trusted him more than I have ever trusted another Being. I've known him for weeks, but it feels like years, like lifetimes, and I suppose that's because he has been there my entire life.

Now, all that's *irrelevant*. I suppose death does that to you. "I know," I sob, as I trail my hand down his cheek, catching a tear as it rolls down his face.

"No, Paege, you don't know. How could you when I didn't even know myself? I didn't care much for anything before, but since. . .I've needed. . ." Laz stammers, not finishing his sentences as if he can't find the words to say. Which is strange because Laz is a male of many words. I also understand because what is there to say? "Always, and I've—I've—When you told me to get out, I've never felt more remorse in my life. The thought of you never talking to me again broke something in me, and I. . ."

Although he never finishes his words, the garbled mess spilling from his lips has never made more sense. The sweetest melody, a song with no words, sung just for me. I know exactly what he's trying to say. Yet, the truth seems impossible.

"Laz." His name slips from my lips, a whisper weighted with nothing but longing and regret "I. . ."

"Sh, Paege."

A sob cracks out of my chest. "I didn't want to die, Laz. I didn't. I never wanted any of this."

"I know, little wolf."

"I'm scared." I cough.

He places a gentle kiss against my lips, his thumb wiping away a tear rolling down my cheek.

He tastes of sin and decadence. He feels like darkness and fire. He kisses me deeply but thoroughly, and it's heady, wearing down my resolve and stirring something in me, igniting something I had buried. It is as if his touch, his kiss is awakening me, pulling me from the brink of death.

For a breath.

For a heartbeat.

For a moment.

I think I might survive.

He breaks our kiss and smiles wearily, and the spark in his eyes that usually accompanies the smile I've come to love doesn't appear.

"What's going to be waiting for me on the other side?" I sob.

"Not what, little wolf, *who*. Your brother. Your mother. Your father," he whispers. "And you will be there, waiting for me when Isra takes me for himself." He swallows thickly. "I will find you again. I will always find you."

Tears stream down my face in a violent waterfall. Quentin, the chamber, the curse, the rest of the world disappear into oblivion as his words slip between my ribs and sear into my soul, branding me like a tattoo. "I'm sorry," I admit.

"I know. I'm sorry too. I'm sorry you never got to know what real love is. What it is to feel safe and respected. You deserve that more than anyone, and I will spend the rest of my Godsdamn near-immortal life paying the consequences of that." He places a soft kiss against my wet cheek, and the warmth of his lips sends a heat coiling around my core. "But I will find you again, in the next life and the life after that. I will keep finding you. I will always keep finding you. I promise." He holds his hand up to his chest, flat across his heart. The Vailenbyrg pledge. The bind that's been constricting inside around my heart explodes into smithereens.

Even in death, words escape me. Because there is nothing I can say to Laz in this moment that can tell him how I feel and how sorry I am for this. "I love you" seems insignificant in comparison to what he just declared to me in his broken fucked up way. But I do think I love him, and I have for some time now.

He places his lips against mine one last time. Leather and sweet cloves envelop me, and my body relaxes at his touch. Laz. His brief kiss is soft and tender. It's pure and real, and this moment is the truth of who Laz is. I can't bring myself to say it, to acknowledge it out loud. Because I *am* leaving this world, leaving him behind. Yet, somehow, I know deep inside that this is not goodbye, not forever anyway. I will see him again. In another time, in another place. We will have time then.

Pain burns through my body, ripping a wild roar from deep within my chest. I writhe as the ache in my chest, not the one from the dagger, but the one from my splintering heart, yanks a sob from me. "Until we meet again."

"I'll meet you among the stars," he whispers in a soothing tone, and the truth of his words settles deep into my dying heart.

I break, not from death, but from love. Tears run down my face, and I find my final words—"I'll be there waiting"—before closing my eyes and letting the darkness carry me to the nothing that lies beyond. To the Hels that now own my soul.

The moment I close my eyes, my mind is hammered with memories of the kingdom's past. Hundreds and hundreds of dizzying memories so intense and overwhelming that I struggle to make sense of what it is telling me. Although my life force is bleeding out of me, pouring out of my veins like the River Plye, I remain focused on what Ardronis is showing me. What the Gods are telling me.

My eyes snap open. Through all the rage and sadness of the past, through all the pain and darkness, I finally see the truth. . . And I am now sure of exactly three things.

I know what I am.

I know who the remaining Grynderwall heir is.

Braxtion blood will not break the curse.

Knowing what I need to do, I try to take in breath, fearful my dying body won't allow me, that the Gods won't allow me to stay here for even one moment past my due. But my lungs rapidly fill with air, my chest rising like the sun on a warm summer's morning, and my body jolts.

I blink, and a deluge of tears falls quickly down my face. A burning pain sears through my body, and a fire now blazes so fiercely from my fingertips, and I stare at the handsome male kneeling before me. His head is buried in his hands. "Laz?" I rasp. Tears fall through cracks in his hands, covering his face and into his lap.

He snaps his head up, eyes widening as he sees my face, and realises I have not yet left this world. "Paege. Oh, Gods, Paege. I thought you were dead."

"I am," I reply tenderly. Despite my eyes being open and my heart still beating, *barely,* I am still not in this world, and I don't have much time to do what I need to do.

"I can get you out of here and get you help." His arm reaches out to me, but I shift my body, rolling myself away from his touch, away from him.

His brows pull together, and his jaw slacks from the plethora of his powerful emotions.

"It's too late, but it's going to be alright," I try to reassure him. "Trust me." I take a deep breath, forcing the unfurling power to quell for just a little bit longer. *I just need a little bit longer.*

Scanning for my captor, I see Quentin's body still lying over the other side of the chamber. Is he dead? Did—

He groans, rolling over. Nope, not dead, just unconscious.

Good. I know she said our lives were bound, but now, I know what she meant.

"I need you to get back," I rasp. The growing power pushes at the edges of my body. I breathe in deeply, trying to subdue the heat building inside, yearning to escape. *Not yet.*

"Let me take you out of here," he pleads. The warrior I have come to love is not kneeling before me; it's a male stripped bare. It kills me, but I cannot stray from my path. My destiny.

"Please, Laz, I need you to get back." I shift my body again, forcing myself to move through the pain. I push myself up, my hands slipping in the crimson pool beneath me, until I sit up against Guy's body.

The energy building is fierce, and I have no idea how long I can contain it for. I hold out my hand, bloodied palm facing up, and heat gathers under my skin. A little spark ignites from my fingertips, my skin tingling with the power and heat churning beneath the surface as it zaps through my digits and releases from the tips of my fingers. I suck in a shuddering breath, and a small blue flame erupts violently from my palm, dancing in the silence of the room.

Hold it together a little longer, Paege.

Laz gasps and scrambles back. "Paege, what in the Hels?"

"It's alright, Laz. Trust me."

"I don't understand." His hands plant into the ground beneath him, steadying him.

"Tell Dad and the twins I love them. Tell Asheron, Lumeilia, and Mhelodic, tell them all I'm sorry. I understand now." I smile softly, and before Laz can respond, I break the connection of our eyes as I lean back into Guy's body. I reach behind me for his arm, lifting it and placing it across my legs, and take his hand in mine. Our bodies are now entwined. I need to take him with me. *I am his other half. Together we are whole.* This won't work without him. Twins.

We have said everything we needed to. I have said everything I needed to. I don't want to say anything else because there is nothing that I could say right now that wouldn't be thought of as crazy or insane. And if this doesn't work, if this fails, I won't give him false promises. I won't do that to him. But it won't. I know it in my bones.

A pack born of fire, a pack born of ash. You all shall rise from the flames with one brilliant flash. A symbol of rebirth, of life anew.

Behind Laz, Quentin rolls to his side, his eyes blinking one, two, three times before fully opening. "Paege, what are you doing?" he asks wearily as he pulls himself into a sitting position. His eyes widen as he notices the flames that are slowly building across my skin.

I slide the ring onto Guy's finger. "I'm taking Guy with me."

Quentin's face freezes, fear seeping from him like an icy river flowing through the depths of his deception, igniting a frenzied panic as he clambers to his feet and closes the space between us. I shoot a saccharine smile to that handsome Wolf now standing before me, next to Laz. But it's a smile that doesn't reach my eyes, a smile that no longer grows from my heart, and I say the only words that I can muster up the courage to say.

"I'll be seeing you soon, *asshole.*" Then I let go.

I let go of every emotion, every feeling I have ever held in.

I let go of all the pain that I locked within that vault.

I let go of all the sadness that stole love from my heart.

I let go of all the hatred that crept its way into my soul.

I let go of all the loss I have been trying to bury, and it erupts out of my body in one violent flash.

My father.

Sylas.

Remi.

My brother.

My mother.

Quentin.

Laz.

I let go.

I let it all burn.

Flames explode from the surface of my skin, igniting a fire that rapidly dances across my body. A heat so intense, so powerful, it instils a sense of calmness within the chaos of my soul. I close my eyes as the heat of the fire engulfs our bodies, and I allow the flames to erase all the pain of my past, liberating me in their fiery embrace. In this final moment, a strange clarity appears in the form of one final gift from the Gods themselves. I finally understand everything: the trials, the tribulations, the losses. And with that understanding comes an overwhelming realisation. Everything will be alright.

Amidst the roaring inferno building around me, before our bodies become nothing more than embers and ash, I catch one final glimpse of the faces of all those I have loved and lost. And I know without a doubt that this is not the end.

I will see them all again.

And then I feel nothing at all.

CHAPTER 63

Unknown

Twin sapphire jewels were the first things he saw when his eyes opened. He blinked, his vision still hazy at the edges. Another hallucination, surely. He groaned. Gods knew how long he had been running for, trying to escape the emancipated creatures that roamed these lands. It must have been days. His body ached in places he didn't know it could. The balls of his feet, his calves, his back and shoulders, his hands. His head. Everywhere. This was different. This was new. Usually, after he had been pulled into the darkness, he would wake with his body healed, refreshed, and ready to repeat the horrors he had lived through so many times before. Not this time.

He squeezed his eyes as he slowly gripped onto reality. He remembered the rancid creatures of death as they flanked his side, the flying beasts of fire as they tore the sky above him, the forest of refuge sweetly calling his name like a siren in the night, and leaping to *safety* before it all went black. Then there were those terrifying visions that continued to assault him.

Green eyes brimmed with silver tears.

A wolf.

A sword.

A girl.

A scream.

What did they mean? Who was she? He didn't know, but she felt so familiar, and it tugged at his heart. It was as if a memory was trying to escape the confines of his broken mind, smashing through the wall separating him from his sanity. Was it a memory, though, or was it just another cruel delusion designed to break him in this Hels hole?

When he opened his eyes again, his vision cleared, and his sight focused on the magnificent blue eyes looking down at him. He still wasn't sure if this was a dream or if he had passed into another realm, but those eyes, attached to an angelic face shrouded in shadows, beamed down on him as if she had been expecting him, waiting for him. Recognition sparked in her eyes.

She didn't speak. She just studied his face, his body, as if she were searching for something. Wounds? He wasn't sure he had any. Her eyes landed on his left hand. A look of disappointment flashed across her soft features. Or was that anguish? Her gaze lingered on his hand for a long moment, and the weight of her stare had him shifting uncomfortably. He didn't know what it meant.

He couldn't speak. He still didn't know if this was his mind playing cruel jokes on him. Besides, he wouldn't have known what to say anyway.

Slowly, he adjusted his body and sat up. She stood and took two small steps back into the darkness. It was enough space for him to move comfortably without knocking her, but not enough space to suggest she was going anywhere or that she feared him. Now, that was a crazy thought. He didn't even know who he was, but still, he wondered why he would think she would be scared of him. Should she be?

He rubbed the back of his neck, cracking it to relieve some of the stiffness creeping into his bones. Her eyes never left him. She waited patiently while he adjusted himself and took in his surroundings. They were in the sparse-looking forest he had seen while escaping those creatures. Relentlessly thumping wings boomed through the canopy above. A piercing screech split the sky, and it sent a shudder racing down his spine.

He flinched.

She didn't.

His heartbeat was mirroring the winged beasts, angry and erratic. What were those flying leathery beasts? They looked almost as if they were part Wolf, part Dragon. He didn't know. Whatever they were, they couldn't enter the forest. Neither could the emancipated creatures that had chased him for days. The female standing before him didn't seem to even notice the chaos in the sky above. He was safe. He was sure of that.

Drag marks across the dirt ground met his body. He was deep in the forest now. She had dragged him to safety. Why?

Who was she?

How long had she been here?

Where was here?

All questions he desperately wanted answers to. Whoever she was, she saved his life.

He should say something. Thank her. Ask her where he is, who she is. He swallowed down a breath. Yes.

He opened his mouth to speak. But nothing came out. The words fell dead on his tongue as she cleared her throat and said in a voice born of the heavens, "We've been expecting you, Guy."

THE END

Glossary and Pronunciation Guide

Names

Adriel (AY-dree-el)

Amarax (AH-mah-racks) Vailenbyrg (VAY-len-berg)

Amalyah (am-ah-LEE-ah) Millenford (MIL-en-ford)

Ardronis (ard-RO-nis)

Arnrun (AHRN-run)

Asheron (ASH-er-on) Millenford (MIL-en-ford)

Blaire (BLAIR)

Bridgette (BRID-jet) Ishaan (ih-SHAHN)

Callum (KAL-um)

Camelia (ka-MEE-lee-ah)

Deekon (DEE-kon)

Enderlene (EN-dur-leen)

Grynderwall (GRIN-der-wall)

Guy / Guygar (GUY-gar) Braxtion (BRAX-tee-uhn)

Halexander (HAL-ex-an-der)

Hallie (HAL-ee)

Hawkins (HAW-kinz)

Hera (HAIR-uh)

Huntley (HUNT-lee)

Israykiel (iz-RAY-kee-el)

Jesstar (JESS-tar)

Juno (Joo-noh)

Keene (KEEN) Thornsten (THORN-sten)

Kholann (KO-Lahn) Vailenbyrg (VAY-len-berg)

Laz / Lazarus (LAZ-ur-us) Cadieux (cad-EEO)

Lilith (LIH-lith)

Lumeilia (loo-MEEL-lee-uh) Faulksing (FAWKS-ing)

Marlow (MAAR-loh)

Mhelodie (MEL-oh-dee) Ravenswood (RAY-venz-wood)

Monella (MON-ell-uh)

Glossary and Pronunciation Guide

Nassurah (NAS-uh-rah) Vailenbyrg (VAY-len-berg)
Niaxon (NAI-aks-on)
Paege (PAYJ) Paegence (PAY-jence) Vailenbyrg (VAY-len-berg)
Perrin (PEHR-in)
Quentin (KWEN-tin) Ishaan (ih-SHAHN)
Remildiaz (rem-EEL-dee-ahz)
Ruhaul (roo-HAHL) Ishaan (ih-SHAHN)
Samuel (SAM-yoo-uhl)
Selene (seh-LEEN)
Sydney (SID-nee)
Sylas (SYE-lass)
Synthony (SIN-thuh-nee) Vailenbyrg (VAY-len-berg)
Tiergan (TEER-gan) Braxtion (BRAX-tee-uhn)
Tyrone (ti-ROHN)
Vaelencia (vay-LEN-see-uh)
Vharkus (VAR-kus) Braxtion (BRAX-tee-uhn)
Whisky (WISK-ee)

Places
Aridor (ah-REE-dor) Desert
Blaxheild (BLAX-hee-uld)
Blethyn (BLEH-than) Sea
Cedrus (SEE-drus)
Darthick (DAR-thick)
Dasturn (DAS-turn)
Elyndria (eel-LIN-dree-uh)
Ferinini (feh-REE-nee-nee)
Lochswick (LOK-swick)
Medelia (meh-DEE-lee-uh)
Mountains of G'phen (guh-FEN)

Glossary and Pronunciation Guide

Neopolis (nee-OP-poh-lis)
Orphelios (or-FEE-lee-ohs)
Owenstown (OH-wenz-town)
Quespelia (kwes-PEEL-lee-uh)
River Plye (PLIE)
Welveryn (WELL-vuh-rin)

Gods
Aesther (EST-er) Goddess of Elements
Amara (AM-ar-ah) Goddess of Life
Edom (EE-dom) God of Blood
Isra (ISS-rah) God of the Stars
Pyrrhia (PEER-ee-uh) Goddess of Fire
Terra (TEH-rah) Goddess of Earth
Tidryn (TID-rin) God of Water
Zephyra (ZEH-fie-rah) Goddess of Air

Beings
Fae, Star-Borne, Israykiel Guards, Witches, Wolves, Heretics,
Sirens, Lupa-Centaurs, Centaurs, The Hallowed,
Naga Guardian, and Eagles

Wolf Packs
Crescent Wolf, Silver Tongue, Scorpion Wolf, Shadow Walkers,
Dragon Hides

Rituals
Unification, Ascension, Emergence

Glossary and Pronunciation Guide

Generic Terms
Fyre: A type of alcohol, or liquor, genric
AmberFyre: Whiskey
BlossomFyre: Gin
CrystalFyre: Vodka
DesertFyre: Tequila
VineBrew: Wine, generic
VineBlood: Red wine
VineDew: White wine
VineMist: Champaign or sparkling wine
VineStar: Sweet syrup wine, port
Ale: A fermented drink
AppleAle: Apple Cider
BarleyAle: Beer
Clays: Currency, low value coins
Drops: Currency, moderate value coins
Gales: Currency, high value coins
Sparks: Currency, highest value coins
Scribe: A device to send written messages or make voice calls
Vision Box: A device to watch entertainment
Music Box: A device to listen to music
Chordo-grande: Instrument, piano
Chordo-bowstring: Instrument, violin
Chordo-strummer: Instrument, guitar
Chrodo-bass: Instrument, bass guitar
Centaurion: An open air carriage pulled by Centaurs
Arrowlets: A dart-like game
Gridcakes: Pancakes

THANK YOU

Thank you to all my readers out there who have taken a chance on reading A Bloodline of Secrets: The Unification. Without you, this could not be possible.

If you enjoyed Paege's story, please head over to Amazon or/and Goodreads and leave a review. As a self-published indie author, every review counts. And please follow me on my social media pages and/or sign up to my newsletter for exciting updates regarding the release of the next instalment of Paege's journey.

instagram.com/dani.drummond_author

tiktok.com/danielleddrummond_author

facebook.com/.danielleddrummondauthor

Acknowledgements

First and foremost I want to thank you, the readers, for all your support over the past year. I am honestly so grateful for all of your support. When I first released my debut, I was worried that my story would not reach many readers, but the overwhelming amount of heartfelt messages I received gave me strength to persevere through the hard times, and continue my writing journey.

Sam, I don't even know where to begin. Remember when we were just two bookish strangers on other sides of the continent coming together over a book convention? Now look at us. Your friendship means the world to me. I would love to say you are my sanity, but I fear you are my insanity. And I am here for it. I love you so much. My world would be a very different and boring place without you in it.

Charla, don't even know if I have words to tell you how eternally grateful I am for your friendship. You are my strength on the hard days, my light in the dark and my anchor in the storm. Oh look at that, words. . . Not only are you my best friend, you are my family. I chose you. I hate that we are literally oceans apart. And the fact that I get to call you my editor too, I am truly blessed. Thank you for teaching me everything you know, and helping me become the best version of myself as a person, but also as a writer. And thank you for all your help in making this book the best it could possibly be, for challenging me, and supporting me through my mania.

To my beautiful friend and proofreader and PA, El. I am extremely lucky to have found you. You have supported me well before we started working together, and I cannot express my gratitude to have you by my side. To all the other wonderful authors in my incredible writing groups (there are too many of you to mention, but you know who you are), I am completely honoured to be surrounded by such inspiring and talented people. Thank you.

A massive shout-out to all my Alpha and Beta readers. Thank you for taking the time out of your lives to read my manuscript and provide feedback to help me build this incredible world and my characters. Your comments on Paege, Guy, Quentin and Laz honestly brought me so much joy. I hope I get to continue working with you all in the future.

And last, but certainly not least, thank you once again to my amazing family for always supporting me and staying positive, even when I couldn't. Our family has had a tough year, there were many highs and lows, but we have all come out the other side so much stronger. My sisters, Jaclyn and Sarah and my brothers Michael and Josh, I am incredibly lucky to have you as family. Your support over the last year has meant the world to me. You have all stood by my side through this journey and given me so much strength. Your encouragement has got me through some rough days, and I know I would not have taken the steps to continue without you. Mum and Dad, I love you. I love you both more than the world itself. You are my everything. Without you, none of this would have been possible.

About the Author

Danielle D. Drummond has been spinning stories since she first learned to talk. She wrote her first storybook, about an injured penguin, at around ten years old and has been crafting short paranormal tales and poetry ever since. Today, she writes epic fantasy novels infused with romance—okay, a lot of romance—because she's a sucker for a happily ever after. Based in Perth, Australia, Danielle shares her life with her two beloved dogs. You'll often find her at a local coffee shop or bar, fully immersed in the worlds she's bringing to life.

Also by Danielle D. Drummond

ORIGINAL SIN SERIES

Book 1:
A Kingdom of Curses: The Emergence

Book 2:
A Bloodline of Secrets: The Unification

Book 3
AHBOA:TR Releasing late 2026.